Wynthrope licked a bit of icing from his fork. Moira shivered.

He set his plate aside, his cake unfinished. "Is the fire too much for you, Lady Auburn?" he asked softly, politely.

"No, I am fine, Mr. Ryland. Thank you."

"I ask because you look a little overheated. You are flushed."

"You are impertinent, I think, Mr. Ryland." And she liked it.

"No doubt you are right, but you have just reminded me of something, my lady."

"Oh? What is that?"

"You still owe me a kiss, and if you insist on looking at me as though you would like to cover me in chocolate icing, you had better be ready for me to collect."

Moira's lips parted, but no sound came out. She could only stand there and stare at him, burning from head to toe.

A slight flush crept up his cheeks as his gaze settled on her mouth. "Good lord, woman," he murmured. "You make me wish I *was* covered in icing."

Other **AVON ROMANCES**

KATHRYN SMITH

In The Night

AVON BOOKS
An Imprint of HarperCollinsPublishers

This is a work of fiction. Names, characters, places, and incidents are products of the author's imagination or are used fictitiously and are not to be construed as real. Any resemblance to actual events, locales, organizations, or persons, living or dead, is entirely coincidental.

AVON BOOKS
An Imprint of HarperCollins*Publishers*
10 East 53rd Street
New York, New York 10022-5299

Copyright © 2005 by Kathryn Smith
ISBN: 0-06-074066-3
www.avonromance.com

First Avon Books paperback printing: February 2005

Avon Trademark Reg. U.S. Pat. Off. and in Other Countries, Marca Registrada, Hecho en U.S.A.
HarperCollins® is a registered trademark of HarperCollins Publishers Inc.

Printed in the U.S.A.

10 9 8 7 6 5 4 3 2 1

For Dave.
What a wonderful man you've become.
Love, Aunt Kathryn

Chapter 1

London
December 1818

"I *dare* you."

She did, did she? What did she think he was, a boy unable to resist any gauntlet thrown down before him?

Probably. And she would be right—to an extent. Her words needled him, but it would take more than a taunt to spur him to action. Wynthrope Ryland turned to his companion with a cool but charming smile. "I am afraid that is a challenge I cannot take."

The buxom woman waved her fan before her cleavage in a slow, seductive manner. Her surprise at his refusal was evident on her fair features. "Why on earth not?"

Returning his attention to the dancers twirling and prancing before them, Wynthrope allowed his smile to cool even further. This was why he despised winter parties—conversation

1

was unavoidable. "Because I already know what would happen should I ask the lady in question to dance."

Lady Dumont was not satisfied with so cryptic a reply. "And what is that, dear sir?"

He polished off the rest of his champagne before replying, gesturing with the empty flute as he did so. "Her sister would no doubt pitch a fit of hysterical proportions."

Melodramatic delivery to be sure, but that did not take away the truth of the words. Most women seemed intimidated by him, and that suited him just fine. Those who did end up presented to him like so much Christmas goose were generally those in need of finances, or simply trolling for connections. Obviously, *good* connections were not a consideration, not when they involved his family. The Rylands—even the more distant branches—were not exactly known as "good" *ton*.

Still, that part of him that could not back down from a dare of any kind forced him to cast his gaze in the direction of the very pretty and popular Minerva Banning and her watchful elder sister Moira, Viscountess Aubourn.

Personally, he thought prettiness was a much overrated quality. And popularity among this bunch simply meant one knew the right things to say. How utterly boring. Still, his gaze had been straying to the sisters all evening. He must have been totally obvious for his companion to notice. Usually he was much more careful than that.

Now, if Lady Dumont had challenged him to steal a kiss instead of begging a dance, *that* might be a dare worth accepting. Begging was not something he did—ever. Stealing, on the other hand, was something he was quite adept at.

Apparently Lady Dumont had no interest in extending such a challenge. More's the pity. "Do you plan to attend your sister-in-law's soiree tomorrow evening, Wynthrope my dear?"

Setting his empty glass on the tray of a passing footman, Wynthrope turned once more to face his companion. Ten years his senior, Lady Dumont was an attractive woman with silvery blond hair and a lush figure. Calling him by his Christian name was not a forced attempt at intimacy—that had taken place years ago. He had shared her bed for a good many months, before and after relieving her of some of her late husband's artwork.

Of course, back then he had thought his criminal activity was all for the good of England. Shagging had been a lovely perk. How young and stupid he had been.

"Of course I plan to attend Octavia's party," he replied, putting thoughts of the past out of his mind. "She has given me no other choice." And even if she hadn't, he wouldn't dream of letting her down. Octavia had earned his loyalty the moment she became his brother North's wife. North was his confidant, his conscience. If Octavia was good enough for North, she was good enough for him.

Lady Dumont flashed a coy smile as she continued the lazy flourish of her fan. "Ladies. The sole weakness of the Ryland men."

Wynthrope made a scoffing noise low in his throat—better that than the expletive he first thought of. "Hardly the sole, rather one of many."

"That is rather harsh, is it not?"

He shrugged. This conversation was quickly becoming tiresome. It was boredom that made him want to turn his back on his former lover and walk away, not a perverse need to keep silent about his family, even though he had been the one to remark against them. He had never spoken of his past to this woman when he shared her bed; what made her think he would do so now?

"I think I may take you up on that challenge after all. Please excuse me, my lady." Out of habit, he bowed, but his

attention was already diverted. Focusing on his quarry alle-
viated the restlessness gnawing at Wynthrope's mind. He
would never admit, not even to his brothers, that he felt as
though something was missing from his life. If only one of
his brothers were close at hand, he might use him to ease the
feeling. Even Brahm quieted his spirit, damn him.

But his brothers weren't there. North was at home with
Octavia. His younger brother, Devlin, was currently traveling up from Devonshire with his wife for Christmas, and
Brahm wasn't generally welcome in society, although the
general opinion of him had improved somewhat since the
season. Perhaps that was why he was so intrigued by this
woman—she had her sister at her side almost constantly.
Realistically he knew that would become bothersome after a
while, but for now he envied it.

Winding through the crowd, Wynthrope worked his way
toward the two sisters. Aside from their hair color and strong
jawlines, there was very little resemblance between them at
all. Minerva was shorter and rounder, her hair spirals of
sable curls, her skin a shade darker, her cleavage far deeper.
She looked like a delectable little confection in her pale yellow evening gown. The viscountess was a tall, almost
waifish bit of work. Her skin was pale; her expression as
aloof as her sister's was open. How odd that she wore the
stronger color of the two of them. Her gown was a rich forest green—a color that brought out the gold in her hair.

She seemed a humorless woman, but he knew that to be
untrue. Everyone he had ever heard speak of her remarked
on her easy nature and quick wit. Perhaps the loss of her
husband two years ago had robbed her of her joy as well. Or
maybe it was the stress of trying to marry off a younger sister outside of the London season. There weren't many eligible young men in town at this time of year, although one

would never know it from the number of male admirers flocking around Miss Banning.

It was no secret that the viscountess was terribly protective of her dear sibling—and terribly picky about whom she allowed the chit to stand up with. More than once since her arrival in London, Miss Banning had been known to vocally protest her sister's tight rein. Minnie, as she had come to be called by the *ton*, liked attention, and didn't appreciate her sister taking any chance she had of being noticed away from her.

Which was exactly why he should stop right there, turn around, go find himself another drink, and not put himself between two such obviously high-strung females. A solid idea.

He turned on his heel only to find Lady Dumont watching him from across the floor. Damn London society for being so thin that one could actually see from one end of the ballroom to the other. His former lover raised an inquisitive brow. He could almost hear the question her expression asked. Had he lost his nerve?

Nerve had nothing to do with it. He had plenty of nerve— Lady Dumont had no idea of the depth of his nerve. She would if she ever figured out who stole those four paintings right out from underneath her nose, he thought with dry amusement.

Not that it mattered what Lady Dumont thought. Let her think him a coward. There was nothing wrong with wanting to avoid being at the center of a sisterly conflict.

And yet, despite that threat, he continued toward the two women. He was going to follow this through, and not because of anything Lady Dumont might say to or about him, but because he wanted to. Despite the potential danger with his quarry's sister, he wanted to ask her to dance, wanted to hear her say yes.

And of course he wanted to hold her in his arms, discover if her skin was really as clear as it looked from a distance. Why? Because just a few days ago he had seen her outside a shop in Bond Street—with her sister, of course. Her cheeks had been flushed from the cold, her eyes bright with laughter. He hadn't been the only man to notice her—others had as well, but it had been he who had captured her attention.

For one second she had looked at him as though she could see right to the very heart of him—and understood what she saw there. It shook him right to the very source of his being, leaving him more than a little raw and vulnerable. Even now, the thought of meeting her gaze again agitated the beating of his heart.

No one had ever made him feel vulnerable before, not even that son of a bitch who had deceived and made a fool of him. Not even Brahm or his father had ever made him feel quite so open, so *naked*, as this female had. Such a strange person to elicit such a reaction from him. Self-preservation told him to turn around now while he still could. No matter what happened, he would not emerge unscathed from this encounter. If he was rejected, his pride would suffer, but if he was accepted, more than just his pride could be at risk.

What the hell was he thinking? More than his pride could be at risk? What else did he have? Certainly not his heart. That piece of shriveled-up meat wouldn't know real attachment if he glued it on his sleeve. Any connection he had ever made that mattered was made through blood. Nothing else had lasted. Nothing else had been real.

This attraction he felt wasn't real. The next few minutes would prove that. She would look at him, and her gaze would be the same as any woman's. He would discover there was nothing special about her after all, and he would lose interest. And then he would no doubt end up drinking more than he wanted and going home with Lady Dumont after all.

A good, unpolished shag would clear his head and rid it of all this foolishness. In the future he would know better than to give credence to such notions.

The sisters glanced up as he neared. Each wore an expression of surprise, though the younger seemed slightly more pleased than the elder.

Luckily, it took more than a little displeasure to stop him once he'd set his mind to something.

He sketched a bow before them, flashing his most charming smile. "Lady Aubourn, Miss Banning, how lovely to see you again."

The younger sister dimpled. "Good evening, Mr. Ryland."

The older sister frowned. Was that disappointment in the depths of her clear hazel eyes? "Mr. Ryland."

Undaunted, Wynthrope pressed on. "I was wondering if perhaps I might request the pleasure—"

The viscountess did not allow him to continue. "I am sorry, Mr. Ryland, but my sister's dance card is completely full."

Wynthrope deliberately raised his brows at her brusque tone, but before he could speak, the younger sister cut him off.

"My card is *not* full." Minerva shot her sister a venomous look.

Lady Aubourn blushed. She was actually quite engaging with some color in her cheeks. "Minnie, do be quiet."

The younger woman's color was high as well, her eyes flashing with indignation. "I will not! I do not need you to speak for me."

"Quite right, Miss Banning," Wyn added, deliberately adding fuel to the fire. "You should never allow anyone to speak for you, sibling or not." God knew he wouldn't want one of his brothers speaking for him. He could only imagine the trouble it could lead to.

The viscountess shot him a look that was half shocked,

half furious. It was the fury that got his attention. He never would have pegged her for a woman of strong emotions. She always seemed so cool and poised.

"Mr. Ryland, while I appreciate your suit and support of my sister, I think you will have to agree with me that you and she would make an entirely unsuitable match."

Disbelieving laughter caught in Wynthrope's throat, choking him. He didn't know whether to laugh at this woman or tell her exactly what he thought of her assumptions. "Is that so?" he asked with a chuckle.

For a moment, Lady Aubourn seemed confused, as though the mocking tone of his voice hadn't been completely lost on her. This time when her gaze met his, questions glinted between her narrowed lashes. Wynthrope could almost feel her trying to pull the answers from him.

"Yes, Mr. Ryland. That is so." Her tone was distracted, but firm.

Minerva stomped her foot, wincing as she did so. Wynthrope wasn't surprised; those thin little slippers of hers wouldn't provide much protection against the hard marble floor. "But Moira, I want to dance with him!"

"Why thank you, Miss Banning," Wynthrope replied with a smile, tearing his attention away from the more compelling sister, "But it was not you whom I was asking."

The admission was worth the expressions on their faces. Ah, here was the sisterly resemblance. It was amazing how much they looked alike when their mouths were gaping open.

"But perhaps your card is filled as well, Lady Aubourn?"

She was magnificent when she was embarrassed. Color bloomed high on her cheeks and throat, and there was a brightness to her green-gold eyes that hadn't been there before. Suddenly Moira Tyndale didn't seem quite so cool and aloof anymore. And suddenly it didn't matter that she couldn't seem to see inside him at this moment. He could see inside *her*. It hadn't occurred to her at all that he might want her over her fluffy little sister.

"I—" The words stopped before her mouth did. She stared at him helplessly. She didn't know what to say, that was obvious. He wanted her to say yes. He wanted to discover if she smelled as good as he imagined she would. She would smell like winter—cool and crisp with a hint of something warmer lurking just underneath. Cocoa and cinnamon on a bitter wind.

"You are very kind, Mr. Ryland," Minerva began, her face tight. "But I am afraid my sister is still in mourning for her dear husband and has given up dancing."

A baldfaced lie if he ever heard one—and the chit knew it too, but that didn't stop her from staring him straight in the eye as she said it. Spoiled or not, Wynthrope had to admire the girl for being so brazen.

He nodded in acquiescence, his gaze locked with Moira's. "My apologies, my lady. I bid you a good evening." Before leaving, he flashed the younger woman a slight grin with a click of his heels. "Enjoy the rest of the ball, Miss Banning."

He made it two strides before his love of mischief made him turn. "Oh, Lady Aubourn?"

Both sisters looked.

Wynthrope smiled—really smiled. "If you ever decide to take up dancing again, please let me know."

The viscountess's gaze widened, and Wynthrope walked away chuckling, her image wonderfully frozen in his mind.

He had eyes so rich a blue, she couldn't think of anything to compare them to. Sapphire was too trite. Turquoise too unnatural. Indigo just plain wrong. His eyes were—

"Blast!"

"Are you all right, Moira?"

Wincing, Moira Tyndale shoved her smarting thumb in her mouth, licking away the drop of blood that beaded there. She turned from the window with a sigh. "It is nothing a mind that works properly could not remedy, Octavia. I poked myself with a tack again."

Octavia Sheffield-Ryland smiled teasingly as she decorated the mantel with sprigs of holly. She was a tall, slender redhead with bright blue eyes and the glow of a newly married woman, something Moira envied. "You are strangely distracted today. Did something happen at the ball last night?"

Moira busied herself with tacking decorations around the window so her friend couldn't see the flush in her cheeks. "Of course not."

"No one asked you to dance?" There was a strange note of interest in her friend's voice.

Moira closed her eyes as a wave of embarrassment washed over her. Octavia knew. Of course she knew. Gossip was thin this time of year; every little thing that happened at a ball or public place was considered news.

"Certainly not." That wasn't a complete lie. Wynthrope Ryland, he of the nameless-blue eyes, hadn't actually been given a chance to ask her. Not properly at any rate.

"Hmm. I must have heard incorrectly."

The best course of action would be to ignore that pointed remark. The best course of action would be to continue tacking up the decorations and pretend ignorance.

Her shoulders sagged with resignation. "What did you hear?"

Holly forgotten, Octavia hastened closer. Thank the Lord the servants were going to help with the decorations. At this rate, the two of them wouldn't be done by the time the guests started to arrive.

The redhead's expression was gleeful, as though Moira's humiliation the night before was a good thing. Obviously, whatever her friend had heard, she had heard wrong.

"I heard," Octavia murmured, as though there was a chance they might be overhead, "that a certain gentleman paid particular attention to you."

Well, that was one way to put it. Moira opened her mouth and paused. How best to respond?

"I made a proper ass of myself, Octavia. *That* is what happened."

Gone was the happy insinuation, replaced by an expression of confused concern. "Surely not."

Moira turned away, choosing to toy with the decorations on a nearby table rather than face her friend's sympathy. She rubbed a strand of crimson ribbon between her thumb and forefinger. The velvet was butter-soft to the touch. "I thought he wanted to dance with Minnie."

"Instead of you?"

What was that surprised tone for? She faced the other woman with a frown. "Of course."

Octavia mirrored her expression, the pale flesh of her brow furrowing tightly. "Why would you think that?"

Moira chuckled in disbelief. Was it not obvious? "Because every gentleman who approaches the two of us at a ball wants to dance with Minerva."

"Ah!" Octavia raised a finger as though she was about to impart great wisdom. "My brother-in-law is not 'every' gentleman. In fact, I'm not certain the term 'gentleman' applies to Wynthrope at all."

Just the mere mention of his name had Moira blushing again. Ever since she first laid eyes on Wynthrope Ryland several years ago, she had thought him the most attractive man in England. He hadn't spared her a second glance, and why would he? Back then she had been an overweight, shy country miss. The only man who paid any attention to her at all had been Anthony, her best friend—her husband.

Late husband. Dear Tony. She missed him still. He had remarked upon Wynthrope Ryland's looks on occasion as well.

But Octavia didn't know that Moira admired her brother-in-law's face and form. It was too humiliating to admit. Like an infatuated schoolgirl, she often looked for him at social events. Odd, but she hadn't thought of him at all during her mourning period. She hadn't thought of much at all other than the fact that her best friend was dead and the world was a grayer place for his loss.

But her mourning period was over, socially as well as personally. Shame on Minnie for leading Mr. Ryland to believe otherwise. Although her sister's quick thinking had stopped Moira from potentially making an even bigger cake of herself.

"I wish you had some idea of your own worth, Moira."

Jerked from her thoughts by her friend's voice, Moira glanced up. "I know my worth. You would have me inflate it beyond reason."

"No. Just to the point where you realize you are every bit as comely as your sister."

Was it Octavia's righteous tone or the words themselves that made her laugh so sharply? "You are a dear friend, but I am not so fragile that you need lie to me so kindly. Minnie is ten times prettier than I am."

Octavia's expression was dark. "Prettiness is not the only virtue a woman should aspire to."

What a lovely way to say that Moira was a nicer person than her younger sister. Octavia needn't be so careful with her words. Moira wasn't insulted for her sister. It was true. She was a better person than Minnie, but only because she hadn't been spoiled by their parents. And Tony had given her so much—taught her so much. Minnie simply hadn't been given a chance by life yet. Someday, Moira was certain of it, her younger sister would become the woman she should be.

And even if she didn't, Moira would still love her. Being an only child, Octavia wouldn't understand that. She would wager ten pounds, however, that Wynthrope Ryland would understand perfectly.

Unfortunately, Moira would wager another ten that he would understand her just as well. Ever since that day on Bond Street, when their gazes had met, she had the unnerving feeling that he had been able to peer inside her soul. Certainly it had felt as though she had seen inside his. For one intense, perfectly clear moment, she had looked at him and known that he was not what he appeared to be.

Which was nice, because he often appeared to be a cold, unfeeling rake.

Smiling sincerely, Moira took one of her friend's long, slender hands in her own. "I know you have little patience where my sister is concerned, Octavia. Thank you again for offering to host this party for her."

Octavia's lips thinned into a disgruntled curve. "I am doing it because I want you to have one evening for yourself."

"I could hardly refuse when you offered to do all the work as well."

"Not all of it," Octavia replied coyly. "Or you would not be here."

True, but Moira harbored her no ill will for it. "I enjoy dressing a house for Christmas. My own has been for days already."

Octavia arranged a pair of porcelain turtledoves on the mantel. "Yes, it makes the season seem that much more festive, does it not?"

Retrieving her holly and tacks, Moira smiled as she returned to work. "That and good friends."

"And hopefully some new ones." Octavia stepped back to admire her handiwork. "I think the entirety of London's aristocratic winter residents will be here this evening. I hope we have enough room."

Whether it was Octavia's invitation, or the lack of society during the colder months, Moira wasn't certain, but she had no doubt that Covent Garden would see more *ton* tonight than it did during the height of the theater season.

Again, if she were a betting woman, she would wager a large sum that the guests who arrived that evening were there either to see Minnie or to see Octavia and her somewhat famous husband. North Sheffield-Ryland had made quite a name for himself as a thief taker before entering into politics. He was already a great favorite of the regent's and the prime minister's.

Moira tacked more holly along the window frame. "Will North's brother be coming tonight?"

Octavia flashed her a sly look as she placed fresh candles in the silver holders on the mantel. "Wynthrope?"

Moira rolled her eyes. Her friend simply did not know when to give up. "You mentioned that the youngest was coming up from Devonshire."

"Ah yes, Devlin. He and Blythe should be here sometime this afternoon. Brahm has accepted as well. Thank you for allowing me to invite him."

Moira frowned at the thanks as she sorted through the leafy greenery for the next piece to arrange. "I could hardly tell you who not to invite to your own home. Besides, I have no reason to dislike the viscount. He's always been perfectly charming to me."

Octavia smiled. "The Ryland men can be terribly charming when they want to be."

Was it an accident, or did Octavia intentionally not mention whether Wynthrope would be there that evening? Well, Moira wasn't about to make an idiot of herself by asking.

As though fate wanted to aid her with that resolution, a maid appeared in the door at that very moment.

"I beg your pardon, my lady, but the man is here with the flowers you ordered. There seems to be some sort of problem with the order."

This was obviously not what Octavia wanted to hear. Casting an apologetic glance at Moira, she begged to be excused. "I shall just be a moment, I promise."

"Take your time. I will try not to puncture my thumb again in your absence."

Her friend smiled and left the room. Unless the flowers were completely dastardly, Moira was fairly certain no one would give them much notice, so whatever mistake the flower man made, it was nothing to fret over. Still, Octavia had yet to return by the time Moira finished decorating the last window.

What to do now? She could go find Octavia, but she had no desire to get involved in the floral dilemma. The only thing left to do was hang the mistletoe in the doorways and in various locations throughout the room.

Moira took the ladder Octavia's massive butler, Johnson, had brought in earlier and began tacking the sprigs of mistletoe up around the room. There would be no shortage of kissing going on that evening. Of course, it would all be entirely proper and in the spirit of the season. Many an eligible bachelor would steer Minnie beneath these boughs—in front of Moira's ever-watchful eyes, of course.

Climbing the ladder to hang the last sprig, Moira stretched to tack it into place. She had misjudged when placing the ladder against the wall, having to position it to maneuver around a painting.

She pushed up onto her toes, straining to her right. Just a little farther . . . *Oh oh.*

The ladder tipped, wobbling backward as Moira's arms windmilled. Desperately she struggled to regain balance, but it was no use. The ladder fell, flinging her toward the floor.

But instead of landing on the hard slats, Moira landed against something almost as solid. A band of unyielding strength closed around her, flattening her breasts to her chest, pinning her to a wall of warm, spicy-scented man. She didn't have to see him to know who he was. Her luck was so rotten, there was only one man it could be.

"Steady," he murmured as her shaking knees threatened to buckle beneath her.

As though near-injury wasn't enough to send her heart into a frantic pounding, his voice added to the chaotic rhythm. Stiffening, she turned, even as common sense ordered her to run as far away as she could.

He didn't release her as any decent gentleman would have. He just stood there, holding her in an entirely improper manner, waiting for her to look up and meet his indescribable gaze. Well, she wouldn't do it. She refused to let him bait her. She would demand that he let her go.

Her resolve lasted all of three seconds. Bold blue eyes stared at her from beneath gently arched brows. His lashes were long and tilted upward at the ends. It seemed everything about him was almost perfectly straight but not quite—even his nose. Such imperfections could have harmed a less impressive face, but not his. Sweet mercy, but he was one splendid-looking man. No doubt he knew it. Beautiful men usually knew they were beautiful.

Of course, in her experience, beautiful men often preferred the *company* of other beautiful men, and she knew that wasn't true in the case of Wynthrope Ryland. He certainly seemed to have enjoyed his share of women.

Strange, but she had the feeling he hadn't necessarily liked them. For that matter, she wasn't all that certain he liked himself that much either, even though he gave all the appearance of just the opposite.

His dark hair was slightly mussed, his cheeks rosy from the cold. His blue eyes sparkled with mischief, crinkling at the corners as a slight dimple appeared in his cheek. Was he laughing at her? Could he feel her heart pounding through the thin material of her gown? And why couldn't she be wearing something pretty instead of a plain blue morning dress? She must look a fright.

So why was he looking at her as though he liked what he saw?

"I must say, Lady Aubourn, that while I have often wished a woman would simply fall into my arms, this is not quite the way I imagined it."

Low and gentle and perfectly modulated, his voice was that of the quintessential gentleman.

It was also so patently false that Moira winced at it. There was something mocking about his tone, as though he wanted people to know it was false.

"Is it not, Mr. Ryland? How lovely that you have had such imaginings. Usually I only think of falling when I am actually doing so."

His eyes widened. Good, her tone hadn't been lost on him either. Such caustic politeness was not her usual mode of speaking, though she knew many members of the *ton* who had it perfected to an art form.

How disappointing that Wynthrope Ryland appeared to be one of them.

Eyes glinting, he continued to hold her, even though her feet were solidly planted on the floor beneath her. He had to know what he was doing was highly improper. He had to know that she could feel him pressed against her through her gown, that she was far too aware of the length of his legs against her own.

"You are welcome," he murmured.

This was his real voice. She knew from the shiver rippling down her spine. Low and soft and dark—like snuggling beneath an ermine-lined blanket on a winter's night. She flushed—not just from her reaction to him, but from his words as well. There was no excuse for rudeness, not when he had saved her from certain injury.

"Thank you." Her eyes downcast, Moira placed the flats of her hands against his shoulders and pushed firmly. "You may let me go now."

"Not yet, my lady."

Not yet? Whatever did he mean, not yet? Lifting her chin, she vowed to ask him that very question, but the minute she looked up, she realized what he meant.

They were standing beneath the very mistletoe she had managed to hang just before she fell.

Horrified, Moira dropped her gaze to his. He was smiling that cool, sure, crooked smile.

"Will you kiss me, Lady Aubourn? Or shall I kiss you?"

Chapter 2

Just one kiss. That was all Wynthrope wanted. Just one kiss and he'd let her go.

He didn't know why he wanted to kiss her so badly, only that he did. She was so delicate, but not fragile, he suspected. Her eyes were huge, her nose straight and sharp. Her brows were sharp, her chin was sharp. The only softness was her mouth—the gentle slope of her top lip giving way to a much fuller bottom one. And her skin . . . it was as fair and clear as he imagined it would be.

She could have slapped him—many women would have for being so bold, but not the viscountess. She just stood there, surprisingly soft against him, her hands braced against his shoulders. She had stopped shoving. She was trembling.

Trembling. Christ, when was the last time a woman had trembled in his company? It wasn't because she was frightened—he knew that simply by the light in her wide hazel eyes. She was wary of him, yes, and perhaps a little intimidated, but

19

she wasn't afraid. Nor did she seem terribly bothered by whatever it was she saw inside him, and she must have seen something inside him because he could feel her looking, even in the most secret regions of his soul.

Her long, thin fingers flexed against the wool of his coat. "This is truly unkind of you, Mr. Ryland."

"Unkind? Do you find me cruel?" As cruel as the tightening in his trousers? As cruel as being denied the promise suggested by her supple form?

"Is it not cruel to torment me as you are?" Her normally low voice was even lower, slightly hoarse. "You should not play such games."

So she thought she was tormented, did she? She did not know the meaning of the word. Neither had he until this moment. "What I find cruel, Lady Aubourn, is that you will not allow me to kiss you, no matter how much I wish you would."

Her eyes widened at that. Perhaps she had thought he was teasing at first. Perhaps she hadn't realized that he wasn't merely flirting with her, but she had to know now. How innocent did a woman—a once-married woman at that—have to be to not realize when a man was sincere in his attraction? And he was attracted. He had thought of little but her since their encounter the night before. She was an intriguing slip of a woman, and he wanted to know her better.

And he meant "know" in the Biblical sense.

"Is this punishment?" she asked, obviously piqued. "Are you trying to exact retribution for my behavior last night? You needn't bother, I assure you I have already berated myself enough for both of us."

Wynthrope scowled. "What kind of nonsense is that? I want to kiss you, woman, not chastise you. Or do you find me so repulsive a kiss would seem like punishment?" Now he was the one spouting nonsense. He might not be as tall as his brother Devlin, or as well built as North, or as handsome as Brahm, but he knew he was not displeasing to a large portion of the opposite gender.

He also knew that if Lady Aubourn found him that distasteful she would have slapped him by now and demanded that he release her.

"Repulsive?" She stared at him in disbelief. "Surely you cannot be that stupid."

What else could he do but laugh? It had a bit of a rusty, dry sound to it, and it felt odd as it worked its way up his throat, but it wasn't an unpleasant experience. He was still chuckling when his gaze locked with hers once more. The laughter died; his smile faded.

She was staring at him with such awe that he was instantly contrite. His heart, nasty little fig that it was, twisted at the sheer wonder in her eyes. All this for a little laughter, a bit of a smile? His laughter was rare, but did it deserve such a reception?

Apparently Lady Aubourn thought so.

If he had wanted to kiss her five minutes ago, he was dying to do so now.

Her lips parted. Was it an invitation, or was she about to speak? Whatever it was, he was doomed not to know.

"Moira?" Octavia's voice drifted from the corridor. "Are you all right? I heard a noise."

His sister-in-law had rotten timing. Had Octavia been watching from some secret spot, waiting for just the right moment to save her friend from his lecherous clutches? Or was fate simply toying with him again as it liked to do?

The gaze he bestowed on his viscountess was rueful at best. "Denied again. You owe me, my lady."

"Please." She pushed against his shoulders as the noise of Octavia's approach grew louder. "Let me go."

Reluctantly he did as she commanded, careful to put a suitable amount of space between them as he did so. "Sooner or later I intend to collect." Then, with one last glance up at the mistletoe, he flashed her a slight smile. "Perhaps tonight."

"Wynthrope." His sister-in-law's voice was as warm as a summer's breeze as she flitted into the room. Not as husky as the viscountess's, and thankfully not at all as arousing. "It is about time you arrived."

He faced her with a humorous but slightly mocking smile, not offended by her tone. "You did not specify a time in the note you sent."

Octavia's expression was one of gentle amusement. "I assumed you would arrive at a decent hour."

"I do not even get out of bed at a decent hour."

"Well, I am glad Moira had someone to keep her company while I was gone."

He glanced at the viscountess out of the corner of his eye. Was she as suspicious as he was of Octavia's intentions? His sister-in-law rarely requested his attendance before dinner. Perhaps Octavia wouldn't try to keep him away from the viscountess at all. Perhaps just the opposite. She looked the very picture of innocence. That in itself was reason enough to distrust her. She was just as good a liar as North, but Wynthrope was better.

"Lady Aubourn is very charming company." He tilted his head. "Now, I assume you called me here for a reason?"

"Oh yes." Her reaction seemed a bit more natural now. "I need you to teach me how to tie the mathematical cravat. Your brother wants to wear that style this evening."

North rolled his eyes. "Why does he not simply hire a valet?"

Octavia looked at him as though the answer was obvious. "He does not want one."

Ah yes. How could he be so daft? "Why hire a valet when he has me."

His sister-in-law grinned. "Exactly."

"Fine. I will show you." There was no point in denying her—he couldn't even if he wanted to. He would never deny her or North anything, no matter how small.

"Thank you." Octavia turned to her guest. "Moira, you will excuse us, will you not?"

The viscountess nodded. In fact she looked rather pleased to be rid of him, the intriguing little baggage.

Wynthrope bowed to her. "I look forward to continuing our conversation tonight, Lady Aubourn."

That stole the satisfaction from her face, but she couldn't very well snub him in front of Octavia without admitting their little encounter. Somehow he didn't think the lovely viscountess wanted his sister-in-law to know anything that happened between them. Not yet, at any rate. Eventually she would tell—women always did.

"Until tonight then, Mr. Ryland," she replied politely with a slight dip of her head.

He smiled, his blood thrumming with anticipation. It had been far too long since he'd felt so challenged. "Until tonight."

Tonight she would not escape him so easily.

"He did *what*?"

Sitting on her bed in her dressing gown, Moira sipped at a cup of sweet, hot tea and offered a sugar biscuit to her dear friend Nathaniel, who lounged across the coverlet like a long, lazy cat.

He shook his head at the plate, and she took it away, stealing another biscuit for herself first. She was going to have to skip dinner. "He said he wanted to kiss me."

The memory of Wynthrope Ryland's words and the darkness of his compelling blue eyes twisted her stomach in knots even as it growled for more biscuit.

"And you did not let him?" Nathaniel's fresh, youthful-looking face wore an expression of horrified disbelief. "Have I taught you nothing?"

Moira smiled sweetly. "Nothing at all."

Lying across the foot of her bed as he was, Nathaniel Caylan was all rumpled elegance and uncaring grace in dark blue and buff. No wonder Anthony had adored him so; Nathaniel was the perfect mix of boy and man. His blue eyes sparkled with a lust for life, even though the *love* of his life had been dead for nigh on two years. His cheeks glowed with health, even though his usual pattern was to stay up all night and sleep most of the day. It was late afternoon, and Moira was fresh from the bath, taking some time to relax before getting ready for the party at Octavia's. Nathaniel had just gotten out of bed an hour ago.

"Wynthrope Ryland is one of *the* most attractive men society has to offer." Nathaniel took a sip of tea. "Any woman—or man—would be mad to refuse him."

Moira chuckled. Her friend was always saying such outrageous things. She was so used to it that he had to be very wicked to surprise her. "Then you had better cart me off to Bedlam, because I refused him."

Pale brows waggled suggestively. "There is still tonight."

Shame on him for throwing Ryland's words back at her. She had just gotten her heart slowed to its normal pace, and now it tripped foolishly once more.

How could she allow herself such a reaction? Surely she was old enough now not to harbor girlish notions where men were concerned. Wynthrope Ryland would be no more interested in her than Tony had been—although for different reasons. Tony would have loved her if he had been capable of it. He had loved her as much as he could, given the circumstances, but he had taken the time to get to know her. Anyone could win the heart of another if given enough time. She truly believed that. Perhaps she might even woo Wynthrope Ryland if given the time, but this interest he showed in her had no time behind it. It was new, too new for her to trust in it. In the past such attention generally meant that someone had made a wager about her, or that they were wanting to use her to get close to one of her sisters.

Everyone who came near her had an agenda of his own—even dear Tony had approached her out of his own interests. It seemed her own interests would be met as well, and they were, for a time.

"Tonight I wager Mr. Ryland will have found someone else to flirt with." She dunked her last biscuit in her tea before popping the entire thing in her mouth. "He will ignore me once more."

Nathaniel brushed a smattering of crumbs from his coat with a careless wave of his hand. "And if he does not?"

"Then I will ask him what exactly it is he is up to." Too bad she didn't feel as brave as she sounded. She would stay true to her word, however. She had been made to feel foolish one too many times in the past to allow it to happen again.

"And what if he says he wants you?" her friend demanded, regarding her with more severity than Moira was accustomed to from him. "What if the only thing he is guilty of is wanting to be with you?"

Flushing, Moira shook her head. "He does not want me." He probably wanted Minnie, despite his blatant dismissal of her younger sister. He could be playing difficult to entice the younger woman—Lord knew her sister had talked of little else since the incident. One minute Minerva hated Wynthrope Ryland, the next she was determined to have him.

"Whyever not?"

"Because he just does not." It was just that simple.

A dog with a bone, he would not let go. "Yes, but how do you know?"

The answer tore free of her with a nasty snap. "Because no one ever wants me!"

Oh dear. That was more than she wanted to reveal. Poor Nathaniel, he looked so horrified. He really needn't put so much upon himself. It wasn't as though he was the pathetic one of the two of them.

"My dear Moira." She flinched at the sympathy in his tone, pulling her hand away as he tried to take it in his own. "How can someone so wonderful think so little of herself as you do?"

She smiled sardonically. "It is surprisingly easy."

"Yes, I do not doubt that it is." Nathaniel shot her a pointed stare. "Well, it stops tonight."

Moira chuckled. As though she could undo a lifetime of self-doubt in one evening.

"Tonight you are not allowed to be so disparaging toward yourself. Tonight, if Wynthrope Ryland or any other man approaches you, you will believe that it is because he is intelligent to see just what a catch you are."

"Oh will I?" Why should she believe that when it had never been true in the past? For heaven's sake, men had made sport of her! And all because she was so "unapproachable" and "immune" to seduction. How those descriptions had hurt. She was neither of those things, nor any of the other words they had used to describe her. She simply had no idea what to do when it came to men, and didn't want to embarrass herself.

Or reveal her secret and lose the life she had made for herself. She would rather die a virgin than return to her parents.

"Yes, you will believe any man who approaches you does so because he cannot deny your charms. Now finish your tea and let us begin preparing for the evening."

Moira stared at him in disbelief. "But it is hours yet before the party!" Was she that unpresentable that she needed almost a full five hours to prepare?

"Exactly. We must begin if I am going to make you see what a goddess you are by eight."

A goddess.

Good Lord, Nathaniel hadn't been kidding.

"What have you done to me?"

Standing before her looking glass, Moira stared at her reflection with fascinated horror. Was this truly she? Yes, she could see the lips move as she spoke. It was she—and yet, it did not *look* like herself.

"I did not do a thing," Nathaniel quipped, looking entirely too pleased with himself. "I simply told your maid what to do. Delightful girl. Very talented."

Moira's gaze slipped from his smiling face back to her mirror.

Where had all that hair come from, so artfully styled and curled atop her head? Those dark arched brows were thinner than she remembered, and her eyes seemed all the bigger for it. Her nose and chin had been powdered, eliminating the shine and giving her skin a shimmery glow. Nathaniel had insisted that the powder extend down her throat and chest, so that the flesh just above the neckline of her gown gleamed in the lamplight.

All those things he had put her through—the bath, the creams, the potions—all of it had been worth it. Her skin felt as soft as a newborn's. She smelled of strawberries and honey, every inch of her tingling from her friend's pampering.

"How do you know so much?" she asked, watching her skirts swish as she twirled around.

Nathaniel chuckled. "I spent many hours with my

mother's maid as a youngster. Everyone thought I was infatuated. I was—but with what the girl could do rather than the girl herself."

"And now I reap the benefits of your education. Oh, Nate! I can scarcely believe my eyes! I am actually pretty!" Was it vain of her to admire her own appearance? But it was true—she felt so very, very pretty.

"You always have been pretty, my love." Nathaniel's smile was kind. "All I did was help you notice."

She swished her skirts again, enjoying how the fabric felt against her legs. "I'm so glad I allowed you to talk me into buying this gown. It is perfect for a winter party."

The gown was soft, luminescent satin in a shade not quite white. The skirt and bodice were dotted with tiny crystals that sparkled in the light, and little pearls that added more shimmery warmth. Her gloves and slippers were the same shade of cream as well. Her only other adornment was the delicate diamond tiara on top of her head. She wore no other jewelry at all.

"I hope Anthony is watching," Nathaniel said, his voice tinged with regret. "He would love to see you this way."

Moira squeezed his hand. "He would be happy to see me wearing the tiara. He always wanted me to wear it more."

"It suits you."

Moira chuckled. "He told me if I married him he would treat me like the queen I was. The tiara was a wedding gift."

"He adored you."

Moira smiled. She didn't need to be told. She knew what her husband had thought of her. "Is it still painful for you to think of him?"

Nathaniel shook his head. "Not like it was. There is more happiness than pain when I think of him now."

Poor Nathaniel. He had gone through full mourning with

her, feeling Anthony's loss as Moira should have. How could she mourn Anthony as a wife should when he hadn't truly been her husband? She had mourned him as one would mourn any dear friend, but Nathaniel had mourned him as a lover, and Moria's heart had wept more for Nathaniel than it ever had for dear Tony.

Two years had come and gone. Moira's mourning clothes were packed away, but Nathaniel still wore somber shades—grays and dark blues, plums and browns. No one but someone who truly knew him would notice the change. Once upon a time he had worn bright colors, the very height of fashion, now he was more subdued. Still, not even Brummell himself could find fault with his appearance.

Moira's only wish was that someday the sparkle would return to her friend's eyes. To think she had often envied Nathaniel's relationship with Tony. Perhaps she envied it still, but she did not envy him his pain. The idea of loving someone so much that they took a part of you with them when they died was terrifying.

And yet . . . How wonderful it must have been for both of them while Tony was still alive. Never mind that they could never love publicly—they could have been imprisoned for daring to have such a relationship. They had loved perfectly, without shame and without regret. Yes, Moira would always envy them that.

"Come," Nathaniel's voice cut through her thoughts. "He would not want us to ruin this evening by being maudlin. We have a party to attend."

How right he was. No one thought anything of Nathaniel accompanying her to so many social events. His longtime "friendship" with Tony made it understandable. It also provided an excuse for neither of them to form romantic attachments. Everyone simply assumed that one day the widow would marry her late husband's best friend. It was the perfect arrangement. This way no one found out the truth about Nathaniel, and no one found out that Moira, for all her years of marriage, was three-and-thirty and still a virgin.

All those years of starving herself so she'd be thin enough to attract a husband, and the man she married hadn't wanted her body.

So why was she still trying so hard to be what society thought she should be when she had no intention of marrying again—not unless she met a man who made her believe in love?

Because she was an idiot, and because she had always had difficulty doing what she wanted. Once she might have blamed her mother for that, but now that she was a grown woman, she could blame no one but herself. She was a viscountess—even if a dowager. If she couldn't bring herself to act as she pleased now, she never would.

"What will people say when I arrive looking like this?" she asked, a shameful echo of fear in her voice. "They will talk, for sure."

Smiling, Nathaniel draped a ermine-lined cape around her shoulders. "Only until someone else arrives for them to whisper about. They will remark on how fine you look, my friend. Nothing more. And those who are nasty will be so because they are small in mind and feeling."

He was right; in her heart Moira knew it too. Secretly she wanted to be looked at and admired.

It was just so bloody unfortunate that she had to go out in public to have it happen.

Would Wynthrope Ryland admire her appearance? Would he know that she had dressed to attract his attention? Would she want that attention if he gave it? What if he ignored her?

No, he wouldn't ignore her. As much as part of her hoped he would—and put an end to this foolish dream of hers—

Moira knew he wouldn't let her have her peace, not yet. Ryland hadn't gotten what he wanted out of her, and he wasn't the kind of man to give up until he had. Regardless of his reasons for flirting with her—it might have been an accident for all she knew—he wanted to kiss her, and he wouldn't stop pursuing her until he had done so.

Perhaps she should kiss him at the party and get it over with. Perhaps she should ask him what he stood to gain by stealing a kiss.

Nathaniel offered her his arm, his smile giving her courage to face the evening. "Shall we depart?"

Placing her hand on his sleeve, Moira exhaled a deep breath. "Yes. I wager Minnie is just about ready to throttle us both for taking this long."

Her friend shrugged. "It will do the chit good to wait for you for a change. I daresay she will be positively green with jealousy over your appearance."

"You shouldn't say such things about my sister." It was a halfhearted rebuke, and they both knew it. As much as Moira loved her younger sister, the girl was a trial at times.

They walked down the corridor to the stairs in the silence. Somehow the pale blue walls seemed closer, as though the town house had shrunk while Moira was in her room. It was impossible, of course. Even the stairs, which were composed of many gentle steps, seemed steeper, each foothold narrow and tenuous.

"You are shaking," Nathaniel remarked as they descended. Were it not for his guidance, she would have tripped for certain.

"I am nervous. Is that not ridiculous?" Holding her skirts out of the way of her leaden feet, Moira kept her gaze focused straight ahead. "Octavia and I have been planning this party forever, it seems, and now that it is here, I am all a-flutter."

"It is not the party that is to blame for the fluttering in your stomach and the tremor in your limbs."

"Do not say it." She knew what he was implying.

"I do not have to. You know who is to blame as much as I."

"*He* has nothing to do with my anxiety." Why was she bothering to deny it? She never hid her feelings from Nathaniel, why do so now? So she wouldn't have to face the sympathy in his eyes when Wynthrope lost interest in her?

Nathaniel appeared not to have heard her—or was willfully ignoring her? "I used to feel the same way every time I knew I was going to see Anthony."

Moira swallowed against the hard lump of envy in her throat. "It is hardly the same situation. I have only just met the man."

"You have thought he was beautiful since you first laid eyes on him."

Yes, that was true. For as long as she could remember, she had believed Wynthrope Ryland to be the finest man in Christendom. Odd how they had never actually met before this. "So?"

He stopped on the steps. She had no choice but to stop as well. He waited until she looked at him to speak. "So stop acting like you are the one who could be clapped in irons for daring to be attracted to someone and take some pleasure from your life."

Moira glanced away. He knew just where to poke her to get the reaction he wanted. He was right. He was the one who had to conduct every relationship in secret, under the threat of persecution, not her. All she had to face was a little public embarrassment. Surely there were worse things.

Like having to return to her parents. Just the thought made her blood run cold. *That* was why she couldn't risk an affair.

She couldn't risk anyone finding out she was still a virgin and her marriage void.

Unless, of course, her lover promised not to tell. Unless he fell in love and wanted to marry her. Such a man wouldn't betray her secret, not if he loved her and she him.

It was such a big risk, and Moira wasn't entirely certain it was worth it, not when she'd been made sport of in the past.

"I will consider it," she promised her friend. Considering was a far cry from actually doing. And by making such a vow to Nathaniel, she was ensuring herself at least a brief reprieve from his well-intended pushes to "take some pleasure" from her life.

Minerva was indeed waiting for them, pacing the drawing room carpet as though she sought to wear a hole in the delicate fleur-de-lis pattern. Her jaw dropped when her gaze fell on her older sister.

Moira hid a smile. "Sorry to keep you waiting, dearest."

The pretty younger woman simply stared at her, her brown eyes as wide as saucers. "Moira! You . . . you look so lovely."

Her surprise wasn't meant to be hurtful, Moira knew that. Still, it was all she could do not to wince at her sister's tone.

"I shall be the envy of every gentleman present," Nathaniel remarked, saving Moira from having to respond. "How fortunate I am to be escorting two such lovely ladies."

Minnie beamed under his praise, even though she must know just how charming she looked with her glossy ringlets and flattering peach gown. She was all hair, eyes, and bosom, her little sister. She knew she was attractive to the opposite gender, and yet she seemed to always need reassurance of it.

They arrived at the party ahead of the other guests. It was only right that Moira be there to welcome guests along with

Octavia. After all, it was because of her and Minnie that Octavia had offered to host the gathering to begin with.

Octavia was content to let Moira stand beside her and her husband, North, until the house began to fill with partygoers, then she sent Moira off to mingle—something Moira found as painful as having a tooth pulled. She never knew what to say to people. Fortunately, she knew that most people liked to talk about themselves.

She was standing by herself near the ballroom mantel, sipping champagne and listening to Varya Christian, the Marchioness of Wynter and a Russian princess, play the pianoforte when Minnie scurried up to her.

"He is here."

This was more enthusiasm than Moira had seen in a long time. It worried her. "Who?"

"Wynthrope Ryland," her sister responded, her eyes bright and her color high. "I wonder if he will want to dance with me tonight."

Oh, this was not good. Minnie had decided that Wynthrope Ryland was a challenge to overcome. "Do not allow him to affect your evening, Minnie."

Her sister shot her a sharp look. "You do not think he will ask me."

"I do not know if he will or not." Was it wrong of her to hope that he wouldn't? Minnie was no match for Wynthrope Ryland. For that matter, neither was Moira.

Minnie frowned. "You want him for yourself."

"Of course I do not, but what matter if I did? You only seek his attention because he snubbed you." She took a drink of champagne to still her tongue. Minnie's temper did not need much encouragement, and the last thing Moira wanted was a scene.

"That is not true." The tone of Minnie's voice told otherwise.

Moira turned to her sister with a gentle hand on the arm. "Dearest, why not put that energy into finding a man who does not have to be convinced that he likes you?"

Maybe she was being a bit harsh—and a bit selfish. Maybe she did want Wynthrope Ryland for herself, but she also didn't want to see her sister injured.

But Minnie obviously didn't see things the same way. With her jaw set defiantly, she turned her back on Moira and wandered into the crowd, swallowed up by a whole host of people who no doubt would soothe her ruffled feathers as the dancing began.

Perhaps there was some truth in Minnie's hopes. Perhaps Ryland had known what kind of reaction his asking Moira to dance would cause in Minnie. Perhaps that was exactly what he wanted—Moira's sister.

Or maybe, a little voice in her head whispered, *he really is interested in you, you great foolish article.*

"I think too much," she mumbled under her breath as pain pulsed in the front of her head.

"A thoroughly unattractive trait in a woman, I assure you."

Oh no. Her cheeks burning, Moira raised her gaze to the dark, mocking blue eyes of Wynthrope Ryland. His mouth lifted slightly to the right—a satiric imitation of a smile if Moira ever saw one.

"Good evening, Lady Aubourn. Would you care to dance?"

She could not escape him now.

Her gaze was wary as it met his, her cheeks stained with a becoming blush. She really was a striking woman, if a little on the thin side. She looked especially lovely this evening, as though she had taken particular pains with her toilette.

Had her efforts been for his benefit? His pride refused to believe otherwise.

She looked away. "I am afraid I am not much of a dancer, Mr. Ryland."

Ah, so it was to be like that, was it? "Very well. Perhaps your sister—"

"No." The wary gaze was determined now.

He smiled. He really shouldn't find her as amusing as he did. "I thought that might make you change your mind."

Some women would have flushed, others would have chuckled flirtatiously. Moira Tyndale stared at him as though they were two dogs after the same bone. "If you are trying to get to my sister through me, it will not work."

Wynthrope didn't bother trying to hide his amusement. "My dear woman, I would rather lay upon a bed of nails than go through you for anything."

That brought a darker shade of pink to her cheeks. "Then why are you doing this? Why this sudden interest in me?"

"By God, but you are a bold baggage." He wasn't certain if he liked it or not. Yes, yes he did.

"I am not bold," she replied, her gaze not quite so sure now. "I have simply been made a fool of often enough that I have no wish to have it done to me again."

"I have no idea what you are talking about. I simply like the look of you and had a mind to make your better acquaintance."

Her eyes widened. "You do?"

He still had no idea what she was talking about. Did she refer to his ignorance, the fact that he liked the look of her, or that he wanted to know her better? Or perhaps she meant all three. Regardless, Wynthrope was beginning to wonder if perhaps the viscountess didn't require more effort than any woman deserved. It was unfortunate, really.

"Why don't I just walk away?" he suggested, disappointed. "We can pretend this never happened."

He had just turned his back when a hand on his arm stopped him. "Wait. Please."

He faced her again, half expecting her to toss a glass of champagne in his face, or accuse him of wanting her pretty sister again. Perhaps she'd surprise him with some other act of lunacy.

Instead she bowed her dark head, the stones in her tiara glittering violently under the chandelier. She looked like a queen—a white queen. Then, she raised her gaze to his.

No, not a white queen. She was the black queen—with a solemn dark beauty and hidden secrets and depths yet unexplored. There was vulnerability in her hazel gaze, along with a steely strength Wynthrope could not explain. If he didn't know better, he would almost think she was afraid of him, challenged by him.

He waited for her to make her move.

She swallowed, the fragile length of her throat straining with the effort. Good Lord, it wasn't as though he'd asked her to run away with him—just for a dance. "Forgive me, Mr. Ryland. I was inexcusably rude to you just now."

He nodded. "Yes, you were." He let her digest that before adding, "But perhaps I have given you reason to be wary."

Her gaze never wavered. "You have. I am not accustomed to such . . . attention."

Why the hell not? Were the men of England so bloody stupid they didn't know a treasure waiting to be discovered when they saw it? Moira Tyndale was a diamond still rough and uncut, odd for a widow married so many years.

He wanted to be the man to discover her facets—all of them. Never before had he felt such an attraction to a woman. As unnerving as it was, he wanted to follow the pull wherever it led him.

"I would be honored to help you become accustomed to such attention, my lady." It was truth, not flattery.

She blushed as though he had told her he wanted to strip her naked and kiss her from foot to head. Not a bad thought, actually.

"Good evening, Mr. Ryland."

Wonderful. The sister had returned. He met her with a cool smile. "Miss Banning. You look lovely this evening." The chit always looked lovely—not as compelling as her sister, but pretty in a totally uninteresting way.

Minerva dimpled. No blush, no fluttering pulse at the base of her throat. She was as accustomed to such flattery as her sister was not. "What are you and my sister discussing?"

"Dancing," Moira surprised him by answering. Her gaze met his for one brief, hot moment before turning to the younger woman. "Mr. Ryland just asked me to dance."

Was it Wynthrope's imagination, or did Minerva look as though she'd like to kick Moira in the shins?

"I am still waiting for your answer, my lady." If she asked her sister for permission, he'd walk away. He really would.

But Moira cast only the briefest—and most apologetic—glance at her sister before offering her hand to him. "I would love to."

Relieved beyond reason, Wynthrope took her gloved fingers in his and led her out into the crowd of dancers without so much as a glance at Minerva. Getting this woman to allow him access to her was going to take more effort than he was used to exerting. A moment ago he had thought she was not worth that exertion. Now he began to entertain the notion that she might be, after all.

Good thing there was nothing else he would rather spend his energy on.

The music signaled a waltz. Had she realized that before agreeing to dance? No, there was no way she could have. Finally fate was being kind to him. He could have her all to himself for a few minutes with no chance of interruption.

"I think your sister wanted to dance with me," he remarked, placing his hand on the small of her back. How delicate she was.

Her slender hand curled around his. "She is eighteen and you snubbed her. She regards you as a challenge that must be conquered."

"How do you regard me?" He would gladly be conquered by Moira.

Her chin lifted. "I have not yet decided."

He chuckled at her candor as he guided her through a gentle turn. "You are a hard woman, Lady Aubourn."

She stiffened in his arms. "I am sorry. I have offended you again."

"Relax." He splayed his fingers against her gown, softly massaging the rigid flesh beneath. "You have not come anywhere near offending me, I assure you."

"But I thought—"

"Ahh, but you think too much." He grinned at her.

She smiled then, an unexpected flash of straight white teeth. Wynthrope's heart gave a mighty thump at the sight of it. No doubt that knocked some of the dust off.

"I have made a decision, Mr. Ryland."

This sounded interesting. He could feel the tension easing out of her as he guided her through another turn. She wasn't a bad dancer at all when she relaxed. "About what, my lady?"

Her gaze was level but incredibly shy and uncertain. "I believe I have a mind to make your better acquaintance as well."

A thrill shot from the middle of Wynthrope's chest straight to his groin. The black queen had made her first move. Now it was his turn. He had a kiss to collect.

But not tonight. Tonight he would enjoy this small victory, and allow Moira to think she was in control of their game. She might have started the play, but he intended to win.

He always won.

Wynthrope arrived at his apartments several hours later to find a lamp burning in the parlor. His valet must have forgotten to snuff it out. It wasn't until he was well into the room that he noticed he wasn't alone. There was someone else in the room.

Someone who looked very much like a man he'd once thought of as a father. A man who'd lied to him and betrayed him right to the bone. A man whose very presence was like a shard of ice in Wynthrope's chest.

It couldn't be him. God, don't let it be him.

"Hello, boyo."

Chapter 3

❧

Those two words cracked the façade of composure Wynthrope tried hard to always project. This was a nightmare—his worst nightmare—coming true.

He launched across the room to where his uninvited guest lounged. Seizing the older man by the lapels, he hauled him to his feet with a snarl, his heart hammering wildly in his chest, blood thrumming in his veins. Their faces were mere inches apart and yet his "guest" did not flinch. At one time he had respected this fearlessness, now he despised it. He wanted to pound it off his face until there was nothing left.

"What the hell are you doing in my house?"

Smiling easily, William Daniels pushed at the hands creasing his coat. "Easy, boyo. Is this any way to treat an old friend?"

"You were never my friend." What the bastard was, was lucky—lucky Wynthrope had some control over himself and didn't just kill him.

Some of the leprechaun charm faded from the older man's craggy features. "Let me go, boy. I've a proposition for you."

Strangely enough, Wynthrope did as he was bid. Releasing Daniels's coat, he dropped the Irishman back into the winged chair. He should have killed him when the thought occurred to him.

"You have five minutes to explain yourself before I throw you out." Why was he even giving the bastard a chance to talk? Had he not learned the hard way that William Daniels was not to be trusted? The longer he spent in the Irishman's company, the worse it would go for him.

Daniels watched him with an expression that bordered on amused. He straightened his coat haphazardly, seemingly unconcerned with Wynthrope and his rage.

The son of a bitch always had been too cocksure by half. To think that one time Wynthrope had looked up to this man; thought of him as more of a father than his own father had been. Of course, that had been the plan. Daniels knew exactly what to say to him, the things to do to make Wynthrope a willing participant in his illegal activities.

And when Daniels hadn't been able to give Wynthrope what he wanted to hear, what he wanted to see, he made it up—never to the point of actually lying, however. Daniels was a master of bending reality to his will.

"Aren't you going to offer me a drink?" the Irishman asked lightly, his tone as smooth and oily as the pomade in his salt-and-pepper hair.

Folding his arms across his chest to ease the shaking in his muscles, Wynthrope leaned against the solid frame of his desk. "You will not be here that long."

That got a grin from the old man. "M'boy, you of anyone should know how fast I can toss back a whiskey."

How could he talk as if nothing had happened? Wynthrope had betrayed him after discovering the truth. Daniels was not a man to forget such a cross. "I know you will talk that much faster without one."

Daniels sighed, regarding Wynthrope as a father might a disappointing son. It was a look Wynthrope had received often enough from his real father. "You've become a hard man, Wyn."

"I wonder why." He couldn't keep the sarcasm from his voice.

"Ah, so it's my fault, is it?"

Was five minutes up yet? "What do you want, Daniels?"

He tugged a crease from his sleeve. "I have a job for you."

That was it. This was the reason for the chummy attitude. Daniels needed him. He had humored the old man long enough. "Get out."

Daniels stayed where he was, an arrogant expression settling over his lamp-shadowed features. "I do not think you want to toss me out just yet."

"Yes, I do." He wanted to do more than toss him out. He wanted to hit him, pummel him with his bare fists until Daniels couldn't smile that mocking smile anymore. He wanted to make Daniels tell him why he had betrayed him as he had, why he had played him for a fool. But most of all— and most pathetically—he wanted to ask if Daniels had been lying when he told Wynthrope he thought of him as a son.

"There is something I need," the old man told him. "I want you to get it for me."

Wynthrope choked on bitter laughter. "There is no payment you could offer to make me work for you again."

Some of the old man's pleasant façade faded. "No payment, boyo. You owe me."

Owe him? If either of them was owed anything, it was Wynthrope.

A few years ago Wynthrope had been a thief, and a very

good one. He enjoyed the risk and danger of his job, and he had been still young enough that he enjoyed the approval Daniels lavished on him. But that was before he had found out that it was all a sham. North had come to him all grim and anxious. Did Wynthrope work for a man named William Daniels? Was he aware that William Daniels was little more than a high-class fence?

Wynthrope hadn't been aware. He had been told that Daniels worked for the government. He had been told that he too was working for the crown, that everything he stole, every intrigue he involved himself in, was to benefit England and the war effort against Napoleon. Daniels's ruse had been elaborate and convincing, but that didn't stop Wynthrope from feeling thoroughly stupid when the truth was finally revealed. He would not be so stupid again.

Daniels's gaze locked with his, dark and deadly. "I see your brother has taken up political ambitions."

Wynthrope said nothing, the blood in his veins turning to ice. He should have seen this coming.

"It would be a right shame if his adorin' public was to find out he purposely tampered with a Bow Street investigation to save his brother from a prison cell."

"Who would believe you?" It was more bravado than certainty, and Wynthrope despised himself for it.

Daniels shrugged. "No one, most likely. They might believe the evidence I have, however."

"What evidence?" But dread was already taking hold of his soul.

The cocksure expression returned. Daniels was enjoying this. No doubt he'd been planning it for some time. "Come on, boyo, you know I kept records of everything. A package to Bow Street, and Duncan Reed would know all about you workin' for me. A smart man like that wouldn't take long to realize you were the reason your brother left Bow Street."

No, it wouldn't take long. "You still cannot prove it."

"I don't need to prove it. I just have to make people wonder. I send this information to the newspapers, and your brother will find himself at the center of a nasty scandal. What do you think that will do for his political aspirations?"

Wynthrope's tenuous grasp on his control snapped. Once again he grabbed Daniels by the lapels, but this time when he hoisted the older man to his feet, he didn't stop. He hauled him toward the door, even as Daniels protested and dragged his feet in an effort to stop him.

Pausing only long enough to open the door, Wynthrope tossed his former employer into the corridor and glared at him, breathing heavily from exertion and rage.

"Get the hell out of my sight," he rasped. "Do not come near me again."

Daniels brushed the wrinkles from his dark green coat once again. "Do not be so hasty, m'boy. I know you don't want to be the ruin of your brother's career, not after all he did for you."

Grinding his teeth, Wynthrope inhaled deeply. Any second now he was going to lose all control and strangle Daniels with his bare hands.

"I'll give you a few days to think about it," the older man continued in his charming tone. "It's just a small job, one you could do in your sleep. You'd be repayin' me for that little double cross years ago, and think of all the embarrassment you would be keepin' from your family. I'm sure your oldest brother would appreciate that."

Former father figure he might be, but Daniels knew exactly where to strike. He knew Wynthrope would not want anything to happen to North. He also knew that Wynthrope would do almost anything to keep Brahm from finding out just how royally he had made a mess out of his life.

But he would not allow himself to be blackmailed, especially not by an Irishman as adept at lying as he was at picking locks.

Slowly, his gaze unwavering, he closed the door, the heavy oak eventually obliterating Daniels from his view.

"Three days, boyo," the singsong lilt carried around the closing door. "I'll expect you to have changed your mind by then."

The door shut with a click that echoed in Wynthrope's mind like the sound of a hammer on steel. Let Daniels come back. It wouldn't make a difference.

Three days wasn't going to change anything.

"I cannot believe he chose you over me."

It had been two days since the party at Octavia and North's, but Moira did not need her sister to explain who "he" was. Despite her usual chatter about her various beaux and their marriageability, Minnie kept coming back to one topic: that Wynthrope Ryland had wanted to dance with Moira rather than her.

"You are being very rude," Moira told her without sympathy. They were having breakfast in the front parlor, the morning sun twinkled through the windows warming the pale blue walls. "Mr. Ryland undoubtedly has sense enough to know that he is far too old for you. Unfortunately, I believe that very sense is what makes him so attractive as far as you are concerned. Please pass the jam."

Minnie shot her a pointed look as she handed her the porcelain pot from the other end of the gleaming oak tabletop. "Do not eat too much. You do not want to get fat again."

Moira froze. Her breakfast consisted of toast and tea,

hardly cause for concern, yet she was tempted to push the plate away and listen to her sister.

Which was just what the brat wanted, of course. Minerva didn't like being tossed over for her plain, older sister. The girl absolutely *had* to be adored by all who met her or life was a disaster. Lord knew their parents weren't very capable when it came to showing affection for their children, perhaps that was why Minnie wanted it from everyone else.

In fact, Moira was amazed the girl hadn't gotten herself compromised.

"Whether or not I am fat is no concern of yours," she replied, deliberately slathering her toast with a thick coating of strawberry jam. Of course she didn't want to be fat again, not when Countess Lieven had complimented her on her looks just a few months before. Of course, some of her gowns were a bit big on her now, but that couldn't possibly be a bad thing, could it? And it certainly meant she could afford to eat a little extra jam on her toast.

"I doubt Mr. Ryland likes fat women."

Moira didn't even look up. "Then perhaps you should reconsider eating that third sausage."

Minnie's fork clattered against her fragile cream china plate. "You are so cruel!"

Sipping her tea, Moira cast a glance at her sister. "So are you. Do you suppose that means we are related?"

Oddly enough, that remark drew a smile from the younger woman. "It is silly to argue over a gentleman, isn't it? After all, there are so *many* of them out there."

Moira couldn't help but chuckle. She couldn't stay angry at her sister for long. "That's the spirit."

"Still—" Minnie took a thoughtful bite of that third sausage. "I am envious. Wynthrope Ryland is very handsome."

"Is he?" Lifting her cup, Moira pretended innocence. "I had not noticed."

Now it was Minerva's turn to laugh. "I am not quite ready to give him up to you just yet."

Moira rolled her eyes. "He is over thirty, Minnie. You are not even twenty yet."

"So? Father is fifteen years Mama's senior."

Was that the best example she could think of? "Yes, and we both know what a happy union that has been."

Her meaning was not lost on her sister. "Good point. I will take it under advisement."

A smile curved Moira's lips. Sometimes, when Minnie wasn't being a terrible headache, Moira rather liked her younger sister. She might even miss her when she was gone. She would not, however, miss her mother's frequent letters demanding to know what Moira was doing wrong that Minerva wasn't betrothed yet.

The only thing keeping Moira from inviting her mother to come to town and take over the search for Minnie's future husband was the fact that Moira couldn't stand her mother. It was an awful thing to admit, but Moira couldn't bring herself to feel too badly about it. Most people who met Eloise Banning didn't like her. She really was a deplorable woman.

How thankful Moira had been to meet Anthony Tyndale. She hadn't had many friends in her life, and dear Tony was probably the most significant. She jumped at the chance to marry him, to bid farewell to her family and never look back. It hadn't occurred to her at the time that she might have regrets, that she might one day wish her husband could love her—that she could love him—the way husbands and wives should love.

Life as a viscountess was very demanding. Never had Moira thought that parties and balls could ever be a chore, but there had been times when she would have rather had a tooth pulled than leave the house again. She had lost more weight in her effort to become elegant and regal. Tony cautioned her not to become too thin. Was there such a thing?

And then there were the nights that they entertained in their own home. Tony had given Moira carte blanche to do whatever she wanted with the house, and she had taken full advantage, making sure their staff was top-notch and pristine in their duties. She made certain every room was a study in style and elegance, that the fabrics were soft to the touch, the colors pleasing to the eye. She had made it her career to be the best viscountess she could be, so no one would find fault with Viscount Aubourn's wife.

She read countless books on etiquette, manners, and entertaining. She read the papers so she could discuss current events with gentlemen, and *La Belle Assemblee* so she could converse with the ladies. She made herself familiar with all the popular poets and novelists—and even some of the more obscure ones. She practiced her needlepoint even though she hated it and made certain she could play at least four selections on the pianoforte and two on the harp. No one ever asked her to play, however. Thank God they never asked her to sing. She even learned to play whist and piquet, although she still wasn't certain she understood all the nuances of the games. She had never been much of a card player. As a viscountess, however, she was exemplary.

Regardless of all the efforts she had made and the headaches they had given her, her life with Tony had been a good one, and she missed his smiling face. She missed his laughter and his wicked wit. Most of all she missed how he made her comfortable with herself. Tony never asked her to be anything but exactly what she was. She never felt as though she had to impress him.

She wanted to impress Wynthrope Ryland, and the knowledge both annoyed and frightened her. How did one set about impressing such a man? And why should she want his good opinion? Had he done anything to deserve hers? No, save for wanting to make her "better acquaintance." Wasn't that reason enough for her to want to make the experience pleasant for him? How often in her life did a plain woman garner the attention of such a man?

Still, she didn't think so little of herself that she was prepared to throw herself at Wynthrope Ryland's feet. Nor was she prepared to be anything but herself in her efforts to win his approval. It didn't matter how lovely he looked, or how deliciously smooth his voice was, if he could not like her for who and what she was, then he would not like her at all.

Perhaps, upon closer examination, she would not like him either. Perhaps a pretty face and charming manner were all he had to recommend him.

And perhaps she could eat an entire chocolate cake and not gain an ounce.

After breakfast, Moira summoned her maid and the carriage and went shopping. It would be Christmas soon and there were still one or two things she needed to purchase. She also needed to get out of the house by herself for a while, even though it was cold and looking as though it might snow. Since Anthony's death she had become accustomed to having all the time to herself she could ever want—or sometimes not want, as was often the case. Having Minnie in the house was both a treat and a torture.

Several hours later, after she had finished her shopping, and satisfied that the snow would not start for some time yet, Moira continued on to Covent Garden to visit Octavia. Only Octavia and her husband, North, could get away with living in such an unfashionable area of London. Between the two of them they had enough charisma to enable them to do almost anything, and society would think them charming.

They were the perfect example of how two people could come together to form a single entity. Not just lovers, they were incredibly good friends, and they loved each other more than they loved life itself.

Naturally, Moira hated them. Unfortunately, she liked them so much that they were impossible to dislike for long.

"Moira! You are just in time," Octavia greeted her in the foyer. She was all grace and refinement in a stylish day gown of dark peach sarcenet, her coppery gold hair twisted into a neat coronet.

"In time for what?" Moira inquired with a smile as the massive butler, Johnson, relieved her of her outerwear.

"Mrs. Bunting has been experimenting with different recipes for our Christmas cake. You must come try some and advise me as to which one to pick."

Cake? Oh God, it was a good thing she hadn't had much for breakfast. "I have never heard of Christmas cake before. Is this a family tradition?"

They strolled together down the corridor, their arms linked. There was something so warm and bright about this house that made it feel like a home. It smelled of lemons and baking, and bustled with the activity of busy, contented servants. Whenever Moira visited, her mood lifted to the point where all she wanted to do was smile. It was love. Love made this little corner of Covent Garden a special place.

"You could say that," Octavia replied with a sly smile. "When North and I were children, his mother would have Mrs. Bunting make us a special cake for Christmas. It was the only way she could keep us in some semblance of decent behavior—with the promise of cake. It was North's idea to have Mrs. Bunting make one this year to celebrate our first Christmas as husband and wife."

Good heavens, North Sheffield-Ryland was certainly possessed of a romantic nature. Were the other Ryland brothers of a similar disposition?

Somehow, she could not imagine Wynthrope making such a sweet gesture. At the same time he struck her as the kind of man who would do anything for someone he loved—even sacrifice himself. That was very romantic in itself, if not perhaps melodramatic in theory.

Octavia led her to the parlor where a lively fire burned in the hearth, crackling in warm invitation. The room was decorated in rich, sumptuous colors and comfortable furniture, and standing at one end of it, not far from the fire, were two men—North Sheffield-Ryland and his brother Wynthrope.

Speak of the devil. Moira stared at him, committing to memory the straightness of his spine beneath his dark blue coat, how dark his hair was in the fading daylight, how graceful and careless he seemed. Even his profile bespoke a blasé arrogance, and yet . . . She sensed there was much more to him than a fine coat and a sometimes caustic wit. At the party he had spoken to her bluntly, with less assurance than she was accustomed to seeing him show.

The tone of his voice when he told her he wanted to get to know her better had almost stopped her heart. A thin thread of uncertainty had colored his voice, made her realize that whatever his motives, he was at least sincere in his quest. The only question was how far was she willing to go to indulge him. Dare she risk exposure for what might prove nothing more than fleeting pleasure? Was the company of Wynthrope Ryland worth the consequences she might have to pay?

He chose that moment to look up, his gaze colliding with hers. It was nothing more than a flicker, but for a second, she thought that he looked happier to see her than anyone else in memory.

Yes, perhaps he would be worth whatever consequences were attached to him.

After Moira greeted both North and his brother, Octavia offered her a slice of the cakes.

"Just small slices," Moira told her friend as she lifted a silver handled knife. Yes indeed, it was good that she'd eaten sparingly at breakfast. There had to be at least six cakes on the tray! If they were as rich as they looked, she was going to have to miss luncheon and possibly supper.

"Small slices will not do justice to Mrs. Bunting's mastery, Lady Aubourn."

That butterscotch voice sent a tremor of delight down Moira's spine. The sound of him speaking was more delicious than any confection Mrs. Bunting could ever conceive. Did the man have any idea how delectable his voice was?

She met his gaze with good humor. "But large slices, Mr. Ryland, will not do justice to my waistline."

His scrutinizing gaze drifted slowly along the length of her. Any other man, and she might have felt soiled by such an appraisal. All Wynthrope's appraisal made her feel was hot. Very hot.

Finally his gaze reached hers. Moira's temperature rose another notch at the warmth she saw in his eyes. "A larger waist only means there is more for a man to hold on to, my lady."

Moira flushed right to the roots of her hair.

"Wyn!" Octavia brandished an icing-covered blade at her brother-in-law. "You forget yourself."

Wynthrope didn't seem the least bit affected by her words, but he bowed to Moira all the same. "My apologies, Lady Aubourn. I meant no disrespect, quite the opposite."

Oh, Moira knew exactly what he meant. He was watching her with barely veiled predatory interest. Perhaps his brother and Octavia were ignorant, but Moira knew without doubt that Wynthrope had meant to shock her. He might be able to play the gentleman, but he wasn't, not underneath his carefully crafted façade. In fact, she'd be willing to bet he wasn't what he pretended to be at all.

Such knowledge served to make him even more attractive. Dangerously attractive. Did she follow his lead and be brazen right back, or did she retreat as she so desperately wanted to?

"Do not trouble yourself, Mr. Ryland. I took no offense." She would not let him see how deeply he affected her—she couldn't, not if she wanted to maintain some kind of control within their budding relationship. Her entire life had been built on control. She would not allow a man to change that.

Again he raised that mocking brow, staring at her with dark eyes that glinted with challenge. Dear God, what was she doing entering into any kind of relationship with this man? He was too much for her. He would be too much for any woman who wished to retain some semblance of self. Wynthrope Ryland was a maelstrom of a man, drawing women into his path and whirling them around until they were too dizzy and free to care what he did next.

Just once it might be thrilling to experience such a sensation, but it was much too frightening to entertain this early in their game.

Game. Odd that she should think of whatever they were doing as a game, but she supposed it was. Each of them wanted to set the rules and each of them was determined to be the less vulnerable.

Octavia passed her a plate. On it were slices of each cake—all of them thicker than Moira would have cut for herself.

Well, there was nothing saying she had to eat all of it. With Wynthrope watching her, it was amazing she could eat at all.

He turned to his sister-in-law with his empty plate offered. "I will have some more of the chocolate please, Vie."

"*More?*" The redhead's face lit with surprise. "You've eaten half the cake already!"

He shrugged, seemingly unaffected by her teasing. "It is good cake."

As she slid another slice of velvety dark cake onto his plate, Octavia turned to Moira with an amused, questioning gaze. "I reckon men do not pay the same attention to their figures as we women do, Moira."

"We are simply not as obsessed with our appearances," North spoke, his own empty plate on a table beside him. "Is that not true, Wyn?"

His brother cut a bite of cake with his fork. "Quite right. However, you are even less concerned than most of us, brother." He smiled at Moira as he lifted his fork to his mouth. "Will this little indulgence damage my appearance, do you think, Lady Aubourn?"

Moira flushed once more. "Why? Do you plan on rubbing your face in it, Mr. Ryland?"

He laughed at that—they all did.

"Serves you right for asking such a bold question," Octavia chastised, but she shot Moira an amused glance. "It seems that Moira's wit is as quick as yours, Wynthrope."

Wynthrope licked a bit of icing from his fork. Moira shivered. Oh, to be that fork.

"It is not my wit that is quick, my dear sister, but rather my tongue." He smiled sweetly at Octavia, but when his sister-in-law's attention shifted to her husband, Wynthrope turned his cobalt gaze to Moira, and what she saw there made her bones turn to custard.

Good God, had he read her mind when she envied his fork? It certainly seemed so.

He set his plate aside, his cake unfinished, and closed the

distance between them. Moira watched him approach, her heart tripping in her throat. Her fingers gripped her plate to stop from trembling.

"Is the fire too much for you, Lady Aubourn?" he asked softly, politely.

"No, I am fine, Mr. Ryland. Thank you." How serene she sounded!

"I ask because you look a little overheated. You are flushed."

Moira's gaze flashed to his. Her heart thumped. "You are impertinent, I think, Mr. Ryland." And she liked it.

His sculpted lips curved to the right. "No doubt you are right, but you have just reminded me of something, my lady."

Dare she ask? "Oh, what is that?"

He leaned closer, as though he was about to impart something of a secretive nature. "You still owe me a kiss, and if you insist on looking at me as though you would like to cover me in chocolate icing, you had better be ready for me to collect."

Moira's lips parted, but no sound came out. She could only stand there and stare at him, burning from head to toe.

A slight flush crept up his cheeks as his gaze settled on her mouth. "Good Lord, woman," he murmured. "You make *me* wish I was covered in icing."

And then he was gone, taking his leave of them in a matter of minutes. After he left, Moira stood there, holding her plate, staring at the slivers of cake lying there. Wynthrope Ryland wanted her. *Her*. How could this be? And what did it say about her that she enjoyed the wicked things he said, the way he looked at her, as though . . . as though he wanted to *eat* her? Just the memory of his gaze sent pinpricks of sensation flooding the surface of her skin. Yes, he was a dangerous, bad, naughty man.

God help her, she more than liked it. She *craved* it.

"Octavia," she said, holding out her plate to her friend. "Do you think I might have a little more of the chocolate?"

He should be thinking about Daniels, but instead his head was filled with thoughts of Moira Tyndale. The hours that had passed since the cake incident had not diminished his want, but intensified it. He had known she was at the party the minute he walked in, even though he hadn't been able to see her.

The woman drew him in as though his will was no longer his own. He couldn't help but flirt with her, make an idiot of himself. He would do anything to have her—anything. It was an awful feeling, knowing he was so desperate for a woman that he would reveal weaknesses to her.

But his past was something he would never admit, not to Moira Tyndale, not to anyone. Even North did not know the extent of things he had done, the shame he held so close. His brothers did not know the things he held inside, the fears he kept hidden from the world, save in the darkest hours of the night, when his entire life seemed to close in around him, crushing him. To give voice to such things would be the greatest humiliation he could ever face. He could not imagine ever making himself so very vulnerable to another person—he could barely do it within himself.

He was the kind of man who made himself wanted by others. Society matrons loved to have him at their gatherings, gentlemen liked to talk or play cards with him. Women found him charming and men found him amiable, but none of them *knew* him. He could stand in the middle of a crowded ballroom, such as the one he was in now, surrounded by people, and be totally alone.

Sometimes it felt as though this person he pretended to be, the person everyone knew him to be, was taking over, pushing the real him out. Other times he was just so bloody tired of always pretending, of always having his guard up. But his true self was so pathetic, so vulnerable and easily hurt that it was easier to hide behind this charming mask.

But it wasn't just vulnerability he sought to conceal. There were other things as well—things that weren't so gentle—things that had hurt or scared the few people who had ever seen them. He kept those locked up tight, so tight that sometimes his head ached with the effort. He'd drink to ease his own suffering if he didn't think the drink would allow all these things to come to the surface.

Moira Tyndale, Lady Aubourn, knew he was hiding things. He could see it in her eyes. She knew he was just acting. How did she know? What was it about her that made her able to see though him? There was nothing terribly special about her. She was tall, too thin, too sharp and angular. Her features were strong, her gaze far too keen, and yet she pulled him to her just like a siren calling a hapless sailor.

She stood not far away, clad in a gown of muted wine, talking to a small group of chaperones as her vivacious sister danced a lively reel with a young baronet. There was something about the days before Christmas that made people more social, music louder, laughter jollier. Winter in London was not normally brimming with social activity, save for the weeks before and after Christmas. Granted, company was certainly thin compared to the season, but there were still enough women to make dancing appealing and enough gentlemen that it was an option, not an obligation, to ask a female to stand up.

And all evening, not a single gentleman had asked Moira to dance. She didn't even seem to mind. How could she not mind just standing on the sidelines while her sister garnered all the attention? And what was wrong with these men that they preferred Minerva Banning's jarring youth to Moira's subtle maturity?

What was wrong with *him* that he hadn't asked her to dance? He had wanted nothing else all evening. Several times he had caught her gazing at him, only to glance away when he met her stare. A little skittish she might be, but she certainly wasn't sly. For a woman who had been married a decade, she seemed to have little practice with the feminine arts. She was awkward when it came to flirting and seemed more apt to flee than to turn on her natural charm when a man approached her.

So why was he approaching her? he wondered as he moved toward her. Probably because he wanted to see if she was as drawn to him as he was to her. It was one thing for her to flirt with him at Octavia and North's, and another for her to dance with him at a Christmas party, but what would she do if he interrupted her conversation and asked her to go outside with him, even if for just a moment?

The women with her watched as he approached. Perhaps they wondered why he was so intent on them. Perhaps they already suspected that Moira was his target. It hardly mattered to him what they thought. All that mattered was the woman staring at him with a mixture of wariness and excitement in her wide eyes—eyes that weren't hazel as he originally thought, but layers of gold, blue and green. Fairy eyes.

"Good evening ladies," he said, not sparing a glance for any of them. His gaze was focused solely on Moira. "Pardon my intrusion. Lady Aubourn. I wonder if I might beg a moment of your time."

To his relief, she didn't hesitate. "Of course, Mr. Ryland. Ladies, if you will excuse me."

He offered her his arm and she took it, following gracefully as he led her toward the terrace doors. Outside it was chilly, the darkness illuminated by the glow of moonlight on snow. There wasn't much—two or three inches at best, but it was enough to coat the world in a delicate layer of white and bring beauty to what might otherwise be sparse and barren.

He could not keep her out there long, even though he wanted nothing more than to keep her to himself. She was not dressed for such weather, even though the neckline of her gown was demure and the fabric a heavy velvet.

If he couldn't have her to himself for long, he would just have to make the most of what brief time he had.

"Lady Aubourn?"

"Yes, Mr. Ryland?" Her eyes were large and reflective in the moonlight, drawing him closer with a magic he was powerless to resist.

"I'm going to collect on that kiss now."

Chapter 4

Moira had no time to react, no time even to think, before Wynthrope's lips touched hers.

He took her totally by surprise. Every muscle in her body tensed at his unexpected and exciting possession of her mouth. His lips were soft and warm—far more yielding than she ever would have believed. He tasted sweet and salty, his chin smooth with just a hint of scratch as it brushed hers. The evening air was chilled, frigid even, and the heat of him pulled Moira even further into the delicious wrap of his arms, melting her very bones.

His lips coaxed. Hers parted. Pinpricks of sensation assaulted Moira's skin as his tongue tasted her. Finally, after all those years of waiting, wondering, *this* was what it was to be well and truly kissed. Other mouths had pressed against hers, but never like this. Never had another man made her want to shove herself against him. Never had she wanted to tangle her fingers in his hair and hold his head so he couldn't escape. Never had she wanted more than just a kiss.

For this brief, magical moment, she wanted everything Wynthrope Ryland was willing to give her.

It was he who broke the contact between their mouths. His breathing shallow puffs in the murky light, Wynthrope rested his forehead against hers. The feel of his flesh was almost as delightful as the touch of his lips, and Moira had to resist the urge to rub her head against him like an affectionate cat.

Lightly, his hands rubbed her upper arms, instilling warmth where chill threatened to settle. "Go back inside," he murmured, his voice husky.

Moira's heart plummeted. "You did not like it?"

Was that a growl or a groan low in his throat? Whatever the sound was, it sent a shiver down Moira's spine.

"I liked it too much," was his reply, his eyes black in the night as he lifted his head. "I will not have you the subject of ballroom gossip."

Moira glanced around them. She could see no one else on the balcony, but the light from the lamps and the ballroom only extended a few feet on either side of them. They were alone, and she did not want to leave. "There is no one watching."

"That you know of." His caution was as endearing as it was annoying. "Right now I am guilty of stealing but a kiss. If you stay here much longer, I will take much more than that, I assure you."

His words should have sent her scurrying to protect her secrets and Anthony's memory, but they did not. Instead, his voice conjured a tight, insistent hum low in her abdomen. She pressed her thighs together to ease the ache, but that only made it worse. She might be afraid to give her virginity to this man, but her body wanted it as badly as a flower wants the sun.

When she did not move, he regarded her with a questioning gaze. "For a woman with a reputation of being cool and proper, you are doing a very good job of playing the temptress, Lady Aubourn."

A temptress? Her? Surely he was jesting! No, that part of him pressing hard and high against her hip was no jest. He was as aroused by their kiss as she was. How amazing to think that she could affect him so.

She took a step backward, allowing the bracing night to breathe between them. The chill did nothing to ease her torment. It only made her nipples even tighter, the tremor of her spine more acute. "Is this better, Mr. Ryland?"

Bowing his head, he raised his gaze. "I do not know. I cannot seem to decide whether to thank you or kiss you again."

Heat stung Moira's cheeks. "Perhaps we should return to the ball."

"You go. If I return now, we will certainly set the gossips aflutter."

He meant his erection, of course. Moira supposed she should be shamed by her behavior, and by his reaction to her, but she wasn't. Nor could she find any reason to doubt or suspect his attraction to her. For now she had to accept that this glorious example of a man wanted to touch and kiss her. What a strange, wrong, and wonderful thought.

Nodding, she backed toward the glass doors, hesitating only as curiosity and insecurity got the better of her. "Will I see you inside?"

There was that self-deprecating, slightly mocking smirk of his. "My dear madam, I plan to be as close as your very shadow."

Dear heaven. Did he mean that? How could he possibly hope to avoid making fodder for the gossips if he planned to watch her so very closely for the rest of the evening?

Slowly, the full chill of the evening sinking into her bones, Moira returned to the warmth of the ballroom. The chandeliers glared down upon her, the noise assaulted her ears. So many voices vied for attention over the rousing melody of the orchestra. Perfume assailed her nostrils, along with the scent of cinnamon. Her stomach growled. She should have gone to the supper table earlier. Would anyone notice if she snuck out to the other room where sandwiches and sweetmeats awaited those who liked to nibble through-out the evening?

Unable to resist her insistent stomach any longer, she drifted through the crowd toward the neat little cucumber sandwiches that had her mouth watering in anticipation. No one paid her any attention.

Well, *almost* no one.

"Where have you been?" Minerva demanded, seizing her by the arm. "You are cold."

Moira dismissed her with a wave of her hand. "I am fine."

Her sister began babbling about something—Moira wasn't listening. Her mind was back on the balcony with Wynthrope. She was in his arms again, his lips succulent against her own . . .

"Moira?"

Blinking, Moira glanced sideways. "What?"

Her sister's doe eyes widened. "What is the matter with you? You have not heard a word I have said."

Moira smiled at her tone. Poor Minnie, was she truly con-cerned or merely worried about what effect Moira's oddness might have on her own evening? "I am sorry, dearest. I went outside for a breath of air and got a little chilled. It is nothing a little mulled wine wouldn't cure."

"Allow me to fetch that for you, Lady Aubourn."

Whatever warmth Moira's body was lacking came rush-ing back at the sound of his voice. It had been little more than minutes since she left him on the balcony, and yet it felt as though she had not seen him for a fortnight, so pleased was she to see him.

She lifted her gaze to his, surprised by her own outward display of calm. "That would be very kind of you, Mr. Ryland. Thank you."

His smile told her it had nothing to do with kindness. He wanted to do everything he could to put her in his debt. He'd travel to India for silk if she wanted, just so she would owe him something in return. It might be worth asking outrageous things of him just so she would have to eventually pay when he wanted to collect.

Regardless of this *thing* between them, Wynthrope was still a gentleman, as his attention to Minerva proved. "Miss Banning, may I bring you refreshment as well?"

Minnie shook her head, corkscrew curls bobbing near her cheeks. The poor dear looked absolutely flabbergasted. "No, thank you, Mr. Ryland."

He bowed to them both, flashing Moira another naughty grin that had her blushing like a schoolgirl, and then was swallowed up by the dancers.

Minnie turned to her with a openmouthed stare that was part amazed, part resentful. "How did you do it?"

Moira's brow puckered. "Do what?"

Her sister scowled at her as though she were a simpleton. "Snare Wynthrope Ryland, that's what!"

"Lower your voice!" Moira whispered, grabbing her sister's arm and hauling her closer. "I have not snared anyone."

Minnie's full lips thinned. "Hmpf. You cannot lie to me, Moira. That man looked at you as though he wanted to dip you in sugar and have you for dessert. Now how did you manage to achieve what so many other women have not?"

Dip her in sugar? Sticky, but not a distasteful thought. What was it about her that made everyone talk in terms of food? She knew she was no longer fat, quite the opposite. Perhaps she wasn't as adept at hiding her natural tendency to gluttony as she thought.

"I have not done anything," she replied. It wasn't quite a lie. She hadn't done anything—except kiss him back, but she wasn't about to tell her sister that.

"Has he kissed you yet?"

"Minerva!" Moira cast a quick glance around them to make certain no one was listening. "That is entirely improper of you and none of your business!"

Her eyes wide, Minnie hid a chuckle behind her hand. All traces of jealousy now seemed to be eaten away by youthful curiosity. "He has! How was it? Is he as delicious as he looks?"

Moira would have cheerfully strangled her sister were it not for the crowd and the trembling in her limbs. How could she be so transparent?

"I am so jealous," Minnie admitted with a rueful shake of her dark head. "You have snared the attention of the one man I thought of as a challenge."

Oh, to be young and stupid. "A challenge does not necessarily mean the man is worth the effort, Minnie."

Her sister arched a thin brow. "Somehow, I do not think you mean Mr. Ryland when you say that. Of course, he hasn't been a challenge for you, has he? Oh well. Since you have snagged him, I must find someone else to amuse me. What about Sir David?"

"Yorke, the baronet?" Moira gave a little nod. "A very nice young man from a good family. I have never heard a harsh word about him."

"So he's boring, you mean."

"So he is the kind of gentleman who will treat you well. Either that or he's just been smart enough to never get caught at any mischief."

The surprised grin Minnie flashed her made Moira smile in return. "Why do you not investigate him for yourself?"

"I think I might." With a swish of her dark blue skirts, Minnie glided toward the unsuspecting baronet. Poor young man.

"I hope your sister did not leave on my account."

Moira's smile became a little guarded as she looked up into eyes so blue they seemed black. If at all possible, he was even more handsome under the glow of the chandeliers than he had been under the silver light of the moon.

"My sister never does anything on any account but her own, but thank you for your concern."

He tilted his head. "Concern? Hardly. I was just being polite. Frankly I'm glad she's gone. I do not want to share you."

She should chastise him for that—it was her sister he was talking about after all—but Moira couldn't do anything but preen.

"Your mulled wine, my lady."

She took the delicate crystal cup he offered her. Through the thin silk of her gloves she could feel the warmth of the fragrant drink. The smell of wine and cinnamon filled her head, making her close her eyes in sheer pleasure.

He watched her intently. "You make me envy food whenever we are together, Lady Aubourn."

"Am I paying more attention to my drink than you, Mr. Ryland?" Was she flirting? That cheeky smile certainly felt like flirting.

He leaned closer. She could smell the warm, spicy scent of his cologne. "Perhaps, but I envy it more for the fact that it will touch your lips many more times than I will this evening."

Oh! There were those shivers down her spine again. "But no more potently, sir." *That* was flirting. Odd, she never thought she knew how to flirt. Wynthrope Ryland seemed to draw it naturally from her.

His eyes changed as they stared at her. She knew there was no way they could darken any more, but they seemed to do so anyway. A strange inner light seemed to glow from within him, shining through that unreadable gaze.

How many layers did this man have? Most people were

pretty much as they appeared to be, but not Wynthrope Ryland. He flirted and strutted around like cock of the yard, but that wasn't him at all. He was just as affected by their game as she was, and he had infinitely more experience with this kind of thing than she.

"I want to kiss you again."

His voice was so honey-smooth, it made her mouth water. She looked away. "You mustn't talk like that. Someone might hear you."

"And you have a reputation to protect."

Was that mockery in his velvety tone? Raising her gaze, she met his levelly. "I am not accustomed to the attention of gentlemen, Mr. Ryland, but I do know that your flirtation might do me more harm than good if the gossips decide to make an example of me."

His head tilted to the left as though in contemplation. "By saying I've made a mistress out of you, I suppose."

"That is one thing they might say."

He seemed amused, but more than a little intrigued. "And what might they say about me?"

She shrugged and sipped her wine. Flavor exploded on her tongue as warmth filled her belly. "Nothing. You are a man."

"Hardly fair, is it?"

"No." A smile tugged at her lips despite herself.

A mockingly resigned sigh escaped his lips. "Then I had better do you more good than harm, hadn't I?"

Was he jesting or serious? It was so difficult to tell sometimes. She searched his face for some kind of indication.

All traces of humor evaporated from his expression. "Do something for me."

This could be trouble. "What?"

"Take another drink of your wine."

A strange request, but there was nothing improper about

it. After all, he had fetched the drink for her, it only made sense that he would want her to finish it.

Raising the cup to her lips, she took a sip of the sweet, warm wine. It was cooling, but no less flavorful. Fruity spiciness washed through her mouth and down her throat. She licked her lips to savor every last drop.

Wynthrope's gaze was fastened on her mouth. When her tongue touched her lip, he closed his eyes, his nostrils flaring slightly with an inhaled breath. She could swear he actually shuddered.

Sensual heat flooded her skin as she remembered his earlier remarks about envying the wine. Moira took another drink to ease the sudden dryness in her mouth.

"I'm finished," she whispered, amazed at the hoarseness of her voice.

Lazy lids opened, regarding her with thinly veiled want. "Would you like another?"

Yes, she would. Her head was already feeling the effects of the first, and the way he watched her did nothing to clear it.

"Perhaps we might share a glass?" It was the most brazen, suggestive thing she had ever said—mostly because it implied so much more than she could say.

The implication wasn't lost on him. Rosy color blossomed high on his sculpted cheeks. Moira swallowed, waiting for his response. Never before had she allowed a man to know that she wanted their relationship to continue—that she wanted him in a physical manner.

His expression was unreadable. "I was going to say that there is none left."

"Oh." Was that a rejection, or merely a truth? She was too inexperienced to tell, and too embarrassed to do anything but stand there, wondering.

"Do you have mulled wine at your house, Moira?" He

took a step toward her as he spoke, bringing the distance between them down to an entirely improper intimacy.

She frowned, unsure why he was asking and strangely thrilled at the sound of her name on his lips. "Yes. As a matter of fact, I do. I always do at this time of year."

"What time shall I come over?"

Moira's heart stopped dead in her chest. Then, with a mighty thump, it started to pound so hard, she thought it might break free. "Come over?"

He caressed her with a gaze that burned. "To your house."

"Tonight?" It was a ragged whisper at best.

He nodded.

"I—" Dear God, what did she do?

His lips twisted into that mocking smile, but there was a flash of vulnerability in his eyes. "My apologies. I overstepped my bounds. Good evening, Lady Aubourn."

No. He could not go back to "ladying" her after calling her by her Christian name. Nor could she allow him to simply walk away as he was now doing.

"Wynthrope." Thank God he was still close enough that she didn't have to raise her voice.

He halted, then turned his head to gaze at her over his shoulder—his wide, gently rounded shoulder.

"Three o'clock," she told him, her mouth so dry she could scarcely speak. "Come through the garden."

This time his smile wasn't mocking at all. It wasn't vulnerable either. It was a seductive smile, full of wicked promise—the promise of pleasure.

He simply nodded and then was gone, leaving Moira staring after him, a fearful tightness in her throat.

What had she done? Wynthrope Ryland was coming to her house later that night!

And Moira had a feeling she was going to want more than wine.

* * *

Moira Tyndale lived in an elegant house in a fashionable West End neighborhood. It was tall and narrow—much like the lady herself—fair of façade and simply ornamented. It wasn't a pretentious house, and yet it didn't seem to be quite comfortable with itself either—were it possible for a house to have such sentiments. Yes, this house suited its owner. It strove to appear a certain way, just as the viscountess did.

Street lamps lit the front of the house, as did the moon's reflection on the light layer of snow blanketing the ground. Normally Wynthrope would curse such a moon when skulking about, and perhaps he should this night as well, but as soon as he saw Moira's garden, he was nothing more than thankful.

There were no flowers, as to be expected at this time of year, but hearty shrubs and thistles glistened with ice. Pale, ghostly statues, embroidered with moss and ivy, kept silent vigil as he walked past. This was no ordinary lady's garden. This garden was wild and untamed and somewhat sinister in the diminishing hours of night. No doubt in summer it was a variable thicket of bright blossoms and tangled vines. How amazing that such a house should conceal such a garden.

It made him wonder what delights Moira concealed.

That she had taken the bait and invited him to her home at such an hour had been a surprise in itself. Who would have thought that the prim and proper Lady Aubourn could be so bold? Everything he heard about her indicated just the opposite, and yet here he was, standing at the garden doors of her house, almost afraid to knock.

This attraction he felt toward her was not rational. It was wild and intoxicating and left him with the same feeling a successful heist used to award.

That very acute, shamefully piquant feeling should be reason enough to return to the relative safety of his apartments. It was also what kept him from doing just that. He wanted to see Moira—*needed* to see her. Little over an hour had passed since he last saw her angular face, and he was already starving for another glimpse. He longed to see his own face reflected in the clear, noncritical depths of her fairy eyes. He wanted to talk to her, and in return listen to what she had to say—another danger.

And he also wanted to kiss her again. He desired that above all else.

Raising his fist, he lightly rapped on the glass. He should have brought something. Flowers perhaps, or chocolate. Ladies liked flowers and chocolate. He would enjoy watching Moira's face as sweet, rich chocolate melted on her tongue. The very thought of it made him hard.

Yes, he really should have brought chocolate.

The door opened, and all chance of turning back evaporated. One look at the woman before him and all rational thought vanished as well.

She hadn't changed out of her evening clothes, but she had removed her jewelry. Somehow she seemed all the more lovely without adornment. She stood in golden-hued warmth, in the cozy confines of her home. He stood in the silvered darkness, the barren night wide open and showering him with a light dusting of snow. The differences between them couldn't be any more obvious even without such presentation.

"I did not think you would come," she said.

Somehow he managed a smile. Thank God it was so cold; that embarrassing erection was almost completely gone. "I thought you might have changed your mind."

Her wide lips curved. "I have not."

"Perhaps you should."

She didn't even pause to consider the wisdom of his suggestion before offering her own. "Perhaps you should come in before you catch cold."

She stood aside, gesturing for him to enter. For one awful

moment it was as though he were trapped in a dream—one in which he was trying to run, only to discover his legs had turned as heavy as lead. He couldn't seem to lift one foot in front of the other no matter how much he wanted to cross the threshold into that welcoming interior.

And then somehow—magically, it seemed—he was inside and she was closing the door behind, sealing them both inside and condemning them both to whatever fate or folly awaited.

The room was decorated in shades of olive, cream, and gold and softly lit, most of the light coming from the fire banking in the hearth. Shelves of books lined all sides, broken only by the paintings of angels. But Moira Tyndale's angels weren't serene and sweet, these were vengeful, wild, mournful angels with wings that ranged from pale ivory to rich indigo. Some were in flight, some in contemplation, and one gazed heavenward, her face ravaged by grief as she held a dying woman in her lap.

"Good Lord," Wynthrope murmured, moving closer to the large, gold-framed canvas. "This is amazing." Then he took a good look at the angel. It was Moira—a younger, rounder Moira, but undeniably her. She looked softer with a little extra weight, but she was just so heartbreakingly sad.

"The woman is my aunt Emily." Moira's voice drifted over his shoulder. "I was very attached to her."

Hence the expression on the angel Moira's face. He turned to face the original. "It is beautiful. Are you the artist?"

She chuckled as she offered him a heavy crystal goblet. He noticed that she avoided looking at the portrait. Perhaps she was embarrassed by having her grief so scrutinized. Or perhaps she feared he might catch a glimpse of vulnerability in her. "Heavens no. My late husband painted it. He painted all my angels."

The way she said it—the very wistful quality of her voice—brought a rush of envy and jealousy over Wynthrope. The late viscount had obviously been very talented, but more than that, he was obviously very much missed by his widow. Wynthrope envied not only the talent, but the sentiment. Would anyone speak of *him* with such a nostalgic tone after his demise?

And yes, he was jealous of the viscount as well. Jealous that the man's wife had thought so much of him—and had the nerve to intimate such devotion in *his* presence. It was enough to make him wish he hadn't come—enough to make him feel like a libertine for knocking on her door, hoping she'd screw him right there in this room under the watchful eyes of her tortured angels.

He took the glass she offered; mulled wine as promised. The cut crystal was warm against his palm and fingers, the fragrance of the wine as potent and inviting as the woman who served it. "Thank you."

She nodded. "Please, sit."

Such cordiality. Either she had no idea that he had come there with every intention of seducing her, or she was toying with him.

He took a swallow of wine as he followed her to a nearby sofa. It tasted as good as it smelled. Cinnamon, cloves, and rich wine flooded the recesses of his mouth, tart yet sweet against his tongue. This was much, much better than the sugary stuff served at the party earlier.

Moira seated herself on one end of the sofa, turning herself ever so slightly inward to face him when he sat on the other end. Only he didn't sit at the other end. He sat right beside her, bringing his knee up onto the cushion beside her so that the entire length of his shin rested against her thigh. His entire body faced her.

She jumped at the contact and regarded him with raised brows, but he wasn't fooled by the hauteur in her expression. The pulse at the base of her throat was pounding so hard he could see it. "There is more than enough room for the two of us on this sofa without you sitting quite so close, Mr. Ryland."

"My name is Wynthrope." He took her glass of wine from her and set it on the table along with his own. "And if I sat at the other end of the sofa, Moira, I would not be able to do this."

Before she could ask what "this" was, he wrapped his hand around the back of her neck and pulled her toward him. The moment his lips touched hers, Wynthrope knew he would be successful in his quest. Moira opened her mouth to his plunder, her tongue twining with his. She did not object to his advances, that was obvious. She wanted him almost as much as he wanted her—there was no way she could possibly want him as much. Once he was inside her, perhaps he would be better able to understand why it seemed as though she could see so easily inside him. Once he had emptied himself within her, perhaps he would no longer feel this rotten, hollow feeling that seemed all the more acute whenever she was near.

The taste of her was more potent than the wine that sweetened the recesses of her mouth. She was warm and wet, soft and pliant, and he held her tightly, ashamed of just how afraid he was that she might try to escape. One of her hands rested on his thigh, the fingers digging into his muscle. He did not know where the other was.

Slowly, Wynthrope slid his left hand up her leg. His right still held her by the neck, fingers aching to pull the pins from her hair. Her gown was soft beneath his hand, and he could feel the heat of her, feel the delicate curves, the fragile bones of her body beneath the fabric. Her hip was gentle, the valley of her waist a tiny dip leading to her ribs. Her breast was larger than he expected. His hand cupped the fullness there, pleasing and arousing him with the softness yielding to his fingers. His thumb brushed the hardened crown of her nipple. Moira gasped against his mouth, her body stiffening. Inwardly Wynthrope crowed.

Ah, there was her other hand. It covered his, stopping him from slipping inside her bodice. To make matters worse, she broke their kiss as well. Raising his head, Wynthrope stared at her in surprise. Had he done something wrong?

She regarded him with something that appeared very much like wariness. "I am not so easy to seduce, Mr. Ryland."

Easy? No. She was practically virginal in her resolve. That did not mean he had given up hope, however. After all, she still held his hand—and it was pressed most pleasantly against her hip. "I am rarely denied what I want."

She regarded him with an expression of mocking disbelief. "You poor man."

He would have laughed at her sarcasm if not for the ache in his groin. "I persuaded you to invite me here, did I not?"

"You are here because I allowed it, and if our 'relationship' becomes more intimate, it will also be because I allowed it, *not* because you willed it."

His smile was one of admiration, he couldn't help it. "You are made of sturdier stuff than you appear, Lady Aubourn." Her resolve didn't stop him from rubbing his palm against her hip.

Now it was his turn to surprise her. "Do you find my appearance lacking, Mr. Ryland?"

"Nothing a few lazy mornings of breakfast in bed could not cure."

His brazen innuendo was rewarded with a soft flush in her cheeks and a subtle widening of her eyes. "You reckon I am too thin?"

"Yes."

She looked completely dumbfounded, but not insulted as most women would have been. "You are very bold sir."

She didn't chastise him for his sexual remarks, but did for commenting on her weight? Such strange creatures were women.

"I am. I believe that is what you like about me, my lady."

"Only one thing? Surely you can do better than that? I imagine you have a whole list of things women find appealing about you."

And now she was making fun. Charming. What a difference being in her own home made. What a difference mulled wine made. He liked this fun and flirtatious side of her. She didn't play games or try to make it seem as though she was acting against her will. She simply didn't want to go as fast as he did, and strangely he respected that. She made him feel young and carefree, and it had been a long time since he felt as though he hadn't a care in the world, or the weight of it on his shoulders.

"I am concerned with no other woman but you, Moira. I warn you, I want you and I have every intention of having you."

Her blush deepened, but she did not look away. "You will not find me an easy mark, Wynthrope."

At least he had her calling him by his Christian name. "I cannot resist a contest of wills. I accept your challenge."

She became thoughtful for a moment. He felt her withdraw from him even though her body didn't move at all. "Are the pages of the betting books filled with wagers concerning the two of us?"

Wynthrope shook his head to clear it, for surely he had not heard her correctly. "I beg your pardon?" He couldn't have heard her correctly.

Finally she peeled his hand away from her hip and released it. "I will be blunt; do you pay attention to me in order to win a wager for yourself or someone else?"

He'd be affronted if it wasn't such a ludicrous suggestion. "Do you try to offend me on purpose, or is this just some kind of defect of your character?"

The flush that rode up her neck and face was nothing short

of magnificent. "I would rather offend you than end up the object of ridicule again."

"Again?" That meant it had happened before. Who had dared ridicule her? He'd have the bounder's head on a platter—his balls too.

Now she looked away. "After the death of my husband, while I was still in mourning, I was befriended by a gentleman. I thought him a friend, at any rate. He was a great comfort to me and I trusted him." Raising her chin, she turned a level gaze on him, allowing him to fill in the rest.

"He made a wager concerning you?"

Moira nodded. "He and his cronies thought it would be good sport to play with my emotions. The only reason he befriended me was in the hopes of worming his way into my bed, and five hundred pounds."

Wynthrope held her gaze despite the urge to glance away. He knew such things happened. Men made foolish wagers all the time in the books at White's and various other clubs—bets concerning everything from when someone would sneeze to when someone would die. Women were considered fair game.

He could apologize for his sex, but not all men were such scoundrels, and he didn't want to sound as though he had something to apologize for. "The only prize I want to claim is you."

She smirked. "Yes, I can well imagine."

"No, I do not think you can," he replied dryly. "There's much more to you than just your body. I want *you*."

The skin between her brows puckered as she tried to process the meaning of his words.

If he had to spell it out for her, then he would. "I want more than one night in your bed."

Her eyes widened. "How much more?"

Wynthrope shrugged. What the hell was he doing? He had no idea, but it felt so right, he couldn't stop himself.

"Much more. As much of you as I can possibly take. I cannot make you any promises—neither of us can at this point—but I do not think one night could possibly be enough for either of us."

"You are very sure of yourself."

"Yes." Why deny what was true? "Sure of you as well."

Her eyes narrowed. She seemed to be trying to peer inside his mind. He wished her luck getting past his thick skull. "And you swear you are not making sport of me?"

"Hand me a Bible, I'll swear on it. Give me paper and I shall sign an oath—in blood if you want."

"That will not be necessary," she replied, a strange, thoughtful expression on her face, even as she smiled. "I will take you at your word."

For some reason her words sent a shiver down his spine. Dread or delight, he couldn't tell. "So you will allow me to seduce you?"

A hand on his chest pushed him back when he tried to come in for another kiss. "You may try."

Wynthrope grinned. "Excellent."

"But not tonight." She gave him another push and a smile that a mother might give a child—a sweet, kindly smile that brooked no opposition. "Now it is time for you to leave."

There was no point in arguing, and he didn't want her to feel pressured. He didn't want her to succumb to him because she felt she had no choice—he didn't want there to be a choice at all.

"Fine." He rose to his feet as she did. "When may I see you again?"

"Two days from now," she responded. "Octavia and North are coming for dinner. You may join us."

Spectators were *not* what he had in mind. "Until then." And he kissed her—hard and brief and not nearly thoroughly enough to last until he saw her again.

She closed the door behind him, and Wynthrope stared at it for but a minute before finally willing his feet to move. It was colder now, the snow falling in fat flakes that were quickly piling up on the grass. He jogged through the garden, following the path around to the street and then down to where his carriage waited. The coachman was inside as Wynthrope had instructed. It wouldn't do to have the man freeze to death while his master was doing his best to wet his wick.

"Home, John."

"Aye, sir."

At one time "home" had been Creed Manor, where he and his brothers had grown up. It wasn't far from Moira's in the wealthy confines of Mayfair. Now he lodged in apartments suitable for a bachelor of his station on Grafton Street, a situation that put him close enough to Mayfair to be fashionable, and far enough away that he didn't feel as though he was living in a fish pond. It was a comfortable arrangement. He had a valet that attended to his fashion needs, a woman who came once a week to clean, and he ate whenever and wherever he wanted—usually at North's house. He lived his life on his own time and by his own rules. Anyone would envy him his existence.

But not if they knew how bloody lonely it was at times.

There was a lamp lit in his study. Wynthrope's heart stopped. He had company.

"Hello boyo."

Wynthrope closed his eyes. *Not again.* "I really must get my locks changed."

"Not a lock on this earth I can't open."

"There has been at least one." The holding cell at Bow Street, for example.

Daniels chose to ignore his barb. "It's a quick in and out, my boy."

"No."

"Be a real shame for your brother's supporters to find out about his involvement in your escaping Bow Street's notice. Mayhap the two of you could share a cell in Newgate. The Marquess of Wynter probably wouldn't like findin' out his sister married the brother of a dirty thief neither."

Daniels was right. "I should kill you."

"If I'm not back at my lodgings in half an hour, a package will be delivered to Duncan Reed at Bow Street detailing your involvement with my gang—and all the details of the cover up by Sheffield. And if you think of double crossing me, I'll see your family ruined, I swear it."

Clenching his jaw, Wynthrope faced his former mentor, fighting to contain his hatred for the man. "If I do this, you'll go away and never come back?"

Daniels nodded. "I can't wait to put as much distance between myself and England as I can. I don't have to tell you that I have more enemies than friends here."

That was true. Daniels had turned in many of his contacts in the underworld as part of a bargain with the authorities. He escaped the noose by sending others in his place. Wynthrope could just tell him to sod off and let his enemies do him in, but he couldn't risk ruining North or Devlin.

"What do I have to do?"

Daniels's weathered face lit up. "Appropriate a bit of glitter for me—a trinket really. A tiara from a wealthy widow. No doubt she's got a dozen."

Wynthrope nodded, barely listening. "She lives in Mayfair, I take it?"

"Aye. In a house she bought after her husband stuck his spoon in the wall."

"And do you know where the tiara is kept?" He couldn't believe he was asking these questions. Common sense told him to go to North, but he couldn't risk it, not after all his brother had sacrificed for him already. North would want to get involved, and that was a chance Wynthrope wasn't prepared to take.

"No. You'll have to find that out on your own. The lady's beyond the sphere of most of my acquaintance, that's why I've come to you."

Wynthrope tilted his head, his face as immobile as granite. "Why are you doing this?"

"Let's just say I've been offered enough money to make certain I never have to work again."

Wynthrope made a scoffing noise. "You've never worked a day in your life."

The old man smiled, revealing the myriad lines around his eyes. "Well, it wouldn't do for me to start now, would it?"

He might have smiled were he not so damn angry. "So I do all the work and get none of the reward."

"You'll protect your family."

Wynthrope nodded. So that was it then. It had been years since he'd stolen anything. He thought he had left that life well and far behind him. Now he was being forced back into it, and a part of him . . .

A part of him was *excited.* Not so much about committing a crime, but about taking the risk. It had always been about the risk for him.

"Who is this widow I'm supposed to relieve of her 'trinket'?"

"A viscountess," Daniels replied. "A Moira Tyndale, Lady Aubourn."

Chapter 5

This was a jest—a cruel jest that normally Wynthrope would appreciate with a healthy bark of laughter. He'd laugh now if he didn't think he'd choke on it.

"No."

Daniels looked puzzled. "No?" Then his expression changed to something crafty and calculating. "You know her."

Shite. That's what speaking before thinking got him; in deeper than he wanted to be, and dragging Moira with him.

"Not well," he replied, his tone deceptively casual. "I know her to speak to her, of course. We do travel in the same circles."

Daniels wasn't quite convinced. "Then why the hesitation?"

"She's just come out of mourning for her husband. It wouldn't be right." How easily the half truths rolled off his tongue, and he was glad. Daniels had always been good to him when he was younger, but the old Irishman wasn't above using Moira to force Wynthrope into doing what he wanted. He might think twice about hurting her, but in the end, he'd do it if it meant the difference between getting what he wanted and not.

And to think Wynthrope used to admire that aspect of him.

Daniels shrugged. "Just means she's still vulnerable. She's a pigeon just beggin' to be bagged."

Hearing Moira described in such a cutthroat manner set Wynthrope's blood to simmering. He couldn't argue, couldn't defend her because Daniels would figure out he had been lying about not knowing her. He had already indicated that his employer was a wealthy man. If he was a member of the *ton*, then he might be feeding Daniels information—including the fact that he and Moira had been seen together.

Stealing from Moira. Christ, why couldn't Daniels have picked someone else? He'd do it in a minute if it was someone else, if for no other reason than to protect his family. Now it seemed he was going to have to betray Moira and their fledgling relationship. He had no choice. If he tried to go to the authorities, his family—and possibly Moira—would suffer. If he killed Daniels, his family would suffer.

If he stole Moira's tiara, only Moira would suffer. No, not only Moira. He would suffer as well, but he would deserve no less.

He moved to the oak sideboard and uncapped a decanter of whiskey. He didn't bother to offer any to the Irishman as he poured himself a glass. "Do you have a sketch of the tiara?" There was no turning back now.

Daniels grinned—such a unthreatening expression. "I knew you'd come round."

Coming "round" had nothing to do with it. Daniels had him over a barrel and he knew it. "Well, do you know what it looks like?" He took a swallow of whiskey. It burned and tasted bitter.

The Irishman took a folded paper from his inside jacket pocket. "Here."

Wynthrope took the paper, the bitterness in his mouth intensifying as he did so. He should have known there would be no outrunning his past. He should have known he would have to pay for what he had done.

The urge to laugh came upon him once more as he gazed at the sketch. The tiara was none other than the very one Moira had worn that night—the one that made him think of her as a queen. How appropriate that it be his prize.

"It shouldn't be difficult for a charmer such as yourself to sweet talk your way into the lady's life," Daniels was saying. "Might as well have yourself a bit of sport while you're at it—provided she's to your tastes."

This time Wynthrope did laugh—bitterly, harshly. To his tastes indeed. A bit of sport. This couldn't be real. There was just too much irony involved. It had to be a dream.

"No," he agreed, his lips twisting into a malicious smile. "It should not be difficult at all."

It was going to be hell.

"I have died and gone to heaven!"

Lounging on a sofa, Moira glanced up from her book with a welcoming smile as Nathaniel swept into her library, his fur-lined greatcoat billowing about his buckskin-clad legs.

"What's his name?" she asked, amused by Nathaniel's animated behavior.

Her friend slipped his coat off his shoulders, carelessly tossing it on a chair as he approached. "Matthew."

Moira eyed the discarded outerwear. "You should hang your coat up."

"That is exactly what Tony would have said."

Anthony had been forever after Nathaniel for being so nonchalant with his personal effects. Their good-natured

bantering about it always led to flirtatious remarks that usually made Moira feel like an intruder—and more than a little
envious.

"So tell me about this Matthew," she suggested quickly,
not wanting her friend to slip into melancholy at the mention
of his late lover. It was time for Nathaniel to move on. She
had loved Tony as well, and she missed him still, but he
wasn't coming back. Holding on to the past didn't make for
much of a future. And Tony wouldn't want either of them to
stop living just because he had.

Gesturing for her to move her legs, Nathaniel plopped
himself down on the other end of the sofa. Moira immediately took advantage of the situation and propped her feet
on his lap. How grateful she was for this relationship, this
ease between them. Theirs was an intimacy that she could
not have with anyone else, as no woman could provide the
same friendship, nor could a man who preferred female
"companionship."

"Matthew," Nathaniel began with a dramatic roll of his
eyes as he patted her knee, "is an angel. Definitely worthy of
these walls."

Moira smiled. She hadn't heard her friend express this
much enthusiasm for anyone since Tony. The fact that he
believed this Matthew to be worthy of Tony's talent spoke
volumes.

"And does he share your enchantment?" Could he hear
the trepidation in her voice? Nathaniel had to be so careful
about whom he set his cap for. If the wrong person found out
about his preferences . . .

"I believe so. He has been very flirtatious, and made a
point of telling me that he was going to a particular coffee
house this afternoon."

"Well, that is encouraging." It certainly sounded it, but
she had no idea how these things worked between two men.

Perhaps they understood each other better than women could. "Are you going to just happen to be there as well?"

"Yes, and you are coming with me." Shoving her legs aside, he leaped to his feet, almost knocking her to the floor. "Now."

Laughing, Moira allowed her friend to pull her upright. "Fine, I will go, but you are buying me chocolate."

"Done." He didn't release her hands, but squeezed them in his own. "Thank you, my friend."

Moira shrugged off his thanks, even though it warmed her to the bottom of her feet. "One of us should at least be happy."

Nathaniel's grin was nothing short of wicked. "Oh, I believe Wynthrope Ryland could put a smile on your face."

"You really are incorrigible." She couldn't help but grin at him, though.

"A boy has to have something to recommend him." Still holding her by one hand, he pulled her toward the library door. "Come, let us get you into a warm coat and gloves."

Moira stumbled behind him. "Anxious?"

"Of course," he tossed over his shoulder. "Unlike you, I have realized I actually want to fall in love again."

Again? "I do not believe I've ever been in love."

He came to a dead stop and whirled to face her, his expression one of anguish. "Oh, dearest."

She placed her free hand against his chest lest he attempt to hug her. She would no doubt do something foolish like burst into tears if he embraced her. "Do not pity me, Nate. Not everyone is meant to have the kind of love you and Tony had."

His gaze was so honest and sincere. "Perhaps not, but you are."

Moira only smiled. "Thank you. Now, no more of this depressing talk. Take me to see this angel of yours."

They took Nathaniel's carriage to Blakney's coffee house

in Covent Garden, where such establishments flourished. Blakney's however, had no political distinction, nor was it a thinly disguised brothel. Both gentlemen and ladies alike were invited to sit and partake of the various refreshments, which included not only coffee, but tea and chocolate as well. Today it was far from full, but neither was it lacking in patrons as Moira and Nathaniel entered.

They had barely sat down when Nathaniel pointed out Matthew. True to his earlier description, the young man certainly looked as though he had just fallen from heaven. He also made a great show of pretending not to watch Nathaniel out of the corner of his eye.

Perhaps men weren't that different from women after all.

"Oh my God," Nathaniel murmured, stripping off his gloves. "We were meant to come here."

Moira, whose back was to the door, tried to peer over her shoulder to see what he was looking at. The brim of her bonnet obstructed her view, blast it. "Why?"

"Do not look, but your Mr. Ryland is here."

She froze. Surely her heart had stopped in mid-beat. "He is?" Oh, why didn't she have her maid do something with her hair before she left the house? Thank heaven for her blasted bonnet.

Nathaniel nodded, his blue eyes bright. "And he's coming this way. Dear Lord but there should be more men like him in the world."

"One is quite enough, I assure you."

"Good afternoon, Lady Aubourn. Caylan."

Moira inclined her head in greeting, afraid to open her mouth and do something stupid like call him by his Christian name, or kiss him. He looked so fine indeed in a dark wine coat and tan trousers.

Nathaniel smiled brightly. "Good day, Mr. Ryland. Will you join us?"

Moira kicked him under the table. To his credit, he didn't make a sound, he hardly even winced.

"I am meeting someone," Wynthrope replied, glancing toward the door, "but I would be honored to join you until they arrive."

Moira watched helplessly as he pulled out the chair next to her own and sat down. He set his hat on the table and tucked his gloves inside. Raking a hand through his thick, dark hair, he smiled at her. "How are you today, Lady Aubourn?"

"Very well, sir. You?" And just who the devil was he meeting? A man or a woman? Hardly a question she had the right to ask, given her own situation, but jealousy stabbed at her breast anyway.

"I cannot complain."

"Oh look," Nathaniel remarked brightly, interrupting their banal exchange. "There is Matthew Sedgewick. I must say hello. Will the two of you excuse me?"

Were it not for the fact that he was up and out of his chair before Moira could reply, she would have kicked him again. The traitor.

She cast a glance at Wynthrope. There was something different about him—a tension she couldn't quite identify.

Well, one of them had to speak eventually. "It is a fine day, is it not? How lovely that the snow hasn't been rained away yet."

Wynthrope turned his head to meet her gaze. "What is your relationship with Caylan?"

Well, that was blunt and to the point. She made a show of removing her gloves so she could avoid his gaze. "What business is it of yours?"

He didn't seem the least bit perturbed by her brusqueness. "I would like to know if I have competition."

It occurred to her that she had never thought before this

day to ask whether he was already involved with someone. She had simply assumed he wasn't. "Perhaps I should ask whether or not I can expect the same courtesy?"

"Of course." His expression was one of extreme boredom. She already knew him well enough to know it was false. "One woman is trial enough."

She smiled. "The same could be said for men."

"So you are not involved with Caylan?" Was it her imagination, or did he sound hopeful?

"No. We are merely friends." Perhaps she was revealing too much of her life to him, but if their relationship continued, he was going to discover much more about her than the fact that she and Nathaniel were just friends. If she wasn't honest with him from the very beginning, she would never feel as though she could truly trust him—nor would he feel as though he could trust her.

"Friends," he repeated, as though he had never heard the word before. "Such devotion is a commendable trait in a friend."

"Yes, it is." Moira ran her finger down the side of his hat, which sat beside her on the table. It was velvety. "I do not know what I would have done without him after my husband's passing."

"No doubt he will be there for you should you ever need him again."

This was such a strange conversation. "I expect so." She dared to glance at him, noting the color the frosty day had placed upon his cheeks. "Do you have such a friend, Wynthrope?"

He nodded, directing his gaze to the door once more. "My brother, North."

That must be who he was waiting for. "How fortunate to be so close to a sibling. I am not close to any of mine, although I am enjoying becoming better acquainted with Minerva."

He seemed surprised by that answer. Surprised enough that he jerked his gaze back to hers. "Really?"

Moira chuckled at his candor. "Really. She is simply young and spoiled. There may be hope for her yet."

"If there is it will be all thanks to your influence."

She regarded him thoughtfully. He was so very serious, not his usual glib self at all. Whatever was the matter with him? It was so very difficult not to wonder if she had done something to offend him, or if he had changed his mind about wanting her. "You flatter me."

He shrugged. "I am honest."

"Are you always honest?" It was an awful question to ask, and she knew it.

"No. Who is?"

"True enough." Silence followed. "Are you quite all right, Wynthrope? You seem different."

He seemed surprised that she noticed. How could she not? "Forgive me. It is no reflection upon you, I am simply preoccupied with something."

"Would you care to talk about it?"

Again, he seemed surprised by her suggestion. "Thank you, but no. It is merely one of those bothersome things which must be done and cannot be escaped."

Moira nodded. "I understand."

He looked at her as though there was no way she possibly could.

"It will not prevent you from coming to dinner tomorrow evening, I hope?" Lord, there was nothing like being overly obvious. If he didn't know how eager she was for him now, he never would.

Wynthrope's head tilted a bit as he shook it. "No. I would not allow anything to interfere with seeing you again."

Now this was more like the man she was becoming accustomed to. "The others are coming at seven. You are welcome to come earlier if you like, although I cannot promise to be much of a hostess."

He brought his head closer to hers, his gaze darkening. His arm on the table was so very close to hers. The barest shift and their sleeves would touch. "I'm more concerned about later. What happens after everyone else leaves? May I remain?"

Heat rushed to her cheeks. He had been serious about wanting to seduce her, then. She glanced around the shop. Was anyone watching them? Thankfully, no. "You should not say such things."

He smiled that lopsided smirk that she was starting to like. "But it is so much more amusing than merely thinking them."

She couldn't argue with that. "Do you always say what you think?"

"No, not always. I believe you to be the kind of woman who does more thinking than saying."

Was that an insult or a compliment? Neither, she thought. It was simply an observation, and a fairly astute one. The only people to whom she had ever let herself say anything less than proper had been Tony and Nathan, and occasionally Minnie. Wynthrope Ryland, however, was quickly becoming someone she felt she could say anything to, and he wouldn't think the less of her for it.

"It is easier to take back things when they are not spoken aloud," she informed him.

His reply was quick. "I make a point of never saying anything I would want to take back."

"Never?" Her tone was dubious.

"Never." He jabbed the tabletop with his finger. "If there are consequences I will face them."

How amusing it was to hear him be so sure, so unmoving about something. "Is it not better to avoid them all together?"

His jaw tightened, and the hand on the table curled into a fist. "There are things one cannot avoid."

Why did she think they were no longer discussing the same thing? What had started out as simple flirtation now felt like something much more serious. There was something amiss with Wynthrope. Perhaps he was simply allowing her to see his true self, or perhaps something had happened to put him in this strange mood. Whatever it was, she couldn't quite put her finger on it, and she couldn't help but think it had something to do with her.

If it weren't for the fact that he was still being very bold with her, she might believe he had lost interest. Or perhaps her fears had been right, and he wasn't truly interested in her at all.

Or maybe he had more on his mind than flirting with her. Not everything had to be of her doing, or involve her. The man had a life that had nothing to do with her.

"You look very pained, my lady."

He said "my lady" as more than just a social nicety. He said it as though she really was *his*.

She regarded him with open honesty. "I am concerned about this curious mood you seem to be in, sir. Is that blunt enough for you?"

His lips curved into a mocking smile, but the warmth of his gaze told her he appreciated her concern, and softened the caustic tilt of his lips. "I promise to be myself again tomorrow evening at your gathering."

Moira smiled in return. "Good."

"But only if you allow me to stay after the others have left."

Oh, he was a dangerous man! And as impossible to say no to as a precocious little boy. "Fine."

"Excellent." His fingers inched closer to hers on the tabletop. "Do you play chess?"

Chess. His hand was no more than a fraction of an inch from hers and he wanted to talk of chess? No talk of seduction or kisses, or likening her to food?

"I have played," she admitted, her fingers itching to touch his. "I have my husband's old set."

He nodded. Did it bother him when she mentioned Tony? "We shall play then."

"I would have thought you more of a gambling man than a chess player." Men who played chess were usually the intellectual sort. That wasn't to say that she thought Wynthrope unintelligent, she knew he was quite the opposite, it was just that he seemed the type to prefer something more . . . stimulating.

His expression was both patronizing and endearing. "My dear Moira, chess is a game of strategy and cunning. It is not about luck, but about systematically defeating your opponent."

How positively divine. "When you put it like that, how could I possibly say no?"

Her sarcasm was not lost on him, and he grinned like a mischievous boy. She preferred this grin even more than the charming crooked one. "Do not tell me that the idea of having me at your mercy doesn't appeal to you."

At her mercy? Him? She could scarcely imagine such a thing. But there was some truth in his words. The idea of having him under her power, even if only for a little while . . .

"I can see from your expression that the idea *does* appeal to you." The light in his eyes burned like the hottest flame. "Best me and I will cater to your every whim for the rest of the evening, until you set me free."

Oh, he certainly knew how to tempt her! "And if you win?"

His gaze flickered over her briefly—long enough to set her entire body aflame—before returning to hers. "I have some whims I would like you to cater to."

She should have known. She had known. She had willingly walked into this situation, knowing full well where the path led. She could not pretend to be shocked when in the deepest part of her she had hoped their conversation would lead to this point.

"You will not make me do anything I do not want to do?" Her question was so softly voiced, even she had difficulty hearing it.

Apparently he hadn't the same trouble. His smile was tight, as though he resented her even suspecting he might do something so dishonorable. "You may be surprised by what you will want to do, Moira, but no. I will not force you."

Part of her had known he wouldn't, but still she'd had to ask. "All right. We will play. And we will see who caters to whom."

Dark blue eyes glinted as he leaned ever so slightly closer. "Either way, I do not see how I can lose." Then he winked at her and straightened. "Ah, I see my brother is here."

His timing was perfect, as Nathaniel had just returned. "Until tomorrow evening then, Lady Aubourn." Setting his hat on his head, he touched the brim to her.

Moira nodded. "Mr. Ryland."

And then with a word to Nathaniel, he was gone, and her friend was seating himself across the table from her, a cup of hot, fragrant chocolate in either hand.

"How did it go with Matthew?" she asked.

"We'll talk about that later," Nathaniel began as he slid a cup toward her. "First, I want you to tell me everything that you and Ryland just said."

Night came early to London this late into December. It wasn't yet evening and already the city was wrapped in darkness. Wynthrope sat alone in his apartments, in a winged chair by a window that overlooked the street below.

The room was dark save for the fire blazing in the hearth. The heat should have been comforting, but it wasn't. The flames cast sinister shadows on the walls, shadows that threatened to overpower him and drag him down into their world. He waited, but they didn't come. Perhaps they didn't want him. Perhaps his soul was too black even for them.

A half-finished glass of whiskey languished in his hand as he propped his booted feet up on the sill, crossing them at the ankle. He could go out. There wasn't an abundance of society in town at this time of year, but the clubs still did business, and there were those like him who stayed in London year round. No doubt he could find someone to amuse him somewhere in this city, but he didn't feel like being diverted. He felt like obsessing over every little detail of his life, and he needed to be alone to do that.

Gazing past his own reflection in the glass, he stared out at the bustle beneath him. The street was wet and bare save for the odd streak of dirty snow and pile of horse droppings. Carriages rolled by in a steady rhythm, though a far cry from the bustle the season usually brought. People strolled along the sidewalks, men and women arm-in-arm, gentlemen engaged in convivial conversation. Occasionally a solitary lady walked past. They probably weren't "ladies" at all—not the proper sort, not if they were alone. Where were they going? Would they be safe? Did they care? Did he?

The street lamps were lit, haloed like bizarre metal angels in the night. Perhaps it was just his mood, but he fancied there was something mystical about them, something magical and otherworldly. Maybe if he waited long enough, one of these lamps would offer him the answers he was looking for.

Beyond the lamps were other windows in the buildings across the street, illuminated by lamps and candles. Not one of them had someone sitting before them. It was just he, staring out into the night with no one staring back.

Above those windows, snow clung to the roofs and eaves. So pure and white, the snow seemed to have a luminosity all its own, and of course the sight of it, paired with the velvet black of night, made him think of Moira.

It had been both awful and delightful to see her earlier at the coffee house. He had wanted to haul her into his arms and kiss her until everything felt right with the world once more. He had also wanted to run away, because looking her in the eye had been more difficult than he ever would have thought.

He wasn't betraying her. They weren't involved deeply enough yet for it to be that. He simply had to use her to protect her and his family. It was for her own good. If he didn't do it, Daniels wouldn't stop at ruining his family. The old man might get someone else to do the job—someone who wouldn't flinch at physically harming Moira to get to the tiara.

What a load of horse shite. What difference did it make why he was doing it? He was going to do it and that was the end of it. It wasn't personal and it didn't change the fact that he wanted her. And it certainly didn't change the fact that he intended to have her. Moira Tyndale had something he wanted—something besides the tiara. He didn't give a damn about the tiara. He wanted to know what she saw in him. He wanted her to make him feel like he was something special without having to be someone else.

True, she wouldn't think he was so damn special if she knew that he planned to steal from her, but she would never know—provided he hadn't lost his touch. She wouldn't be the first woman he stole from while having an affair with her. Though, he hoped she would be the last.

It didn't change the fact that he felt dirty just thinking about it. It didn't change the fact that it pretty much ensured that his relationship could go no further than a physical

one—not that he wanted more, of course. Stealing this tiara
would not ruin his life, nor would the loss of it ruin Moira's,
but the simple truth was that if he didn't steal it, both North
and Devlin would suffer. Wynthrope could not allow that to
happen.

As much as he liked her, Moira came second to his brothers. And he himself came second to her. It did not matter
what he wanted, or what he wished. All that mattered was
the trial awaiting him. He would steal her tiara, and when he
tired of her, or when he discovered that she no longer made
him feel special, he would walk away and keep looking for
that someone or something that did. Because the alternative
was to face the possibility that he wasn't special at all, that
there was nothing about him worth loving, and he wasn't
ready to accept that, no matter how much he feared it might
be true.

It had taken a force of will he hadn't known he possessed
to keep his secret from North. A voice in his head had insisted that he confess all, that North would know what to do.
Another voice argued that North had already sacrificed
enough to save Wynthrope's arse. He could not allow his
brother's desire to do the right thing to cloud his judgment
again. He would not allow North to put him first, not when
North had a wife to think of.

His brother probably suspected something was wrong, but
he hadn't asked. He had just watched him with pale blue
eyes and waited for Wynthrope to confess. Somehow, Wynthrope had managed to keep it all inside. Knowing that the
truth would put his brother in harm's way had helped. Knowing that Brahm would eventually find out—his eldest brother
always found out—was another reason. It wouldn't surprise
him if Brahm knew about his past and was just sitting on the
knowledge, waiting to use it for his own advantage. He
would not give Brahm the opportunity to lord anything over

him. It had been bad enough growing up in his shadow, always being held up to him and found lacking. He would not spend his adult life being compared to a man who was a social pariah because he had no self-control.

It didn't surprise him that North had noticed that he wasn't quite himself—or rather, that he wasn't the self he liked to project. He and North had always been close. What surprised him was that Moira had noticed as well. He was normally so good at hiding his emotions. Until now only his brothers had ever been able to see through him. Perhaps he wasn't as skilled at hiding as he believed. Or perhaps Moira Tyndale was some kind of witch. Lord knew she had woven some kind of spell around him. He would have to be careful around her. If she caught even the slightest hint that he was deceiving her, she'd withdraw from him and make finding that damn tiara all that much more difficult.

And he had yet to claim her, he wasn't ready to lose her just yet. Why it was so important that he have her was a mystery. He only knew that she held the answer to a question he couldn't put into words, that he himself didn't quite know the significance of.

Just this one last job and then he was done with thievery forever. He could finally close the door on that part of his life.

At least until Daniels decided to blackmail him again.

No, the old man meant what he said. Daniels was many things, but he was still a man of his word—honor among thieves and all that. He wanted to get away from England and the enemies he had made, and once he was gone he would not return. After this, Wynthrope would never see him again.

And what of Moira? When this was over, would he ever see her again? Unlikely. Continuing any kind of relationship with her after using her so badly was beyond even him. That was the true sin of this whole situation. He liked Moira. He didn't just desire her; he enjoyed her company. Their acquaintance had only just begun, and already he was counting the hours until he could see her again. He was jealous of her friendship with Nathaniel Caylan; they actually did things together. Caylan knew her better than Wynthrope did, and that annoyed him. He would have to remedy that.

Unfortunately, the next time he saw her was also when he would start trying to ascertain where she kept the tiara.

Why did she look at him in the street that day? Why did she ever have to peer into his soul with those damn eyes of hers? If only he had never noticed her. If only she had never noticed him. This would be so much easier if he didn't like her.

Then again, his seduction of her would give him ample opportunity to search her house.

Sighing, he leaned back in his chair. "I am such a bastard."

As he spoke the words, a gust of wind blew hard against the window, rattling the glass. It was as though the night itself agreed with him.

Chapter 6

At exactly one minute past seven the following evening, Wynthrope knocked on Moira's front door. He had wanted to come earlier, so strong had been his desire to see her, but it wouldn't do to appear too eager—especially since he was going to be staying after the other guests had left.

Even so, it had been a struggle to be even a minute late. He stood on the step, his greatcoat open despite the wind, grateful for the cold drops of rain that spattered against his cheeks. He needed to cool this fire in his blood, this awful excitement he felt every time he knew he was going to see Moira.

He had to keep his wits about him. She was business, not just pleasure anymore. If he was going to find out where she kept that damn tiara, he couldn't get too caught up in his enthusiasm for her, no matter how much he wanted to.

He usually was so careful in everything he did. He never got too close, never let people inside. How ironic, how amusing and terribly painful that the only person to ever make him want to let someone in was someone he had to use—someone he had to take from, despite all that she freely offered.

The door opened. A butler—or at least Wynthrope *thought* this was the butler—greeted him.

"Good evening, good evening!" Round, red cheeks glowed. Sparkling blue eyes smiled up at him. "Come in, good sir!"

Bemused, Wynthrope did just that, never taking his eyes off the corpulent little man who stood no higher than his chest and had hair as white and untamed as lamb's wool. He wore not the usual austere uniform of the highest ranking household servant, but a bright scarlet coat and matching shoes. His waistcoat was a dark green.

The gnome caught him staring and didn't seem the least offended. "Christmas colors, my good man. I like to think of myself as a holly berry this time of year."

Strangely enough, Wynthrope found himself nodding. "That is the very thing I thought of when you opened the door."

The old man grinned, turning his face into a creased ball of little more than cheeks. He certainly was an odd choice for a butler—nothing the least bit subservient in his demeanor at all. "That's the spirit. Now, you must be Mr. Wynthrope Ryland. I am Chester. Lady Aubourn's expecting you. If you would just follow me."

Most butlers asked for a guest's name when he arrived, or for his card. It was strange, this man knowing who he was when they had never met before. True, Moira's gathering was undoubtedly small, but it was nice to feel so welcomed.

This was the first time he had been in Moira's house, other than his clandestine visit the other evening. As he followed the portly but spry Chester through the hall, he took this chance to commit what he could of the house's layout to memory.

The hall was spacious and decorated in shades of taupe, cream, and slate blue. Paintings adorned the walls. More of the late viscount's work, perhaps? Some were portraits and others were scenes from the Bible or Greek myths. Anthony Tyndale had been a very talented artist. His work appealed to Wynthrope on an emotional level that few others achieved.

One thing was for certain, it was unlikely Moira kept a safe down here. The best he could hope for was that it was located in one of the rooms downstairs, or perhaps her private apartments above. The worst was that the housekeeper was in charge of storing such valuables and had a safe tucked somewhere in the bowels of the house. He'd faced such a situation before and it had been a pain in the arse to find.

The hall branched into a wide corridor, brightened with even more cream paint and delicate plaster work. Two doors on the right, three on the left. It was the last of these doors that Chester led him to.

"Mr. Ryland," the woolly-haired butler announced before stepping back and favoring Wynthrope with a smile. Then he bowed and took his leave.

"Wynthrope," Moira's voice greeted him with a pleasant huskiness, as welcome to him as the sun itself. Clad in a gown the color of rich, fragrant cloves, she came to him with her hands outstretched, and he gave her his own without hesitation.

"That Chester fellow is amazing," he remarked, kissing her cheek. She even smelled of cloves. "Wherever did you find him?"

It took all his strength to lift his head from hers, even though he wanted to bury his face in the warm hollow of her neck, where a tiny tendril of dark hair curled against the paleness of her skin.

"Anthony hired him when we married. I couldn't bear to

leave him for the new viscount and his family, so I brought him with me." She squeezed and then released his hands. "I'm so glad you could join us."

It was then and only then that Wynthrope realized they were not alone. Idiot. He should have been aware of the others as soon as he entered the room, but he'd had eyes for Moira and no one else. Her sister Minerva sat near the hearth, eyeing them with youthful interest. North and Octavia, his brother and sister-in-law, blinked almost in unison before exchanging glances that said more than Wynthrope could ever hope to read. One thing was for certain, both of them knew there was something between himself and Moira. They looked so smug and pleased. If only they knew what he planned, they would not be so content.

"Good evening," he said, bowing to the three of them. He avoided his brother's gaze. The last thing he wanted right now was to see North laughing at him.

"Would you care for a drink?" Moira asked. "Wine? Or perhaps something a little stronger?"

Was it his imagination, or was she baiting him? The twinkle in her multicolored eyes told him she sensed his discomfort and was enjoying it.

"Nothing, thank you," he replied, his gaze locked with hers. "I wish to keep a clear head for our game later."

Judging by the delectable blush that tinted her cheeks, she knew he referred to more than just their chess match.

"Game?" North asked. "What game?"

"You are so nosy," Wynthrope remarked with more smirk than scowl as he turned to face his sibling. "If you must know, Lady Aubourn has challenged me to a game of chess."

Moira shot him a surprised glance. She didn't expect him to admit that he had issued the challenge, did she? North and Octavia would know for certain he was interested in her then.

"I thought I told you to call me Moira," she said, holding

his gaze. "After all, you made such a fuss about me calling you Wynthrope."

Touché. So she was not going to let him get away with embarrassing her without a jab of her own. A slow smile curved his lips, and he was about to reply when he caught sight of his brother out of the corner of his eye. Both North and Octavia were practically vibrating with speculation. He would have to be careful just how much eye contact he made with the seductive viscountess.

"I hope you have not wagered any money, Wyn," Octavia warned jovially. "Moira is very good."

"Are you joking?" Her husband's expression was incredulous. "My brother would wager his firstborn before he'd risk any blunt."

Wynthrope's eyes widened. Did he slap his brother or laugh? "Are you implying that I'm tight with my money?"

North nodded, as though it should be obvious. "Yes. That is exactly what I am saying."

"I'm not the one who doesn't own a carriage and hasn't a valet."

"No, but your valet is your only servant other than a woman who cleans once a week and you live in rooms when you could afford a house."

"What is the point in having a house when I would be alone in it?" Bloody hell. Too late he realized all that he had said with that one idiotic sentence, spoken more testily than he'd meant. The room fell silent, the other occupants looking decidedly uncomfortable.

Except for Moira. She fixed him with a sympathetic but understanding smile. "I know exactly what you mean. Sometimes it is lonely living alone. The solution is to fill the house with possessions that have meaning and people you love as often as possible." She shared her smile with her sister and her friends.

What a pity he was going to have to hurt her. This was a woman Wynthrope could actually imagine falling in love with. Love. Whoever would have thought that *he* would entertain such a notion? But if love was an intense longing, a desire to spend the rest of his days in a house with one person, then love was definitely an emotion Moira Tyndale could inspire.

"Here, here," North remarked raising his glance. What was he agreeing to? Oh yes, Moira's notion of filling a house with loved ones as often as possible. Too bad Wynthrope hadn't taken that drink. He would have drunk to that himself.

It was only a few moments later that Chester came to announce that dinner was ready. Wynthrope escorted both Moira and Minnie to save the young woman from being left out, and allowed Moira to direct him toward the dining room.

Dinner was a casual affair, with good food, good conversation, laughter, and good company. They were all comfortable and easy with one another, even Minerva, whom Wynthrope often thought of as disagreeable. Tonight she was all youthful smiles and inquisitive innocence. Perhaps it was the influence of her older sister. Who wouldn't be a better person after a few weeks with Moira?

Lord knew she made him want to be a better person, and a few weeks was all the acquaintance he had with her.

Throughout the meal, he could scarcely take his eyes off her, and he didn't give a damn if his brother noticed or not. She kept sneaking glances at him as well. Was she waiting for the end of the meal as he was, counting the minutes until they would be alone?

Finally, after dessert and after port in the drawing room, North and Octavia took their leave, and Minnie went off to read in her room.

"Shall we have our game now, my lady?" he inquired softly when they were finally alone.

Moira eyed him with an expression that made his blood run hot. She reminded him of a fawn, unsure of whether to bolt or come closer. Curiosity and interest won out and she nodded. "I hope the library is a suitable venue?"

Ah, the library. That room where he had tasted her lips just two nights before, where Anthony Tyndale's sad portrait of her hung among the other angels.

"The library is fine." Strangely enough, it was. Though this house had many reminders of the late viscount, Wynthrope didn't feel as though the man's memory posed any kind of hindrance to his seducing Moira. Jealous he sometimes was of Anthony Tyndale, but he wasn't threatened by him.

He followed her down the corridor, admiring the gentle sway of her hips as she walked. She might not be a lushly figured woman, but she was all grace and ease, moving with a sensuality she seemed totally ignorant of. He'd follow her on foot to Scotland just to admire her walk.

There was a table already set up when they entered the library. A small, gilt-trimmed, black-lacquered affair, with ebony and ivory squares inlaid on the top, held matching pieces on their corresponding colors, waiting for the first move to be made.

Wynthrope gestured to the seat on the white side of the board. "Ladies first."

She flashed him a narrow glance. "Are you suggesting that I need all the advantage I can get, Wynthrope?"

"Not at all." Smiling came easy with her. "Would you prefer I make the first move?"

He could see her shiver and knew she had taken his words in a context far removed from chess. To hell with the game. Maybe he should kiss her instead.

"No retracting now." She slid into the chair. "I will play white."

She was much more suited to black, but he didn't tell her

that. In truth, he didn't care what color she played, or who won. He wasn't leaving until he had tasted her lips once more.

Moira made the opening move, firmly grasping one of her pawns and moving it toward the center of the board. He countered by moving one of his own pawns forward to hers. Moira moved again.

"We should have a little conversation, should we not?" he asked as he considered his next move.

"If you wish."

Obviously she wasn't much for talking as she played. A point he could no doubt use to his advantage, especially if conversation threw her off balance.

"What do you plan to have me do if you win?" He moved another pawn, setting it up for her to take.

"*When* I win," she corrected, jumping at the bait and taking his pawn. "I have not thought about it."

"Liar." He smiled at the chagrined look she tossed him and casually offered up another pawn. "Do you plan to start with kissing, or do you want to force me to your bedroom?"

Color bloomed in her cheeks as she took the second piece. "I plan to do neither. Now, are you going to treat me as a serious opponent, or are you going to purposely allow me to win?"

Ah, she didn't like thinking he might "allow" her anything. Did she believe he wanted to be at her mercy? What a joke. Perhaps if she were a bit more sure, a bit more skilled at seduction, he would want just that, but she was no more prepared to seduce him than he was to let her win.

"Do you want me to let you win?" He brought out his bishop. "Are you that desperate to have your way with me?"

Moira was thoroughly flustered. He could see it, even though she tried to hide it. She brought out a knight. "I do not believe I would have to sink to desperation, sir. You are quite ready to offer yourself on a platter as it is."

Wynthrope laughed at that—a loud guffaw that almost hurt, it was so sudden and strange. He made his next play. "I am no challenge, is that what you are saying?"

Moira countered his move. "None whatsoever."

Now she was getting cocky. Time to prove to her just how much of a danger he truly was. She believed he was out to simply seduce her, and in a way she was right, but he wanted more than that. He wanted to *win* her, and that took considerably more skill than seduction.

He simply smiled and moved once more. Moira frowned at the board. She was now realizing that her queen was in peril while he had managed to fortify his king with a row of pawns. She hesitated only a moment before moving in to take one of his pawns, too late realizing her folly. He reached over the board, picked up the rook, and used it to block her queen. There was no way for her to retaliate or else her king would be lost.

His smile was smug, victory awakening his blood with a thrill. "I believe, Lady Aubourn, that the game is mine. And therefore, so are you."

He had won.

Moira stared at the board, at her king and queen, so neatly pinned by his rook. How could he have beaten her? She'd been so certain of her victory. He hadn't been about to let her win at all. He had only wanted her to *believe* she stood a chance against him.

She had played right into his hands. In fact, part of her had almost hoped it would happen this way.

Slowly, she raised her gaze to meet Wynthrope's. He leaned back in his chair, hands behind his head, and smirked.

"You are not going to renege on our agreement are you, my lady?"

His lady. Yes, he was going to make certain of that, wasn't he? If only she weren't a virgin, this situation wouldn't cause her so much anxiety. It was a totally improper thought, but she couldn't help thinking it.

"No," she murmured, her tongue thick and heavy in her mouth. "What do you want?"

He made a tsking sound as he rose. "You sound as though you are going to your execution." He paused beside her. "Come sit with me on the sofa."

Moira stared at his proffered hand. Long and slender, it was graceful and nonthreatening. Why was she so afraid to take it? So afraid of where it might lead her?

Tentatively, she slid her fingers into his and stood. His hand was warm, strong, and sure. Her knees were shaking.

He led her to the sofa—the same one they had shared that night they drank mulled wine. He sat and gently pulled her down beside him. Moira couldn't even breathe as she waited for him to make his move—to kiss her, or touch her, anything.

They sat in silence for several heartbeats as he made himself comfortable. He held her hand, stroking her palm with his thumb. "How old were you when you met the viscount?"

All the breath came rushing out of her in one astonished burst. "Excuse me?"

Wynthrope's head tilted, his lashes fluttering guilelessly. "Are you quite all right, Moira? You are flushed."

He knew perfectly well she wasn't "all right!" "You put me through that awful game, all that anxiety, and all you want to do is talk?"

His expression was all innocence. "What else would I want?"

She could hit him! Was this relief or annoyance burning in her chest? "You said you had whims for me to cater to!"

He nodded. "I do. I want you to tell me about yourself." Again that innocent blink. "Were you expecting something else?"

Moira glared at him, more embarrassed than angry. "You know very well I thought you referred to seduction."

He had the nerve to appear affronted. "I do not recall saying anything about seduction, but if that is what you would prefer—"

She raised a hand as he leaned toward her, stopping him before he could kiss her and feel the wild pounding of her heart. She was such a coward. "Nineteen. I was nineteen when Anthony and I met."

He settled back against the sofa with a smile that was both satisfied and mocking. He was toying with her, of that she was certain. Like a cat with a mouse, he was simply mauling her until he felt like taking a bite. "Was it love at first sight?"

She could lie and tell him yes, but she didn't want to lie to him. If they ever did make love, he would find out her marriage had been a sham, and that was going to be difficult enough for her to explain.

"No. It was never like that." She swallowed and gave in to the urge to reveal more, "Tony and I adored each other, but not like that. Ours was a marriage of convenience. He needed a bride and I needed to escape my family."

Fortunately he didn't press the issue of her marriage. Unfortunately he found a different topic to seize upon.

"To escape your family? How fortunate that you could. Did it work?"

Was he making fun or genuinely astounded? Moira smiled. "For a time. You have met Minerva, so you know I still have some contact with them."

His gaze was shrewd. "More than you would like."

"Yes." How easy it was to admit these things to him. "I am somewhat close to two of my sisters, and I believe Minnie and I might form some kind of bond, but I do not wish to have contact with any of the others."

He nodded, apparently satisfied. Did he not want to know

why she disliked her family? Or did it simply not matter why, only that she did?

"What were you like as a young girl?"

She replied without thought, grateful that he had changed the subject, "Bookish. Fat."

"Fat?" His expression was laughable. "No."

"It is true." Her cheeks warmed at his continued disbelief. "My mother constantly belittled me for my weight."

His gaze raked over her in a clinical fashion. There was nothing the least bit brazen about his appraisal. "But you are so thin now."

Moira's brow puckered. This was not the first time he had mentioned her size with a hint of concern. "You think I am too thin, don't you?"

He met her gaze evenly. "I think you could stand to gain a stone or two, yes."

She laughed. It came out more harshly than she intended, but she wasn't sure what these emotions raging through her were. "No one ever thought I was pretty when I was heavy. They do now."

His gaze never wavered, his expression was resolute. "You're beautiful, but whether you are thin or fat, that will never change."

Moira turned her head, her throat constricting as she fought the tears burning the back of her eyes. All those years when she was plump she had wanted someone—anyone—to tell her she was pretty, and all she ever heard was how attractive she would be if she were thin. Now this wonderful, intriguing man was telling her he didn't care what size she was. Dare she believe he meant it?

He was silent for only a moment. It was as though he knew she didn't want to continue this particular conversation. "What would be the worst fate in the world, do you think?"

God love him for being able to read her so easily, no matter how much it frightened her. "To end up living out the rest of my days with my mother."

He laughed, and his sheer delight brought a smile to her own lips. "Honestly?"

She shrugged and changed the subject. "I would like to know real love before I die."

The fingers entwined with hers squeezed gently. How right it felt to sit here holding hands with him. "Wouldn't we all."

The wistful quality of his voice gave her pause. She leaned her elbow against the back of the sofa and rested her temple on her fist as she studied his face. "I wouldn't have thought you the kind of man who believes in love."

Was he insulted? He jerked a little bit, as though she had struck a nerve. "I believe love exists. I don't think everyone is lucky enough to have it find them."

Spoken like a man afraid love might come looking. "Perhaps we have to find it on our own."

"Perhaps." Now he shrugged, as though tossing off her idea. "Regardless, I do not think it and I are bound to ever cross paths."

"Why not?" When had the balance of power between them changed? When had she become the inquisitor? And why it did hurt to hear him say he expected to never know love? "Surely you do not believe you are unlucky?"

He folded his arms across his chest. Yes, he was definitely withdrawing. "Undeserving."

"That's absurd." It was time to bring him back out of his shell, even if she had to browbeat him out. "You are as deserving of love as anyone."

He cocked a brow. Oh, but he had perfected the sarcasm in every expression. "As deserving as you?"

It was tempting to slap him. Was he trying to trap her with words? "Of course."

"I think you are more deserving than I."

Oh for heaven's sake! "I will not allow you to be so self-pitying."

"It is not self-pity." Then why did he sound so defensive? she wondered. "It is simple honesty," he said.

She scowled at him as she lifted her head. What a pile of malarkey. "Honesty? You are not honest with yourself, how can you be honest with anyone else?"

His jaw dropped. "I beg your pardon?"

This conversation had gone way beyond light and frivolous since shortly after it started. He would not hesitate to tell her exactly what he thought—she was still smarting over his telling her she should gain weight—why should she hesitate with him?

"You tell yourself you are undeserving of love—for some long-ago sin, no doubt. You needn't share it with me, it is of no consequence. All that matters is who you are today. And that man deserves to be loved."

He stared at her, his face pale. Obviously she was close to the truth. "How can you possibly know that?"

"Because I have seen glimpses of him when you forget to pretend to be someone else. Regardless of the mistakes you've made, or will make, I believe that you are a good man."

For one brief, awful second, Moira thought he might jump up and run away. He looked so stricken, so confused, and she realized that he really did think he was an awful person.

And it broke her heart.

But he didn't run away. Instead he turned to her, reached for her. She didn't move, didn't even breathe. Any hesitation on her part and he might withdraw from her forever, and she would rather be fat again than lose him now.

His head neared hers. She held her breath, her heart

pounding as she saw the darkness in his gaze. Then her eyes closed, and she saw nothing at all.

Wynthrope's lips were firm and warm yet undeniably soft as they moved against hers. Moira followed his lead, breathless as his mouth teased her lips apart. Opening her mouth to his exploration, Moira sank deeper and deeper into the darkness of his kiss. He tasted warm and faintly of the wine he'd drunk during their chess game. Odd, but she had drunk the same wine, and it hadn't tasted as good then as it did now.

Tentatively, she slid her palms up the soft wool of his coat to clutch at his lapels. She probably should push him away, but her hands refused to act. They couldn't even pull him closer as her body demanded, they just clutched and held him near.

His hands were in her hair, deftly removing pins one by one. There was a soft smattering sound as he tossed the entire handful on the carpet. Then he unwound her elaborate hairstyle, soothing the ache in her scalp with gentle fingers, combing through the waves until her hair fell down her back. No one had seen her with her hair down since she was a girl. Not even Anthony had seen her hair like this. Anytime she had worn it down in front of him, it had been braided, or tied back. Now this man, for all intents and purposes a stranger, was going to see her as no one else ever had.

It seemed appropriate, really.

But he didn't break their kiss to look. His lips still clinging to hers, still demanding and insistent, he pushed her backward, down onto her back on the sofa. Moira went willingly, still clutching his coat in her hands.

Wynthrope wasn't a huge man, but he was strong and solid, his shoulders broad and his limbs long. She expected him to be heavier than he was, but he supported most of his weight on the forearm by her head as he pulled her skirts up above her knees. He settled between her thighs, resting most of his weight there, against a spot that instantly came to life at the sweet hardness of his body.

One of his hands hooked behind her knee, drawing her leg up so that it cupped his hips. The pressure between her thighs intensified. Instinctively, Moira's hips lifted, pushing against him. The fingers on her leg flexed against her calf as Wynthrope's hips pushed back.

Moira gasped against his mouth. So this was what it was all about. This was why women had affairs and got themselves ruined. Now she was beginning to understand. A hard ridge threatened to bruise the tender flesh between her legs, was almost painful in its force, but still she ground herself against it, and wanted more.

She shouldn't be doing this. It wasn't proper, and she had always been most proper. Still, a part of her argued, what could possibly be wrong about something that felt so right? She was a widow, and not bound by the same rules that kept unmarried women in their place.

Her tongue moved against his. Their hips rose and fell in time with the rhythm set by their kiss. The throbbing deep inside Moira grew, until it was a steady, humming ache.

A virgin she might be, but green she wasn't. She knew what happened between a man and a woman—she had her imagination, and had seen drawings in a book. She knew how their bodies fit together. She knew what arousal was and how it felt, and she knew how to relieve the ache. But none of those things had prepared her for the urgency that having Wynthrope's body pressed to hers wrought. She wanted this man to touch her in places no one but she had ever touched. She wanted him inside her, even if it hurt.

And yet she was afraid to have it happen. If he took her now, would he turn his back on her tomorrow? Was she to lose him so soon?

His weight shifted and eased. Moira felt the loss of him

keenly. Without the pressure of his body, her own cried out in something very much like pain, so acute was the longing within.

Hands braced on either side of her head, Wynthrope stared down at her. The planes of his cheeks were flushed in the soft light. His hair was mussed and his jacket was a wrinkled mess. His lips were slightly parted, and dark from their kisses, and his eyes glowed with a fire that made Moira want to be burned alive.

"You look like one of the angels in your paintings," he told her, his voice strangely husky.

Moira's throat constricted. She'd always thought Tony's angels to be among the most beautiful creatures she had ever seen. "Thank you."

"Shall we continue, Moira? Or do you wish me to stop?"

So he was going to make her decide, was he? She supposed it was very gentlemanly of him, even though she knew what he wanted her to say. *She* knew what she wanted to say, and yet the words wouldn't come. She could give him her virginity now, on this sofa, and let the secret out, trusting him not to reveal it, or she could hang on to it, and hope that he didn't tire of waiting, and of her in the meantime.

He rose from the sofa. "Your silence is answer enough."

Quickly, awkwardly, Moira followed him into a sitting position. "It is not that I do not want to—"

He silenced her with a finger to her lips. "When I make love to you, I do not want there to be any hesitation on your part. It will happen because you tell me not to stop."

Moira bowed her head. How embarrassing this all was. "I'm sorry."

The same finger that had touched her lips now raised her chin. His gaze was gentle, even understanding, with no hint of mockery. "Seduction is like a chess game, Moira. All the pieces have to be in place for the king to stake his claim."

She smiled at his analogy. "A king now, are you?"

He returned her smile, along with a soft brush of his lips against her own. "Of course, and you, my black queen, are a prize I am prepared to wait to win."

Moira stared at him, her eyes wide. He was prepared to wait. Prepared to give her time. In the meantime, did that mean he was going to take every opportunity to make his winning move? To strip away all her defenses until she had no recourse but to surrender? Yes, that was exactly what he meant. God help her, but she needn't have worried about his turning away from her, she should be worried about what would happen when he discovered she had given him the ultimate prize a woman could give a man.

She had a feeling Wynthrope Ryland held on to what he thought was his, and that was even more frightening than the idea of him walking away.

Chapter 7

∽◯⌣◯∾

Christmas Eve came as crisp and perfect as it ought. The night was dark and quiet for London. Houses looked warm and cozy with lamps burning in windows. Stars were bright in the sky, and despite the lack of snow, the air was cold enough to turn one's breath to visible wisps of vapor. There was something about Christmas that made the night seem more inviting, and one's heart fuller.

"Minnie, do stop fidgeting. You look fine."

The younger woman pulled a face as the carriage gently swayed back and forth as it rolled ever forward over the bare cobblestones. "Perhaps you can be satisfied with that, but I want to look better than 'fine.'"

Moira's brows arched, but the expression went unnoticed by her sister. Of course Minnie wouldn't notice, the girl was too wrapped up in herself, as she should be. She was young and on her way to a Christmas Eve party that a young man—a new young man—she had her eye on was also going to attend.

119

But Moira was also on her way to a party where a man she had her eye on was going to be, and she resented the implication that she looked merely "fine" as well. Her hair alone had taken her maid more than two hours to style, shape, and pin, and if she tilted her head it felt as though the whole thing might fall off. Her eyebrows had been shaped, her lips lightly tinted with color. Her jewelry consisted of a yellow diamond choker and dangling earrings that Anthony had bought her on their fifth anniversary. Her gown was new, and of a rich, shimmering golden-green silk that seemed to change color depending on the light. Her gloves and slippers had been dyed to coordinate, but not quite match, as Moira's modiste, Madame Villeneuve, had been adamant that the dress stand out.

Moira didn't care if the gown stood out. She cared only for Wynthrope Ryland's reaction to her in it.

Over the course of the last week and a half, he had become something of a regular fixture at her house. He had been by four evenings out of the ten for dinner and a game of chess, which he always won, even though she made it as difficult for him as she could. Sometimes he demanded her kisses in return, other times he asked her questions about her life, about her house—things she wouldn't normally expect him to care about, like whether she kept her valuables in a safe place, given the fact that she and Minerva were alone in the house.

His questions bothered her—not because she found them intrusive, but because they were so often personal. It reminded her of her idea that a person could make anyone fall in love with him, if only the other person were given the time to get to know him. Wynthrope Ryland was certainly getting to know her. Was he starting to love her as well? God knew she was trying to guard her own heart from just that same thing, because not only had he learned a lot about her over the course of their developing relationship, but she had learned a lot about him as well.

Such as the fact that he and North were best friends as well as brothers, and that while he claimed to dislike his eldest brother Brahm, he still seemed to desperately want his approval. Mostly she learned that for all his wit and caustic talk, he was a very vulnerable man, reluctant to offer his real self for anyone to see because he was afraid of being rejected. It was this vulnerability that drew her in, because she rather liked the softer side of him. She preferred his genuine smiles to the practiced smirks, and she preferred his teasing and his laughter to his droll remarks and sarcastic humor. He came across as little more than a dandy, and there was so much more to him than that. He was intelligent, and he liked to discuss things other people ridiculed her for. They discussed the existence of God, the religions of other cultures, mythology, and so many other topics that she wondered about. Never once did he scoff at her. In fact, he had many ideas and questions of his own, so that most of their time was spent talking about, even debating, the world outside their own.

Oddly enough, the more time they spent talking, the more often she wished he would kiss her, and the less time she spent worrying about where kissing might lead. In fact, she wanted the kissing to lead to something more, but Wynthrope was careful that it didn't. She knew he wanted her too, but he seemed to be holding back, and she knew why: he was waiting for her to let him know she was ready. When the time came for them to make love, he wanted her to be completely aware that it was her idea—and that his seduction of her was complete.

The realization sent a shiver of anticipation down her spine.

She was still not certain she could trust him with her secret, but she was beginning to lean in that direction. Wynthrope was many things, but she could not imagine him betraying her in such a manner. He was not the kind of man to use others for his own personal gain.

"Are you coming?"

Jerked out of her thoughts by the sound of her sister's voice, Moira looked up. Minnie was poised near the open door of the carriage, both she and a footman watching Moira expectantly.

Good heavens, they had arrived and she hadn't even noticed! Mumbling an apology, Moira followed her sister out of their carriage, assisted to the ground by the expressionless footman.

Tonight's party was at Wynter Lane, the Palladian-style London home of the Marquess of Wynter and his wife, Princess Varya. Just last year the marquess's sister, Blythe, had married the youngest Ryland brother, Devlin. Moira suspected her invitation to the festivities was owed mostly to Wynthrope—or possibly Octavia, as men weren't naturally given to such considerations.

Still, it was an honor to be invited to what was essentially a family gathering. Outside of the Rylands, Miles and Varya Christian had invited only a few other close acquaintances and Moira. She was extremely grateful for the courtesy, as she and Minnie would have no doubt spent the evening at home alone.

Inside the house, their outerwear was taken by the butler, who smiled and wished them both a pleasant evening before handing their clothing off to a footman and then escorting them to the party.

Minnie's eyes were wide as they drifted through the great hall. Indeed, Moira found it hard not to stare herself. She was used to luxury and elegance, but Wynter Lane was opulent beyond her imaginings, and just saved from being gaudy. She supposed much of it could be owed to Varya, who was Russian and no doubt used to excessive grandeur.

They were shown to the music room. The walls between it and another room had been opened up to allow room for refreshments and dancing if the guests so desired. It was lovely. Lamps burned throughout the rooms, bathing everything in a soft, warm glow. Men wore the usual evening attire of black and white, while the women were a veritable rainbow of colors.

Princess Varya was dressed in a gown of rich forest green that enhanced her impressive bosom. Her thick black hair was piled high on her head in a style that must have taken almost the entire day to perfect. Diamonds glittered in her hair, from her ears, and around her neck. It was so very obvious she was royalty, and Moira was struck by the sight of her.

She came to them with a bright smile on her lovely face, her blue eyes shining. "Lady Aubourn, Miss Banning. How delightful that you could join us!" Her accent wasn't heavy, but just rich enough that she sounded terribly exotic to Moira's English ears.

Returning the smile in what she hoped was a relaxed fashion, Moira curtsied. "Thank you for the invitation, Your Highness."

Varya waved a gloved hand. "Pish. None of that. You are a friend of Octavia, and therefore a friend of mine. I will presume to call you Moira and you will call me Varya and we will ignore the silly rules society likes to put upon us."

Moira could only stare for a moment. Good gracious, the princess had made short work of the niceties of becoming acquainted! Perhaps she might have found such a quality overwhelming in another woman, but somehow Varya managed to put her quite at ease. This was a woman Moira could like very much indeed.

After extending the same warm friendliness to Minerva, Varya took Moira by the arm and led her toward a group in the center of the room. Minerva went off to talk to some of the younger people, most of whom she already knew, and one of which was this young man she had been talking much about as of late. Moira was just relieved the boy was closer to her age, and not out of her sphere like Wynthrope.

Speaking of that very devil, he was part of the group Moira joined. He was deep in conversation with a giant of a man and didn't seem to notice her right away, although Moira thought she caught him glance at her out of the corner of his eye.

He was dressed like the other gentlemen, in stark black and white, but somehow he seemed to make the uniform his own. His lean frame made him seem relaxed and easy in his clothing, rather than stiff and restricted like some of the others. His cravat was tied in an intricate knot and his shirt points were high, but not too much so.

A redhead of amazonian proportions joined Wynthrope and the other man. Good heavens! The woman was almost as tall as Wynthrope! Only an inch or two separated them. This must be his sister-in-law Blythe, who was also Lord Wynter's sister. That meant the giant was his younger brother Devlin. She should have known. Out of all the men present, only the Rylands and one or two others were wearing trousers instead of the usual evening wear of breeches and stockings. These brothers were not the kind of men ruled by fashion and societal preferences.

Varya introduced her to many of the guests, including Blythe, whom Moira found a little intimidating at first, but soon warmed up to. It was very difficult not to like someone so very open and friendly. Blythe in turn introduced Moira to her husband, Devlin. Moira tried not to stare as she offered him her hand. She was a tall woman herself, but this man was at least a whole foot taller than she was! He was a perfect match for the statuesque Blythe, but Moira wouldn't want a man this big at all. She much preferred Wynthrope who, though tall, was nowhere near as intimidating.

In fact, she didn't find Wynthrope physically intimidating at all. Physically exciting, yes, and perhaps emotionally intimidating, but his size and stature didn't make her uneasy at all. If anything, his build made her wonder what he looked like beneath all those neat, perfectly pressed layers. Certainly then she might find his nakedness a little unnerving.

He was watching her, smirking that infuriating smirk that told her he knew exactly what she was thinking. "Good evening, Moira."

If anyone arched a brow at his use of her Christian name, Moira didn't notice. All she heard was the challenge in his voice. He was deliberately allowing these people to know that they were intimate acquaintances, no doubt to unsettle her.

Or perhaps to lay claim.

"Wynthrope."

"You are in exceedingly good looks this evening."

Was he suggesting that she wasn't normally in good looks? No, he thought she had gone through all this effort for his benefit. Well, he was right, blast him, but she wasn't about to admit to it.

"As are you," she replied with false innocence. "I wonder whose toilette took longer, mine or yours?"

Blythe and Devlin laughed, their amusement as robust as they themselves. Even Wynthrope chuckled, revealing the startling white of his teeth as he did so. He grinned at her, his eyes bright with appreciation and humor.

"Mine, no doubt," he replied. "Such natural loveliness as yours requires little ornament."

Oh. What a lovely response. The brute no doubt knew she would be lost for a reply. "Those are very pretty words, sir. Thank you."

"My brother is very good with words," Devlin commented somewhat dryly. "I have seen him do more damage than a bayonet with that tongue of his."

Wynthrope shot his brother a sardonic look. "Oh yes, but I'd much rather use it to bestow pleasure than pain."

Moira flushed right to the roots of her hair. Even Blythe looked somewhat shocked by his brazenness. Devlin, however, merely shook his head. "Perhaps if you followed that canon you would be married by now."

Wynthrope shook his head with a wry smile. "Bayonet. Cannon. Marriage. It always come back to war with you, doesn't it?"

Rolling her eyes, Blythe laid her hand on Moira's arm. "This could go on a while, Moira. Why don't you and I go talk to Octavia and Varya?"

Moira would never admit it, but she was loath to leave Wynthrope's presence. With him she felt relatively safe and secure. With these other people, she didn't know what to say and was nervous about making a fool of herself. Still, she allowed the taller woman to lead her away and soon found herself laughing and carrying on as though she had known these women for years.

Sometime later, her grumbling stomach drove her to the refreshment table. Unable to fight the hunger any longer, she loaded a plate with tiny cucumber sandwiches, her favorite. Turning so that her back was to most of the party going on in the other room, she began stuffing the sandwiches into her mouth.

Oh! They were so good!

"Will you share or do you intend to eat them all?"

Turning to face him, Moira flushed as she swallowed a large bite. The plate was still half full. "I have not eaten since this morning—"

Wynthrope smiled faintly as he folded his arms across his chest. "No need to justify yourself, Moira. I like a woman with healthy appetites."

Oh dear. That raised all sorts of delicious thoughts and

questions. And some not so delicious. "Is this more of your campaign to have me gain weight?"

Either he missed the sharpness of her tone or he was willfully ignoring it. "You do what you feel comfortable doing, but I wouldn't mind having a bit more of you to hold on to, no."

Her cheeks warmed even more. "You say the most devilish things."

"You think that was devilish?" His amusement was palpable. "My initial urge was to tell you that the softer the woman, the sweeter the coming."

Moira burned right to the tip of her ears. "My God."

He nipped a sandwich off her plate and took a smug bite. "So if you want to devour this whole plate and come back for more, I will support you wholeheartedly."

She raised her gaze to his, even though she knew eye contact would just make the tingle in her stomach worse. "Why do you talk to me like this?"

He finished the sandwich. "Because you like it."

"I do not." How indignant she sounded. Whom was she trying to convince?

He shrugged and stole another sandwich. "The way you look at me says you do."

She denied it, even though she knew there was truth in his words. "I am simply not accustomed to such speech."

"Of course you are not." He folded his arms again. "You are so wonderfully prim sometimes, Moira. It is delightful."

She narrowed her eyes. "And you are extremely vexing at times, Wynthrope."

"Part of my charm." Oh how that little smirk irked her at times!

"Indeed." She lifted another sandwich to her lips. He watched as she did so. Feeling brazen, Moira moistened her lips with her tongue before slowly taking a bite. She chewed and swallowed, aware of his gaze on her mouth the entire time.

"And what will you do for me?" she asked.

He blinked. "I beg your pardon?"

She smiled sweetly. She was playing with fire here, but she couldn't help it. She liked it. "If I soften myself up, *sweeten* myself for you, what will you do for me?"

His Adam's apple bobbed as he swallowed. "Anything you want. I would be entirely at your command. All you have to do is say the word and you may do to me whatever you please."

Moira's stomach fluttered. He was serious. This conversation was getting out of hand. Forcing a flirtatious smile, she kept her tone light. "And that word would be?"

Wynthrope leaned toward her until his mouth was right beside her ear. She could feel his breath on her skin, feel the heat radiating off him. Was there a man on the earth who had ever smelled this good?

"Yes." His voice was little more than a breeze, but it tore through her like a cyclone.

Trembling, she met his gaze as he raised his head. His eyes were so dark they were indigo, so intense they seemed fathomless.

She couldn't speak, couldn't remember how to make her tongue and lips work together to form words. Dumbly she glanced down at the plate in her hands. What had she been thinking, loading it with all these sandwiches? There was no way she could eat them all—not with her stomach so tied in knots.

"Would you like me to help you eat those?" There was no hint of mockery or innuendo in his tone.

Moira nodded, raising her chin. She was in grave danger of falling in love with this man. Did that frighten her? Thrill her? Make her want to weep?

"*Yes*," she murmured, and took another sandwich for herself.

After dining with North and Octavia on Christmas Day, Wynthrope departed for Moira's. He had yet to determine where she kept the tiara, but that wasn't something he was going to think about this evening. This evening, he promised himself, was strictly for the pleasure of Moira's company.

This was becoming a regular occurrence, his spending an evening with her at her home. He wasn't kidding himself—only part of it was his search for the tiara. The only reason he gave a damn about the tiara was to protect North and Dev. If he really wanted to search the house, he'd just wait until she was out or asleep and break in. No, he spent so much time there because he craved Moira's company.

She was waiting for him in the parlor, clad in a simple gown of violet muslin. His heart leaped at the sight of her. Only one day had passed since he had last seen her, and it felt as though he had been deprived of her for months.

This was not good, not good at all, and yet he couldn't make his heart believe it.

"Are you ready to play, or would you like a drink first?" she asked.

Smiling at her readiness, Wynthrope offered her the small ebony box he had brought with him. "I have something for you first."

Moira's expression was one of dismay. "Oh, you shouldn't have! I do not have anything for you."

It had never occurred to him that she might. "That is of no consequence. Please, take it."

She did, her reluctance giving way to delightful curiosity. "Thank you."

"Do not thank me until you see what is inside."

Like a foolish boy he held his breath as she opened the box, exhaling only when her face lit like a candle with pleasure.

"Oh! It is beautiful." Reverently, she withdrew the small, intricately carved ivory angel from the velvet lining.

Wynthrope puffed his chest, inordinately pleased with himself. "I thought you might like it."

She came to him, her face aglow, and kissed his cheek. That kiss alone was more gift than he deserved. "I love it. Thank you."

Moira set the angel and the box on the little table near the chair where he knew she most often sat, giving it a little caress before turning to him. How happy she looked. What he would give to see her always so content.

How her expression would change if she knew the truth about him.

But he wasn't going to think of that tonight. Tonight he wasn't a coldhearted bastard out to relieve her of a treasure. Tonight he was just the pathetic man who couldn't get enough of her. The lucky man allowed to be this close to her.

They sat in their customary places, with him playing white and her playing black. How fitting that she would play black when he'd long thought of her as the black queen. Wynthrope, playing white, made the first move.

It was Moira, however, who ended their game by eventually taking his king.

"You won." He was more shocked than she was. Realization dawned. "You've been practicing!"

She turned the sweetest shade of pink, but didn't look the least bit contrite. "So?"

He laughed then. "Good enough. Well, as the winner you get to name your prize. What will you ask of me?" With his luck she would probably make him read to her from some horrid romance, or worse, poetry.

Her blush deepened. She truly was so maidenly for a widowed woman ten years married. "I want you to kiss me," she informed him in a somewhat shaky voice.

She what? This was an interesting turn of events. So his patience was finally paying off, was it? Wynthrope's heart leaped in anticipation. She wanted him. He would have to go slow. He didn't want to appear too eager.

He leaned across the table and kissed her cheek. "There you go."

She flushed even more. How red could she get before she burst into flame? "On my mouth."

Smiling inwardly, Wynthrope leaned across the table again and brushed his lips over hers. He wanted to devour her, but resisted. He sat back. "How was that?"

She looked positively murderous now. "That is not how I meant and you know it."

Feigning ignorance, he blinked at her. "I am afraid I have no idea what you mean. Perhaps you should show me."

She glared at him. She knew that he was deliberately toying with her. If he wasn't careful she would turn the tables on him just as she did at Wynter's party the night before. Perhaps he would do better to not be careful. She did turn the tables on him in such a *stimulating* fashion.

Pushing back her chair, Moira rose to her feet and came around the table to where he sat. Wynthrope pushed back his own seat as she approached.

"Stand up," she ordered.

He smiled lazily. "I do not feel like it. Why do you not sit on my lap?"

For a moment he thought she might tell him to go straight to Hades, but then a strange glint lit her eyes, and he knew he was in for torment.

Deliberately, she lowered herself onto his lap, squirming against him in a pretense of making herself comfortable, but he knew it was for no other reason than to drive him to the brink of insanity by rubbing him to full erection with that delectable bottom of hers. For a woman so unsure of herself at times, she certainly had a natural knowledge of seduction.

"Are you comfortable?" he growled when she finally stilled.

She smiled sweetly. "Yes, thank you." Taking his face in her hands, she tilted his chin, stroked his jaw with soft fingers. And when she began to gently massage his scalp, it was all he could do not to close his eyes in ecstasy.

"You like this, do you not?" Her fingers combed through his hair. "You seem to enjoy it."

"I do," he answered, finally giving in and closing his eyes. "My grandmother used to brush my hair for hours when I was a boy."

"Were you close to her?"

"I adored her. I never had to worry about pleasing her or being good enough for her. She loved all four of us equally and just as we were."

The fingers in his hair stilled. "You were very fortunate to have her."

Wynthrope opened his eyes at the longing in her voice. "I was." Looking at her, he realized that Moira hadn't had anyone to make up for her parents' stupidity as he had. No one to make up for thoughtless remarks or blatant favoritism. No wonder she tried so hard. No wonder she sometimes still felt inferior. No wonder she had wasted herself on a marriage of convenience when she deserved so much more.

Had her husband ever realized how blessed he'd been to have her, this woman who could make a man feel ten feet tall with a simple glance?

"You amaze me, Moira Tyndale."

He had astonished her—that was obvious in her wide eyes and soft gasp. "I do?"

"I have no idea how you could have grown up where you did and turned out so good. You make me ashamed."

"But you have nothing to be ashamed of."

Her confidence in him cut him to the quick. "You have no idea what I have done thinking it was within my right to do it. I spent so much of my life feeling bitter, carrying a huge chip on my shoulder, when I had no right to feel so sorry for myself. I had my brothers and my grandmother. Who did you have?"

Her smile was kind. "I had myself. And I had my aunt. I did not see her very often, but her visits and her letters gave me something to hold on to. Do not pity me, Wynthrope, I will not stand for it."

Something gave way in his heart as he stared into her eyes. It was as though the hardened shell around it cracked and splintered, the shards piercing him from every angle.

"I'd like to kiss you now," he murmured. "Will you allow it?"

"Yes." Her face neared his. "Did you not tell me I only had to say that word to have you at my command?"

"Yes," he whispered. "I did."

Her lips brushed his. "Then kiss me. I command it."

Lifting his arms, he caught her head in his hands, holding her still as he claimed her mouth with his own. She was warm, moist, and sweet. He should take his time, cajole her into surrender, but finesse escaped him. He trembled with hunger for her, his muscles quivering with restraint. His tongue assaulted hers as her kiss consumed him.

Her hands caught at his coat, undoing the buttons to slide inside. Could she feel the erratic pounding of his heart against her palm? Could she feel his hardness against the back of her thighs? Had she any idea that he was practically beside himself with wanting her?

He had to do something to alleviate the tension threatening to overpower them both. Releasing her head, Wynthrope reached down and clutched at her skirt, pulling the soft fabric upward. Shoving his hand beneath, he pushed the layers of fabric aside, sliding his fingers up the silky stocking covering her calf, past a garter, to the satiny flesh of her warm, bare inner thigh. Moira jumped.

"What are you doing?" she demanded, breathless against his mouth.

"You said you wanted to give me a present," he reminded her, his breathing equally as shallow. "This is what I want, Moira. I want to touch you. Open for me."

Her eyes wide and dark, her gaze held his as her legs parted for his hand. He watched her face as he brushed his fingers along the springy curls there. She gasped, her body leaping at the contact. Her eyelids fluttered, color rose in her cheeks as he slowly stroked the fine, dampening hair.

Christ, but he wanted her! He wanted her beneath him, on top of him, any way he could have her, but most of all, he wanted to see her face when he gave her pleasure. It meant more to him than he could ever say to know that he could arouse such sensations in her.

He slid his fingers along those moist curls, easing one into the cleft between. He watched as her brow puckered and her mouth parted. She was hot and wet and slick against his finger, her flesh clutching at him like an eager hand. She would be deliciously, maddeningly tight, he knew that instinctively.

Her thighs parted as far as her skirts would allow— enough for him to ease his hand fully between her legs. Slowly, deliberately, he slid the length of his finger into her, his own body tightening as he watched her expression change ever so slightly. Her fingers tightened on his lapels and her hips began to move, setting the rhythm for his now wet, questing fingers. Beneath her, his cock pulsated with need, irritated by the friction of his small clothes, demanding to be released. Gritting his teeth, Wynthrope concentrated on Moira's pleasure rather than his own discomfort.

Easily, his thumb found the apex of her sex as his finger moved inside her, stroking the hooded nub. His entire body throbbed in response when Moira cried out, lifting herself against his hand. Driven by his own lust to hear her cries, his desire to feel her spasm around his finger, Wynthrope worked her body with a teasing but insistent rhythm.

Still gripping his coat with one hand, Moira slid the other between them, finding the hard ridge that pushed against the fall of his trousers. He groaned as she caressed him through the fabric, and when her fingers tore at the fastenings, he made no move to stop her.

Her fingers closed around the naked length of him, eager and unschooled. They caressed and squeezed and made his sac tighten with their sheer enthusiasm.

Shifting her weight, she moved on his lap so that she was on his thigh more than his groin, giving herself better access to his heated cock. The hand at her head now slid down to her back, supporting her as she stroked him.

"Up and down," he growled. If she wanted to jack him, he wasn't going to stop her, but he was going to make certain she did it right. Tentatively, then with more confidence, she began moving her fist up and down to the cadence his own hand set between her legs.

"That's it." He gasped as the tightening in his groin became more insistent. He increased the pressure of his thumb, drawing a low moan from her lips.

Sweat beaded on Wynthrope's upper lip. The need for her release was almost as sharp as the need for his own. He matched the tempo of her hips with his thumb, and when her cries became more and more urgent, the grip on his prick tighter, he increased the pressure.

Her coos and cries became more encouraging, more frequent. When she tossed her head back, her mouth opening in wordless cries of delight, her body clenching at his hand as spasms rolled over her, Wynthrope lost all control. His own neck bowed, his forehead pressed somewhere in the region of her breast as his own climax erupted.

He waited until the stars behind his eyes faded before opening them. Moira had collapsed against him and was watching him with an expression he could only term as bewildered contentment.

Wynthrope knew his smile was one a cat might give after swallowing the canary, but he didn't care. He was sated and languid and he was smug, damn it. Drawing his handkerchief from his pocket, he handed it to her. No doubt she would want to wipe her hand.

Slowly she returned his smile as she accepted the folded linen. "Well, that was certainly better than the hair comb Minnie gave me."

Unable to contain his laughter, Wynthrope gathered her to him in a fierce hug. "Indeed. Merry Christmas, Moira."

She kissed his cheek before snuggling against his chest. "Merry Christmas, Wynthrope."

Chapter 8

The following morning, Nathaniel swept into Moira's breakfast room in a fashionable flurry of coats and scarves. He took one look at her and froze, his mouth dropping open.

"My Lord, you bedded him!"

Thankfully they were alone, or Moira would have been tempted to throttle him. As it was, she leaped to her feet to go shut the door behind him. "For heaven's sake, Nathaniel! Do lower your voice."

He seemed unaffected by her reprimand as he tossed his outerwear onto the back of the sofa before sinking into a chair at the table. "You must tell me all about it. Every detail. Was he amazing?"

It was impossible to be angry with him, even though he was impertinent beyond belief. "I did not 'bed' him as you so politely put it," she informed him as she sat down as well.

Nathaniel's cherubic face took on a dubious countenance. "Something happened. I can tell."

She frowned and poured him a cup of coffee from the silver pot near her elbow. "You cannot."

"I can," he insisted, gesturing at her with his hand. "You have this glow about you."

Oh dear, now she was starting to blush. She offered him the cup. "I do not."

"You do. He gave you *la petite mort*, didn't he?"

Moira wasn't an experienced woman when it came to sexual matters, but even she knew what the French referred to by "the little death." She didn't have to reply, her face felt as though it were on fire, and surely it must have looked just the same.

"He did!" Nathaniel cried with a delighted clap of his hands. "Oh, how I wish Tony was here!"

Mortified beyond belief, Moira stared at him. "If Tony was here, it never would have happened."

Of course, that didn't seem to faze him at all. He merely shrugged, as though everyone had extramarital affairs. "It might have. Tony often remarked that he wished you would have an affair."

"He did?" She lifted her own coffee to her lips and drank, her mind mulling over this new piece of information. Tony had dropped hints, but she always believed them to have been out of guilt, or at the very best, jests.

"Of course he did." Nathaniel sounded a little put out that she might have thought otherwise. "He wanted you to be happy. It was never his wish that your marriage would be so unfair to you."

Moira's brows and shoulders shrugged in unison. "I suppose I took my vows seriously, no matter how insincere they might have been."

"Not insincere." Nathaniel patted her hand. "Unconventional."

Moira smiled. "What a wonderfully polite way to put it."

Her friend leaned back in his chair, all ease and elegance. "So, are you going to tell me what happened between you and the beautiful Mr. Ryland?"

Make that all *nosy* ease and elegance. "I most certainly am not!"

"Oh come on!" Nathaniel lurched forward, bracing his forearms on the table. "I will tell you what happened between the angelic Matthew and myself."

It was an interesting proposition. Not only was there a vibrancy about her friend that hadn't been there for some time, but Moira had long harbored a curiosity about what two men did together, and she did so yearn for someone to talk to about Wynthrope—someone who didn't know him. Someone who had experience with this sort of thing.

For example, what did what happened between them the night before mean? It had been so very pleasureful, so very intense. Afterward, they had been a little awkward with each other, though he had stayed for another two hours before departing for his own home. And he had kissed her so thoroughly before taking his leave. It had to mean *something*, didn't it? But what? Did it mean he had feelings for her beyond the sexual?

He could have had her last night. She probably wouldn't have put up any resistance if he'd tossed her on the floor and had his way with her. Instead he had shown her what he was capable of and backed away. Why? Did he think she was still reluctant? Was he still trying to make her come to him? Hadn't she done that last night as well?

"He could have taken things further last night," she confided sotto voce, "but he did not."

Propping his chin on his hand, Nathaniel made a perfect O with his lips. "How far did he get in the first place?"

Her face burning, Moira took a deep, fortifying breath. "He touched me in places only my hands have known, though not as intimately as his."

Nathaniel's blue eyes widened. "No! Did you like it?"

Moira glanced at her feet. This was so embarrassing! "Really, Nathaniel."

Her friend tossed his hand in the air in a dramatic gesture. "What? If you did not like it then he is not doing it right, and either needs to be taught or is not worth your time."

She could barely meet his gaze. "I liked it."

Her confession was met with a rakish grin. "Excellent." He snatched a bite of ham left over from her breakfast off her plate with his fingers and popped it in his mouth. "And did you reciprocate?"

Good heavens but this conversation was scandalous! Moira had never discussed such things with anyone. Then again, she'd never had such things to discuss.

"Yes."

Nathaniel practically howled in glee. Moira was tempted to crawl under the table and stay there.

"And did he seem to enjoy it? Do you need some pointers?"

Moira scowled at him. "Yes, he enjoyed it. Well, I think he did. He . . . he . . ."

Nathaniel nodded, sparing her further embarrassment. "Ah. I understand. You obviously did it right then." He thought for a moment. "Course, I'm not sure there is a *wrong* way."

"Can you teach me?" Moira asked, curiosity overcoming her humiliation. "Can you tell me other things he might like me to do to him?"

Nathaniel's pale brows shot up on his high forehead. "Well, look who has become a temptress! Of course I will share what I know with you. Besides appreciating men, I am one myself, you know. And I do know what I like."

Of that Moira had no doubt.

"But," her friend amended, "before you go casting your pearls before swine, let me ask you something."

"Anything." How could it be worse than anything else he had already asked?

"Do you have any idea how deep Ryland's regard for you runs?"

She shook her head, touched by his concern. "I'm not certain. We spend many evenings together—sometimes doing nothing but talking. He seems to enjoy my company, and I know he enjoys the . . . physical aspect of our relationship, but I am not certain of the depth of his attachment, no."

Nathaniel seemed to consider this. "The fact that he could have bedded you last night but didn't is a large indication."

Moira's heart plummeted. "I take that to mean that he is not very attached at all?"

Now it was he who scowled—scowled at her as if she were the veriest of simpletons. "No, you goose. It is an indication of a great level of attachment."

That was more of a relief than she cared to admit. "It is?" But wouldn't greater attachment have forced him onward? That was how she would have acted, but then men were so very difficult to predict.

"Of course it is!" Nathaniel fixed her with a patient stare. "He obviously senses your reticence. Whether you act it or not, you are a virgin, and virgins, like anyone about to experience something new, have a natural reluctance to jump into the unknown. He no doubt wants you to know he is not going to pressure you. He wants to earn your trust."

How she wanted to believe him! "I must admit, that does make sense."

"Of course it does. I was terrified my first time."

Moira's natural curiosity leaped, but there was time for hearing about Nathaniel's own experiences later. Right now she wanted his insight into *her* romantic life.

Her earlier embarrassment all but forgotten, she leaned forward. "So you think what happened between us last night was a good thing as far as the development of our relationship is concerned?"

He rolled his eyes. "My dear, you had an amazingly handsome man give you pleasure. What could possibly be bad? Of course, you have given me so little detail . . ." He allowed his voice to drop off with a naughty grin.

Moira laughed. "I cannot believe you are so interested."

A scoffing noise cleared his throat. "Who would not be? Not everyone is fortunate enough to have a romantic encounter with one of London's most eligible bachelors."

"Who had a romantic encounter with one of London's most eligible bachelors?" Of course it would be just at that moment that Minerva chose to bound into the room, all youthful exuberance and fresh scrubbed beauty.

Moira's face flooded with icy heat. Oh yes, underneath the table was looking very good to her right now. Unfortunately, Minnie would probably follow her under the tablecloth.

"It is impolite to eavesdrop," Moira reminded the younger woman.

Minnie made a face as she seated herself beside Nathaniel. "I was not eavesdropping. I was coming in for breakfast when I heard the two of you talking." Grabbing a roll from the bowl in the center of the table, she turned her attention to Nathaniel. "So, who are we talking about?"

Nathaniel smiled sweetly. "Wynthrope Ryland."

Moira could have kicked him, but she probably would have hit Minnie instead. She settled for glaring at him. He ignored her.

Minnie's dark eyes widened. She cast Nathaniel a conspiratorial glance. "He *is* one of London's most eligible bachelors."

"Divine," he agreed with a wink. Obviously Nathaniel was almost as at ease with Minnie as he was with Moira. Moira wasn't certain she liked that. She was used to being the only person who knew Nathaniel's secret.

Minnie's smile grew. "I would have a romantic encounter with him any day."

Nathaniel only nodded in response as they both turned their gazes on Moira. Defiantly, she stared at them both.

"Unfortunately," Minnie remarked, popping a bit of bun in her mouth. "Wynthrope Ryland chose Moira over me. His loss of course."

Moira smiled mockingly. "Of course. I am certain he feels it every day as well."

Minnie's eyes brightened with mirth. "Moira, how very caustic you can be! Did you know she could be so biting?" she asked Nathaniel.

Her Judas nodded. "She hides it behind that prim and proper exterior, but she has the tongue of a viper, believe me."

Minnie took another bite of bun, chewed, and swallowed. "The more time I spend with you, Moira, the more I wish I had come to visit you earlier."

Her words seemed to hit Moira square in the chest, knocking the air from her. "You do?"

The girl nodded. "I thought you were going to be like our sisters." She wrinkled her nose. "I thought you were going to be like Mama. I'm so very happy that you are not."

"No," Moira agreed, a little dazed. "I am nothing like our sisters, or our mother." In fact, she was nothing like anyone in her family. Odd how she used to think that was a defect in her makeup. When had she realized that it was actually a virtue?

Probably right around the time she started feeling comfortable in her own skin—when Wynthrope Ryland walked into her life and told her she should eat whatever she wanted.

Her gaze shifted to the bowl of rolls. She loved bread. She could live on bread alone. She wanted bread. She wanted the whole bloody bowl.

She snatched a bun and slathered it with butter. Then she took a huge bite. Oh, it tasted heavenly!

Minnie watched her with an expression of angelic innocence as Moira chewed. "So did you have a romantic encounter with Wynthrope Ryland?"

Moira choked. It took several coughs and a gulp of coffee to ease the bread down her throat. She regarded her sister through watery eyes. "That is none of your business!"

A wide grin split the younger woman's face. "You did!"

"You two are incorrigible." Moira wiped her mouth with her serviette.

"Is he a good kisser?" Minnie asked with a dreamy expression. "He looks like he would be. He has a nice mouth."

"Very shapely," Nathaniel agreed.

Moira stared at the both of them in openmouthed astonishment before addressing her sister. "What do you know about kissing?"

Minnie rolled her eyes again. It was an annoying skill apparently perfected by those under the age of twenty. "I have been kissed before, Moira."

"Ooh!" Nathaniel was suddenly sitting upright again. "By who? Anyone I would know?"

Smearing more butter on her roll, Moira took another bite. How had this morning happened? How had this conversation turned into such a farce? This was ridiculous—and way out of her control.

"Adam Westlake," Minnie informed Nathaniel with a smug smile.

Nathaniel's expression was suitably impressed.

"Do you think you might marry him?"

It took a minute for Moira to realize that the question was directed at her, but who else would it be meant for when Minnie was the one asking?

"Wynthrope?"

Her sister nodded. "Will you marry him?"

Poor Moira's already boggled brain could scarcely take any more scrambling. "I . . . he has not asked. I have no reason to think he ever will." The admission caused a strangely hollow feeling in the pit of her stomach, but it was true. She had known all along that whatever happened between her and Wynthrope would no doubt be nothing more than temporary. He didn't strike her as the kind of man who wanted to settle down.

"Why not?" Minnie demanded.

"Yes," Nathaniel joined in. "Why not?"

Frustration flared. Had neither of them been listening to her? Did they know nothing?

"Because I have no idea how he feels about me, or for that matter, how I feel about him." There it was, the whole foolish truth of just how lacking she was when it came to knowing herself, or anyone else.

Minnie shrugged. "The two of you spend enough time together. That must mean something."

How to explain to her sheltered sister that there was a reason Wynthrope kept coming back? Of course, if intercourse was all he wanted, he could have gotten that already—she knew that for a fact.

"After all," Minnie continued, picking up another roll. "If all he wanted was someone to warm his bed, he could find that anywhere. He actually seems to *like* spending time with you."

Apparently she didn't have to explain it at all. Minnie

seemed to have a worryingly clear understanding of the situation already.

Nathaniel nodded. "That was my point exactly." He lifted his gaze to Moira's. Were her eyes crossing? "Be cautious until you do ascertain his intentions, but do not constantly assume they are the worst."

"He must like you," Minnie added. "He'd be daft not to. You are a good person, you are pretty, and you are rich. And you like him. Why wouldn't he like you?"

There it was, the way the world should be in the mind of an eighteen-year-old. Why wouldn't he like her indeed?

And why did Moira suspect that deep in her heart she wanted so much more than mere "like"?

He couldn't escape her.

Lying on the brocade sofa in his little brown and gold parlor, Wynthrope stared at the ceiling, counting the swirls in the plasterwork.

No matter what he did, or how much he counted, he could not get Moira out of his head. She haunted his waking hours with memories of conversations, laughter, kisses—and that unforgettable night in her library. When he went to bed it became even worse, because every time he replayed that fateful chess match and her demand to be kissed, his dreams turned it into a much different situation—a situation in which he came in her, not in her hand.

He spent most of his time frustrated, wracked with longing when he wasn't ravaged by guilt. He wanted her with a vengeance. He missed her when she wasn't around, and he could not reconcile his feelings with the fact that he was going to have to steal from her, no matter how much he tried, or pretended. Most days he simply tried not to think about it.

But today he had done nothing but think of it. He was going to betray her, and no one but he and Daniels would ever know the truth. Moira would never know it was he. Could he continue the charade? Could he lie to her just to keep her in his life? He couldn't tell her the truth. She could go to the authorities and make matters worse. She might tell Octavia, and Octavia would tell North in an instant. Or worse, she might do something that would put her in danger. If Daniels had any suspicion that Wynthrope had exposed him, he wouldn't hesitate to harm Moira to get that tiara.

Moira would blame him for whatever Daniels did to her, and she would be right to. No, she was better off not knowing—if for no other reason than that he couldn't bear to see the hate in her eyes. He would rather turn his back on her and have her think him a heartless cad than realize what a fraud he was.

She thought he—the real he—deserved love. What did she know? She was a woman of a certain age who obviously had experienced no sexual gratification in her marriage or outside it. He wasn't a rake by any stretch, but he knew the look of a woman who had been brought to her first orgasm. She might have roused similar sensations by herself, no doubt she had at her age, but he had been the first man to make her come.

And in turn she had made him a god, if only for a few minutes, and only in his own mind.

By Christ she had been beautiful, all wild and wanton in his arms. So wet and willing. He should have taken her. He could have.

So why didn't he? Some foolish sense of chivalry had kicked in. Perhaps it would have been wrong of him to take advantage of her. Perhaps he wouldn't have been able to achieve another erection. No, he could have been hard again in a minute if she had commanded it. He had been afraid to do it. He had promised to seduce her, had told her that he intended to do just that, and she rose to the challenge. But what happened after he succeeded? He didn't want to walk away. It wouldn't be easy to walk away, and unless he wanted to spend possibly the rest of his life lying to her, he would have to walk away.

The rest of his life. Had he ever entertained the idea of spending his life with one woman? No. He had always thought marriage a prison. Certainly his parents and many of their contemporaries had proven him right. But Devlin and North, they were the exceptions. They had good marriages, to women they adored. They were adored in return. He had seen both of them changed by their women, and not changed in a negative way, as many men liked to joke. Blythe and Octavia were positive additions to the Ryland family, helping to heal the wounds his brothers had both carried for far too long.

Could Moira help heal him? Would she want to? Was it too much to ask that she give him anything more than he was already poised to take from her? She trusted him, or at least he feared she did. She let him into her home thinking he was there for no other reason than her. Perhaps she suspected he had seduction alone on his mind. Perhaps she had no idea that it had become so much more than that.

God willing, she had no idea just how much he had come to need her in his life. He hoped she would never know how much of a coward he was, but he couldn't risk his heart, not when there was a job to be done, not when he couldn't be certain she would want the shriveled little fig.

Not when he had no idea whatsoever of how to give it to her. The idea of it terrified him more than the thought of prison or death or being responsible for North's ruin.

"What are you doing in here all alone in the dark?"

Speak of the devil. Was it dark? He hadn't noticed. And he should have thought twice before giving North a key to his home.

"Light a lamp if it bothers you," he replied, not bothering to get up.

There was the sound of footsteps behind him and then the striking of the flint. Soon, golden light flooded a corner of the room. Yes, it was dark. Very dark. What would he do when the days lengthened again and there was no night to hide in? He would have to draw the shades and pretend.

"Are you ill?" his brother demanded, coming around to stand before him.

"No." Not in the manner North meant, at any rate.

"Then why are you just lying about?"

Turning his head on the cushion, he smiled weakly. "I felt like it."

North scowled. "This is not like you."

Wynthrope chuckled dryly. "Not like me? Of course it is like me. I'm the brooding one, remember? I brood. I like to think about things and be melancholy. I'm thinking about giving lessons."

His brother was unimpressed by his wit. It was just as well. It seemed to take more effort these days just to be flippant. Sarcasm didn't come as easily as it once did, and the only person who seemed shocked by anything he said or did was he.

He sighed. "Why are you here, North?"

His brother seated himself on the arm of a large chair. "Do I need a reason to visit my brother?"

"No, but you always seem to have one regardless." Perhaps flippancy wasn't so difficult after all.

North's expression was totally blank, but he could not hide the disquiet in his eyes. "Octavia thought you might like to join us for dinner. She doesn't think you eat enough."

Wynthrope smiled at that. "Your wife is too good for you."

Of course his brother did not argue. "I tell myself that daily. Will you come to dinner or not?"

Folding an arm behind his head, Wynthrope shifted position on the narrow sofa. "Give Octavia my thanks and apologies, but I think I'll remain where I am."

"Damn it, Wyn!" So much for that blank expression. It had quickly given way to one of frustration. "What the devil is wrong with you?"

Now it was his turn to be expressionless. "Nothing."

North scowled. "You are a frigging rotten liar."

Laughing, Wynthrope faced his brother with a thankful smile. "I am fine. I just do not feel like company this evening."

North tilted his head, his mouth curving slightly. "Not even the lovely Lady Aubourn?"

He should have seen that coming. Perhaps if his head wasn't lodged so far up his own arse he would have.

"Since she is a lady, and not very likely to come to a bachelor's lodgings unescorted, I sincerely doubt that will be an issue."

He also should have known that his brother was just getting started. "You've been spending a lot of time with her lately."

Facing the ceiling again, Wynthrope closed his eyes. "Yes, I have."

"People are talking."

"Yes, they are." Was there a point to this conversation?

He could hear North shift on the chair. "She's a good friend of Vie's, you know."

Ahh. Now they were going somewhere. So much for his brother not needing to have a reason to come calling. "I know."

"I think very highly of her as well."

Wynthrope raised his brows but still did not open his eyes. "No doubt."

"Octavia and I would hate to see her . . . *disappointed* in any fashion."

"As her friends, I imagine so." How calm he sounded, even though the future was already laid out before him. Moira was going to be disappointed by him, one way or another.

"For Christ's sake, Wyn, will you look at me?"

Another sigh as he opened his eyes and rolled them toward his brother. "What do you want me to say, North?"

His brother fixed him with a scowl that threatened bodily harm. "Tell me what your intentions are toward Moira."

"I do not know. To get to know her better, I suppose." *Liar.* It was a wonder he didn't choke on the words.

"She deserves more than a tumble."

He was right. She deserved much, much more—more than he could probably ever hope to give her. "Is that what you think I am after?"

North's gaze was shrewd as his lips flattened into a grim line. "I do not know. What are you after?"

Damn. He should have known North would know how to trap him. Carefully wiping his face of any emotion, Wynthrope replied, "More than a tumble, obviously. I could get one of those anywhere for considerably less effort than I'm putting into the lovely widow Aubourn."

"Is that what she is to you, an effort?"

Something within him snapped, and he bolted upright, swinging his legs over the side of the sofa. "What she is to me is none of your frigging business!"

North stared at him, his jaw slack. Wynthrope might have laughed if he weren't so angry at himself for losing his temper.

He ran a hand through his hair and exhaled a deep breath before speaking again. He was calmer this time. "What is this inquisition about, North? You and Octavia think I am out

to harm Moira, that I'm toying with her in some manner?"
He supposed he was, but that wasn't the point.

North shrugged. At least he had the grace to look uncomfortable. His pale blue eyes didn't quite meet Wynthrope's. "You never stay with one woman for more than a
week or two."

"I have been seeing Moira for almost four." Good Lord,
had it been that long already? Yes. He had met her early in
the month. Today was the twenty-ninth of December.

"That is why we are concerned. It is obvious Moira is not
some casual affair."

Wynthrope slumped against the back of the sofa. Christ,
he was tired. "If you are so certain she's not a casual affair,
why the questions?"

"Because Octavia and I are concerned that she might be
expecting more than you are prepared to offer her." His
brother raised a brow as though to make a point.

"Marriage?" How spiteful and bitter he sounded.

North nodded. "You are the first man she has shown any
interest in since the death of her husband. She is still unsure
of herself."

"She wasn't unsure when she had her hand wrapped
around my cock the other night." The second the words left
his mouth Wynthrope wanted to snatch them back. This
wasn't about Moira, and he had no right befouling her in this
way. He made the other night sound cheap and tawdry, and it
had been anything but.

"I am going to forget you just said that," North informed
him, his gaze as cold as his tone.

Wynthrope rubbed his eyes. "Good. Maybe I can as well."

His brother wasn't about to let up just yet, however. "The
way I see it, one of two things is happening here."

North was little more than a blur when Wynthrope opened

his eyes. Blinking, he watched his brother, wishing to hell he would just leave. "And those are?"

North folded his arms over his broad chest. Wynthrope had always envied his muscular build. "Either you are out to destroy Moira for some reason, or you are in love with her."

Wynthrope's heart slammed against his ribs—at which suggestion he wasn't certain. "Perhaps it is both. Perhaps I want to destroy her by falling in love with her."

The scowl on his brother's face deepened. North really could be an intimidating bastard when he wanted. "What the hell does that mean?"

Chuckling hoarsely, Wynthrope shook his head, his hands limp in his lap. "I do not know."

Obviously North wasn't prepared to give up. "You do know, else you wouldn't have said it."

Good point. "I do not want to destroy Moira, North. I think too much of her to ever *want* to hurt her, but I'm not sure I am capable of doing anything else."

There was little more than a few months separating them by birth, yet Wynthrope felt as though he were years older than his illegitimate brother at this moment. Poor North, he looked so confused.

"You sound as stupid as Devlin did when he first met Blythe."

Wynthrope made a sound of disgust. "There is no way I could ever sound *that* stupid." Poor Devlin. He was a happily married man now, but there had been a time when he had risked turning his back on his feelings for Blythe because he thought he wasn't good enough for her.

"Can you not hear yourself? You talk as though you do not deserve a woman like Moira." North's tone was incredulous.

Was he insane? "I don't."

"Do not be an idiot." If words were whips, he would have been flayed alive then and there.

"I'm not. If I were a monk and did nothing with my life but perform good deeds I would not deserve a woman like Moira." He sighed and raised his weary gaze to his brother's. "It does not mean I would not aspire to such heights if given the chance."

His reply seemed to surprise North as much as it surprised him.

"You are falling in love with her."

Again there was that uncomfortable thumping in his chest. Perhaps North had struck too close to the truth, or perhaps it was guilt that made him feel this awful. "I do not know what I am doing. Before you showed up I was trying not to think about it."

"If you are afraid of falling in love, it is all right. It happens to all of us eventually."

His words were little comfort, though Wynthrope knew that's how they were intended. "Thank you, oh wise one."

The scowl was back. "Why do you always have to be such an ass?"

"Why are you still here?" Wynthrope shot back.

North exhaled a harsh breath as he stroked the stubble on his jaw. "Because you are my brother and I love you."

Wynthrope regarded him blankly, even though his words tugged at his heart. "I would love you as well, but I'm too afraid."

For a second North looked as though he would dearly love to pummel him. It was going to hurt if he gave in to the urge. Fortunately for Wynthrope, North laughed instead. "You really are an arse, Wyn. You know that?"

Wynthrope nodded, a hesitant smile pulling at his lips. "I know."

His brother regarded him through a tilted gaze. "Are you sure you do not want to come for dinner?"

"I am sure. I had some bread and cheese earlier."

"And I won't have to defend you to my wife when you've broken her friend's heart?"

Wynthrope's smile faded. "I cannot promise that, North, you know that."

Straightening, North shrugged as he strode toward the door. "I suppose that is all I can ask."

Wynthrope lowered himself onto the sofa again, his forearm over his eyes. Soon there would be nothing but silence and he could wrestle with his demons in peace.

His brother's voice drifted over him. "Will you be all right here alone?"

He grimaced. "I'll be fine."

But when he heard the gentle click of the door closing, and the silent darkness closed in on him once more, Wynthrope knew he wasn't going to be fine. He wasn't going to be fine at all.

Chapter 9

Moira was as nervous as a new bride when Wynthrope came to collect her for the evening.

It was New Year's Eve and she hadn't seen him since Christmas. It was the longest they had ever spent apart in the whole duration of their relationship. She had filled the days and evenings as much as she could, but troubling questions and nagging doubts plagued her all the same. She knew she should have more faith in him—and in herself—but she couldn't help wonder at times if he had lost interest.

"I was beginning to wonder if I was ever going to see you again," she informed him as they faced each other across the interior of his carriage. It was an expensive vehicle, well appointed, softly lit, and delightfully warm on this chilly night.

He appeared uncomfortable, and for a second she regretted speaking. She should probably pretend not to care and not let on that she had missed him, but she was too old to play those kinds of games. If he didn't want to see her, or

156

wanted to put distance between them, that was his prerogative, but she would prefer it if he told her outright and saved her the embarrassment of being slowly cast aside.

Shadowed features remained impassive. "I thought you might need some time alone after what happened Christmas night."

Maybe a day to think about it, but he had ignored her for five. His excuse was weak at best. "Why would you think that?"

His eyes were beyond dark, and far too difficult to read in this light. "Because I needed time myself."

"Oh." What else could she say? She hadn't expected him to be so honest with her in return. And what did he mean that he needed time alone?

"I like you, Moira."

She stared at him in the flickering lamplight. He made it sound like he was imparting some great secret. He looked as though he was as well. "Thank you. I like you as well, though I think that should be obvious."

"Should it?"

Her cheeks burned. "I do not normally shove my hand down the trousers of men I do not like." She had never shoved her hand in anyone's trousers, but he didn't need to know that.

He chuckled. "And you accuse me of saying scandalous things."

Moira smiled in return, her embarrassment waning. She felt far too comfortable at times in his presence. "I suppose you must be a bad influence on me."

Wynthrope's good humor seemed to fade before her eyes. "No doubt I am."

He was in such a strange mood, it made her uneasy. Was he trying to tell her something? This was all so very confusing. Just when she believed things were a certain way between them, he did something that made her doubt her judgment.

"Do you not want to see me anymore, Wynthrope?" She braced herself as the carriage hit a rut in the road—and for his reply.

This time his laughter was harsh as he turned his face toward the window. The shade was down, so Moira had no idea what he was looking at. "I want to see you all the time."

He did? She didn't know what to say. "I enjoy our time together." What an understatement that was.

Tilting his head, he regarded her as though she had no idea what he was talking about. "Do you? These last few days have been empty without you in them. Tell me, did you think of me at all?"

She met his gaze evenly, openly. "Every waking hour of every day and even in a few of my dreams."

He seemed so pleased, and yet so pained by her admission. He glanced away, then lifted his gaze again, his expression earnest and strained. "Moira, I—"

The carriage rolled to a halt. They were at their destination.

"You what?" Her question was hurried. She wanted to hear his reply before the door opened.

Wynthrope smiled. "I missed you."

That wasn't what he meant to say, of that she was certain, but it would do for now. It was nice to know regardless. Moira returned the smile. "I missed you too."

The carriage door opened and Wynthrope alighted first, turning to help her down. Holding up her skirts and ermine-lined cape, Moira took his hand and stepped to the ground. Looking up, she saw that they were in front of an elegant-looking building on King Street.

"What is this place?"

"Eden," he replied, placing her hand on his arm. "Surely you have been here before?"

Moira shook her head. She had heard of the popular club, certainly, but she had never stepped foot through its doors as it had opened while she was in mourning for Anthony. "No, but I have heard so much about it, I have long wanted to come."

"I'm glad I could be here to witness your first time." He didn't look at her as he spoke. "I hope it lives up to your expectations."

She glanced at him out of the corner of her eye as they climbed the steps. Was he being flirtatious, or did she simply hear it in everything he said now? "Does the first time ever live up to one's expectations?"

His arm jerked beneath her palm. She had caught him off guard! "My dear Lady Aubourn, whatever do you mean?"

"Do not play innocent, Wynthrope." It was difficult not to smile. "It does not suit you."

He grinned. "You are with me. I will make certain your first time is everything you could ever dream it would be."

A shiver practically fell down Moira's spine. If he only knew how much she wanted to put that theory to the test. "And if my expectations are not met?"

He paused at the door and fixed her with a gaze that just about melted the soles off her slippers. "Then I will keep trying until they are. Now stop looking at me like that or I'll have to shove snow down my trousers."

Moira didn't know whether to chuckle or preen at his words. The idea that she could have such an effect on him was a heady thought indeed.

Inside the club they were met by a hulking majordomo who took their outerwear and led them to the ballroom where the private party was being held. The club was owned by Lord and Lady Angelwood, who ran the business as partners, much to the chagrin of many of the *ton*. That didn't stop most of society from frequenting the club, however.

Tonight the club was open by invitation only. Wynthrope had been invited because he had known Lord Angelwood for

years, and because Octavia's friendship with Lady Angelwood made them and the Rylands meet frequently on a social basis.

The ballroom was a cavernous room with marble pillars
and floor. The Italian marble was a delicate peach under the
light of the glittering chandeliers. Chairs lined the outer wall
where people could sit and chat and watch the dancing. On
the left wall were a set of French doors opening to another
room where Moira could see a small group of gentlemen
gathered around the refreshment table, no doubt collecting a
glass of punch for their ladies.

The musicians were hidden behind an ivory and gold
screen, giving the illusion of music being conjured rather
than played. A few couples were already dancing while others milled about.

Yes, for a private party in the middle of winter, it was a
decided crush.

Moira was well aware of the stares that met them as they
strolled toward where Devlin and Blythe stood talking to another couple. Wynthrope was not known for being the kind
of man who often escorted ladies to social affairs, and she
was not known for attending any function with a gentleman
at all. That was what had made her a target for those vindictive men in the past, her lack of "companionship."

What did the gossips say about them? Did they wonder what
he saw in her? Or why someone like her was with a man like
him? Did they think the relationship was purely physical, or
did one or two of them actually possess the intelligence to
speculate that maybe they simply liked each other's company?

Could they tell that she was so happy to see him again that
she could dance a jig? Could they see how pleased she was
that he claimed to have missed her? Served him right, the
bounder. If he hadn't been such a fool and simply came to
call, he wouldn't have had to miss her at all.

And why had he needed five days to think about what had happened that one night? Even she hadn't obsessed about it to that degree.

"Moira!" Blythe exclaimed, gathering her up in an exuberant embrace. "How marvelous to see you again."

Moira was happy to see her as well, but Blythe's exuberance felt as though it might have cracked a rib.

"It is so nice to see a friendly face," Moira admitted once the larger woman had released her. "I am not that acquainted with many of the guests."

"We must remedy that." Taking her by the hand, Blythe made their excuses to the men, and tugged Moira along behind her. Moira had no choice but to follow. If she dug in her heels and grabbed hold of another guest, she still would not be able to slow the force that was Blythe.

Within the course of the next twenty minutes, Moira had met Lilith, Lady Angelwood herself, and her friends the ladies Braven and Wolfram. Moira liked each of them exceedingly well, and accepted an invitation to take tea with the three of them some afternoon.

After that, Blythe introduced her to Viscountess Praed, a businessman by the name of Dunlop and his charming wife, and a whole host of other people whose names she could never begin to keep straight. Her head swam with nameless faces, all of whom she hoped to see again—and hopefully remember.

"Oh no," Blythe murmured as a group of three ladies approached them. "Moira, I'm sorry, but I do not think we can avoid them."

Moira arched a brow at her new friend's apology. Who were these ladies that they made a woman such as Blythe cringe?

Ladies Dumont, Pennington, and Brightstone, apparently. "Lady Brightstone is a notorious gossip," Blythe informed her in a hushed, hurried whisper as the women neared. "Pennington is a viper. She tried to make Varya's life miserable when she first came to London. And Dumont . . ." Blythe's expression turned almost sympathetic. "Lady Dumont is a former *friend* of Wynthrope's."

Heat rushed to Moira's cheeks. "Oh." She knew exactly what Blythe meant by "friend." She also knew that if the lady still had feelings for Wynthrope, she was bound to see Moira as competition.

The women were almost upon them now, so there was no chance of escape. They were like harpies bearing down on helpless victims, each of them dressed in the height of fashion with feathers in her hair and cosmetics accentuating her features. They looked more like fashion dolls than real women.

"Lady Blythe!" the oldest of the women greeted. "Oh wait, it is simply Mrs. Ryland now, isn't it?"

Blythe's smile was as serene as an angel's. "Lady Ryland, actually, Lady Pennington. My husband was knighted, you will remember."

"Oh yes." The plump woman turned her false congeniality on Moira. "And this must be Lady Aubourn."

Blythe made introductions and Moira did her best to be cordial to each woman, even though the buxom Lady Dumont looked as though she'd like to take her eyes out. Competition indeed. Although Moira didn't think the fleshy blond much of a rival. True, she had a luscious figure, but there was a jaded aura about her that Moira knew would not hold Wynthrope's interest for long.

"You came here tonight with Wynthrope Ryland, Lady Aubourn?" Lady Pennington questioned.

They certainly didn't waste any time getting to the point. Moira kept her countenance as emotionless as she could. "Yes, I did."

Lady Pennington's narrow eyes were bright. "He is a very handsome man."

Moira nodded. "I believe most women would agree with you." She would not be baited. She would *not*.

Apparently Lady Pennington was hoping for the opposite. "He is truly a remarkable specimen of manhood."

Lady Brightstone cast her a puzzled glance. "You make him sound like an insect or an animal."

Lady Dumont smiled at her companions. "Well, he is equipped like a horse."

God, had they orchestrated that entire conversation just for that one remark? Moira made a face. Even she knew that Lady Dumont was exaggerating. "Now that's just ridiculous. No man could ever be *that* large." Oh dear, had she said that aloud?

The other women seemed surprised by her outburst as well, especially Blythe, who hid her laughter behind her hand.

Lady Dumont regarded her through narrowed lashes. "I assure you, Lady Aubourn, I *know* all about Wynthrope Ryland's *equipment*."

The woman was deliberately trying to goad her, trying to make her look foolish—trying to make her jealous. Moira straightened her spine, conscious of an equally annoyed Blythe beside her. "And I assure *you*, Lady Dumont, that I *know* he is not built like a stallion. Perhaps you are not as acquainted with his *equipment* as you believe."

Oh, if only she could have captured this moment somehow. All four of the women stared at her with wide eyes and open mouths. Though while Blythe looked positively thrilled, the other three were less than impressed. They never expected for a moment that *she*, the prim and proper viscountess, would be so scandalous. Wynthrope Ryland was a bad influence on her indeed.

"Now, if you ladies will excuse me, I think I need some air."

She hadn't made it very far before Blythe caught up with her. "That was hilarious. You are my new favorite person."

Halting, Moira raised a hesitant gaze. All the anger and bravado drained from her being. "What do you think Wynthrope will say when he hears?" And he was bound to hear, of that she was certain.

Blythe waved a dismissive hand. "He'll laugh, especially when he hears what you said in return."

Oh yes, no doubt he'd be just thrilled that she told one of London's biggest gossips that he wasn't incredibly well endowed. Men loved that kind of thing.

"You are really bothered by it, aren't you?" Blythe's expression was wonderfully sympathetic. If Moira hadn't already liked her before this, she adored her now.

Moira nodded. "I'm not accustomed to these things. I suppose I've been a wallflower for too long." She had spent so many years being the perfect viscountess, and to ruin it now by saying something so base and scandalous made her feel as though she was somehow besmirching Tony's name.

And her own.

The tall redhead gave her a reassuring smile. "You held your ground. Do not let them ruin your evening."

Reaching out, Moira gave Blythe's arm a thankful squeeze. "I will not, but I am going to see if I can find someplace to be alone for a moment. Will you excuse me?"

"Of course. In fact, I'll tell you where you can find some privacy."

Following Blythe's directions, Moira left the ballroom by a side door and found herself in a dimly lit corridor. She walked down to the second door on her right and slipped inside.

There were no lamps lit in the room, but the curtains were open, allowing the moon and the outside lamps to cast a silvery glow along the softly painted walls and elegantly pat-

terned carpet. Crossing to the window, Moira skirted a low
table and a sofa to press her forehead against the cool glass.

Why had she fallen to Lady Dumont's level? Why had she
opened her mouth? Why couldn't she have been one of those
cool, elegant ladies who let everything roll off them? Instead, she had to act like she was Minnie's age.

"What is this I hear about you impugning my manhood?"

Oh dear Lord. He had heard already? How had he managed to find her? And why hadn't she heard the door open?
The man was as silent as a ghost.

Moira didn't even turn. "I could not help it."

"Could not help it?" Wynthrope's incredulous tone grew
louder as he approached. "Could not you have said something a little more flattering?"

Moira turned to face him with a frown. "Such as what,
that you *are* equipped like a stallion?"

He grinned. "At least a bull. A ram perhaps."

The tension drained from Moira's shoulders as she realized he wasn't upset with her at all. In fact, he seemed every
bit as amused as Blythe had said he would be. "I am sorry."

His grin became smug. "And jealous. Do not forget
jealous."

She scowled again. "I am not!"

He came closer, so close that she could smell the warmth
of his skin and the soft spice of his soap. "Of course you are.
She wouldn't have been nearly as successful in goading you
if you did not feel threatened by her."

"I do not feel threatened by that overly busty pigeon," she
insisted hotly, then added, "That's not her real hair color you
know."

His grin grew. "I know."

"How—?" Then she realized and her face blazed. He had
shared her bed, of course he knew her "natural" hair color.

He probably knew all kinds of intimate secrets about the Lady Dumont. "So is that where you spent the last five days, with her?" Oh dear. Perhaps she was jealous after all.

Suddenly Wynthrope was all seriousness. His hands came up and caught her by the shoulders. "There has been no other woman since I met you. And I fear there never will be again. Not one that will ever compare to my black queen."

Moira opened her mouth to reply, to tell him that was the sweetest thing she ever heard, but she never got a chance, because he covered her mouth with his own and kissed her. And he kept kissing her until her bones turned to putty and she forgot where she was.

Suddenly the last five days didn't matter. He had missed her, and she apparently had ruined him for all other women. Who could ask for more?

Not long into the new year of 1819, Wynthrope decided he'd had enough of sharing Moira with others. Common sense told him he shouldn't be alone with her. It would just make things more difficult later if he was alone with her, and yet he didn't care about later. Tonight all he could think about was *now*. He wanted to enjoy what time he had left with her, however long that was. He wanted to enjoy her, because it was true that he would never meet another woman quite like his black queen.

"Did you enjoy the evening?" he asked once they were in his carriage and on their way home.

Across the carriage she nodded, her head wobbly on her neck. "I did, thank you. You?"

He smiled. "Aside from the jokes about my privates, yes."

She giggled. It was the strangest sound coming from her. "I am sorry about that."

"I can tell."

Suddenly she lurched across the carriage at him. Luckily

she didn't have far to go because her feet tangled in her cape and sent her sprawling in his lap. Only his quick reflexes kept her from tumbling to the carpet.

She laughed again as he arranged her on his legs. "I drank too much champagne tonight."

That was probably going to be the understatement of this next year. "Did you?"

"Yes." Her eyes were bright and slightly unfocused in the lamplight. "You are a remarkable specimen of manhood, you know."

Biting his tongue to keep from laughing, Wynthrope simply nodded. "Indeed. Though not as remarkable as a stallion."

She rolled her eyes. She looked so young when she did that, although the motion seemed to throw off her equilibrium. She wavered on his lap. "Why would you want to be? There's not a woman in all the world who would want to make love to a horse."

Lord, but she really was naive in some respects. "How about a bull or a ram?"

She wrinkled her nose as she squirmed against him. Even being a drunken fool she could still make him harder than anyone else ever had. "Or those. Why would you even want to be compared to such animals?"

"Because every man wants to think his manhood is huge, the biggest his woman has ever had." It was a universal truth, and she scoffed as though it were utter nonsense, which he supposed it was. But it didn't change the fact that when the time came for them to make love, he wanted to be the best lover—the biggest lover—she'd ever had.

"Manhood," she repeated. "It sounds like some kind of head covering."

Wynthrope tilted his head in contemplation. "I suppose it is, in a way."

She leaned against his chest, her weight a slight, delightful pressure. "Why is it so important that a woman thinks you are big?"

Had her husband taught her nothing? For all he'd heard about how wonderful Anthony Tyndale had been, he didn't seem to have been much of a husband—not in the way Wynthrope thought he ought to have been. "Because much of a man's confidence resides in his crotch."

Her eyelids were heavy from drink. "That's just ridiculous. Women judge men based on their character, not their endowments."

She obviously did not know some of the women he had known, which was probably a good thing.

"We often judge ourselves based on our endowments." Foolish, yes, but there were very few men alive who didn't wonder if their "equipment" was up to the task at one time or another.

She wrapped her arms around his neck. "Well, I'm going to judge you based on your character."

He breathed in the sweet scent of her perfume and was overwhelmed by a sensation of keen and desperate longing. "Not my character."

She pressed her bottom against him. "Shall I judge you based on something else?"

His heart cracked at the humor in her voice. How she had changed since he first met her. She was so amusing, so open and wonderfully brazen at times.

He brushed the back of his fingers against her cheek. She was so soft, so fair. "Not that either."

She drew back, gazing at him as seriously as one could when their eyes couldn't quite focus. "What shall I judge you on then?"

"Kisses," he suggested, seizing the first thing that came to mind. "Judge me based on my kisses."

She smiled. "I like that. I like your kisses."

He curled his hand around the slender curve of her hip. "I like kissing you as well."

Moira lowered her head. "Kiss me now."

Wynthrope didn't need any more encouragement. Here, in the gently lolling darkness, he raised his face to hers and allowed her to claim his lips with her own. She tasted of champagne and vaguely of cucumber sandwiches. Inwardly, he smiled at the combination. She had eaten like a horse tonight, but perhaps he shouldn't judge her based on her appetite.

She looked as though she had put on a little weight—and he liked it. There was no need of her being so slim, not to fit some kind of ideal someone else had leveled on her. But even if she never got any bigger, he would still adore her. She was perfect just as she was, and no matter how she looked, she would still be perfect to him.

She broke their kiss and stared down at him with wide eyes. "Let's make love."

His head bounced on the squabs. "What?" Good God, he couldn't have heard her correctly.

"Let's make love," she repeated.

"Here?" His voice actually cracked.

She shrugged. "Here. My house. I don't care." She pressed herself hard against him.

Sweet Christ, she must be more foxed than he thought. "Not here."

"My house then." She moved to kiss him again.

He stopped her, holding her at a distance with his hands on her shoulders. "Not there either."

She actually pouted. "Why not?"

He chuckled. The moment was so preposterous, he had to. It was either that or cry. He had a woman he wanted as he wanted air practically begging him to take her, and he refused to do it.

"Because you are drunk, that is why." *And I'm not certain*

I can make love to you now and then screw you later. And he was going to screw her. Screw her out of a tiara.

"Don't you want me?" Everything about her betrayed her hurt—her expression, her plaintive voice.

The fissure in his heart widened. At this rate the rotten little nut was going to crack in two. "More than you will ever know."

"Then take me." Her hips undulated, grinding her against his aching cock. "I want you to."

He bit back a groan. God, surely this noble gesture would go far in keeping him from the pits of hell when his time came. "You are too foxed to know what you want. Trust me, you would regret it when you're sober."

"I will not." She was so defiant, so sure.

"Yes, you will." Now they were arguing about it. Could this get any more farcical? It was bad enough that he was denying himself the only thing he had wanted in a long time. Hell, he had told her weeks ago that he planned to bed her, and now that she was offering herself, he couldn't do it.

She was going to regret knowing him bad enough some day, he didn't want to add to it. His conscience wouldn't allow it.

Reason must have broken through her drunken fog. Either that or she saw that there was no convincing him. She slid off his lap onto the seat beside him.

"If I were sober, would you do it?"

He smiled as she rested her head on his shoulder. "In a minute."

She yawned. "Good. I was worried that maybe you had lost interest in me."

Wynthrope swallowed against the lump in his throat. "Never."

Her only reply was a contented "mmm." A few minutes later

they stopped at her house and Wynthrope carried her snoring form inside, leaving her on the sofa in the parlor, a blanket over her. He didn't trust himself to carry her to her bedroom. If she woke up and asked him again to make love to her, he didn't think he'd be able to resist. He was only human, after all.

He arrived home tired and with a heart more confused than it had ever been. He could rant and rave about how unfair his life was, but somehow he didn't think it was unfair. Somehow it seemed fitting that after all the awful things he had done, he be denied something sweet and good.

Christ, North was right. He did sound like Devlin. It could be worse. He could sound like Brahm. Then he would know he was in real trouble.

He entered his apartments and kicked the door closed behind him. He didn't bother to light a lamp as he flicked the lock into place, but rather stripped off his coat and began tugging at his cravat. He had given his valet the night off as it was a time for celebration.

He was unbuttoning his waistcoat when he realized he wasn't alone.

"Good evenin', boyo." Daniels rose from a chair in the shadows and moved into the beam of moonlight streaming through the windows.

"Damn it, would you stop sneaking into my home?" With a sigh of frustration, Wynthrope tossed his coat and cravat onto a chair. The last thing he needed tonight was Daniels on his back.

"I hope you were out stealing my trinket for me."

He ran a hand over his face. He was so tired. All he wanted was to crawl into bed and pull the blankets over his head. "I have yet to discover where she keeps it."

The older man leered as he casually closed the distance between them. "Then why aren't you there right now, swiving the answer out of her?"

Had Daniels been this crass when Wynthrope had liked him? Or had it been some façade that he had thought of as a father? He had undoubtedly seen what he wanted to see in this cold bastard, not what truly was.

"I will get it."

Daniels thrust a finger in his face. "You had better. I've been patient because of our past relationship, but I'm not going to wait much longer. You get me that damn tiara on your own, or I'll make you get it."

Bravado took hold before Wynthrope could stop it. He pushed Daniels's finger aside. "Just how do you propose to do that?"

The old man smiled, the face of a sweet old man with the soul of a devil. "Be a real shame if anything happened to one of those brothers of yours, or one of their wives."

Ice crept into Wynthrope's veins. "You wouldn't."

Daniels shrugged his bowing shoulders. "Maybe I would, maybe I wouldn't. Perhaps nothin' will happen to them at all. I've heard stories about you and Lady Aubourn. I've seen how much time you spend at her house. Did you think I wouldn't notice? Did ye think I wouldn't put two and two together and figure out there was more goin' on than you scoping out a pigeon? You'd have no one but yourself to blame if she met with a little accident."

Wynthrope's spine straightened.

"Course, it would make it easier for you to steal the tiara if she was out of the way. Maybe that's the way to go. What do you think?"

Jaw tight, Wynthrope fought to rein in his temper, despite the murderous urges rising in his breast. "I think you had better leave Lady Aubourn out of this."

There was that damn charming smile. "But boyo, 'twould be you who was responsible. If you just do what I want no one will get hurt, but if you don't, someone's going to bleed, and a woman as frail-lookin' as the viscountess is liable to break real easy."

What little control Wynthrope had snapped. He struck out, catching the older man square in the jaw with his fist, knocking him back into the sofa. Seizing him by the lapels, he dragged Daniels to his feet, pulling back his fist for another strike.

Daniels met his gaze, blood trickling from the corner of his mouth. Something in his expression made Wynthrope pause, kept him from moving any closer. Then he felt a pinprick of sensation against his ribs. He didn't have to look down to know what it was. Daniels had pulled a knife on him. It was probably the same knife Wynthrope had seen him use to threaten others years ago. It was a lovely blade, Spanish made with an ivory handle, and sharp enough to cut a man to ribbons with little more than a flick of the wrist.

Slowly he opened his fist, releasing his hold on Daniels. The old man didn't move, but he regarded Wynthrope with a look of pure venom. This was the real Daniels. To think he had once looked up to this man, had wanted to emulate him. His actual father would have made a better mentor than this.

"Don't ever do anything that stupid again, boyo." Daniels's voice was as dark and poisonous as his expression. "Not unless you want to get hurt."

Wynthrope met his stare. "I don't care what you do to me."

Daniels's lips twisted. "No, but you do care about your brothers and even the lovely widow. I know you, boy. I know you wouldn't want their ruination or their blood upon your hands. You'd feel that too keenly."

He didn't respond. He didn't have to. Daniels already knew the truth. And now he knew just how much Moira meant to him, all because he couldn't keep control of his temper. What the hell was wrong with him, tipping his hand like that?

"Now, are you going to do what I tell you, or do you need a little convincing?"

Daniels's idea of convincing usually involved something painful and personal. In this case it wouldn't be a physical pain. He would strike at Wynthrope through the people he cared about. It wouldn't necessarily be family either. It might be a friend. It might be a lover.

It would be Moira.

Swallowing the bile and pride bunched in his throat, Wynthrope lifted his chin. "I will get you the tiara."

If Daniels had noticed that he hadn't agreed to do what he told him, he didn't let on. He simply smiled. "That's me boy. I knew you'd see reason. When?"

Wynthrope shrugged. "I have to find out where she keeps it."

The older man lifted the knife, pointing it directly at his throat. Wynthrope didn't move, didn't even flinch. Daniels wasn't going to hurt him—he needed him too badly. The old man might have been something in his day, but he was just an old man now, and there was no way he could break into Moira's house and find the tiara on his own without being caught. Wynthrope knew that, and Daniels knew it too.

"You have until Twelfth Night. The longer you make me wait, the more impatient I'm going to become, and you know how I get when I lose my patience."

Wynthrope's reply was a slow blink. Yes, he knew how Daniels got. He had to find the tiara soon or the old man would make good on his threat to start hurting people.

"I said I'd get it and I will."

Lowering the knife, Daniels backed away. "Good. We understand each other then." He sheathed the knife in his sleeve. "I'll be in touch in a few days. Don't disappoint me, Wynnie."

Wynthrope watched him leave in stony silence. It wasn't

until Daniels was gone that he allowed his shoulders to slump. He crossed to the door and reset the lock, resisting the urge to put a table in front of it as well. Daniels wouldn't be back, not tonight.

He went to his bedroom and undressed, crawling into bed with a sigh. Lying on his side, he stared out the window at the night and brought his knees up toward his ribs. Closing his eyes, he refused to think of Daniels and his threats. Instead he made himself think of pleasant things.

He thought of Moira, her smile and her wit. He thought of how little alcohol it took to turn her into a complete wanton, and when his throat tightened and the backs of his eyes burned, he kept on thinking about her. He thought about her until he felt the wetness seep from between his lashes onto his face, and then he stopped.

Because Wythrope Ryland hadn't cried since he was a boy and he would be damned if he'd do it now, just because he felt like one.

Chapter 10

Twelfth Night came as surely and unwelcome to Wynthrope as a storm cloud on the day of a spring picnic.

He dressed as he might for a friend's funeral—carefully and with great consideration, as though clothing made a difference on some level. His black trousers were the perfect length and fit. His shirt and cravat were white as freshly fallen snow. His waistcoat was unblemished ivory and his coat hugged his shoulders and torso like second skin, yet allowed freedom of movement. He would at least dress the part of the perfect gentleman, even though he was far from it in truth.

As he checked his appearance for the third time in his looking glass, he felt as though he were about to go to his execution, though he was not the one who would suffer if he didn't have the tiara for Daniels by the morning.

He had spent much of the past few days with Moira. Every chance he had, he searched her house for a safe, but found none. He plied her with carefully worded questions and received no satisfactory answers. Maybe he hadn't asked the right questions. Maybe some part of him had purposefully sabotaged his own perfidy just to postpone the inevitable.

Tonight was the night; the last night he would spend with her. He had decided sometime since the new year that there was no way he could deceive her and continue to see her on a personal basis. As much as he wanted to continue their relationship, he couldn't allow it to grow on a lie. It was a decision that part of him cursed, because there was a side of him that wanted to be with her so badly, it didn't care if he had to lie to her. It didn't see the problem with carrying on. After all, it wasn't as though Moira would ever know he was the culprit.

She would never know that he was the man who stole a priceless gift given to her by her dead husband. He might not have learned where she kept the damn thing, but he knew everything else there was to know about it—such as the fact that she hardly ever wore it because she was afraid of something happening to it. Or at least that was the impression he got from her.

If it weren't for the fact that Daniels might hurt North or Dev, or Moira herself, he would say to hell with it all. But Daniels knew just how to get to him, and he knew that threatening someone Wynthrope cared about was the only way to control him. The old bastard would follow through on his threats, if for no other reason than to keep Wynthrope under his thumb.

"We have outdone ourselves, Mr. Ryland," his valet said with more than a touch of pride.

Wynthrope couldn't even summon a half smile. "Indeed. Take the rest of the night off, Charles. I won't be needing you."

The valet asked no questions, simply nodded, said good night, and left, leaving Wynthrope alone with nothing but his conscience as he slipped into his greatcoat. It was black as well, as were his hat and gloves and shoes. It was really no different from what he wore to any evening party, but tonight he felt very much like an undertaker.

His carriage was waiting outside as he exited the building. The crisp night air smelled of snow and horse and city. The cobblestones beneath his feet were dry for now, but that storm cloud that hovered somewhere over his head was sure to bring a tempest before morning. If he managed to get to Moira's house, he would have to do so before the snow fell. It wouldn't do to leave tracks of any kind for Bow Street to follow.

He climbed into the carriage and rapped his knuckles against the roof for the coachman to depart. Too bad he wasn't a hopeless drunk like his father and Brahm. He would dearly love to lose himself in a bottle, but as much as he wanted to be a coward, he couldn't afford to be. Or rather his family and Moira couldn't afford for him to be.

It was time to face the consequences of his past.

What an idiot he had been. Young and full of piss and vinegar, he had jumped at Daniels's offer to serve his country during the war with Napoleon. It never occurred to him to investigate Daniels, to go to the Home Office, or to ask detailed questions. If he had gone to North, all of this might have been avoided, but he had believed Daniels when the Irishman told him that all the secrecy was necessary for England's safety. That in itself was a testament to just how young he had been, but it was no excuse for his stupidity.

If he hadn't grown up in the shadow of Brahm the heir, he might not have done it. If he had felt as wanted by their father as North so obviously was, perhaps he wouldn't have fallen for Daniels's deception. But the truth was, he had wanted so desperately to prove himself as worthy as Brahm the future viscount and North the fearless Bow Street Runner that he had made the biggest mistake of his life to do it.

No, the biggest mistake of his life had been staring back when he caught Moira watching him in the street that long ago day. He shouldn't have paid any attention to her. If he hadn't, she would not matter to him now. Certainly she would still be his intended victim, and perhaps he would even be trying to seduce her to get to the tiara, but he wouldn't care about her, because he would never have gotten to know her. Moira's appeal, her charm, her very essence was like a fine wine. To get to the flavor of the bouquet, the process took labor and patience and a degree of concentration. To appreciate Moira, one had to take the time to get to know her. And *that* had been his folly.

Because, as with any fine wine, the more he had of Moira, the more he wanted.

There was no point obsessing over it any longer. Thinking about it only made things worse. He was going to take advantage of this night—their last night—and then he was going to walk away from her. Not right away, of course—that would cause suspicion. He would have to wait at least a few days for news of the theft to die down, then he would end their acquaintance. He would have to take up with someone else. Lady Dumont was still interested. Perhaps he'd dally with her for a while until Moira was convinced he was a heartless bastard, then he'd go back to being alone.

He hated being alone. Almost any company was preferable to his own.

It was almost a relief when his carriage rolled to a stop. Arriving at the party put him that one step closer to betraying Moira, but at least it would provide a bit of a distraction as well. There was some comfort—albeit a very little—in knowing it would all be over soon.

Stepping out of the carriage, he donned his hat and slowly climbed the steps to the front door of the Elizabethan manor. Another carriage pulled up as he knocked.

Tonight's gathering was at the house of Leander Tyndale, the new Viscount Aubourn, a bachelor whose sister Annabelle was playing hostess. They welcomed Wynthrope with smiles and great cordiality, surprising since Wynthrope wasn't well acquainted with either of them. Perhaps they were closer to Moira than he had been led to believe. He could see no other reason for his invitation.

The ballroom was well lit; the crystal drops of the chandeliers casting tiny rainbows all around. Jewels sparkled on a number of illustrious persons chatting and dancing. Laughter and music filled his ears. Perfume filled his nostrils. He wanted to turn around and leave—not just this party but England. Just for a second, he allowed himself to entertain the idea of running away.

Then he saw her. Of course he saw her. His eyes had refused to see anyone else since that night she'd told him to leave her sister alone. God, how could she have ever thought he would be interested in Minerva when she was there?

She was with Octavia and one of her new friends, the Countess Angelwood. Both Octavia and the countess were attractive women, but they faded into the woodwork next to Moira. She laughed at something Octavia said, her lips parting sweetly as her multicolored eyes sparkled.

She wore a gown of deep plum that revealed the slender line of her neck and the delicate rise of her bosom. The color of her gown was bland compared to the natural wine of her wide, curved lips. The diamonds at her ears and throat were dull compared to the sparkle of her eyes. She had turned him into a goddamn poet and he couldn't even bring himself to be annoyed about it.

His natural inclination was to go to her, perhaps ask her to dance or drop to his knees and confess everything. He would gladly suffer every public humiliation if it meant she and his brothers were safe, but fate was not that kind. The idea of

Daniels harming her in any way was worse than having to hurt her himself.

But he didn't go to her. He went to his brothers instead. North, Devlin, and Brahm stood just to his right. That he chose Brahm as company was a great indication of just how badly he wanted to avoid Moira. In fact, he was astounded that Brahm had been invited. Most of society avoided his eldest brother, and with good reason. Brahm might be sober now, but at one time he had been the kind of drunk that ruined more than just parties. He had ruined lives and reputations as well.

"Good evening," he said brightly as he joined them.

All three of them looked at him. Their faces were so different, but the expression was the same. They knew there was something gnawing at him.

Brahm said nothing. Devlin said, "Good evening, Wyn."

North said, "Moira's here. Why are you not with her?"

Wynthrope attempted a look of mock innocence. "I thought I would stop and greet my brothers first. You were on the way to the lady, after all."

Luckily, that seemed to appease his nosy brother, and it was all Wynthrope could do not to sigh in relief. He daren't do anything, lest North catch on. The one thing he did not want this night was a former Bow Street man watching him, especially not one who knew about his past. Once word got out that Moira had been robbed, North would immediately turn to him. His brother didn't share Moira's naive trust of him. North wouldn't want to think him responsible, but the investigator in him wouldn't be able to ignore the evidence— or his gut.

"Now that I've fulfilled my familial duty, I believe I will greet the lady. She is much prettier than you lot." It was a carelessly tossed remark, delivered by that part of him that he donned like a suit whenever in a social situation. It was a part of him Devlin and North were much accustomed to. Brahm, on the other hand, didn't seem quite convinced.

For a second, Wynthrope's gaze locked with that of his eldest brother. Brahm's whiskey brown eyes weren't judgmental, they weren't filled with disappointment. No, it was worse than that—they were filled with understanding. He could take almost anything from Brahm but understanding.

Brahm did *not* understand him. He never had and he never would.

Devlin and North said farewell. Brahm continued in silence, but he smiled. His smile was understanding as well. Wynthrope was torn between wanting to hit him and wanting to beg for his help. A bastard he might be, but Brahm was still the eldest, and there were some things that even resentment couldn't change.

His heart hammering, he approached Moira and her companions. As if by magic, the other women drifted away when they saw him. Normally it would have been amusing that they knew he was there for Moira and Moira alone, but tonight it disturbed him. Would no one come to her rescue?

"Mr. Ryland."

He bowed. "Lady Aubourn. May I say how lovely you look this evening?"

Moira smiled, a delightful blush suffusing her cheeks. She colored so easily, like an inexperienced girl rather than a once-married woman. It was every bit as charming as it was annoying. Why couldn't she be jaded and cynical? Why couldn't she be one of those women who didn't believe a word he uttered? Why did she have to believe them all?

No, that wasn't it. A few weeks ago she wouldn't have believed him because she didn't think herself lovely at all. She only blushed now because she knew *he* believed it.

"You look very fine yourself, sir."

There was faint fluttering in his chest, as though his heart were trying to preen under her praise. He smiled, then deliberately allowed his gaze to travel down to the gentle slope of her cleavage before rising to the stones around her neck. As he had hoped, his appraisal of her breasts disconcerted her.

"I hope you keep those baubles in a safe place."

She eyed him curiously, rose still staining her cheeks. Damnation. He should have known not to be so blunt with her. Moira was not a stupid woman—it was one of the things he adored about her, but now it was a definite obstacle.

"You have shown an abundance of concern about where I keep my valuables as of late."

He shrugged, trying to seem disinterested while his heart pounded like mad. "I worry about you and Minerva living alone as you do. You are prime targets for a thief." If she only knew how prime she was.

She smiled at him. Perhaps she wasn't that intelligent after all. No, that was the hardened side of him trying to make this easier for him. She smiled because she believe him, because she trusted him. It wouldn't occur to her that he was someone she should protect herself against. Why would it? He had played her so very well.

"That is very sweet, but you may put your mind to rest. I have a safe in my bedroom where I keep all my jewelry."

His heart dropped. "Is it well concealed?"

She obviously mistook the irritation in his voice for trepidation, because she answered without hesitation, "Of course. Behind an oil of Narcissus that Tony painted."

Finally his questioning paid off. Wynthrope waited for some part of him to triumph, but there was nothing but a feeling of sickness in the pit of his stomach.

"A painting is the first place a thief would look."

Now it was she who shrugged. He wanted to shake her, make her realize just how gullible she was being. "If someone takes the time to break into my bedroom, search behind my paintings, and break the combination on my safe, they are welcome to the contents of it."

His fingers clenched into fists. "You might feel differently if it ever happens. There has been a rash of thefts lately." Yes, thefts that he himself was behind. Nothing major, a necklace here, some silver there—small things that had all turned up at local fences and been reclaimed by the owners with little effort. It had taken a bit of planning, but he had succeeded in letting the *ton* know there was a thief about, but not enough to raise much alarm.

Just enough that he wouldn't be the first suspect that leaped to Moira's usually sharp little mind. It was just a precaution, though. He knew he was one of the last people she would suspect.

Bitterness flooded the back of his throat.

Moira's hand settled on his arm. It was meant to be reassuring, but he wanted to toss it off like an insect. How could she touch him? More importantly, how could he let her?

"Thank you for your concern, but there is nothing for you to be anxious about. I am not careless when it comes to security."

No, just when it came to men, or rather one man. Him.

His mind set, already planning his next course of action, Wynthrope asked her to dance. He went through the steps mechanically, flawlessly, as his head worked out timing and details. Then, after the dance, he led her back to his friends, with the excuse that he saw a business acquaintance he wished to speak to, and the promise that he would be back for another dance after.

After he stole the tiara, he planned to make good on his promise. He had it all worked out. After going home for a change of clothing, he would break into Moira's house, steal the tiara, and then take it back to his place and hide it in the secret compartment under his bed. Then, he would change back into his evening clothes and return to the party. With any luck, no one would notice his absence, and if they did, Moira would deliver his defense. It was all very simple.

His apartments were quiet when he entered. He half expected Daniels to speak from the shadows, but the old man was thankfully absent. The Irishman was counting the money he would soon have, no doubt.

Wynthrope walked to his bedroom and lit the lamp. Then he slowly and methodically stripped off his evening clothes and replaced them with black wool trousers, sweater, and boots. Over the sweater he tugged on an old black coat that would keep him warm but not hinder his movements. He'd thought about wearing a mask or a hood, but that would work against him if he was caught in the neighborhood. Dressed as he was, he would raise some suspicion, but he could probably talk his way out of it.

Back outside, he rounded the building to the stables where he housed his horses. He saddled King, a black gelding who ran like the devil himself was on his heels, and hoisted himself up onto the horse's back. Then, putting his heels to King's flanks, he started off in the direction of Moira's house.

He wasn't yet halfway there when it began to snow.

Wynthrope had lied to her.

It was unfair of her to think it, but Moira couldn't help it. He said he was going to talk to a business associate, but that had been more than half an hour ago and she had yet to see him again. To be sure, there were quite a few people milling about Leander's ballroom—the same ballroom she used to preside over as hostess—but not enough to conceal a man like Wynthrope for long.

Perhaps he and this acquaintance were elsewhere in the house, somewhere they could sit and enjoy relative quiet while they talked. That was a very plausible answer, and Moira didn't believe it for a second. In her heart, she knew that Wynthrope had left the property altogether. He had left without saying good-bye.

It would be easy for her to think his absence was due to her, and that part of her that was still uncertain of her own appeal was convinced it was just that. However, none of his brothers seemed to know where he was either, especially North. He was closest to North. If he was leaving with no intention of returning, wouldn't his brothers know? Or perhaps he had feared North would say something to her?

Nonsense. Wynthrope Ryland didn't fear very much. People without much joy in their lives never did. It was an unfair assessment, perhaps, but a valid one. There wasn't much in this world that Wynthrope would miss should he leave it. He would miss his brothers, and that was about it.

He might miss her, but Moira wasn't certain. Was she someone he would regret losing? He certainly didn't act like it, disappearing like this. She just knew it had something to do with her. She could feel it. Regardless of the fact that she believed him to be much more straightforward than that, his strange behavior over the past few days only served to reenforce her misgivings. His kisses hadn't changed, the way he spoke hadn't changed, but there was an underlying tension in him that she couldn't quite put her finger on. He seemed preoccupied and a little distant.

Perhaps he had tired of her and didn't want to hurt her. That would be reason to not be his usual blunt self. Given their conversation of New Year's Eve, that was unlikely, but not impossible. A lot could have changed over the last few days.

It was just her luck. She had finally found someone she thought she could trust with the secret of her marriage, and he was already withdrawing from her. The first man she ever truly wanted to give herself to, and it seemed as though he no longer wanted her.

No. She refused to think this way. That was the old Moira talking. It was so easy for her to blame all this on herself, but that didn't make it right. Wynthrope wasn't the kind of man to play games without a reason. Perhaps he was involved in something he didn't want to discuss with her. Perhaps there was trouble with some kind of business venture he had invested in. That could very easily be the reason for the change in him, and it had nothing to do with her.

Regardless of his reasoning, the party had lost much of its luster without him there. She had danced with many gentlemen, some of whom had flirted shamelessly with her. If nothing else, she had Wynthrope to thank for this newfound popularity. He had changed something in her. She felt more comfortable in public now. She could make conversation and not feel foolish. She was more at ease in her own skin. The changes were obvious to her, and they were obvious to others as well.

Still, that didn't change the fact that she didn't want to be there any longer.

"Octavia," she said, turning to her friend. "I'm not feeling that well. I think I might go home."

Her lovely face a mask of concern, Octavia frowned. "Do you want me to come with you?"

What a dear. "Heavens, no. I am not that ill. Merely tired."

Blue eyes narrowed. Octavia saw too much at times. "It is Wynthrope isn't it? He has upset you."

Moira shook her head. "Not at all." It wasn't a whole lie. She cared about Wynthrope, but she wasn't about to give him *that* much power over her.

That seemed to appease Octavia, even if she didn't look totally convinced.

"Might I ask you to watch over Minerva, though?" Moira asked before Octavia could voice any more concern or questions. "See that she gets home, if it is no trouble?"

It would be unfair to ask her sister to leave now, when she was so obviously enjoying the attention of Lucas Scott, a young man of good fortune from an old and respected family. It looked as though Minnie had finally met someone who could hold her interest. Perhaps this was it. Minnie had found the man she would marry. The house would seem so quiet with her gone. Funny, just a few weeks ago, Moira would have done just about anything to be rid of her sibling, now she realized she was going to miss her. Life was so very puzzling at times.

Her friend's smile was reassuring. "Of course it is no trouble. North and I will deliver her to the door ourselves."

Moira gave her a brief hug. "Thank you. I will talk to you tomorrow. Be sure to keep track of any good gossip for me."

Octavia would also be sure to tell Wynthrope that she had left should he choose to return. She would do this of her own accord, because Moira would never ask her to. Octavia had never made any secret of the fact that while she thought Wynthrope a good man, she also thought he needed a "strong hand" to guide him into a relationship. For some reason she thought Moira had such a hand. It made her smile. Everyone seemed to think she was stronger than she felt. Even Tony had thought her capable of so much more than she ever dared attempt.

She said her good-byes and made her way out of the ballroom. A footman had gone to collect her cape, leaving her relatively alone in the hall.

"You are not leaving, are you, Moira?"

She smiled as Tony's cousin approached her. Leander Tyndale was a sandy-haired man, possessed of the Tyndale kind countenance and laughing brown eyes. He was taller than Tony had been, and larger, stockier. He was the kind of person who made one feel safe and secure in his presence.

"I am afraid so, Leander. You will forgive me, I hope?" She kept her tone light, teasing almost.

A small frown puckered his brows. "You are not unwell, I hope?"

He was sweet to be so concerned. Everyone was so concerned about her. Obviously they didn't think her *that* strong. "No. Just tired. Nothing a good night's sleep will not remedy."

"You are perfectly welcome to rest in one of the rooms here." He gestured toward the stairs. "Your chamber is exactly the way you left it."

A thoughtful offer, if not a strange one. If was as though he didn't want her to go home, but what difference did her continued attendance make?

Good Lord, he didn't have designs on her, did he? No, that was ridiculous. Leander had never shown any more interest in her than a cousin might. Perhaps that was why his solicitous behavior now was so strange.

"Thank you, but no." Her gaze traveled around the hall of its own accord, every corner and nook painfully familiar. "As much as I love this house, it is no longer my home, and I'm afraid that chamber will only remind me of all the nights I lay awake listening for Tony in case he called my name."

Just the mention of it brought back all those awful memories of Tony's sickness. He had suffered more than anyone should have to, and in the end he had almost convinced himself it was because of his "deviance," as he came to call it. Regardless, at the end, the only person he wanted with him other than Moira had been Nathaniel. He had loved him until his last breath, and Moira refused to believe God would punish him for such devotion.

Leander nodded. He seemed a little distracted, anxious

even. "You will be careful, will you not? There has been some thievery in the area as of late. I hate to think of you alone in your house."

Dear God, not him too! Moira gave his arm a reassuring pat. "I am not alone. I have a houseful of servants there with me. You are sweet to worry, Leander, but I will be fine."

So many people concerned with her safety and well-being. Whatever had she done to deserve such regard? It was enough to make one suspicious, especially when one of those concerned was someone who had rarely bothered with her before this.

A footman appeared with her cloak and gloves, and another footman informed her that her carriage had been brought round. Leander had no choice but to wish her a good night and allow her to leave, not that she thought he might try to stop her.

He was still frowning when she looked back at him from the foyer. Moira couldn't begin to fathom what was bedeviling him so. Was he that concerned about the possibility of her being robbed, or was there something he wasn't telling her?

Good heavens, she was in fine form tonight! Everyone had a secret agenda—what a ludicrous thought. Perhaps she really did need a good night's rest. Lord knew she wasn't quite herself at the moment.

It was snowing when she stepped outside, the fat flakes drifting lazily to the still bare ground. It probably wouldn't amount to much, but she was glad that she was leaving now just in case. The last thing she wanted was to be delayed because of poor conditions. At least Minnie would have Octavia and North to keep her company. Moira would have nothing but her own thoughts, and she had quite enough of them already for one evening.

Luckily the drive to her own house was less than a quarter

hour from door to door. A light dusting of white covered the walk and steps, nothing of any consequence. She didn't bother to lift her skirts to avoid dampening the hem, so convinced she was of there being no danger to the fabric.

After handing over her outerwear to Chester, Moira asked for water for a bath and went directly to her room. Normally she wouldn't trouble her servants at such an hour, but she needed something to soothe her mind, something to relax her. A bath and a nice glass of wine would do just the trick. Then she would crawl into bed and, she hoped, spend the entire night in peaceful slumber, rather than plagued by troubling feelings as she was now.

It didn't take long for the water to arrive as there was usually a huge cauldron warming in the kitchen, especially at this time of year. Footmen set the tub near the hearth where a fire banked, and emptied the buckets into it. A maid left her a decanter of wine and a glass while another laid soft, fluffy towels near the fire to warm.

Moira dismissed them all with thanks, telling them to leave the tub till morning and wishing them a good night. Once she was alone again, she added vanilla-scented oil to the steaming water and poured herself a full glass of wine. Then she extinguished all the lamps in her room and slipped out of her clothing and jewelry. Her gown ended up a heap on the carpet, her necklace and earrings left on the vanity. For a moment she thought of Wynthrope and Leander's warnings about a thief. She would put the gems in her safe before crawling into bed.

She left her hair up so it wouldn't get wet and climbed into the tub, wine in hand. A delicious shiver wracked her body as the hot water hit her skin. Slowly, with a sigh of delight, she sank into the copper tub, the metal already warmed by the water and the fire behind. Settling against the curved back, she reclined her head and sipped her wine, her eyes closed. The wine danced on her tongue, warming her on the inside as the bath warmed her outside. The crackling of the fire and the scented water worked their magic quickly, and she felt the tightness begin seeping out of her muscles.

She was in a state of perfect languidness, her head and limbs heavy, the wine long gone when she heard a strange noise. Opening her eyes, Moira was astonished to see a man coming in through her balcony doors. He was dressed entirely in black, his movements almost perfectly silent. Only the lifting of the latch had given away his presence.

Good Lord, was it the thief both Wynthrope and Leander had warned her about? Her gaze darted to the gems on her vanity. Those were her favorite. There was no way she was going to give those up without a fight. She didn't care if she had to jump out of the tub and attack him like a screaming wet banshee!

She was just about to scream when he turned. Their gazes locked, and he looked every bit as shocked to see her as she was to see him. Of course, he probably hadn't been expecting to find her naked in a bathtub. Then again, she hadn't been expecting him at all.

"Wynthrope? What are you doing here?"

Chapter 11

Frozen in the heated water of her bath, her body even more tense than it had been when she climbed in, Moira gaped at Wynthrope. He gaped back, his gaze darting to the water in the tub before rising back to hers.

Heat flooded her cheeks as she crossed her arms over her chest. "Are you going to answer me?"

"I—" He glanced toward the balcony doors, then back again, obviously at a loss. "I did not think you would be in the bath."

It didn't sound as though he thought he'd find her here at all! But that was ridiculous. "Where did you think I would be?"

"In bed."

If she flushed any hotter, the water in the tub would boil. "If you had waited a few minutes I probably would have been. Now tell me, what the devil are you doing here?"

He seemed distracted. "I went back to the ball and was told you had already left. I wanted . . . to see you."

He was definitely seeing her all right! More of her than she was comfortable showing. And yet Moira couldn't deny that there was a part of her that was very aroused by his arrival and his strange appearance.

"Did you go back to the ball dressed like that?" She nodded at his old coat and sweater. Good heavens, she could see the hair on his chest!

He glanced down at himself. "No."

This was such an embarrassing situation! He didn't seem to know what to do any more than she did. Had he come because he thought she was upset with him? And why had he chosen to dress that way? Just to climb up the trellis to her room? If she didn't know better she would suspect him of being the very thief he had warned her about.

Why dissect why he was there? He told her he wanted to see her, and she should believe him. Perhaps this was fate's way of giving her the perfect opportunity to decide whether she should trust him with the secret of her marriage, and risk everything, or tell him to get out.

Whether it was the wine, the night, or the fact that she had taken complete leave of her senses, Moira wasn't certain, but she was suddenly overwhelmed with courage—and want. Lowering her arms from her chest, she placed a hand on either side of the tub and rose to her feet, hot water streaming in rivulets down her cooling body.

"Fetch me that towel, will you?"

Wynthrope stared at her, his jaw as wide as his eyes. Shame made her want to cover herself, but pride made her stay just as she was. She might not have the perfect body, but it was hers, and she had never allowed any man to ever look at it before this night. She was offering him something she had never offered anyone else, whether he saw her as a prize or not, she was not going to think of herself as anything less.

He came toward her, his footfalls silent on the carpet.

There was nothing but the crackle of the fire and the roar of her pounding pulse echoing in Moira's ears. She held her breath as he approached. He stopped before her, the only thing between them the rim of the tub just above her knees.

"The towel?" Her voice was a hoarse whisper.

His gaze raked over her, heating her chilled flesh and puckering her nipples. Warmth flooded between her legs as a pulse there gave a mighty throb. Dark blue eyes locked with hers. "I will be your towel."

Shivering, Moira watched as he removed his coat, tossing it heedlessly to the floor behind him. His gloves followed. His bare hands reached for her, touching her neck like some precious treasure before sliding up to cup her jaw. His skin was dry and warm against hers, his thumbs soft as they stroked her cheeks. His gaze roamed her face.

"You are so beautiful, I cannot believe you are real."

Moira parted her lips to reply, but never got the chance before he lowered his head to hers.

His mouth was like a brand, searing hot as it marked her forever as his own. Her head swam as he overwhelmed her senses. Her hands came up to his shoulders, clinging to his sweater to keep herself from falling. His tongue invaded her mouth, exploring and teasing her own until they both tasted of wine.

One by one, he plucked the pins from her hair. They fell to the tub, making tiny plopping noises as they hit the water. Soon he had her hair free and tumbling down around her shoulders, his fingers combing through the heavy strands, massaging the soreness from her scalp. Moira moaned, her head tilting back into his hands.

The fingers in her hair slid down her back to her waist. Her feet lifted from the bottom of the tub and over the side, dripping on the carpet as he gathered her against him. The wool of his sweater was soft yet scratchy against her breasts and stomach. Her nipples ached at the contact, bringing a soft gasp to her lips, which he swallowed with his own.

Moira clung to him as he carried her to the bed, the full length of her flush against him. Gingerly he placed her on the counterpane, the mattress sinking as he lowered himself beside her. His gaze was earnest and dark with desire as he looked down at her.

"Are you certain this is what you want?"

Moira's heart clenched at the tenderness in his tone. She slid her fingers down his chest to tug his sweater from the waist of his trousers. Her hands slid beneath, hungry to feel the warm satin of his skin. "You are what I want."

He kissed her again, tenderly, reverently. His tongue teased hers with the promise of being devoured, but never followed through. The pads of his fingers were slightly rough as they slid down her chest to circle a nipple. Her breasts pulled and tightened at his touch, wanting more. When his fingers pinched the aching peak, Moira whimpered against his mouth. If all of lovemaking felt this good, she was never going to survive it.

His mouth left hers, trailing along her jaw and throat and down her chest, building the knot of anticipation in her stomach with every soft kiss. Finally the wet heat of his mouth closed over her nipple, replacing his fingers. Moira moaned in pleasure, arching toward him.

Wynthrope's hand slid down past her ribs, down her belly to the aching valley between her thighs. Her body jumped as his fingers parted the curls there, teasing the cleft between. Moira tightened her grip on his shoulders, but made no move to stop him. They were delicious, these feelings and sensations he was arousing within her, more intense than anything she had ever felt before, even that night in her parlor.

One of his fingers parted her, knowing instinctively where to touch her to make her gasp and writhe. Sparks of pleasure flared in her belly, rolling into one tight, pulsating ache that demanded to be assuaged even as it delighted in tormenting her.

Moira pushed his sweater upward with insistent hands, stroking the heated flesh beneath. His skin was smooth against her palms, the hair on his chest springy as she drove her fingers through it. His nipples were tiny pebbles tightening at her touch, and when she slid her hands down to the waist of his trousers, his stomach trembled.

His teeth nipped at her breast, drawing a cry from her. Lifting his head from her swollen, glistening flesh, he gazed down at her, his ruthless fingers still stroking the wetness between her legs.

"Do you want me to take my clothes off?" His voice was low and butterscotch smooth.

Moira nodded, unable to speak. She wanted him naked. Wanted to feel every succulent inch of his skin against hers.

Wynthrope rose up on his knees on the bed, his gaze brazenly fastened to hers as he grabbed the hem of his sweater with both hands and pulled it upward. Fascinated, Moira watched with greedy eyes as the smooth flesh of his stomach and the skin pulled tautly across his ribs was revealed. The black wool slipped over his head and was tossed to the floor.

He was beautiful and golden from the knobby bones of his shoulders to the delicate indent of his navel. He wasn't a bulky man, but the muscles of his arms and chest were well defined, as though sculpted by a master.

With his arms at his sides, his gaze burned into hers. "Shall I continue?"

Again Moira nodded. Her mouth was dry, all the moisture in her body seemingly pooling in one place much lower than her face.

His hands went to the falls of his trousers, his fingers

working with deliberate, slow deftness. He slipped one leg over the side of the bed and lifted himself off the mattress so that he stood beside the bed as he peeled the dark fabric down his legs. Moira watched as he straightened, her gaze traveling up from the muscled curves of his calves and thighs to his narrow hips and the jutting flesh just below his abdomen.

Even though she had felt it that night in her library, and caught a glimpse of it afterward, she hadn't seen it fully erect. Long and thick with a ruddy, bulbous head, it probably should have been somewhat intimidating, but Moira found it fascinating.

And she wanted it. Wanted it inside her with a ferocity that threatened to consume her. She wanted him inside her, as a part of her. Never before had she ever wanted to have one person claim her, take her over as she wanted this man to possess her.

"Do I pass inspection?" His tone was teasing, but his voice was lower than normal, even a little rough. Moira shivered.

"You are beautiful," she told him, repeating his earlier praise of her as she held out her arms to him. "Come here."

She didn't have to ask him twice. He crawled onto the bed so that he hovered above her, and this time when he lowered his head to her, he didn't stop at her breasts, even though he paused long enough to taunt her nipples into aching, distended peaks once more.

His mouth scorched a path down the valley of her ribs, past her waist to the juncture of her thighs. Was he going to do what she thought he was? Yes, he was! Moira's hips jerked as his mouth and tongue explored her in the same manner as his fingers had before. Hot, wet and firm, his tongue was like rough velvet against her sensitive flesh, teasing her even more acutely than his fingers had. She surged against him like waves to shore, not caring if her behavior was wanton or not. She knew only that what he was doing felt incredibly good, and that writhing against his tongue came instinctively.

Holding her thighs splayed wide, Wynthrope lapped at her with his tongue, the fine stubble on his jaw abrading her in the most arousing fashion. Moira's fingers clutched at his hair, pushing his head lower as her hips lifted and fell. The spiraling pressure within her grew, mounting to an intensity that was quickly becoming too much. If it didn't break soon, she was certain she would go mad.

His mouth left her, despite her groan of frustration. Like Poseidon rising from the ocean, he loomed above her, his hips sliding between her legs, the hard length of him pushing insistently at the entrance to her body. Time seemed to halt as he poised there. He was waiting for permission from her, Moira knew it. No matter that he wanted her as much as she wanted him, he wasn't going to do anything she did not want.

The knowledge would have made her weep were it not for the other, much stronger emotions raging through her right now.

This was it. This was where he gave her what she craved. She lifted her hips to accommodate him as he shoved, plunging the full length of him inside her.

Moira gasped. It was though he had pinched her inside.

Wynthrope froze. She could feel him pulsating within her. The expression on his face was one of awful realization, and for a moment Moira feared he might withdraw from her body. She locked her legs around him to keep him with her. She was not going to let him go, not now.

He stared down at her, his arms trembling on either side of her head. He didn't try to hide the confusion in his gaze. "Why didn't you tell me?"

"I didn't know how," she replied, which was true, though not the whole truth. "We can talk about it later, please don't leave me."

"Leave you?" His voice was harsh as he reared up on his knees. Lifting her hips with his hands, he gingerly positioned her so that her bottom rested on his thighs, her legs wrapped around his waist.

"Are you all right?" he demanded.

Moira nodded. "Please don't stop."

He muttered something that might have been an oath, but somehow Moira thought he was more upset at himself than at her. One of his hands came around to her abdomen, sliding down to the mound of her sex. Gently, his thumb parted her as his fingers had earlier, searching out and finding that tiny part of her that gave so much pleasure. He stroked her, rekindling the fire that had banked within her, until her hips began to move despite the burning where his body joined hers.

He moved inside her with deep, gentle thrusts, withdrawing only a fraction before moving inward again. It kept the friction between them, and the discomfort of his possession to a minimum, and allowed Moira to concentrate on the pleasure his hand was giving her. Gripping his flanks with her calves, she arched upward, pushing her pelvis against both his body and hand until the tension became unbearable and then finally broke, convulsing her body as a gale of pleasure swept through her.

Dimly, she was aware of Wynthrope quickening his thrusts, the pleasure of her release masking the soreness his movements brought. Then he was gone, spilling his seed onto the sheet beneath her as he fell onto his forearms above her.

She supposed she should be thankful he had enough control to withdraw, and she was, but she was also strangely disappointed as well. There was something so intimate about the idea of having him come inside her. It was as though he would have been leaving her something of himself, something she could possess as he possessed her. Realistically she knew that something could very well lead to a child, something she as a single woman was not to wish for, but it still seemed *wrong*.

He rolled onto his back beside her, both of them staring at the ceiling in silence as their bodies cooled and the tension between them faded from the physical to something deeper.

Tears prickled the backs of Moira's eyes. Was he angry at her? Was this the part where he withdrew from her completely? Would she find out tomorrow morning that she had been wrong about him? No. He wasn't like that. He had told her he wasn't like those other men who had made sport of her. This wasn't just about his promise to seduce her. There was more between them than that.

His hand moved, closing over hers with a gentle squeeze that made her heart leap and her eyes burn.

He rolled toward her, pulling the quilt from the bottom of the bed over them both as he did so. His arm settled over her waist as his chest pressed against her arm. She could feel the rhythm of his heart against her shoulder. She shifted her bent legs so that they rested against his thighs to avoid the dampness on the sheet below her hips.

She met his gaze, trying to decipher what that unreadable emotion she saw there was when he spoke. "Why didn't you tell me?"

She could lie, but to what end? To protect herself? She had already made herself as vulnerable to him as she could, and if she didn't trust him completely, what was the point in trusting him at all?

"I was afraid," she confessed. How liberating it was to tell him the truth. How utterly frightening.

He raised a brow. "Of me?"

She nodded. "Of what you might do if you learned the truth about my marriage."

He frowned. "It was never consummated."

"And therefore not legal."

He stared at her. "You said it was a marriage of convenience, but I assumed that it was still a marriage."

"Tony had his reasons for marrying me and I married him to escape my family. For years I have been terrified of someone learning the truth. If word got out that my marriage wasn't valid I could lose everything and end up at the mercy of my parents. I would rather dance naked in Covent Garden than do that."

"And you would look very fetching as you did so. But I still do not understand why it was never consummated. The two of you appeared to have a good relationship. Surely you could have been able to share a bed at least once."

This was the sticky part. Telling him her own secrets was one thing, but she had no right to reveal Tony's.

"My husband was not able to perform his husbandly duties." It wasn't a lie. Tony had been no more able to make love to her than he would a stick of wood. In fact, the stick might have fared better than she. It wasn't because he hadn't loved her, he just hadn't found her attractive. He used to lament how much simpler his life would be if he could only be a husband to her.

Her explanation seemed to satisfy Wynthrope—at least on the subject of her marriage. "Why did you never take a lover?"

"The same reason I was fearful of being with you. I was afraid of people learning the truth. I didn't know if I could trust anyone."

He stilled as the full implications of that sank in. "But you trusted me."

She nodded, her throat tight under the weight of his gaze. "Yes."

He kissed her again, fiercely and without finesse, but the raw emotion of it filled Moira's heart with joy. Slowly he released her and she became aware of something hard pressing against her hip. Surprise filled her as she realized what it was.

"Again?" Dear heavens, she didn't know if she was ready to do it again. The tenderness from the first time had yet to fade.

"Ignore it and it will eventually go away," he advised, wrapping his arms around her again. "As eager as it is, I have no wish to hurt you. I'll indulge it when you've recovered."

The knowledge that there would be a next time filled her with a rush of happy anticipation as she snuggled against him. It was so hard to believe that this was real, that she had found someone who gave her so much happiness, who made her feel so complete. She wanted it to last forever.

As she closed her eyes and drifted toward sleep, Moira realized that she was very much in danger of falling in love with him. Not just that, but she wanted to fall in love. Even more surprising was that she believed in her heart that he just might be able to love her in return.

A virgin. Good God, what kind of joke was this? Was fate out to destroy him?

Lying on his side, Wynthrope watched Moira as she slept. He would have smiled at her soft snores if his heart wasn't slowly being shredded in his chest.

She was the most amazing woman he had ever met. Being inside her was the closest thing he'd ever experienced to heaven, but hearing her tell him she trusted him made him feel like hell.

What had she been doing there? He should have had plenty of time to steal the tiara before she returned home from the party. She never returned home before one o'clock, not when she was enjoying herself.

Not when he had been with her.

Damnation. She had left the party because he wasn't there. It had never occurred to him that his attendance would affect her one way or the other. He should have known. If the situation had been reversed, he wouldn't have stayed either, especially if he got the idea that she wasn't coming back.

The horrible thing was that he had intended to return. How differently this night might have turned out if things had gone as planned. They would probably still be at the viscount's house—Moira's former house—dancing until the wee hours. He would have seen her and Minerva home, perhaps he might have stolen a kiss or two, but whether he would have ended up in her bed was a mystery.

Regardless of what might or might not have happened between them, the fact still remained that he had come there for one reason only—to steal the tiara. That fact hadn't changed, it had only been delayed for a bit.

The image of her in that tub, her pale skin gold and glistening in the firelight, was something he would carry with him forever. Never in his life had he seen something more breathtaking or perfect. She was all slender perfection, her form rounder than he remembered. She had taken his suggestion to heart and gained a few pounds—just enough to make her a little softer.

He thought his heart was going to stop when she stood up and asked for that blasted towel. Did she truly believe he would allow her to cover herself again after giving him a glimpse of all she had to offer? He had wanted to wrap himself around her, touch and taste her, and he had succeeded.

The scent of her clung to him, vanilla sweetness mixed with warm, aroused woman. All he wanted was to spoon against her, bury his face in her hair, and sleep forever, but there was a job to do.

Slowly, so as not to wake her, he slipped out from beneath the quilt and gathered his clothes from the floor. The fire in the hearth had burned away to little more than embers, and he had to feel around for all his belongings. Finally dressed, he took a stub of a candle from the mantel and lit the wick with the glowing remains in the grate. Glancing toward the bed to make certain his activity and the extra light hadn't wakened Moira, he moved silently toward the painting on the wall directly opposite the bed. It was a good place to start looking for the safe. Thankfully there were only a few paintings in the room.

He felt around the side of the gilt frame, closing his eyes in regret as his fingers encountered the cool metal of a hinge. Of course he would find the correct painting immediately, it was just his rotten luck.

A bit of pressure and the painting swung forward, the hinges protesting with a soft whine. Again Wynthrope glanced toward the sleeping woman on the bed. Her soft snore assured him that she was still asleep.

She looked so lovely, so peaceful. His heart hurt at the sight of her. He turned away.

Lifting the candle to the face of the safe, he illuminated the locking mechanism. He would have been apprehensive about cracking it if he hadn't staged those other robberies first.

Narrowing his concentration on the safe, trying to block out the fact that Moira slept trustingly behind him, Wynthrope's fingers expertly began their task. He felt, rather than listened for the safe to tell him the correct combination of numbers. If he knew Moira as well as he believed he did, he already had the correct sequence figured out. He tried the combination.

The lock clicked and he smiled grimly. His luck was with him this evening, even though he wished it wasn't. The key to the safe was Moira's wedding date. Most would believe that it was because of her love for Tony, but even if he hadn't discovered the truth of her marriage, he would still know that she had chosen that date because it symbolized her freedom from her parents.

He despised these people and he had never met them, though he despised himself more at this moment.

He lifted the candle to peer inside the confines of the safe. There were flat wooden boxes for jewelry, velvet bags, and soft velvet pillows. There were also papers and other personal items, but he ignored those. He was after one thing, and that's what he needed to concentrate on.

The tiara sat on a velvet pillow, its stones throwing off a blinding array of glittering sparks as the light of the candle touched it. Reaching in, he carefully picked it up, his movements slow and fluid so as to not disturb anything or make a noise.

Outside the safe, the tiara didn't look like much of anything. Atop Moira's glistening hair, it had looked like an adornment fit for a queen—his black queen. Now it was nothing more than an intricate integration of stones and metal—a heavy, insignificant thing.

It was the key to his freedom. All he had to do was take it, wrap it up in the bag he had brought with him, and take it with him when he left. Then he could give it to Daniels and all this would be at an end. He wouldn't have to worry about North or Devlin, or even Brahm being touched by the mistakes of his past. He wouldn't have to worry about Moira and her safety.

He wouldn't have to worry about Moira at all. Not anymore. The moment he turned this trinket over to Daniels, it would signify the inevitable end of his relationship with Moira, unless he could lower himself enough to face a future built on deceit.

At one time he probably could have lowered himself to just such a degree, but he didn't have the heart for it anymore. Somewhere along the line that shriveled fig in his chest had come alive, slowly blossoming under Moira's nurturing attention. It was far from whole, still cracked and dusty, but there was hope within it again, and the knowledge that he wasn't as lost as he had once feared.

If only it had stayed a dried-up, dead thing, this would be so much easier.

He had the prize he had come for. All he had to do was close the safe, so why didn't he? He stood there, frozen to the spot, unable to will his legs to move, staring at the bit of glitter in his hand.

He couldn't do it. He couldn't take this prize because he had been given a far more precious one by the woman sleeping trustfully just a few feet away. He didn't mean her maidenhead—it was much overrated as far as prizes were concerned. Every woman had a maidenhead once in her life, it was hardly a rarity among mankind.

No, the prize Moira had given him was her trust. She had a secret that she had guarded for years, a secret that made her close herself off from life, that made her cautious and careful. He knew all about those kinds of secrets, he had plenty of his own. Had he trusted her with his? Not really— not the deep ones. He kept the secret of his past concealed from her even as she revealed her own.

She had given herself to him. He hadn't seduced her or coerced her. When she stood up in that tub, revealing her nakedness to him, it had been because she wanted to do it. She wanted him to be the first man to know what it was like to be inside her, and, God help him, the idea of her ever allowing another to touch her that way filled him with a cold, dangerous possessiveness.

In the beginning she had been so afraid that he was out to use her in some way—that he was going to make some kind of trophy of her. Christ, if she only knew the truth. She was a trophy—but not as she thought. She was something worthy of winning, a woman worthy of fighting for, of risking everything just to hold. The fact that he embodied everything she feared and mistrusted was sickening because he had convinced her otherwise.

Hell, he had almost convinced himself otherwise.

She was so much stronger than he was. She had faced her fear of what might happen if she revealed the truth to him. If he were the sort of man to spread tales, he could easily ruin her by bragging about his conquest. He knew many men who would do just that, without any thought of what the indiscretion might do to the lady involved. One word from him and Moira could end up with nothing, dependent on her parents once more. She rarely spoke of them, but he knew how much she would hate going back to them. She would starve before she asked them for a penny.

No, he was definitely the weaker of the two of them. He was too afraid to trust her. He could sugarcoat it and justify it by saying it was because there was more than just himself at stake, that he kept his silence to protect his brothers, but that was horse shite. He kept his silence because he couldn't bear for her to look at him with distaste in her gaze. He would rather have her think him a heartless scoundrel than know he had been duped into being a thief.

He didn't want her to think he had used her just to get the tiara. He had wanted her from the first moment he saw her, the tiara had nothing to do with that, but she would never believe that now. If only he had told her from the beginning, perhaps they could have worked something out. Perhaps she would have sold him the tiara. If he had been truly careful he might have been able to get a forgery made—one that even Daniels couldn't see through.

But it was too late for second thoughts now. Now was the time for decisions. He had the tiara in his hand. Did he take it and walk away from Moira? Or did he take it and conceal the truth from her forever?

Or did he put it back and tell her everything and pray to God she forgave him? Which meant more, keeping his secrets and protecting his family, or having Moira in his life?

A bigger man would choose his family. A better man would know that putting others ahead of himself was the greatest sacrifice.

A better man would realize she could never love a liar and a thief. A bigger man would let her go.

He was not such a man. He wanted her, wanted to give her everything he had to offer and more. He wanted to be a better man, but not for his family or himself, but for *her*. And the better man for Moira would not steal from her. A better man would tell her the truth and risk losing her rather than deceive her altogether.

Daniels would have to find another way to get this tiara. North would have to deal with the actions of his past, just as Wynthrope himself would. This ended tonight.

As he lifted the tiara to put it back in the safe, a soft sound made him freeze. He turned his head, knowing full well what he was going to see, but unable to avoid it all the same.

Moira sat up in the bed, the dying fire not dead enough to conceal the bewilderment in her expression. For the second time that evening she asked the one question he didn't want to answer.

"What are you doing?"

Chapter 12

He could not be stealing from her. He couldn't.

Clutching the quilt to her chest to hide her nakedness, Moira couldn't help but notice that Wynthrope was fully dressed, nor could she fail to notice that he held the tiara Tony had given her in his hand.

How had he gotten into her safe? More importantly, *why* was he in her safe?

The candle in his other hand illuminated his face, casting dark shadows across his eyes. He was silent, his mouth set in a grim line. He obviously was not pleased to find her awake.

"What are you doing with my tiara?" Perhaps he'd answer a more direct question if he wouldn't answer her previous query. Whatever he said, she hoped he proved her suspicions wrong.

He returned the tiara to her safe and closed the door, sealing it inside once more. "I was going to steal it."

The breath rushed from her lungs. *Was?* "You're the thief everyone is talking about."

He didn't even attempt to pretend innocence. "Yes."

All the blood rushed from her face, leaving her with a sick feeling in her stomach. "Why? Are you so desperate for money?"

He shook his head, his gaze focused somewhere to her right. "Money had nothing to do with it."

He sounded so caustic, so mocking. "So you do it for the excitement, is that it?"

"I did it because I had to." His tone made it obvious that he didn't expect her to understand. Of course she wouldn't understand. How could she?

"You had to?" How very ludicrous! "Why on earth would you have to steal a candelabra and a set of dueling pistols?"

Now he chose to meet her gaze, and when he did, it was like staring at a stranger. "So no one would notice when I took something more precious."

More precious? Her tiara, or was that simply another ruse to cover his tracks? Oh God, it hurt so much to think that he had only been using her. She had suspected he was after one thing—her body. It never occurred to her that the "one thing" might be something of a more material worth.

"Did you not stop to consider that these items might have sentimental value to their owners, despite their lack of worth?" Such as the fact that she only cared about that tiara because Tony had wanted her to have it.

He closed the hinged painting as well. "It didn't matter. Those other items all found their way back to their rightful owners."

And that made it all right, did it? He sounded so detached, so uncaring. Was this the real he, or was he simply pretending? This cold stranger was not the man she had come to care about. "What about my tiara, would it have made its way back to its rightful owner?"

His silence was answer enough. Moira's chest tightened painfully, making it difficult to draw breath.

"If I hadn't woken up, you were going to simply take it and go, weren't you?"

"No." He gave his head a determined shake. "I was putting it back."

He expected her to believe that?

Anger heated her blood, strengthened her resolve, and spurred her onward. "All those questions you asked me about where I kept my valuables. You were not concerned for my safety, you simply wanted to know where to look."

He nodded ever so slightly. "Yes."

She knew that would be his answer, but it still hurt to hear it so plainly from his own lips.

"And all the time you spent here, that was reconnaissance work, was it?" God, all those kisses, all those conversations that had meant so much, that had changed her . . .

He met her gaze, and it was as though he'd punched her in the stomach. "Not all of it, no."

Even if she took him at his word, that still meant that some of the time he had spent with her he had been planning to steal from her. The imaginary knife in her gut twisted.

"You had this planned from the beginning didn't you?" Her voice cracked. "From the first moment we met."

His expression was beseeching, his tone resolute, "No. Moira, it was not like that."

She clutched the quilt more tightly against her chest. For all its protection, she felt even more naked than she had been in the tub. How very awful it was to find out that she had been so wrong about him when she so very badly wanted to be right. "Everything you said to me, you didn't mean a word."

"I meant it all." His voice was strangely weary, quiet.

She ignored him. "My God, this is worse than any wager.

You weren't out to win a bet, you were out for a bigger prize."

He held out a hand as though he could touch her from across the room. "Moira—"

Tears filled her eyes, constricted her throat. "You came here to steal it, didn't you? I thought you came here for me, but you came for it."

He dropped his hand and said nothing. He didn't have to.

Wetness scalded her cheek as a tear slipped from her eye. "You made love to me for a piece of jewelry."

"No!" He took a step toward her, his tone adamant. "What happened between us had nothing to do with this." He gestured toward the safe.

"It had everything to do with this!" Angrily she wiped at the tears streaming down her face. "Why did you have to do it like this? Why couldn't you have simply broken into my house weeks ago? Why did you have to make me trust you?"

"I never intended for this to happen. You and I had already met before I ever planned to steal the tiara."

Of course he would say that. He would say anything to confuse her. "Why do you want it? There are other more impressive ones among the *ton*."

He raked his free hand through his hair. Was he uncomfortable? *Good.* "I do not want it. The man I work for does."

"Work for?" How long had he been doing this, for heaven's sake? Any amount of time was too long. If he was the kind of person who could take from others without any thought to what it meant, then he certainly wasn't the man she thought he was.

He shook his head. "It is a long story, one that hardly matters now. All that matters is that I do not do this of my own free will. You must believe me."

"Believe you?" She choked on the words. "Why should I believe anything you say? For all I know, everything that comes out of your mouth is a lie."

He pointed a finger at her. "I never lied to you, not about anything that mattered."

Her mouth fell open and disbelieving laughter tumbled out. "You do not think this matters?"

"I'm not lying to you now."

She'd see about that. "No? Who do you work for?"

He pinched the bridge of his nose with his thumb and forefinger and sighed. "No one you would ever want to know."

Moira shut off the tiny remaining part of her that had any sympathy for him. "Why does he want my tiara?"

He dropped his hand. "He plans to sell it to someone else."

"Who?" Who would want it so badly that he would hire someone to steal it? It was a lovely piece, but certainly not worth *that* much.

The same hand he dropped came up again to rub his jaw. "I do not know."

Did not know, or was there no such person? "Why does this other person want it?"

"I do not know."

"Why did this man ask you to steal it?" If he told her he didn't know, she was going to throw something.

"I used to work for him. He knows I'm good."

Good God, he wasn't actually boasting, was he? Of course he was. Not only was he a despicable thief and a scoundrel, but he was a man, after all, and men always had to puff themselves up by crowing about their prowess.

Her fingers tightened on the sheet. "What did he offer you in exchange?"

"Does that matter?" He sounded so defeated.

Oddly enough, it did. "Yes." She wanted to know what his price had been for crippling her this way. She wanted to know if it had been worth his while.

Wynthrope's chin came up almost defiantly. As if he had any right to take such posture with her. She could slap him. "He was blackmailing me. He threatened to harm someone I care about. That's all you need to know."

Another twist of the knife—a reminder of how little she actually meant to him. "So you won't lie to me, but you won't tell me the entire truth either."

He was unflinching—seemingly immune to her anguish. "I'm not going to tell you anything that might get you hurt."

That was laughable. He didn't actually expect her to believe he cared, did he? Not after telling her she knew all that she needed? "Nothing you could tell me could hurt me any more than I already am." Perhaps she shouldn't admit just how deeply his betrayal cut her, but she couldn't help it. She wanted him to know.

His face was ravaged with emotion as he came toward her. For a moment—just a moment—she actually believed he meant it when he said he never wanted to hurt her, but he'd been so cold just a few moments before, she didn't know what to believe.

"Moira, I agreed to steal your tiara because I thought I had no other choice."

The pleading in his voice cut her to the bone. What a skilled liar he was. "You have said as much already."

"But when the opportunity to take it came, I realized that I do have a choice. I chose to put the tiara back." His tone was agitated, frustrated. He was actually upset that she didn't readily believe him!

"You put it back because I caught you! And now it is my word against yours if I alert the authorities. No doubt you'll tell them I accused you out of spite because you rejected me."

He had the nerve to look affronted. "Do you really believe I would do something like that?"

God, she was tired, so very tired and sad. Disappointed.

Disillusioned. "A half hour ago I wouldn't have believed you could steal from me. Now I believe you to be capable of almost anything."

"Moira, please."

No, she wouldn't listen anymore. She had already given him adequate opportunity to explain himself, and so far he hadn't said anything that gave her any cause to believe or forgive him.

"I gave you my trust, Wynthrope. I trusted you with my secret, trusted you to be my first lover because I believed you would not hurt me. You have hurt me more than anyone else in my life. My parents could take lessons from you."

He knew what kind of insult she meant that to be, she could read it in his expression.

"I put the tiara back because I didn't want to betray you. If you had not woken up, you never would have known about this."

Ah yes. Had she only stayed asleep she would still be blissfully ignorant of his duplicity. That led to her next thought. "Tell me something. Would you have stayed until morning? Would you have had the gall to face me after your theft, or would you have snuck out as quietly as you came?"

His hand was in his hair again. She remembered how those silken strands had felt entwined around her own fingers. "There wouldn't have been a need, because I wasn't going to take it."

"What was your plan, Wynthrope? Before you had this sudden change of heart, that is?" Why was she doing this to herself? Did she not hurt enough already?

He didn't bow his head. At least he had the courage to face her, she would give him that. "I was going to stay until morning."

The bastard. He was going to crawl back into her bed, and

stay with her—possibly even make love to her a second time—and then calmly walk out of her house with her tiara.

"I do not know you," she whispered, choking back fresh tears. "I thought I did but I do not."

He was beside the bed now, the flame of the candle detailing every nuance of his ravaged expression. "Moira, you know me better than anyone ever has."

He was a good actor, she would give him that. If his betrayal hadn't turned her heart to stone, she might actually believe him.

"No. The man I thought I knew would never do something like this, not without a good reason, and I do not think you have one of those."

"I told you why. Someone I care about is in danger."

Yes, he had already told her that. "But you will not tell me who?"

He pursed his lips. "No. This person would not appreciate your knowing."

How would this person ever know unless Wynthrope told him? Did he not trust her to keep such information a secret? Obviously not. "So for all I know, this nameless person doesn't even exist."

Earnest blue eyes locked with hers. "You could trust me."

His hopeful tone would have been laughable if it hadn't lit a fuse deep within her. Of all the inane, rotten things he could possibly say to her. "How dare you ask that of me! I have trusted you more than you ever deserved."

His face tightened. "I suppose you expect me to tell all of London about your sham of a marriage now?"

"It would not surprise me." What if he did? She would be ruined. Oddly enough, that hardly mattered to her at the moment. The one thing that she had built her life around for more than a decade meant absolutely nothing to her now that she was faced with the possibility of it.

"And what of you?" There was that mocking twist of his lips again. "Am I to be arrested in the morning?"

The idea of him being locked away sickened her, even though she knew he deserved it. "It would serve you right."

He set the candle on the bedside table, leaning down so that their faces were just inches away. So beautiful, so treacherous. He was Lucifer incarnate. "I will make a bargain with you. I promise to keep your secret if you promise to keep mine."

Bitterness rose in Moira's throat. She had no intention of turning him in to the authorities—for her own benefit as well as his. It was weak of her, no doubt, but she didn't see how she could report him without someone figuring out they had been intimate. And no matter what he had done, she couldn't betray him like that, even though he had betrayed her. The fact that he was so ready to blackmail her only proved that he wasn't the man that she thought.

Some of her distaste must have shown on her face, because sorrow flickered in his eyes. "I do not ask for me, Moira."

A sneer curved her lips. "Let me guess, you are asking for this mystery person you must protect."

"Yes. More people than you and I would suffer if word of this got out."

He was right. There were other people to think of. "I promise not to say anything, but not for you. It is Octavia and North I am thinking of, and the rest of your family."

He glanced away, but not before she saw something in his eyes. Was it his family he thought of as well? Was it one of his brothers he sought to protect?

Good God, she wasn't actually starting to believe him, was she? The only person Wynthrope Ryland sought to protect was himself.

"Thank you," he murmured.

"It is I who must thank you."

His gaze was questioning as it met hers. "Me?"

"Yes." Her tone was so cold, her own bones chilled with it. "At least you revealed yourself before I fell in love with you. That would have been too cruel, even for you."

She had struck a nerve. He recoiled as though she had slapped him. Perhaps she should have, but that wouldn't have been nearly as satisfying as seeing the pain so clearly written in his features. Of course, there was an edge of remorse to her satisfaction. Either he was a better actor than she thought, or he truly was hurt by her words.

Good. She wanted him to hurt. If his heart was broken into one fraction of the pieces hers was, he would suffer enough for her mollification.

"Now get out. And I warn you, if that tiara goes missing anytime in the near future, I will consider my promise not to go to the authorities void. Understood?"

He nodded as he moved toward the balcony doors. He probably thought he was doing her a service by leaving the way he came. Probably thought he was protecting her virtue or some foolishness. Unfortunately, he was.

Pausing at the doors, he turned to face her, his remorseful expression almost lost in the darkness. "Moira?"

Defiantly, she raised her chin as she glared at him. She said nothing.

His lips twisted to one side. "I'm glad you did not fall in love with me as well."

And then he was gone into the falling snow, leaving Moira alone with her tears.

He vomited under the watchful gaze of Moira's garden angel.

Shoulders hunched against the cold and the darkness, Wynthrope wiped his mouth with the back of one hand. The other rested against the angel for support, his fingers clinging to the smooth surface.

The churning in his stomach eased as he leaned into the angel's unyielding embrace. This had to be a dream—a horrible nightmare. Things couldn't have possibly gone this bad.

But they had gone bad. The irony of the situation wasn't lost on him, and part of him might even appreciate it one day. Right now it only served to make him bitter and sick. He had been putting the damn thing back, for Christ's sake, had decided he couldn't betray Moira's trust in such a manner, and then she woke up.

Perhaps it really was fate. Perhaps no one had any control over what direction his life took, he was just a pawn in a much larger game.

If only he could have made her understand, though there was no reason he could expect her to. He wouldn't if the situation was reversed. She was hurt and angry, and it wouldn't matter what he said or what evidence he presented, she wouldn't see past that.

It certainly hadn't helped that he couldn't tell her the whole truth. Telling her about his connection to Daniels wouldn't have mattered because she was in no frame of mind to hear it, but he couldn't tell her about North. That simply wasn't his business to tell. Risking her retaliation against him was one thing, but he didn't want to color her opinion of his brother. North had obstructed a criminal investigation to protect him, and that was something someone of Moira's moral starchiness might not understand.

It wasn't any different than her not telling him why her husband couldn't consummate their marriage, although she was unlikely to agree.

Sweet, innocent Moira. What a fool she must feel like right now. Was she weeping over him, or was she still too angry for tears? If there was any mercy in heaven, she was still angry. He didn't want to think of her wasting tears over him.

Dragging a hand over his face, he straightened, edging away from the sheltering stone of the angel. Dawn wasn't long on the horizon, and he would do well to get home before anyone saw him. It wouldn't do to have the gossips speculating about him being at Moira's at this hour. The last thing she deserved was to have her reputation destroyed on top of having her heart broken.

His horse was down by Moira's own stables where he had left him. Wearily, he hauled himself into the saddle and urged the gelding down the drive. His fingers were cold and stiff on the reins and snow fluttered down his neck, but he didn't care.

She had thanked him for hurting her before she could fall in love with him. If she had been looking for a remark that would cut him to the very quick, she had found it with that one. Had she been in danger of falling in love with him? He didn't know which was more painful, the thought that she might have been in danger of doing so, or the fact that she hadn't developed such feelings for him yet.

He wanted her love, just as a child wanted a toy it was told it couldn't have. And now that it was impossibly far out of his reach, he wanted it with a desperation that made his chest tight and his head ache.

Still, there was a certain amount of relief in having her find out the truth. She knew now what kind of man he had been, what kind of man he was. He didn't have to worry about her finding him out anymore. He probably should have told her everything, but she hadn't been in the frame of mind to hear it. If she ever came near him again, and there wasn't much of a chance of that, then he would tell her everything—if she cared to hear it.

That was the future, and he had other things to think about right now. He had to clear his head of Moira and the tears in her eyes and put his mind to Daniels and what he was going to do now.

Daniels had given him until Twelfth Night to steal the tiara. Twelfth Night was rapidly bleeding into day, and Wynthrope was without the prize. No doubt Daniels was going to pay a call on him within the next few hours if he wasn't waiting for him already. He would not be pleased that Wynthrope had failed to deliver. He would not be pleased that Wynthrope had changed his mind. Daniels was many things, but he was a man of his word; he would do everything he could to ruin North and the rest of the family. If he wasn't able to buy himself time to figure things out, Wynthrope would have to pay a visit to his brothers and prepare them for the worst. He was going to have to tell them everything eventually, but he wanted to have a course of action planned out before he let North loose. He was also going to have to ensure Moira's safety without her knowing about it. A woman scorned was not a rational creature, and he wouldn't put it past her to put herself in danger just to spite him.

But his Moira wasn't a spiteful person. She was sweet and loving, and far too kind for her own good. The notion that he might have damaged those qualities was sickening. She would think twice before trusting anyone again, and she would think of him every time she considered such action. At least she would think of him sometimes, even if it was in a negative manner.

He suspected he would think of her often over the rest of his life, and always with regret.

By the time he arrived home he was covered in a thin layer of snow and his cheeks burned with cold. The chill outside was nothing like the chill inside, however. He was numb, totally numb, sick and tired.

So it was only fitting that Daniels was waiting for him when he stepped inside the darkened confines of his apartments.

"'Bout time you got back."

"Lovely to see you too." At least he hadn't lost his ability to be sarcastic. He would always have that.

The old man made a scoffing noise. "Where is it?"

Wynthrope shook his head to remove any remaining snow and then tossed his coat over a nearby chair. "I don't have it."

The silence that followed his announcement was so dense, he could have touched it. "What do you mean, you don't have it?"

Wynthrope lit a lamp and turned to face his adversary. "Just that. I do not have it."

Daniels's eyes blazed as hotly as the lamp. "Why the hell not?"

Sighing, Wynthrope ran a hand over his eyes. "She caught me."

"*What?*"

The old man's tone would have been laughable if Wynthrope could only remember how to laugh. "She woke up. I couldn't steal it. I was lucky to get out without her raising the alarm." He didn't feel the least remorse for withholding details from Daniels. It was none of his business what transpired between him and Moira.

"So you got yourself some rub 'n' tug, but you didn't get my tiara?"

Wynthrope shook his head. "I did not."

Daniels's fist came down hard on the mantel. "Do you take me for a fool, boyo?"

Meeting his gaze evenly, Wynthrope smirked. "I believe you a lot of things, Daniels, but a fool is not one of them."

"Then you know that I meant what I said. If you do not get me that tiara, I will make you and your brother the talk of London."

He shrugged. "Then you had better give me time to come up with a new plan. I'm no help to you if all of society knows the truth about me." How calm he sounded. No doubt it was because he no longer cared about any of this.

Daniels's face was impassive. "You don't give me orders, boy."

Another shrug. "What do you suggest then?"

Pale blue eyes narrowed. Daniels wasn't stupid, he could sense the change in him. "What happened boyo, did she turn her back on ye? Is that the reason for your lack of respect?"

His lack of respect was due to the fact that Daniels didn't deserve any, but he didn't say that. He didn't say anything, and that was his first mistake.

A slow, knowing smile spread across the Irishman's face, and Wynthrope realized the power he had just handed his former employer.

"I suggest you figure out a way to get me that tiara by week's end, or you'll pay for it."

Wynthrope arched a brow despite the unease in his stomach. What was the old bastard planning? "I'll try."

"That Lady Aubourn's a real pretty thing. I would hate to see her get hurt." Some of the humor left his gaze. "And I will hurt her, and anyone else who strikes my fancy."

He knew it was coming, he knew what the old man was capable of, but that didn't stop the haze of red hot rage from settling over his brain. He acted without thought, only instinct.

"You son of a bitch." Wynthrope's fist caught Daniels in the face, driving the older man's head up as he spiraled backward. Driven by his lust for blood, Wyn moved in for another attack, hauling his former mentor to his feet by his lapels.

It was then that he felt the sharp sting of steel against his throat.

"Easy now, boyo," Daniels advised, his mouth bleeding at the corner. "We·wouldn't want that pretty head of yours to become separated from the rest of ye."

Wynthrope stilled. The blade had already cut him, and he could feel blood running down his neck. He held the older man's gaze, but kept his silence. He was not afraid of dying, but he was afraid of who Daniels might send after the tiara in his place.

"Now that I have your attention," Daniels was saying, "allow me to tell you how it's going to be. You are going to get me that tiara, understand? I don't give a rat's arse how you have to do it, but you will do it. If you don't, someone is going to get hurt. And by 'someone,' I mean someone you care about. Are we clear on that?"

He didn't dare nod. "Perfectly."

Daniels lowered the knife with a satisfied smile. "Good. I'll check with you in a day or so to make certain you haven't forgotten."

As if the wound on his throat wasn't going to be reminder enough. "You do that."

Wiping the blade on his trousers, Daniels shook his graying head. "Oh boyo, you always were a insolent rascal. That was part of the reason I loved you so much."

"You never loved anyone but yourself."

"Ah, now that's not true. I loved you until you betrayed me. That seems to be a habit o' yours, betrayin' people you claim to care about."

"While you prefer to deceive and lie to the people you claim to care for."

Daniels shrugged. "I only told you what you needed and wanted to hear, son. You filled in the rest by yourself."

It was true. Daniels had known exactly what to say to make Wynthrope believe him. He had also known exactly what strings to pull to make a young man behave how he wanted.

If it was the last thing he did, he would make certain Daniels never duped any young fool again.

"I will get your damn tiara. Now get the hell out of here."

Still wearing that smug smile, Daniels slipped his blade up his sleeve and pressed his hand to the back of his mouth, where blood was now pooling. "You had better take care of that cut on your neck. Wouldn't want you to come down with a fever."

Wynthrope said nothing, even though the old man's mocking laughter made him want to strike out in any way possible. He knew better than to push Daniels. Daniels would be far easier to dupe if he thought he was the one with all the power.

But what Daniels didn't realize was that the balance between them had shifted. Yes, there was the chance that Daniels might harm Moira or one of his brothers, but Wynthrope now knew that there were precautions he could take against such a thing. All he had to do was swallow his pride and admit that he couldn't defeat Daniels alone.

The door clicked shut as Daniels made his exit. Wynthrope waited until he was gone before he pulled his handkerchief from his pocket and used it to staunch the blood seeping down his throat. Pulling it away, he glanced down and grimaced at the sticky, dark red stain. Daniels had cut him worse than he thought. Thank God for cravats, else he'd have to think of a suitable story, and no one would believe his valet had cut him while shaving.

One thing was certain. Daniels had turned this into a personal war by involving Moira. Wynthrope and North and even Dev and Brahm were grown men who knew full well the consequences of their actions. They all had demons from their past they had to face at one time or another, and were prepared to do it if necessary. Moira, however, was an innocent. She had nothing to repent, nothing to regret except trusting him. If it was the last thing he did, he would ensure that she did not pay for his mistakes.

He was tired of being a pawn. It was time fate learned who was really in control.

Chapter 13

The gray light of morning came as surely as an un-
wanted guest. Moira watched its approach with hot,
bleary eyes. Every brightening moment took her further and
further away from the sleep that eluded her. Her mind refused to let her rest, it kept running the night before over and
over in her mind—not all of it, just the best and most painful
parts. She must have remembered Wynthrope's touches a
thousand times.

And she remembered his betrayal twice as many.

Yet as many times as her memory forced her to rewatch it,
there was still a part of her that refused to accept that he
could be as awful as she believed. She was more of an idiot
than she ever thought possible.

Finally, unable to stand lying abed thinking about him any
longer, she threw back the blankets and slipped out of bed.
The air was chill on her bare flesh, and she grabbed the
wrapper draped across the footboard.

A smudge of color caught her eye, and she turned her attention back to the bed as she tied the ribbons of the robe. The linen was stained—the result of her time in Wynthrope's arms. A ruined sheet, that was what their relationship had been reduced to. His perfidy had hurt far more than the taking of her maidenhead. If her heart were able to bleed, the bed would be soaked with crimson.

But this stain wasn't much at all, and far easier to conceal from the eyes of her servants, who would be certain to see it and know the truth.

She took deliberate strides toward her vanity, ignoring the twinge of tenderness between her thighs. It would pass, as would the pain in her heart, although a tad more quickly no doubt.

The decanter of wine was exactly where she had left it and she took it back to the bed, pulling the stopper and gingerly tilting the bottle until rich burgundy trickled from the open neck, spilling onto the sheet and completely obliterating the evidence of her folly.

Then, before the wine could soak the mattress beneath, she pulled the soiled linen from the bed and balled them together, rolling them until all trace of wine and everything else was gone, left in a mound of wrinkled white fabric. Now no one would know. And she could try to pretend that it had never happened.

Her gaze trailed across the carpet, up the wall to the safe. The concealing painting hung open still and she ran to it, slamming it shut with far more force than was necessary. No reminders. Not today.

The water lingering in her bath was cold, but she bathed in it anyway. The need to wash his scent off her was overwhelming and all-consuming. Finally, shivering with chattering teeth, she dried herself and slipped into a clean chemise. She was pulling on her stockings when her maid came in—surprised to find her up at such an hour.

"I couldn't sleep," Moira told her, knowing the girl was bound to tell just as much from the darkness beneath her eyes.

"You're freezing!" the maid admonished and hastily scurried to the fireplace.

Within minutes there was a fire in the hearth and Moira was standing before it, warming her hands as her hair was brushed into crackling waves. The fire took the chill from her skin, but it couldn't warm her inside. Nothing could do that.

Finally dressed and warm, she left her room, leaving the footmen to empty her bath and her maid to take care of her unfortunately stained sheets. *I thought some wine might help me sleep, but I clumsily spilled it instead.* Of course the maid asked no questions. Even if it occurred to her, she would know it wasn't her place.

Downstairs she went to the little table in the parlor where she always liked to take her breakfast. She always asked for just a small serving for herself.

Not today.

"I want ham," she told her housekeeper. "And eggs and sausage. Bring me potatoes as well, fried in with the sausage. Oh, and I want bread. Lots of bread and a pot of coffee."

The poor housekeeper looked at her as though she had lost her mind, but didn't argue.

Moira stared out the window at the freshly fallen snow. The tracks of a lone horse were just barely visible in her drive, the impressions almost totally filled in. The sight was like a rapier through her heart.

"Here's your coffee, my lady."

Already? How long had she been staring out that blast window? "Thank you, Mrs. Wright."

Her fingers trembled as Moira lifted the silver pot, filling her cup with hot, fragrant coffee. Normally she drank it black because it helped keep her slim, but she hated drinking it black. Thankfully Mrs. Wright had thought to include cream and sugar with this morning's offering. Moira added a liberal helping of both. The coffee was heaven to her tongue. It gave her pleasure. She would take whatever contentment she could.

Sometime later, when Moira was gorging on her delicious breakfast, Minnie entered the room. She took one look at the laden table and her sister's bulging cheeks, and her cheerful expression turned to one of distress.

"What has happened?"

"Breakfast," Moira replied around a mouthful of egg and ham. "It is amazing."

Almost hesitantly, Minerva slid into the chair across the table from her, warily eying the banquet laid out between them. "Do you plan to share?"

Moira flashed her a look that promised murder if she dared touch her food. "I'm sure Mrs. Wright will bring you your own breakfast." This food was hers. She had starved herself for too long, denied herself for years to be what she thought she should be. She always tried to be what others wanted her to be. No more. Starting today she was going to be whatever—whoever—the hell she wanted, and right now she wanted to be full for once. No more grumbling in her belly, not for anyone.

But perhaps grumbling was better than this sick feeling.

"Maybe you should take a pause," Minnie suggested.

Swallowing what was in her mouth, Moira nodded. "Perhaps you are right. I am sorry to be such a bear, Minnie. Go ahead and help yourself."

Her sister took a bun from the basket and pulled it apart with her fingers. "Has something happened with you and Mr. Ryland?"

If she talked about him now, she really would be ill. "No."

Minnie's gaze was shrewd. The girl was smarter than she pretended. "So you are gorging yourself silly because . . . ?"

"Because I am tired of starving myself."

"Starving yourself? You do that?"

Moira took a drink of coffee. "Do you not remember how plump I used to be?"

Minnie shook her head. "I've heard it mentioned. I'm fifteen years your junior, remember? You were married and out of the house by the time I was six."

Yes, and by that time Moira was a much slimmer version of herself. "You will just have to take my word for it then. I was fat."

Minnie shrugged. "So was I as a child, but I grew out of it. I never starved myself."

"Mama must not have minded fat children when she got to you."

Minnie's eyes widened. "You truly despise her, don't you?"

Yesterday Moira would have said no, but now . . . "Yes. I married a man I did not love to get away from that woman—and her husband. I denied myself food to make myself thin because she would *not* stop harping about it!" She slammed her palm on the table before snatching up another piece of ham with her fingers and cramming it into her mouth.

Poor Minnie stared at her with an expression that was concerned but bordered on fearful. "Moira, you are not yourself."

Moira swallowed. "That is where you are wrong, Min. I am about to become myself. Does that make any sense to you?"

The younger woman shook her head.

"I am going to stop caring what other people think of me, how other people think I should act and look. From now on I will do exactly as I want, say what I want and eat what I want." Proving her point, she took a big bite of buttered roll.

Minnie's expression turned to one of delight. "Good for you! Now, are you going to tell me what brought this about?"

"It is amazing the epiphanies one can have during a sleepless night."

"I thought you looked tired. What kept you awake?"

Her sister, God love her, was obviously not going to stop asking until Moira told her something. Besides being nosy, Minnie actually seemed worried about her, and as much as Moira wished to conceal her shame, she did not want to cause her sister concern.

"I do not wish to discuss it, but I will tell you that it is very likely that Mr. Ryland will never darken our door again." Amazingly, she managed to keep her voice from cracking even though her eyes burned at just the mention of his name.

"Oh, Moira." Minnie's brow furrowed as she reached across the table, laying her soft warm hand against Moira's own. "I am so very sorry."

Moira shrugged. She had to assume an air of disinterestedness, else she'd burst into tears, and she refused to give Wynthrope the satisfaction. She had cried for him enough after his departure; she was not going to waste any more tears on him now. She'd wager her entire fortune that he wasn't sobbing over her this morning, so why should she conduct herself differently?

"Men are swine, Minnie. I am convinced of that."

Her sister's face fell a bit. "I am sorry to hear you say that because I have found one I should like very much to spend the rest of my life with."

That proclamation was just the slap Moira needed to break free of the melancholy gripping her. "I beg your pardon?"

Minnie fidgeted in her chair, a becoming blush blossoming on her smooth cheeks. "Lucas Scott has asked me to marry him."

Moira's mouth fell open. "Oh my goodness!" Pushing

back her chair she jumped to her feet. Minnie followed suit and soon the two were laughing and embracing.

"He wants to do things properly," Minnie continued, taking a step back so the sisters were eye to eye. "Moira, as my guardian here in London, may I count on you to give him permission?"

"Of course!" Everything she had seen and heard of this young man indicated that he was a perfect match for her headstrong sister. And he was the perfect age! She had been so worried Minnie would end up with someone too old for her.

Thank God Wynthrope hadn't set his sights on Minnie instead. Moira would have to kill him if he hurt her sister.

"Oh, thank you!" Minnie gave her another happy squeeze. "But what about Mama and Papa? Will he not want their permission as well?"

Minnie rolled her doelike eyes. "Mama and Papa have never denied me anything, Moira. They certainly will not deny me the husband I want, especially when he comes from such connections and has an ample fortune of his own."

She had a point. After all, they had practically thrown Moira at Tony when they discovered his desire to marry her. They hadn't asked any questions except in relation to his wealth.

"Besides," Minnie was saying, "Your blessing means more to me than theirs."

Tears threatened again, and this time Moira let them come, because they were tears of joy and love, not despair. She hugged her sister tightly to her, laughing and crying at the same time. How had the spoiled little girl who had come to stay with her only months before grown into such a wonderful young woman?

"I owe my happiness all to you, my dear. If you hadn't taken me in hand I never would have found Lucas. Nor would he have wanted me."

"Me?" Moira echoed, pushing her sister to arm's length. "What did I do?"

Minnie smiled lovingly. "You refused to give in to me. You made me see people differently. I saw how much people adore you and I knew that you were the kind of woman I wanted to become."

Moira's throat tightened. "Oh."

Laughing, Minnie gave her another squeeze. "That does not mean I did not resent you for it as well at first, but I am oh so thankful for it now."

Another embrace followed, and the sisters were laughing again.

"Good heavens, whatever is going on?"

Separating, Minnie and Moira shared a smile before opening their arms to a curious Nathaniel. "Minnie is going to be married, Nate."

His cherubic face lit with happiness, Nathaniel came to them with open arms, stepping into their joint embrace and joining in the laughter.

"My dear Minerva, what wonderful news! You must tell me everything. And after breakfast we will begin shopping for your trousseau. Dear God, who is all that food for?"

Moira followed his gaze to the table with a chuckle. "Me. Would you care to help Minnie and me finish it?"

"My dear girl, you would never in a million years fit all that food inside of you. Of course I will help."

The three of them sat around the table, picking from the various plates of hearty fare that were beginning to cool, and discussed plans for Minnie's wedding. Nathaniel had a much better flair for style than Moira did, so she bowed to his superior judgment on most things, except that the bridesmaids should wear puce.

"I do not care how popular a color it is, it reminds me of half mourning and I refuse to wear it." Folding her arms over her chest, Moira leaned back in her chair. "I am sorry, but that is all there is to it."

Minnie and Nathaniel shared a glance. "There will be no persuading her, Nathaniel. She is quite determined to please only herself from now on."

That raised a pale brow. "Has she now?" He turned his attention to Moira. "What brought this on?"

"Is it not obvious?" Minnie took a sip of coffee from Moira's cup. "That scoundrel Ryland has broken her heart."

"Minnie," Moira's tone was rife with warning. Of course she intended to discuss things with Nathaniel, but not right now, not while the pain was still so fresh.

Nathaniel's concern was obvious as he reached out and took her hand in his own. He didn't have to speak for Moira to know exactly what he was thinking. He was wondering if she had made love with Wynthrope.

She was spared having to say or do anything by the arrival of Mrs. Wright. "I beg your pardon, my lady, but Mr. Ryland is here. Shall I send him in?"

The bottom fell out of Moira's stomach. "Which Mr. Ryland, Mrs. Wright?"

The housekeeper looked as though that should be obvious. "Mr. Wynthrope Ryland, my lady."

Gathering all the courage she could to still the quaking in her limbs, Moira began to rise from the table. She wasn't interested in anything he had to say, no matter how badly part of her wanted to see his lovely face again, but she was going to tell him that he was no longer welcome in her home—and to never step foot in it again.

Nathaniel's hand on her arm stopped her. "Let me."

Ire rose in her chest. "You do not have to protect me, Nathaniel."

Her friend stood. "Dearest, I know that. But Mr. Ryland may need protecting from you." His expression changed, as did his tone, from teasing to genuine caring. His voice was hushed, for her ears alone as he spoke, "Moira, if he sees you now he is going to know you spent the night lying awake because of him. Do you want to give him that advantage?"

She hadn't thought of it that way. Trust dear Nathaniel to do the thinking for her. "No." She squeezed his hand. "Thank you, my friend."

He flashed her a smile and then breezed off to face his adversary. Moira sank into her chair and gazed across the table at her sister.

"Maybe he came because he is remorseful," Minnie suggested.

Moira would have laughed, if she were capable of it. "Maybe," she agreed.

But she doubted it.

"May I help you, Mr. Ryland?"

Wynthrope turned from studying one of the late viscount's paintings and faced the voice. It wasn't Moira. Of course, he had known that the minute he heard the footsteps in the hall. His heart would have jumped if the steps had belonged to Moira. His heart had stayed dead.

So she had sent out Nathaniel Caylan, her loyal friend and protector, to face him, had she? He supposed he should have expected as much, but he had half hoped that she had spent as wretched a night as he—maybe that she missed him as much as he missed her as well.

Obviously that was too much to ask.

He skipped all pretense of pleasantries. "She refuses to see me."

Nathaniel nodded, even though it hadn't been a question. "I am afraid so."

He didn't sound regretful at all. Perhaps Caylan hadn't

been sent. Perhaps he had offered to confront him. "What did she tell you?"

The fairer man's smile was cold and unfriendly. "Nothing. She did not have to."

What did that mean? "Is she all right?"

"No, Mr. Ryland, she is not, but she will be. Do not trouble yourself with that."

Wynthrope nodded. The man made it sound as if that might be something Wynthrope would hope against, but he was wrong. He hoped to God that Moira recovered from his betrayal. And more quickly than he himself would.

He should have expected this kind of reception. He hadn't actually thought she'd come to him with open arms and forgive him, had he? Of course not, but maybe a part of him had hoped just a little . . .

"I will not keep you any longer then," he said, donning his hat. "Just tell her that I will keep my promise, will you? And tell her . . . tell her that the white king is hers if she wants it."

Nathaniel frowned. "All right."

Wynthrope managed a half smile. "Thank you." He turned to go.

"Mr. Ryland?"

He faced him again. "Yes?"

Nathaniel's expression was void of any warmth at all. "Whatever it was you did to her, I hope you live long enough to have someone do it to you."

Another smile. "So do I."

He left the other man to think that one over and took his leave. Outside the morning was gray and crisp, and Wynthrope wasted no time as he strode down the freshly cleared steps to his horse.

He cast a glance at the house as King picked his way down the snow-covered drive. His heart gave a mighty jolt as he met the gaze of the woman standing in the parlor window. He couldn't see her clearly but he knew merely by the moss green of her dress, the stiff set of her narrow shoulders, that it was Moira. Then she turned her back to him and was gone.

It was a dismissive gesture, one that would have been disheartening to a more intelligent man, but Wynthrope wasn't disheartened.

He was just happy to have laid eyes on her one more time.

"What the hell do you want?"

Leaning heavily on a gold-topped cane, Brahm smiled wryly. "Good afternoon, little brother. May I join you?"

It was a testament to just how low Wynthrope had sunk that he said yes. He didn't want to be alone with his thoughts any longer, and if Brahm was the only distraction available to him, then he'd take it.

They were at Blakney's coffee house, the warm interior rife with the smells of freshly brewed coffee and fine cigars. Brahm pulled a slim cigar from a silver case before offering the case to Wynthrope. Normally Wynthrope didn't smoke, but these were expensive and it gave him some degree of pleasure to take something from his brother. He took one with muttered thanks.

"That must have pained you," Brahm remarked with a rueful smile. "Thanking me for anything."

Wynthrope simply scowled in reply and lit his cigar from the lamp on the table. It was late afternoon, and night was already descending upon the city.

He didn't really know why he resented Brahm so much. Yes, there had been the constant comparisons growing up, and the constant scandals his eldest brother brought down upon the family, but Brahm himself had never tried to make Wynthrope feel inferior. Perhaps that was why he resented him as he did. Perhaps if Brahm had been a bit more of a bully or a bastard, Wynthrope would be able to tolerate more than a few minutes in his presence.

Brahm ordered a pot of coffee for the two of them and lit his own smoke. When the pot arrived, he poured two cups and slid one across the table to Wynthrope.

"You don't have any whiskey, do you?" Wynthrope asked.

His brother shot him a pointed look. "What do you think?"

At one time Brahm would have pulled a flask from his pocket and dumped half of it in a cup and then poured an ounce of coffee on top. Now he drank his coffee black, and free of liquor of any kind. Wynthrope knew that, he was just being cruel.

"I like being cruel to you." Why the hell was he admitting it? Because he was spoiling for a fight and hoping his brother would give it. He was so angry at himself for the mess he was in, he needed to abuse someone other than himself or he'd explode.

Brahm's brows rose as he inhaled deeply on his cigar. "You don't say."

"Yes. I am not sure why."

His brother leaned back in his chair, his reddish-brown eyes flickering with mild amusement. "I always likened it to the child who torments those he loves most."

That was a joke. "You think I love you?"

Brahm exhaled a thin stream of smoke, his expression changeless. Anyone else would undoubtedly have been hurt by such a blunt retort, but not his brother. "As much as I love you."

What a perfect response. Brahm usually had a perfect reply for everything. It was one of the many things he had always envied yet resented about his brother. Wynthrope might be the most caustic wit in the family, but Brahm was the one who could make an insult sound like flattery and vice versa.

"You love me?" It was damn near impossible to keep the disbelief from his tone. "You, the one who beat on me whenever you had a chance when we were children? The same one who always had to be the best in everything? God forbid I ever best you at anything. You blackened my eye that time I beat you in a foot race."

Brahm shrugged. "I never claimed to always *like* you. That's a different matter entirely."

Wynthrope tapped ash off his cigar into the glass dish on the table. "I never would have guessed."

Brahm smiled at his sarcasm. "You were always such a snarly little ponce."

He couldn't stop the sneer. "And you were always perfect."

Disbelief lit Brahm's features. "According to who?"

He couldn't really be that dense, could he? "Father."

Brahm inhaled smoke with a sour expression. "He was wrong."

"I know." He couldn't seem to stop himself from saying cutting things to his brother, even though he felt badly for them afterward. What did he want, for Brahm to tell him that he wasn't better? It wasn't Brahm's place to do that. The only person who could tell him that and have him even remotely believe it was dead.

Fragrant smoke drifted from his brother's lips across the table. "Yet you resent me for it. He made you feel inferior and you blamed me."

Wynthrope fiddled with his own cigar. "Well, yes."

"And he made me feel that I had to be the best in everything or I wasn't worthy. That's why I blackened your eye that day, because I knew he'd berate me for it later. I sometimes hated you and the other boys for not having such expectations upon you."

Wynthrope stared at him, clenching his jaw to keep it from falling open. He had never known that their father pushed Brahm to excel. He never knew that Brahm resented him in return.

"It was an unfair situation for both of us, do you not think?"

When he put it that way, it did sound unjust, yes. Probably better not to respond.

Brahm smiled. "That is what I thought. I would apologize but since I've done nothing wrong, I won't."

Wynthrope scowled at him. He couldn't simply blame everything on a dead man and erase all the bad feelings. "Get off that high horse of yours, Brahm. You were an arse when we were boys and you're an even bigger one now that you're sober."

His brother simply grinned. It was an infectious expression that soon had Wynthrope's lips curving despite his better judgment. This was the most time he had spent in Brahm's presence for years, and he found his brother strangely comforting. It was probably because he would rather be with anyone than by himself, or maybe it was Moira's influence. She was such a good person, always willing to try to understand someone before judging him. He never gave much thought to how he treated Brahm when they were younger, only that Brahm was the favorite. He had North to be his friend and companion, and sometimes Devlin. Who did Brahm have? Their father was at him constantly to be the best at everything, to learn how to be the next viscount—and in hindsight, the old man probably was the one who taught him to be a drunk as well, or at least drove him to it. Wynthrope should have been more of a friend to his brother. He should have been a better brother.

"I still don't like you," he muttered, fighting a smile.

Brahm laughed. "Ponce."

"Arse."

The situation between them was so comfortable that for a moment, Wynthrope thought maybe he could confide in his eldest brother in a way he couldn't confide in the other two. Brahm didn't know him as well as North and Devlin, and he certainly had no knowledge of his past as North did.

Bracing his forearms on the scarred surface of the table, Wynthrope leaned forward, his cigar temporarily forgotten in the dish. "Have you ever done something that keeps coming back to haunt you no matter how you try to change?"

Brahm regarded him with an expression of irony. "Well, not too many people know this about me, but I was a horrible drunkard at one time."

Wynthrope might have chuckled at his sarcasm if Brahm hadn't been just such a man once upon a time. Of course his brother would understand what it was like to not be able to escape his past, and Brahm had the disadvantage of having his mistakes being public knowledge.

Brahm puffed on his cigar. "Are you being haunted?"

Wynthrope nodded, his lips twisting with regret. "Yes. I thought I had buried it deep enough, but it is back. Do you think I should send for a priest?"

His brother didn't smile at his attempt at humor. "I won't ask you for details, because if you wanted me to know them you would have offered them already, but I will tell you this, your past is exactly that, your past. If you let it affect your present, however, it starts to affect your future, and that is what gets you into trouble."

Sounded like horse shite to Wynthrope, but Brahm had begun to turn his life around, perhaps he knew something Wynthrope didn't. "How do I keep it from affecting my present?"

"By confronting it head on. By refusing to allow it to control you."

"But other people could be hurt."

"There are always those who might be injured, it's part of life. You keep basing your decisions on those people and you are not living your life, they are."

His brother struck too close to the truth. "My God, you are positively enlightening."

Brahm grimaced as he crushed out his cigar. "You know, your mockery does nothing more than tell me I'm right."

Wynthrope glanced down at the table. A sudden feeling of contriteness had taken hold of him and refused to let go. "You are right. I wish you were not. I wish I could be the kind of man who does not make those kinds of decisions, but I am."

"I never would have thought that of you." Brahm's voice was rife with surprise. "I always thought you did exactly what you wanted with no thought to anyone else."

Wynthrope cast him a sideways glance. "That is how I wanted you to see me."

Silence fell between them, and Wynthrope finished off his cigar and the remains of his coffee.

Brahm poured him a fresh cup. "Does this sudden quest for betterment have anything to do with Lady Aubourn?"

Was there any point in lying? "Everything."

"Why so miserable about it?"

He ran a hand over his face. Damn, but he was tired. "Because I made a decision and she suffered for it."

The gleam in Brahm's dark eyes was knowing. "And now you are suffering for her."

His brother was astute, he would give him that. "Something like that."

"Can you not simply talk to her?"

Did he not realize he had already thought of that? "I tried. She refused to see me."

Brahm shifted in his chair. "So keep trying."

"That is easy for you to say."

Turning the hand on the table palm up, Brahm shrugged. "It is just as easy for you to do."

"And if she keeps refusing, what then?" Moira might be an understanding person and willing to give others a chance, but he had greatly wounded her, and she had her pride just like any other woman—pride that could make her very, very stubborn.

His brother leaned forward. There was maybe a foot between them and that was it. "Do you really want to try to make things right with her?"

Wynthrope's voice was little more than a hoarse whisper. "Yes." Before he lost her, he hadn't quite realized how much she was coming to mean to him, but now the idea of living without her, of facing endless days without her in them, was like contemplating the deepest pit of hell.

Brahm's finger beat against the table, punctuating his words as he spoke, "Then you keep trying, and she will eventually see you."

Oh yes, that was a wonderful idea. Wynthrope sneered. "Because I've worn her down?"

Brahm looked as though he'd dearly love to cuff him. "Because she'll know you are sincere."

Would she? If he kept trying, if he refused to let her go so easily, would Moira finally give him a second chance? Would she listen to his whole sordid tale? Would she believe the truth after he had deceived her so badly? He could only hope so.

Right now hope was all he had.

Chapter 14

Rain came upon London with a vengeance, turning the snow to slick ice, then to thick dirty slush before washing it away completely. Even when the streets ran clean and there was no snow to be found in any nook or gutter, the rain continued. Sometimes it was an almost imperceptible drizzle, invisible to the eye until one felt the sheen of it on one's face or saw the diaphanous mist covering one's coat. Other times it was stinging, frozen pellets, or fat, cold drops that chilled and drenched until it seemed there was no chance of ever being dry and warm again.

Sometimes, as was the case today, the rain fell in sheets; a wall of water that poured down from the heavens, flooding drains and casting the entire city in a dismal, sopping-wet gray.

Moira stood at the window, watching the black horse pick its way down her sopping drive. The man on its back had his collar pulled up around his face, the brim of his hat pulled low. What did he hope to accomplish by acting so foolishly? He should be in a carriage where it was warm and dry. Did he think to win her sympathy by appearing on horseback, subjecting himself to the elements? Well, it was working, damn him. He was going to catch his death this way, the idiot.

As was becoming his habit, he turned his face toward the window as he rode past. The endless streams of rain made it difficult to discern his features, but Moira felt the impact of his gaze as surely as a blast of sunshine through the clouds. Her heart imagined it could see sorrow in his eyes, penance even. She knew better than to trust it. Her heart had already proven itself to be blind as a bat.

This time he turned away before she did. It was a small thing, surely not that significant, but it felt as though the world had tipped beneath her. Was he losing patience so quickly? She had thought he'd continue this charade a little longer than this. Perhaps she had underestimated him in all aspects, not just where trust was concerned.

"I do not need to tell you who that was."

Smiling sadly, Moira turned from the window to face Nathaniel as he entered the room. Thank God for her friend. He had been a source of much-needed strength for her these past few days.

"Eventually he will stop coming." As soon as he saw that it would take more than a few martyrish rides in the rain to turn her head, he would give up.

Although why he was trying in the first place was a mystery. Did he hope to somehow worm his way back into her life so he could steal the tiara, or was he truly sorry? Perhaps she should simply face him long enough to ask him herself, but she was frightened of what else might happen if she saw him. That weak, puny side of her missed him so very terribly and wanted to believe that he was as much a victim as she, that it was sure to believe anything he told her. And she didn't know if the rest of her was strong enough yet to resist him, so strong was the pull to forgive him, to take him in her arms and tell him everything was all right.

She wanted there to be some awful reason that he needed her tiara. She wanted to be right about him. She wanted him to be the man she believed him to be. That was why she refused to see him, because she feared she would find out just how wrong she was.

Or, God forbid, that she had been right after all.

More importantly, he kept coming to see her. Did he not realize the risk he was taking? Most women would be threatened by his attention and run straight to the authorities, but not her. She didn't have enough sense to be afraid of him—not in a physical manner. What was he trying to prove? That there was more to his betrayal then he had told her? That he truly cared for her?

So which of them was the bigger idiot now? Him for riding in the rain, or her for wanting to believe his visits actually meant something?

Nathaniel poured himself a glass of sherry from the crystal decanter on the sideboard. "For the past three days he has come to see you, and every time you have me turn him away. I do not think he is a man who gives up easily. Sherry?"

She shook her head. "No, thank you. You are right, he does not give up easily, but sooner or later, he will have to."

Her friend tipped his brows as though he thought cessation might be a long time coming. "Are you certain you will not see him?"

"I cannot." She hugged herself with her arms. If only she could get this chill from her bones. "The pain is still too fresh. If I see him now, I will not be able to discern lies from the truth."

Nathaniel sipped his sherry, his expression sympathetic. "Do you not at least want to know what he has said?"

"No." She hugged herself tighter. "What did he say?"

"Let me see . . . oh yes. Yesterday he said that he would keep coming back until you saw him. Today he simply said to tell you he missed you." Another swallow of sherry. His brow puckered as though he were in deep thought.

Moira's heart pinched. He'd said that, really? It had to be lies, but she wanted it to be truth. She was so torn. Her heart said one thing, her mind another. To which did she listen? Or better still, how to get the pair of them to just shut up for a while?

"Oh—and that first day he said to tell you that he would keep his promise, and that the white king is yours, whatever that means." Shrugging, Nathaniel topped up his glass with more wine.

Closing her eyes, Moira struggled against the spinning that threatened to claim her. She knew what it meant—what he had wanted her to think it meant. He was always white, every time they played chess. Often times he referred to her as the black queen, and in jest, to himself as the white king.

"He means that *he* is mine. *If* I want him."

Nathaniel's lips parted as a pained expression crossed his face. "Oh dear. That is terribly romantic. Terribly romantic indeed." He gave his head a rueful shake. "I swear, Moira, if you can resist this man you are a stronger person than I."

"He just said those things in hopes that I would be stupid enough to believe. He wants the tiara, nothing more." If that were true, why did neither her heart nor her head quite believe it?

Obviously Nathaniel didn't believe it either. "If he wanted nothing more than the tiara, why not just come get it some night?"

"He doesn't dare." Bravado didn't suit her. It sounded stilted coming out of her mouth.

"Whyever not?" Nathaniel's tone wasn't cruel, merely curious as he walked away from the sideboard. "He has you over a barrel, or at the very best the two of you are at an impasse. You cannot turn him in without risking having your own secret revealed and he cannot reveal your secret without risk to him as well."

Moira made a face. "As though anyone would believe me. No doubt he'd make me sound like a fool—a vindictive woman he tossed aside once he'd bedded her."

Nathaniel considered her words. "Which makes it all the more plain that he is after more than the tiara."

It was all Moira could do not to strike herself in the chest as her heart tripped hopefully against her ribs. "All it makes plain, Nathaniel, is that he is not to be trusted. He can't very well come steal it with you here, can he?"

He raised his glass to her to make a point. "Something which cannot continue much longer or the scandal will have us married."

"Just a little while longer, please." How whiny she sounded, just like a child. She was a grown woman and had survived on her own for the past two years. "Just until I'm sure he will not come back."

Nathaniel must have missed the panic in her voice because he continued on with his terrifying hypothesis, "If he's half the man I think he is, he will keep coming back. He's not after some bit of swag, Moira. He's after you."

"That's not true." If she hugged herself any tighter she'd faint. "The reason he hasn't tried to steal the tiara is that he wants to avoid a physical altercation with you."

Her friend laughed at that. "Darling, *you* are more manly than I am. Wynthrope Ryland is not afraid of making me scream like a little girl. If anything, you would end up protecting me from him. He wouldn't risk alienating you even more by harming me."

Nathaniel made him seem superhuman rather than a mere

mortal—a fact that made her sneer in response. "Wynthrope Ryland is not above doing anything to get what he wants."

"Then you had better hope it is just the tiara he wants." Nathaniel dropped onto the sofa, without spilling a drop of sherry. "Because if he wants you, that man is going to have you."

Moira turned back to the window. God help her, but she hoped he was right.

Wynthrope walked into North and Octavia's house in Covent Garden half hoping, half dreading to find Moira there as well. Unfortunately—or fortunately, depending on how he looked at it—she wasn't.

In fact it appeared to be a family-only affair—family being Devlin and Blythe's respective families. Miles and Varya were there, as well as Brahm.

It was unlike Octavia to host a dinner party and not invite Moira, so why wasn't she there? Had Moira told Octavia that she would rather stick pins under her nails than see him? Or was something else afoot? If it weren't for Miles and Varya's presence, he'd suspect his family of plotting against him. But to what end? He had yet to confide anything about Daniels and his blackmail, and aside from Brahm, he hadn't talked to any of them about Moira. Brahm might not be his favorite person in the world, or even in this room, but he trusted his brother to keep his confidence.

North was on him the minute he stepped into the drawing room and greeted everyone.

"What did you do to Moira?" he demanded in a harsh whisper as he yanked Wynthrope into the far corner of the room. It had been a long time since North had resorted to physical brutality with him—not since that night he discovered Wynthrope was the thief he'd been chasing.

Wynthrope made a show of brushing the wrinkles out of

the sleeve of his coat. It gave him a moment to regain his composure. "What makes you think I did anything?"

"Because the last time Octavia called on her she said Moira was not herself. She was withdrawn and pale."

Wynthrope's conscience winced at the description. The idea of his Moira as anything but vibrant and warm was heartbreaking. To know that he was the cause was insufferable.

"Perhaps she ate something that did not agree with her." The words were harsh, even to his own ears.

"Damn it, Wyn. Do not play the cold bastard with me."

"What makes you think I am playing?" It was not a flippant remark, it was an honest question.

North withdrew a step, frowning as he regarded him. "You are not yourself either."

This was not the time and place for this. "If I am not myself, then I have no idea who I possibly could be." Lately he'd been wondering that very thing himself. Who was he? Was he the man Daniels thought he was, or the man Moira thought he was? Or was he the man everyone else thought he was? Perhaps some strange combination of all the above? Perhaps that was why he hardly seemed to know himself. Perhaps that was why he didn't seem to be able to decide what to do, because there were so many options depending on whom he was trying to please.

North gazed at him as though he didn't know who he was either. "Something has happened. What is it?"

Wynthrope pulled a face. "That overly developed imagination of yours is running away with you once again. Nothing has happened."

"It is never my imagination where you are concerned. If anything good falls in your lap you always seem to toss it away."

Toss? North thought he had *tossed* Moira away? Ire sparked deep within him. Did his brother think he would willingly give up someone like Moira if he didn't have to? It was *his* fault Wynthrope had lost her. If North hadn't stuck his face in all those years ago, Daniels wouldn't have had anything to blackmail him with. Of course, he would have had to leave the country or suffer time in prison, but what did that matter now? He'd rather be in France where there was no Moira Tyndale, or wasting away in some fetid cell, than bear the pain of knowing he had hurt Moira.

Even her parents had never hurt her so badly; she had said so herself.

"You want to know if I tossed Moira, is that it?" he asked with a forced sneer. "Of course I tossed her. Tossed her skirts over her head and—"

North held up his hand, his expression one of disgust. He didn't say a word before turning his back on Wynthrope and rejoining the group. Wynthrope watched him go with less regret than he should have. There was no pleasure in angering his brother, but at least he had saved himself from answering questions he didn't want to answer.

All he wanted was one night without the memory of her filling his head, plaguing his thoughts. He should be able to do that among his family, even if all he could think about in this room was how he had caught Moira as she tumbled off a ladder while hanging mistletoe. He had known the second his arms closed around her that he would never be satisfied with simply holding her, so he had tried to steal a kiss, and when he finally claimed it, he had known that he would never be satisfied with just one.

And now that he knew what it was like to be inside her, part of her, he would never be satisfied by any other woman ever again. He had to have her back, even if it was just for one fleeting moment. He had to have her again.

Christ, he had just arrived and already he was consumed by thoughts of her. How could he have thought that he could escape her here? He could leave, but there was nowhere he could go that she would not follow. She was in his head, in his heart, and she dogged his steps and haunted his every waking moment.

Today he had been the one to look away first, just because he could not bear to watch her turn away from him again. Hell was not some fiery pit of damnation. No, hell was knowing you had hurt someone you cared for and not knowing if you could ever make it right.

Salvation came in the unlikely form of Brahm. Something nudged Wynthrope's calf, and he looked down to see the tip of a cane pressing into his leg. He raised his gaze, and his eldest brother seemed to smile without moving his lips.

"I was going through the attic the other day and found some old effects of Father's. I thought perhaps you might like to come by and sort through them."

Was it Wynthrope's imagination, or was everyone watching to see how he would react to Brahm? It wouldn't do to be too friendly, besides, just because he had confided in Brahm didn't mean he *liked* him all of a sudden. Still, he couldn't seem to summon the same amount of resentment toward him either.

"Why would I want to do that?" As if their father would have wanted him to have any of it.

Brahm tilted his head, his expression mildly mocking. "Because you are the only one I could think of who might appreciate an antique chess set."

Wynthrope's eyes widened. Their father's chess set? Brahm wanted him to have it? He loved that set. As a boy he would sit by himself and play with the pieces. His father would sometimes play with him. It was the only thing they ever did together. Brahm hated chess—probably because it was something else Wynthrope was better at than he. Had their father berated him for that as well?

He schooled his expression to hide his eagerness, but not before he knew Brahm had seen it, damn him. He nodded, the movements jerky. "I will come tomorrow if that is convenient."

To his credit, Brahm's smile was nothing more than a smile. There was no smugness, no overt emotion. No one in the room would ever know that the dynamic between them had changed the slightest bit—not by looking at Brahm.

"Good. There are some other things you might be interested in as well, some books and whatnot. I'm sure father would rather they be in the hands of someone capable of appreciating them." Then, before Wynthrope could even try to choke out his thanks, Brahm pivoted on his heel and walked over to a winged chair with a pronounced limp.

Wynthrope watched his brother as he walked away. Brahm's leg must be bothering him in this wet, cold weather. It had been crushed in the carriage accident that killed their father. Both Brahm and their father had been drunk at the time, and to Wynthrope's knowledge, his eldest brother hadn't had a drink since. Brahm never spoke of the accident, at least not that he knew of. Did he ever wonder if he might have been able to do something? Did guilt ever gnaw at his insides as he ran the scenario over and over in his head, trying to think of something he might have done differently? Or had he been so drunk he couldn't remember a damn thing?

And why did Wyn care? He had never given this any thought in the past, so why did it matter now if his brother suffered at all? No one blamed Brahm for their father's death. The accident could have killed him even if he'd been sober. Of course, the accident might not have happened if one of them had been sober. Rumor had it they were racing another carriage when it happened. No one knew for certain. Brahm couldn't seem to remember and there had been no one else present when the wreck was found.

Wonderful. Now he was obsessing over Brahm instead of Moira. He really needed to get ahold of himself. At this rate he'd soon take an interest in North and Octavia's marriage or start inviting Brahm to dinner, and then they'd have to cart him off to Bedlam because he'd gone mad as a loon.

Thankfully, Octavia's voice cut through his thoughts. "Blythe, Devlin, why do you not tell us why you wanted to have us all together tonight?"

Wynthrope's gaze went to his youngest brother and his smiling bride. They sat side by side on a sofa like the king and queen of some mythological race of giants, trading glances as though they shared some great secret.

Devlin put his arm around Blythe's shoulders as she flushed. "In eight months you all are going to have a new niece or nephew to dote over."

There were gasps all around and the women rushed to Blythe with hugs and congratulations. Even Devlin was not saved from their giddy exuberance. They reached up and seized the back of his neck, pulling him down so they could buss his cheek and squeeze him without mercy. The men were more subdued, offering Blythe a kiss on the cheek and their hands to Devlin, except for Brahm, who had always acted a bit more fatherly toward his youngest brother. He caught the taller man in a one-armed embrace and slapped him happily on the back.

After offering his own felicitations, Wynthrope stood back and watched the celebration with a definite feeling of separation. Miles and Varya were ecstatic. They had children of their own and were overjoyed that little Edward and baby Irena were going to have a cousin to play with. North and Octavia, the newlyweds, had yet to start their family, but it was apparent from their expressions that they planned to very soon.

Wynthrope watched them with a strange sense of bewilderment and envy. Having a child was not a new invention. People had been doing it for years, so he wasn't quite certain why everyone was carrying on so. Of course he understood that it was a very happy occasion for his family, but he really didn't think it warranted all this fuss.

At the same time, he wanted them to stop carrying on because the more everyone gushed, the more agitated he became. He envied Devlin and Blythe, just as he envied North and Octavia and Miles and Varya. He envied anyone lucky enough to have found his life mate—anyone fortunate enough to receive unconditional love and trust. He wanted to be such a person, and he really didn't think it would ever happen. One couldn't just be given love, one had to earn it, and he had no idea whatsoever how to go about doing that.

"I suppose you will be next," Brahm said as he came up beside him, also watching the laughing bunch just a few feet away.

Wynthrope cast him a sideways glance. "Doubtful. My money's on you."

Brahm chuckled at that. "Who would want an old wreck like me?"

"A rich, titled wreck," Wynthrope reminded him.

"A *scandalous*, rich, titled wreck."

Wynthrope shrugged. "I'm sure there are more than a few mamas who would love to toss their daughters into your path." There was that word again, "toss."

"You are fairly wealthy in your own right." Brahm's tone was casual. "And if I should die without issue . . ."

Wynthrope turned his head with a horrified expression. "You won't. Promise me you won't."

His brother laughed. "Perhaps you will die before me and the title can go on to Devlin's son." They both knew it didn't matter if North and Octavia produced a dozen sons, none of North's issue could inherit the title.

He nodded. That sounded much better. There was no way he wanted the responsibility of the title to fall upon his own shoulders. "I still believe you shall produce progeny of your own, however. I rather like the idea of you being plagued by a passel of screaming brats." He turned his head to watch the others once more.

He heard the smile in his brother's voice. "I could wish the same on you."

Wynthrope shook his head. "It will never happen."

Silence fell between them as they stood apart from the rest of the family. No one seemed to notice that they weren't as involved as everyone else.

"Thank you for the chess set," Wynthrope said after a few moments.

"You are welcome. There is only one thing I ask in return."

Wynthrope frowned. He should have known there would be a catch. "What?"

Brahm shot him a meaningful glance. "That you will not give up pursuing your viscountess. I should like very much to see her as the mother of your screaming brats."

And with that, he limped away. Wynthrope watched him go with a wry expression. His brother certainly had a flair for exits that was to be envied.

Sometime later, after they had finished celebrating the news of Devlin and Blythe's impending parenthood with dinner and wine and raucous conversation, Wynthrope took his leave. He was the first to depart, but he couldn't bear to be surrounded by such loud, happy people any longer. Everyone wished him a good night, except for North who was obviously still very vexed with him. He told Wynthrope he would call on him in the morning. Wynthrope could scarcely contain his enthusiasm.

His carriage was brought around and he climbed into the warm interior, draping the lap robe over him as he rapped on the roof. He'd caught a bit of a chill riding home from Moira's that afternoon and it lingered still in his bones. It served him right for going on horseback, but he thought it might earn him a little sympathy from her if she saw how truly repentant he was. He would know better next time.

When he alighted from the carriage in front of his own residence, he was surprised to see someone lying on the steps to the building. He was not the only bachelor who lived there, so at first he wondered if it might be one of the other tenants, passed out drunk. It was a rather cold night, and he stooped down to wake the poor blighter.

It was then that he noticed that the person's clothing was dirty and torn in places, and stained with blood. If this was a drunkard, he had been in a bit of a scuffle that evening.

Wynthrope rolled the body over carefully, not wanting to add further damage if the person was injured. As the face came into view, he saw that this person was indeed injured. The features were swollen and bruised and almost entirely covered in blood so thick even the rain had failed to wash it away.

Light from the lamp above illuminated the battered face and then Wynthrope saw who it was.

"Christ, no."

Minnie and her young man joined Moira for dinner that evening. Nathaniel had made plans to see Matthew, and Moira couldn't find it in her heart to ask him to cancel just because she was afraid Wynthrope might come to call. She would have to face him eventually. Perhaps sooner was better, while she still had the pain of his deception keeping her strong.

Just in case the pain wasn't strong enough, she had Minnie and her soon-to-be-betrothed to hide behind.

It didn't take long after Lucas Scott's arrival for Moira to decide he was the perfect match for her sister. At five and twenty he was young enough to relate to Minnie and enjoy many of the same pastimes, but he was also old enough that he had a great deal of responsibility laid across his shoulders. He was not one to be easily fooled or steered from his course, and he was as stubborn as Minnie herself, which would come in handy whenever the two of them argued.

Such a handsome fellow as well. His golden good looks and sparkling blue eyes were the perfect contrast to Minnie's dark hair and eyes and pale skin. And he smiled a lot, which was always a good sign. His family was large and very close, from what Moira had been able to glean from Minnie. He got on well with both his parents and all his siblings—an enviable situation for anyone in the Banning family indeed. It would do Minnie good to be around a loving family.

But the largest trait in his favor was his obvious adoration of her sister. Moira was pleased beyond words at how Lucas lavished attention on Minnie. He talked with her, joked with her, and listened intently whenever she opened her mouth.

Yes, Moira couldn't be happier for her younger sister, or more jealous. Here she was, more than thirty years old and a widow, and her innocent little sister had what she had never been able to achieve. A short time ago she had foolishly entertained the idea of sharing such harmony with Wynthrope, but now . . .

Dear heaven, could she not go at least a few hours without thinking of him? Just a hour or two, that was all she asked. It seemed such an impossibility these days. She had never missed or mourned the loss of a person like this—not even Tony.

After dinner, the three of them retired to the drawing room where a warm fire crackled in the hearth. Moira poured mulled wine for them and then found herself unable to drink hers because it made her think of *him*.

Thankfully neither Minnie nor Lucas noticed she wasn't partaking. They were too busy exchanging secret smiles as they sat together on the sofa. Even though there was a proper amount of distance between them, the joyous tension was obvious. God, she had been relegated to intruder in her own home.

Finally, Minnie took her beau by the hand and turned her attention to her sister. "Moira, I told Lucas that you and I have already spoken, but he has something he would like to ask you."

Trying her best to smile encouragingly—it really wasn't that difficult—Moira met the young man's eager gaze. His smile was sure and genuine—not the least bit hesitant.

"Lady Aubourn, my regard for Minnie is undeniably obvious to you and anyone else who happens to be present when I see her lovely face." He glanced at said face as soon as he spoke the words.

Oh how sweet. Envy tightened its hold, even as joy warmed Moira's heart. This was what love should be. Minnie would never wake up in the middle of the night to find Lucas betraying her.

Lucas turned his attention back to her. "I find the very thought of living the rest of my life without her unbearable and therefore humbly request that you save me from such torment and give me your permission to formally ask her hand in marriage."

She was going to cry. That was all there was to it. Such a well-spoken behest and so very obviously sincere. Only true love could inspire a man to such an overly poetic fancy. When Tony had asked her parents for permission, the topic immediately changed to money and how soon the ceremony could take place. Of course, she had been just as eager to have those decisions made. She had wanted so very desperately to get out of that house that she never once gave thought to the idea that she might be passing up a chance at something real.

Swallowing against the lump in her throat, Moira smiled lovingly at them both. "My dear Mr. Scott, you not only have my heartfelt permission, but my blessing as well." She stood and went to them, kissing them both on the cheek as they beamed happily. They had known she would say yes, but the finality of it seemed to overwhelm them.

"I suspect you would like a few moments alone to rejoice," she remarked, seeing how delighted they both were. They only had eyes for each other, and if Moira didn't leave soon, they were liable to explode.

But just because she envied them and was happy for them did not mean she was going to completely toss her duties as chaperone to the wind.

"You have ten minutes," she warned them with mock severity as she made to depart. "And I am leaving the door open."

Whether they even heard her, she did not know.

Still smiling, she strolled through the well-lit expanse of the hall, stopping beneath Tony's painting of Cupid and Psyche.

"Ah, Tony. If only you and I could have been so fortunate as those two." Wryly, her lips twisted. "Not necessarily with each other, though."

If only Tony had liked women. No, even then things might not have worked between them. If only Moira had been able to find someone for herself—someone who might have been to her what Nathaniel was to Tony. If only Tony had lived.

No. If she had found a lover and Tony had lived, then she might resent him for being what stood in the way of her being with the man she truly loved. All Tony had done by marrying her was spare her—for a few years—the heartache of loving and not being able to have that person. She would rather go through the torment and pain of Wynthrope's deception than resent Tony for anything. At least Tony had never led her to believe he was anything but what he projected. It was everyone else outside his immediate circle he saved that for.

A knock on the door echoed through the hall, saving her from further ruminations. Who could that be? She wasn't expecting any callers.

Straining to hear, she listened as the door was opened. As soon as she heard Chester's dismayed "Oh dear!" she moved into the foyer.

Her heart stopped dead in her chest. At first she noticed nothing except that Wynthrope Ryland was in her house and he was soaked to the skin, his hair clinging to his skull, his eyes wide and dark in the chilled pallor of his face.

And then she noticed that he carried a heavy bundle in his arms. Her brow knitted. Was it a person?

Wynthrope came forward, even though no one had bidden him enter. His back was slightly bowed under the weight of his burden, which, as he entered the lit hall, Moira could see was indeed a person.

She moved forward, her limbs suddenly leaden, her heartbeat a staccato pounding. She reached out with numb fingers as he stopped directly in front of her, offering the person in his arms to her for her inspection like some kind of pagan sacrifice.

Moira gave a little cry as her fingers touched the cold, wet, blond hair. She knew who it was even before she saw the pale, bloody face nestled into Wynthrope's shoulder.

Nathaniel.

Chapter 15

Nathaniel lay on her bed, in exactly the same position as when Wynthrope had put him there. His face would have been pale if not for the myriad bruises and streaks of blood on it. He had yet to wake, had yet to utter the barest sound. Moira sat in a chair by his head as Mr. Griggs, the physician Wynthrope collected, examined him.

"Will he recover?" Fear made her voice thin and hoarse. As much as she wanted, she could not tear her gaze away from the awful sight of Nathaniel's face for fear that he would die while she wasn't looking.

Griggs offered her a kindly smile as he began wiping the blood from his patient's face with a warm, wet cloth. "I do not have the slightest doubt that he will make a full recovery."

Relief washed over her so brutally she could have wept. "What are the extent of his injuries?"

The physician rinsed the cloth in a basin. Moira tried not to notice how crimson the water turned. "His ribs are not broken," he replied, wringing out the cloth, "but the bruising around that area is already significant. My guess is that he will be quite uncomfortable for several days. The cuts on his face will heal with barely a scar, but it is the swelling that will be the real issue for the next while. It will get worse before it gets better."

Moira glanced at Nathaniel's battered face. One eye was already swollen shut. Her poor dear friend. Who could have done such a vile thing?

It wasn't Wynthrope, she knew that without a doubt. He may have harbored some resentment that Nathaniel refused to allow him near her, but Wynthrope was not a cruel man. Not only that, but if he had been the culprit, he wouldn't have delivered Nathaniel to her himself. He would have left him for her to find on her own.

And he wouldn't have looked at her with such a ravaged expression on his face, or such sympathy in his eyes. She could scarcely look at him because of the remorse in his features. He hadn't looked this sorry when she found him with his hands in her safe. Or perhaps he had and she had simply been too hurt and angry to notice.

Could this Matthew person be to blame? Had he only been pretending to like Nathaniel, perhaps pretending to share the same preferences as well? He might be one of those gentlemen—and she used the term lightly—who despised men who seemed the least bit effeminate.

Or maybe someone had seen Nathaniel and Matthew together and attacked them both. Perhaps Matthew was somewhere badly injured as well. Good Lord, what if he was? She would send a note around to his lodgings just to be safe.

Regardless of who had done it, why had he left Nathaniel for Wynthrope to find instead of her? It didn't make sense, unless Wynthrope had been on his way to Moira's when he found Nathaniel. She hadn't thought to ask where he had found him. She had been so very terrified, she'd practically ordered him to fetch the physician immediately after he carried Nathaniel to her room. They hadn't spoken more than a few words to each other since his return. For all she knew he had left.

At least she hoped he had left. But then, she hoped that he had stayed as well. She didn't know what she hoped. No, that was a lie. She hoped her friend would be fine, and she hoped the bastard who hurt him rotted in hell.

Griggs had finished cleaning Nathaniel's face, revealing features that, while swollen and bruised, were far less frightening when free of blood. His injuries were not as awful as they had first appeared, not now that the bleeding had stopped. Still, it tore at her heart to see her friend in such a state. Dear Nathaniel would never hurt anyone, and the idea of someone hurting him in such a manner was inconceivable.

She watched as the elderly doctor washed his hands before collecting a small jar from his satchel. He removed the lid and dipped his fingers into a thick salve, which he then applied to the open cuts on Nathaniel's face.

"This will help them heal," he told her. "I will leave this jar with you. For the next few days you will have to watch these wounds for infection. Change the bandages morning and night, wash the areas, and apply this cream with each new dressing."

Moira took the jar with a confused frown. "Won't all that water prevent the wounds from healing properly?"

Mr. Griggs smiled. "I know it sounds odd, but it has been my experience that wounds which are kept clean tend to heal faster. Water doesn't harm them a bit, provided it too is clean."

Moira nodded. A physician obviously knew more about such things than she did.

After applying bandages to Nathaniel's face, Griggs

wiped his hands on a square of linen and replaced the lid on the jar of salve, which he left on the bedside table. "I have done all I can, Lady Aubourn. If you should require my services again, you know how to find me."

Actually, she didn't. Wynthrope had brought him there, not she. "Could you leave me your direction regardless, please Mr. Griggs?"

He didn't question her reasons, but simply withdrew a small silver case from inside his coat and withdrew a card. "Here. This has all my information."

Moira took it in cold, numb fingers. "Thank you."

As much as she wanted to stay by Nathaniel's side, she knew it would be rude of her not to show the physician out. The calling card she placed on the nightstand next to the jar of salve. She left one of her maids with her friend, along with a bottle of laudanum should he wake up and be in great pain, and personally escorted Griggs downstairs.

He received her profuse thanks with a warm smile, refusing to take payment. "My fee has already been paid, Lady Aubourn."

By whom, she wanted to ask, but there was no need. Wynthrope had paid him, of that there could be no question. Why? Why do all this for her and Nathaniel when it wasn't necessary or welcome?

No, that wasn't true. His help was appreciated. It was his presence that was unwelcome. He had taken care of everything, no doubt to put her in his debt, or something equally as nefarious.

With Griggs gone, her first instinct was to run back upstairs and stay by Nathaniel's side until he woke. Instead she drifted through the warmly lit hall and down the corridor to the parlor where she had sat with Minnie and Lucas. The ten minutes she had promised them had turned into two hours. They were still there, waiting for her to apprise them of

Nathaniel's condition. Somehow she knew she would not find them alone.

She was not wrong, though the discovery both thrilled and frightened her. No, not frightened. She was not afraid of Wynthrope, even though part of her thought she ought to be. She was angered by his continued presence in her home—angered that he presumed to have the right to be there.

He sat in a winged chair near the fire, a glass of what appeared to be bourbon in his hand. She was silent in her approach, her slippers making no sound at all on the tiles. Even still, he seemed to know the exact second she entered the room. His head lifted and turned toward her, his gaze locking with hers as he finished whatever it was he was saying to the young people with him. His words were nonsensical to her ears, so loud was the roaring in them. Slowly, he rose to his feet.

He looked like hell and yet her heart still leaped at the sight of him. He was pale and drawn, his hair a disheveled mess from the rain and wind. His coat was open and she could see that his taupe-colored waistcoat had dark stains on it—blood. Nathaniel's blood. It was on his shirt and hands as well. Had he not thought to ask for water so that he might wash?

No. She could tell that from the hollow look in his eyes. He had asked for bourbon and nothing more.

Seeing that his attention had been diverted, Minnie and Lucas turned and stood as well. Minnie hastened toward her, concern marring her pretty features.

"How is he? How is dear Nathaniel?"

Moira placed a comforting arm around her sister. It did much to soothe the discord in her own soul as well. "He will be sore when he wakes, and his face will not be so pretty for a time, but Mr. Griggs expects him to make a full recovery in a matter of days."

The younger woman sagged in relief. "Oh, that is good news."

Moira gave her a gentle squeeze, but her attention was on the man lounging by her fire. He tried to look so relaxed, so composed, but she could see the telltale whiteness around the knuckles of the hand holding his glass.

She kept her gaze fixed on him as she released her sister. "Minnie, would you and Mr. Scott mind giving Mr. Ryland and me some privacy? There are things I need to discuss with him."

Her sister shot her a glance that spoke volumes. No doubt Wynthrope understood it as well. Minnie didn't want to leave her, especially not with the man who had broken her heart. Dear Minnie. She knew nothing but what little Moira had chosen to tell her, and yet she firmly believed her sister to be the injured party.

Which of course she was.

Minnie also undoubtedly knew that she could not make a scene in front of Wynthrope and her fiancé. Reluctantly she bade Lucas to follow her to the library. He followed after her without question, but he flashed Moira a smile that was as warm as it was resolute.

"Do let me know if I can be of any assistance to you, Lady Aubourn," he said cordially. His meaning was plain in his gaze. *Do let me know if you need me to forcibly remove Mr. Ryland from your home.*

Moira returned his smile. Obviously her little sister had shared some of Moira's tale of woe with her fiancé. Wonderful. Who else knew? All of London, no doubt. There had to be talk about the fact that the two of them hadn't been seen in public together over the last few days. There had to have been remarks about how she had taken to staying so close to home as of late. And society had to have noticed just how ravaged Wynthrope was looking, even if he was still damnably beautiful despite it.

Once they had left, Moira closed the door behind them

and strode across the carpet on trembling legs, to stand not far from where Wynthrope sat. He raised his gaze to hers, and her heart was not immune to the pain there.

"I will leave if you like," he told her, his voice as tired as he looked, "but I thought you might want to talk."

Moira swallowed, gathering all her will in the hopes that she would sound somewhat normal when she spoke. Perhaps his weariness was sincere, but she wasn't about to let him know how awful she felt, not if she could help it.

"What happened?" Even with all her efforts, she still ended up sounding as though she had some kind of blockage in her throat.

He took a swallow of bourbon before shaking his head. "I do not know. I was at North and Octavia's for the evening celebrating the news that Blythe is with child."

How lovely for Blythe! This little tidbit was as welcome as Minnie's betrothal when paired with all the awfulness of tonight and the previous·few days.

"Please give them my felicitations." She meant it, but even that good news could not take away from the terrible tragedy of the evening. "Then what happened?"

He shot her an unreadable glance before continuing, "I left for home. When I got there I found Nathaniel on the steps. I immediately thought to bring him to you."

"Why?" Why her? "Why not take him into your home? Or to Mr. Griggs?"

"Because you love him, and I knew you would want to be with him." He took another drink. "And because I have no frigging idea where he lives."

A few days ago she might have smiled at that, but her lips seemed incapable of such expression now. "Do you have any idea why he went to your home and not here?"

Wynthrope sighed. It was a pensive rather than wistful sound. "I do not believe he went willingly."

Fear jolted Moira's nerves. She had suspected as much, but to have him agree with her hunch unsettled her. "You think he was deliberately left for you to find?"

He nodded. "Yes."

Her brow furrowed. There was something he wasn't telling her, then the awful realization came to her. "You know who did this?"

Another nod as he rubbed his eyes. "Not the man who is physically responsible, but the man who made it happen, yes."

A hot, sick feeling churned in her stomach. "The people you work for, they did this."

He was as ashen as a marble statue. "I presume so."

"Why?" Disbelief and shock drove her to lean on the chair opposite him, one hand pressed against her belly to quell the rolling there. "You and Nathaniel are hardly friends."

Wynthrope met her gaze with dark, despairing eyes. "No, but you and he are."

If it were possible for a person to literally freeze from fear, Moira would have done it at that exact moment. "It was a warning."

"Yes."

"For you." Her tongue felt thick and awkward in her mouth. "Because you failed to bring them the tiara."

His lips thinned. "Yes."

She laughed, harsh and discordant. "What next, they come after me?"

"Or Minerva."

The shock of being right was nothing compared to the rage that shot through her at the mention of her sister's name. "If anyone harms my sister I will kill them."

He seemed unimpressed by her resolve. "How can you kill what you do not know?"

Her gaze narrowed. "You know who they are."

He shook his head. Never had she seen him look so defeated. "I know who one of them is. I do not know who he is working with."

That was not good enough. "But you are in contact with this man."

"Yes, but I will not tell you his name just so you can go and do something foolish like get yourself hurt." He tossed back the remainder of his bourbon and set the glass on the floor beside his chair.

Frustration tightened her fingers into fists. Anger gave her strength. "You tell them that if anyone else I love is injured, I will personally destroy that damn tiara."

A spark of admiration lit the deep blue depths of his eyes. For a moment, he looked like the Wynthrope she had adored. "That is what I love about you, Moira. You look so fragile, but you've a spine of iron."

What he *loved* about her? It was a little late for that, was it not?

"Do not flatter me, Mr. Ryland. My friend is badly hurt and it is all your fault." Her words were harsh, but she wanted him to deny the accusation. She wanted to fight about it.

"Yes." He wasn't going to argue? "And I am sick because of it."

"I do not care how you feel." That was a horrible lie, but she said it anyway. "What I care about is what you intend to do about it."

He rubbed a hand over his eyes, then blinked to clear his vision. "I'm not certain. Try to draw their attention away from you and Minnie."

"And just how do you propose to do that?" This man he worked for obviously knew she was in possession of the tiara, what was to stop him from hiring someone else to steal it? He obviously wanted it badly enough to resort to harming innocent bystanders.

Wynthrope lifted his chin, his gaze locking with hers so intently that she knew whatever he was about to say was nothing less than the honest truth. "If I have to, I will turn myself in to Bow Street and tell them everything."

She stared at him. He would do that? For her and Minnie? No, not for Minnie, for *her*. There was no way she could fool herself about who he meant. His determination to protect her was as plain as the nose on his face.

She moved closer, even though her mind urged her not to. She didn't stop until she was standing directly before him, and then she knelt at his feet, so that they were eye to eye.

"If this is what they would do to someone not involved, what would they do to you?" Her voice shook as she asked the question gnawing at her conscience.

His silence struck fear into the very heart of her. Slowly, against her own accord, she lifted a hand to his face, trailing her fingers along his stubbled cheek. Lightning fast, he caught her hand in his own, pulling it away.

"Don't," he rasped.

Undaunted, she lifted her other hand and placed it against his other cheek. Could he not see that she was trying to bridge the distance between them? That she was trying to tell him that even though he had destroyed her trust and broken her heart, she still cared what happened to him? The very thought of living in a world without him was even more unbearable than the thought that he might not be the man she hoped he was.

He grabbed that hand as well, and before she knew what was happening he had hauled her off balance so that she toppled toward him. He caught her in his arms, holding her gaze for little more than a second before claiming her mouth with his.

He had almost forgotten how she tasted.

Wynthrope kissed her without mercy, his tongue plundering the soft, warm confines of her sweet mouth. He drank her in, his soul sighing in pleasure as she filled him. Warmth seeped into the frigid, barren parts of him, light glowed where just moments before there had been nothing but black abyss. His hands splayed across the delicate width of her back as he spread his knees, hauling her even closer, so that he could feel the pressure of her small breasts against his chest, the soft firmness of her belly between his legs.

She didn't fight him, much to his surprise. At first her slender hands held themselves somewhere away from him, then they settled with uncertain gentleness on his shoulders. Any pressure from her and he would have to stop. He didn't want to but, he would respect her wishes.

There was no pressure—not to push him away at any rate. Her fingers tightened around his shoulders, pulling him closer. He groaned against her mouth as her tongue tentatively stroked his.

For the first time since that awful night—no, for the first time since Daniels first reappeared in his life—Wynthrope felt as though there was hope, that everything might actually be all right. Moira was in his arms, kissing him with such longing that it hurt as much as it filled him with joy. Was there a chance that she might be able to forgive him? That once this whole debacle was over with, once Daniels was gone, they might be able to start over? Was it possible she felt more toward him than just this animosity he knew he deserved.

One of his hands slid down the soft fabric covering her back, around to the fragile rise of her ribs. She had put on a little weight, he could feel it in the way her bones weren't as defined beneath his palm, in the almost imperceptible added heaviness in her breast as his fingers cupped the gentle roundness. Never in the history of man had a woman possessed breasts more beautiful than Moira's.

An exquisite hardness met his questing thumb as it grazed the peak of her breast. Stroking it gently, he drew the tip of his nail over the tightening bud, his cock stirring in response as she moaned into his mouth.

Regardless of anything else she might feel for him, how she might despise him, she still wanted him. There was no denying her body's response to him, no denying the pleasure she found in his kiss. It gave him more hope than he dared confront. It was obvious they still had a physical connection, now if he could only rebuild the trust that had been broken.

His breath came in a ragged rhythm as their mouths continued their slow, desperate dance. His hand slid down her back to caress the soft swell of her bottom. The fingers on her breast became more persistent, rolling her nipple through the layers of fabric, lightly pinching until she gasped and pressed against his hand.

Moira's hands left his shoulders, drifting inward, stroking him through his coat as they glided across his chest.

She untied the knot in his cravat, untwining the length of linen from around his throat. The cravat was tossed aside and her eager fingers came back to his neck, touching him tenderly, stroking the flesh there until she stumbled upon the wound Daniels had inflicted. Wynthrope winced at the contact. The wound was still sore.

Moira drew back, her fingers now still. The gaze that met his was curious, worried even. She glanced down, holding his collar wide as she did so. He knew the moment she saw the cut.

"What happened?"

Reaching up, he closed his hands around hers, pushing them away from his neck. "It is nothing. I cut myself shaving."

She glared at him, her face pale, her expression dubious at best. "Do not treat me like a simpleton, Wynthrope."

"I would never dream of it." No, it would be too much to ask that she had become stupid during their estrangement.

"*He* did this to you, didn't he?"

There was no need to ask who "he" was. She certainly wasn't referring to Nathaniel, and the only other man they had discussed that night was Daniels—although Wynthrope had been careful not to refer to him by name. Nor was there cause to be so pleased that she had called him by his Christian name for the first time since his arrival. She was worried about him, and it warmed him.

"Yes."

She seemed to struggle with something, a puzzling combination of emotions playing across her features. There was concern, anger, fear, and . . . resignation?

"Because you had failed to get what he wanted?" It was obvious she believed that he was indeed working for someone now, at least.

He could lie, but she would see it in his eyes—or perhaps in his soul. He'd never quite been able to shirk the feeling that she had the ability to read the very heart of him when she wanted.

"Because I hit him."

Not satisfied, she pressed further. "Why did you do that?"

Damn her, she didn't really need to ask, did she? For someone who refused to speak to him for the last three days, she certainly had a lot of questions now. Of course, the only reason she was speaking to him now was that her dearest friend had been injured because of him.

He glanced away. "Because he threatened to hurt someone."

"Me?" There was a tremor to her voice, despite the certainty.

"Yes, damn it!" He glared at her, angry beyond measure that she had drawn the confession from him. "He threatened my family and I didn't do anything. He threatened you and I lost control. Happy?"

She looked so beautifully bewildered. "Why would that please me?"

If she were any other woman, it would have. "Because now you know I place you above my family, even though I am no better than dirt in your estimation." That was a gross exaggeration and he knew it, but a part of him wanted her to tell him different, just as she had wanted to hear that a threat against her had driven him to violence.

"Not dirt," was all she said. Served him right for daring to hope for more.

He wanted to make her feel even a hint of the guilt and remorse he felt. "So I hit him when he threatened you, and then he pulled a blade and put it to my throat. When I refused to back down immediately, he cut me to put me back in my place. Nothing makes a person feel more vulnerable than cold steel to the throat—especially when it has already sliced through your skin."

She paled at his description. Good. Maybe he had no right to do this to her, but he needed to see the color drain from her features. He needed to know she was not as unaffected as she wanted him to believe. He needed to know some part of her still cared, damn it. Otherwise there was no point in going on.

She pulled away from him completely and he let her go, despite the urgent insistence from his groin that he try to seduce her into finishing what they had started.

"Wait here," she instructed, something in her tone telling him that he would be wise to do as she bid.

She drifted from the room like a specter, leaving him waiting for her return like an obedient dog. He retrieved his cravat from the floor and rewound it around his neck, tying the now limp linen in as neat a knot as he could with no mirror and fingers that shook. Did he have time for another bourbon? He could use another drink. The brief moments he'd held her were like a cruel jest. He wanted her so badly, but there would be no more kisses this evening, of that he was certain.

He picked up his glass and went to the sideboard, where a selection of crystal decanters sat. Removing the stopper from the bourbon, he poured a liberal amount into his glass and downed it in one swift gulp.

Moira returned just as he was considering pouring another. In one hand she carried a small jar. The other hand held a carved oaken box, which she set on a table. "Come here," she ordered.

Should he bark and wag his tail as well? Moodily he went to her. "What?"

She removed the top from the jar. "Pull down your cravat. This salve will help heal your wound."

His cravat felt strangely tight as he held the layers of linen away from his neck. It had been a long time since anyone had doctored a wound for him, and the gesture struck a chord deep within him, sending a ripple of tremulous emotion throughout his entire being.

Her fingers were gentle as they applied the cool salve. The tincture strung a little, but that was it. Once his cravat was back in place, he offered her his handkerchief to wipe the cream from her hand, refusing it when she tried to give it back. Let her keep it. It would give her something to gaze on when she regretted him years from now.

She dropped the discarded linen on the table beside her and picked up the oaken box. For a second she just stood there, staring at it, as though remembering another time she had held it.

"Here." Snapping out of her reverie, she offered the box to him.

He took it, an uneasy suspicion forming in his stomach. He opened the lid and his stomach plummeted, even though a part of him had known what he'd find.

The tiara. It twinkled up at him from a bed of black velvet.

"Take it." Her voice was firm, perhaps even a little raw.

The lid snapped shut as he raised his astonished gaze to hers. "I cannot." He shoved the box toward her.

She stepped backward, shaking her head. "It is yours now. Give it to the man who wants it so badly."

"Moira—"

She scowled at him, her patience at an obvious end. "For heaven's sake, Wynthrope, will you just take the fool thing? You had no problem trying to take it before."

The remark stung, even though he deserved it. Telling her that he had decided not to take it that night would do no good. She wouldn't believe him.

"Why?" Perhaps he was a fool to ask, but he had to know. Was there a chance she still had feelings for him? Could it be that he had not completely destroyed those precious emotions?

"Because that little bit of shine is not worth someone's life, not Nathaniel's, not Minnie's, not yours."

"Nor yours," he added, pleased beyond reason that he had been included with the two most important people in her life.

Her gaze was impassive. "Nor mine. I think you should leave now."

He blinked. She what? He should have expected this. Had he actually thought anything had changed? No. And no doubt she saw their kiss as a weakness on her own part. She was not about to let him back into her life so easily. Her body—even her heart—might want him, but her mind and her pride did not. And Moira was a very smart, very proud woman.

Her chin tilted defiantly. "You have gotten what you

wanted. There is no need for you to trouble yourself with me anymore."

"'Trouble myself'?" He couldn't contain his annoyance. "Is that why you think I stayed here tonight, in hopes of getting this?" He held up the box.

She shook her head. "No. I believe you were genuinely concerned about Nathaniel, and for that I thank you, but I think you had better leave before I decide that you might just be a good man after all."

That pierced his heart. "Moira—"

She held up a staying hand. "Please, just leave. I was willing to risk scandal to be with you, Wynthrope, but I refuse to risk the safety of my loved ones. It seems you are a dangerous man to be associated with, and even if I could bring myself to trust you with my heart, I have no guarantee that Minnie and Nathaniel will not pay a price for it."

He stared at her, a strange tightness in his throat. There it was. It didn't matter if he managed to win her heart again, she would not give it, not while there was a chance of her friend or sister being at risk—not while he continued to keep the entire truth from her. She had no way of knowing whether more threats from his past would resurface. She had no idea that until recently it had been years since he had stolen anything. She didn't know.

And he wasn't going to tell her, because at the moment, it was better that she knew as little as possible. If she knew the whole truth she might feel sorry for him or, worse, decide that she wanted to help him. She was such a good person, he wouldn't put it past her to make such an idiotic decision. The only reason he cared about Nathaniel and Minnie was that Moira cared about them. His main concern was her, and he would rather die before he put her in danger.

He took a breath. "Thank you for helping me."

"I do not do it for you," she replied quickly, harshly. "I am doing this for my friend who is lying unconscious in my bed as we speak. He is an innocent in all this, and I would not see him suffer anymore."

Wynthrope nodded. "Whatever your reasons, I appreciate them, and I swear I will repay you."

She swallowed, and he could see that her hands were clenched into tight fists. "You may repay me by leaving."

Again he nodded, saying nothing as he tucked the box under his arm and moved toward the door. She was right to feel as she did, but it didn't stop his heart from hurting. He wanted to beg her not to make him go, beg her to give him another chance, to let him make it up to her, but he had some modicum of pride left, and he knew that begging would do him no good. The only way he could show her how sorry he was, was to do exactly as she wanted. He had hurt her so much that walking out on her now was the least he could do.

The very least.

Chapter 16

The next morning Moira and Minnie sat in the library, making up a list of people to invite to Minnie's engagement party that was to be held in two weeks' time. It was the perfect distraction for Moira, who would rather be doing anything this morning but thinking of Wynthrope Ryland.

Had she done the right thing in giving him the tiara? Had he been sincere in all that he told her? Had his regret been genuine? Or had it all been a clever ruse designed to coerce the tiara from her?

Whatever it had been, it hardly mattered now. He had the stupid tiara—may Tony forgive her for handing it over—and if he truly cared for her, he might come back and try to woo her once again someday. If he did not, he would stay away. Would it make a difference in the end? She had told him to stay away; he might just believe she meant it.

She had meant it. As much as it broke her heart not knowing whether she could trust him, she was not about to put anyone she loved in more danger by associating with a thief. Poor Nathaniel had already suffered enough.

"You know we have to invite Mama and Papa."

Moira glanced up at her sister, who was watching her with worried brown eyes. "Yes, they are your parents after all."

"And yours."

Her smile was wry. "It will not be me they come to see. I'm certain Millicent, Margaret, and Marissa will want to come as well."

Minnie wrinkled her nose. "It was terribly unkind of Mama and Papa to give us all names that begin with M."

Yes, it was, but Moira had the sneaking suspicion that neither of her parents—especially her mother—lost any sleep where their daughters' names were concerned.

"You have suffered grievously for it, obviously," Moira replied in a dry tone. "I think we've just about finished the list. Is there anyone else you can think of?"

Minnie licked her lips, worrying the bottom one with her tongue. "Should we invite Mr. Ryland?"

"North?" Moira made a big show of looking over the sheets of paper on the desk before her. "Oh yes, he and Octavia are already on the list."

"You know who I mean."

Sighing, Moira met her sister's anxious gaze. "Do you want to invite him?" If it meant Minnie's happiness, she could certainly survive an evening with Wynthrope. They lived in the same city, for heaven's sake, she was bound to run into him on occasion.

But not often, surely. Hopefully.

"I do not know. I would like to have him there because he was nice to me, and the rest of his family are invited, but I cannot abide what he has done to you, Moira, even though I only know the half of it."

Less than half, actually, but Minnie didn't need to be told

that. She would only ask questions, and Moira spent so much time thinking about it that she didn't want to talk about it.

She made her face a mask of indifference. "You should invite him. I'm sure he would appreciate the chance to extend his felicitations."

That didn't seem good enough for her sister. "He did that last night when Lucas and I told him."

Moira paused, her pen poised above the pot of ink. "No doubt he did, but doing so publicly is another matter." She dipped her quill in the ink and scrawled his name on the list before nerves got the better of her.

"Do you think he will come?"

Good Lord, was she to have no escape from the man? "I do not know, Minnie!" Her patience was at its very end. "Would you like me to personally go to his lodgings and ask him?"

Minnie's eyes widened. "You would do that for me?"

Moira was just about to tell her sister to go away—far away—when she noticed the gleam in the young woman's eyes. She was teasing, and doing a fine job of it too.

"No," she replied with a smile. "But I will have Cook make us some chocolate. Would you like that?"

Minnie clapped her hands like a child. "Oh yes!"

After chocolate, Moira went up to check on Nathaniel. She had sat with him most of the night, getting very little rest in a chair beside his—her—bed. It wasn't merely the chair that kept her awake, it was the fact that her mind kept replaying the night's events over and over again, especially that kiss she and Wynthrope had shared.

Had she no control where the man was concerned? He kissed her and she melted, forgetting every despicable thing he had done to her. While her friend had been sleeping above them, his body battered and bruised because of an association with a dastardly criminal, Moira had been ready to make love to that same criminal on her Aubusson carpet.

Nathaniel's face was peaceful when she peeked around the half-open door. If possible, his features were even more swollen than they had been the night before, and the bruising had deepened to an awful shade of purplish green, but he didn't look as though he was in pain, and that was good.

"I was wondering when you were going to show up," he mumbled, opening his eyes as she slipped into the room. "I am in desperate need of the chamber pot, and I'm afraid you are going to have to help me."

With anyone else Moira would have been embarrassed beyond reason, but not with Nathaniel. During Tony's illness they had both taken turns nursing him, and that included helping him to the water closet, and eventually emptying his bedpans. After all of that, she could certainly help her friend stand while he attended to nature's demands.

"I am happy to see you as well," she informed him, "but for entirely different reasons."

She crossed to the bed and drew back the blankets. He was nude beneath and she caught a glimpse of the bandages wrapped around his ribs before she averted her gaze. Guilt stabbed at her conscience. It was her fault this had happened to him. If only she hadn't given in to her attraction to Wynthrope.

"Stop blaming yourself," he ordered hoarsely. "And get me a robe, will you. I'm cold."

She had never seen Nathaniel in such a foul mood. Of course she had never seen him nude, or beaten before, so it shouldn't surprise her. She fetched the robe that one of her servants had collected from his house and brought it to him. It was a slow and painful task for him to don it, but he stubbornly saw it through. Then, with his arms over her shoulders, Moira wrapped her arms high around his back and helped lift him to his feet.

"Are you sure you wouldn't rather a bedpan?" she asked, gasping for breath as they both struggled for balance. "I can get you one."

"I can make it to the pot, blast it."

And make it he did. It took almost a quarter of an hour to get him to the commode and back, and he was winded and perspiring by the time he settled against the pillows, but they had achieved his relief. Moira made a mental note to have one or two of the footmen move the commode closer to Nathaniel's bedside so he wouldn't have such a struggle again.

Once he was settled against the pillows again—still clad in his robe—Moira finally allowed the tears to come. "I am so very sorry, Nate."

He scowled at her—or at least she thought he did. It was very difficult to tell when one of his eyes was swollen shut. "I told you not to blame yourself."

"How can I not?" Was that whining noise her voice? How very annoying it was.

Apparently he found it annoying as well, because he was positively peevish. "Because it had nothing to do with you."

"Of course it did." It was time to confess all and get it over with. "It was all about that damn tiara!"

He watched her with one pale eye. "I know."

She froze. "You know?"

"Oh yes." He might have attempted a bitter smile, but it was nothing more than a slight hitch of his lips. "They made sure I knew I was intended to be a message for your Mr. Ryland."

An acrid taste filled her mouth. "He is not my Mr. Ryland. Not anymore." She glanced away. "I do not know if he ever was."

"Save the melodrama for when you are alone with your thoughts, dearest." Nathaniel's tone was firm but not cruel. "That man has treated you abominably, to be sure, but he cared about you too."

She shook her head. "No."

"Yes. When I was lying on those steps, on the brink of unconsciousness, I heard his voice. He was begging God and anyone else who might be listening to keep me alive, and he told me he was going to bring me to you because if anyone could save me it was 'our Moira.'"

Moira clenched her jaw to fight the prickling behind her eyes. "That simply means that he knows how much I love you."

"Whatever you say." Nathaniel licked his lips, wincing as his tongue hit the split in the lower lip. "He probably saved my life by bringing me to you."

"How can you say that? It is because of him that this has happened to you!" The more she thought of it, the angrier she became. The anger felt good. It was much preferable to the misery she had been feeling lately.

"It is not his fault either." He cast a longing glance at the pitcher beside him. "Be a love and pour me a glass of this water, will you?"

She rose from the chair to fetch his drink from the tray on the bedside table. "How can you be so forgiving when you know it was the man who hired him behind the attack on you?"

"I assume I was chosen because I am close to you, and whoever was behind it knew that." His face contorted with pain as he shifted himself into an even more upright position. "They also knew that Wynthrope would assume that either Minerva or you would be the next target. They did it to exercise their control over him. He is as much a victim as I am."

She shoved the glass of water at him. Were he not an invalid, she might have thrown it. "You are too forgiving."

That clear, unmarred blue eye regarded her knowingly. "You are vexed with me because you cannot bring yourself to forgive him, no matter how much you want to."

"I have not forgiven him," she countered as she sat, "because he has not asked me to, and even if he did, he does not deserve to be forgiven."

"Why not?"

She couldn't believe he had to ask her that! "Because he used me."

He nodded slightly as he took a sip from the glass. "Tony used you."

"That is not the same thing!" How could he even suggest such a thing? If anyone should be able to understand Tony's motives for marrying her it was Nathaniel.

"Is it not?" He shifted against the pillows again, grimacing as the movement obviously disturbed his abused ribs. It must be so very difficult for him to find a comfortable position.

"Of course not." She was so petulant and defiant. "Tony and I had a mutual understanding."

"Yes, you did." He took another drink. "And Wynthrope Ryland used you to steal a tiara and you used him to lose your maidenhead. I think that was fairly mutual as well, do you not?"

Moira's face flamed. "I did not use him to lose my virginity!"

"Of course you did. You did not fall in love with the man at first sight. You fell in love with him after you came to know him, after you had already decided to take him as a lover. You wanted to know what all the fuss was about and you set your sights on him."

She shook her head. He made it sound so mercenary and it hadn't been like that. She wasn't like that. "No."

He reached out and covered one of her hands with his. "Yes. And it is all right. You did nothing wrong."

"But he did!" Tears filled her eyes. "I gave myself to him and he tried to steal from me! He betrayed my trust!" Anything else she might have said was lost in a sob. She would not cry, not now.

Nathaniel watched as she wiped her eyes with her hands, pulling herself together with a mighty sniff.

"He didn't have to become your lover to steal from you, Moira. He could have entered your house and taken it without you ever being the wiser, that's what good thieves do."

She sniffed again. "Obviously he's not a very good thief."

"I disagree. He stole your heart, and I despaired of anyone ever being able to achieve that."

She didn't bother to argue. "He didn't waste any time in tossing it back at me."

"He did no such thing. He is as much in possession of it as he was when you took him to your bed. You would not hurt nearly so much if he had relinquished his claim."

Moira sagged against the back of her chair. "How I wish I had never met him."

Nathaniel's smile was kind. "Instead of regretting what cannot be undone, you would be better off asking him why he waited so long into your relationship to betray you."

Her eyes narrowed. "What are you suggesting?"

No doubt he would have shrugged if could have without hurting himself. "Only that I believe he was coerced into stealing the tiara after you and he had already begun your courtship."

Courtship. He made it sound as though she and Wynthrope were destined to have more than just one night in her bed.

"I think you might be suffering some kind of brain fever," she told him dryly.

"Did you ask him why he wanted the tiara?"

"He said he had to acquire it for someone. He wouldn't

give me any more information—probably because he couldn't think up a lie fast enough."

"Or because he is protecting someone."

"Who?" It came out more sharply than she intended.

"I have no idea." He raised his brow. "Perhaps you should ask him."

Moira rolled her eyes heavenward. "Now I know you are suffering a brain fever. What guarantee would I have that if I were foolish enough to ask he would tell me the truth."

"You could trust him," he suggested.

"Oh yes, because I have had such good luck with that thus far."

Instead of being offended, Nathaniel smiled. "You sounded exactly like him just then."

Moira wasn't feeling so guilty over Nathaniel's injuries anymore—the guilt was being edged out of the way by a sense of annoyance. "You are only defending him because you have become infatuated with him playing your rescuing knight."

Nathaniel's face darkened. "Ah, because I am such a deviant and must want every man I meet, is that it?"

Moira gasped. "No, that is not—"

He cut her off, angrier than she had ever seen him. "Well I do not want every man I meet, Moira, no more than you do. However, I do know a good man when I see one, and I do not have to become infatuated with him to see his worth."

She should apologize for insulting him, but she couldn't let it go. "How can you of all people claim that he is a good man?"

"Because you love him, and he wouldn't be deserving of you if he wasn't!"

She stared at him. He seemed every bit as surprised by his outburst as she was. Sweat beaded on his brow. This exchange was taxing him. He was so agitated he was aggravating his injuries with every little move.

"Forgive me," she whispered, unable to think of anything else to say.

He squeezed her hand. "Only if you forgive me first."

She smiled, her eyes blurry. "Done."

His gaze met hers. "He is a good man, Moira. I feel it in my heart, and I think you do too."

She was saved from having to deny, or confirm his statement by a knock on the door. Mrs. Wright peered inside with a happy smile.

"Oh bless me, you're awake Mr. Nathaniel! You have a visitor."

"Who is it, Mrs. Wright?" Moira asked.

"Matthew Sedgewick, my lady."

Moira turned to Nathaniel with a smile. Even though she knew Matthew had been unharmed, it was a relief to hear he had come to call. "Would you like a visitor?"

Nathaniel nodded. "I would."

"Send him up, please."

Her friend cast her a nervous glance. "How do I look?"

Rising, she bent down to brush her lips across his forehead. "Like a beautiful mess. I'm sure it will win you much sympathy."

He smiled. "Oh good."

Moira left the room. She met Matthew on the stairs. He stopped to say hello and inquire after her health even though it was obvious he was anxious to see Nathaniel. Moira sent him on his way quickly and continued down the stairs with a fading smile.

Was Wynthrope Ryland a good man? She should know. After all, she seemed to have been blessed enough to have already shared some of her life with two of the best.

* * *

"No doubt you are wondering why I asked the three of you to come here tonight."

Sitting in the room that doubled as parlor, library, and study in his apartments, Wynthrope glanced at each of his brothers. They sat in a semicircle before him, waiting and watching expectantly.

It was Brahm who spoke. "Since you never invite me here, I for one am very curious."

"I need your help." It was like swallowing mud, but he was glad to have it out. "Something—*someone* from my past has come back into my life and I cannot get rid of him alone."

North was watching him with an expression akin to horror. He knew who Wynthrope meant.

"Perhaps you had better tell us who this person is," Brahm suggested, massaging the thigh of his injured leg as he stretched it out before him.

Yes, that was a good place to start. Start at the beginning and leave nothing out.

Wynthrope drew a deep breath. "Several years ago I was approached by a man claiming to work for the Home Office."

"Wyn—" North's voice had an edge of warning.

Wynthrope held up his hand. "I have to do this, North. You will understand soon."

North fell silent, his expression both dubious and worried. What Wynthrope was about to reveal affected him as well, but there was no avoiding it. Wynthrope had to do this—it was the only way to end this nightmare.

And his only chance of ever winning Moira back.

"This man—Daniels—told me I could help my country defeat Napoleon without marching off to fight. Since I was young and foolish and filled with the same fervor every young man at that time was filled with, I jumped at the chance to do my part without having to leave London. After all, I was Father's spare. God only knew what kind of accident might befall Brahm when he was in his cups."

Brahm raised his brows but said nothing.

Wynthrope drew a deep breath. "So I began working for him. He told me we were spies of sorts, stealing back items that had been acquired by French supporters to help fund Napoleon's campaigns. It was my job to repossess those items so Daniels could make certain they helped support England instead."

"You believed all this?" Obviously Brahm could not keep silent any longer.

Wynthrope shot his brother a glance that said he knew just how foolish he had been. "I was but eighteen at the time, and Daniels treated me like a man. He became a father figure to me."

The eldest Ryland brother nodded. "To replace the real father you believed did not care about you."

Perhaps his reasoning really was that crystal clear, but it annoyed him that Brahm saw through him that easily. "I suppose so, yes. Anyway, I did what he asked. I became a thief and a very good one at that. It wasn't until a Bow Street Runner approached me about an investigation he was working on that I began to realize the truth. That I was a stupid boy who had been tricked into becoming little more than a common criminal."

Devlin and Brahm both turned their eyes to North. "Bow Street Runner?" Devlin asked. "How many years ago would this have been?"

North glared at them both, his arms folded across his broad chest. "Yes, it was me. And yes, it is the reason why I left Bow Street. Both of you would have done the same rather than have your own brother arrested for being the burglar all of London was beginning to call the Ghost."

Surprised faces turned back to Wynthrope. "You were the

Ghost?" Brahm's tone was incredulous. "Sweet Jesus, Wyn!"

Wynthrope nodded. In another time, many years ago, he would have been proud of his brother's disbelieving expression. His prowess and reputation had been something he wore like an invisible mantle back then, but not now. Not when he realized it was nothing to be proud of.

"I was," he replied, casting a thankful glance at North, who still didn't look terribly impressed with him. "And if not for North, I would have either gone to prison or had to flee the country in disgrace."

"It would have topped any scandal I was ever involved in," Brahm remarked lightly. Did nothing faze this man? Now he was making jokes. He'd been surprised for maybe, what, two seconds? And now he was acting as though Wynthrope had just admitted to having cake for breakfast.

"Why did you never tell us this before?" Devlin asked, his tone more curious than hurt.

"Better yet," Brahm added, his expression knowing, "why are you telling us now?"

Wynthrope swallowed what was left of his pride. "I never told you because I felt every inch a fool. And I did not want Brahm to know what an idiot I had been."

Brahm glanced up, as though momentarily taken aback. Then he gave a slight nod, as though the explanation made perfect sense.

"I'm telling you now," he said, exhaling a deep a breath, "because I need your help."

North shot him a narrow gaze. "What is it? Has someone uncovered the truth?"

Was his brother concerned for Wynthrope, or for himself? Both, if he was smart. "Worse. Daniels is back."

The announcement was lost on their brothers, but North knew the full implications of it. His face lost some of its usual ruddy color. "What does he want?"

"A diamond tiara. He told me to retrieve it."

North's gaze was hard and shrewd. "And did you?"

It was one of the hardest things he ever had to do to look his brother—brothers—in the eye. "I failed."

"Who does this tiara belong to?" Of course Brahm would ask that.

Wynthrope lowered his gaze, staring at the shine of his shoes. "Moira Tyndale."

There was a chorus of oaths, but North's was the loudest. "You used her? You bastard! She's a friend of my wife's. How am I going to explain this to Octavia?"

A hard gaze shot to his brother. "First of all, you are not to tell your wife anything." He glanced at Devlin. "That goes for you as well. The fewer people who know about this, the safer we'll all be."

"Safer?" Trust North to jump on that.

He tugged his cravat down so they could see the wound on his neck. "Daniels left me with this. I believe him also to be behind an attack on Moira's friend Nathaniel Caylan."

North ran a hand over the stubble on his jaw as he muttered an expletive that would have made even the devil's ears burn. "I cannot believe you allowed yourself to get involved in this. You should have come to me."

Did North really think him fool enough to simply jump back into a life of crime? Did he have so little faith in him? "Daniels threatened to expose your cover-up of my involvement in his gang. He says he has proof that could ruin you. I could not risk bringing scandal upon the family name."

"Scandal?" Brahm echoed. "Who cares a whit about scandal when there are lives at stake?"

Wynthrope turned to face him. "I did not know it would come to this. I believe Daniels will make good on his threats. He is that kind of man. He has only turned violent since I failed to get the tiara for him."

A muscle ticked in North's jaw. "So you tried to steal it, then?"

He nodded.

"Christ, Wyn. How could you pretend interest in Moira just to rob her?"

Of course North would think that was the way it was. North had spent so much time in the underbelly of London that his first instinct was to immediately distrust a person's motives, even if that person was his brother.

"I didn't. Daniels approached me after Moira and I had already begun our . . . relationship. Later, when he started to catch on that I might be developing feelings for her, he started threatening her as well. His attack on Nathaniel is a clear warning that Moira, or perhaps her sister, will be next if I fail to deliver the tiara next time."

"Next time?" North's face was red now. "What do you mean, *next time*?"

"What do you think it means? Daniels has no intention of letting me off his hook. It is not over until I get the tiara."

There was an uncomfortable silence as they all weighed the implications of that threat—not just to Wynthrope, but to themselves and everyone he cared about as well.

"What stopped you from making off with it during your previous attempt?" Brahm asked.

Wynthrope closed his eyes for the briefest of moments, not wanting to think about that night. "Moira found me."

"Found you?" North threw his arms in the air, looking as though he were about to have a seizure—or start laughing. "Excellent. So now she knows about our past as well?"

Wynthrope shook his head. "No. I did not tell her about you. She thinks I have always been a thief. She thinks I used her right from the beginning."

"And you did not tell her the truth?" It was Devlin who spoke, he of few questions.

Wynthrope shook his head at him. "It was not my place to tell her about North. Besides, it is better this way."

"Oh yes," North remarked caustically. "It is much better to have you looking like hell and Moira acting as though she has lost her best friend. Best for everyone involved."

"Would you rather I told her about you?" The fragile string holding Wynthrope's control under wraps was about to break. "You have just begun what is going to be a promising career in politics. You think I would risk ruining that?"

"You would rather ruin yourself." Brahm's tone was remarkably calm against the heightened tension in the room. "You would rather hurt the woman you love than one of us, even me."

It was true, but when it was said aloud it sounded so . . . soft. He didn't bother trying to deny his feelings for Moira. He didn't even argue his feelings for Moira. What difference would it make? Besides, he wouldn't know love if it slapped him in the face. Perhaps he did love her, but he hoped not. It would be much easier if he didn't.

"You are my brothers." And just in case that wasn't explanation enough, "I would do anything for you."

The room fell silent once more. His brothers traded glances, communicating without words, before turning those gazes on him.

"Do you have a plan?" North asked, most of his anger having seemingly evaporated.

"I did, but it changed last evening." Striding across the room, Wynthrope collected the oaken box Moira had given him from a locked drawer in his desk. He returned to his brothers, opening the box for them to peer inside.

Brahm whistled. Devlin was unimpressed by such shiny things. And North cursed.

"I thought you said you didn't steal it." North's pale blue eyes were bright.

O ye of little faith. "I didn't. Moira gave it to me last evening."

Three sharp gazes pinned him, but only Brahm spoke. "She did? Why?"

Wynthrope closed the box and set it on the table beside him. "She said she did not want anyone else to get hurt."

"Including you?" North wondered aloud.

Wynthrope shrugged. "Apparently even me."

Brahm's expression was appreciative, even a little teasing. "Well, that makes her a better person than me."

Devlin nodded. "Me too."

North actually managed a half smile—one that he directed at Wynthrope. "I think we are all in agreement that we would let him rot, but that is not the point. The point is now we are in possession of what Daniels wants. We just have to decide how to go about making him think he is going to get it."

"How do we do that?" Devlin asked, always the first to volunteer for battle.

"*You* don't," Wynthrope informed him before the other two could speak. "You have a pregnant wife to think of. You are going to stay the hell at home so I do not have nightmares about being responsible for my nephew losing his father."

Devlin scowled, ready to argue, but he was outnumbered. Brahm and North both agreed with Wynthrope. Devlin would be allowed to help plan, but he was not to be involved with the execution, and that was final.

"The first thing we have to do," North began as he started to pace. "is to let Daniels know Wyn has the tiara. We will arrange a meeting for the exchange . . . Wyn, get me some paper, will you, and a pencil?"

And so it began. The brothers talked and plotted for what felt like hours, working out every last detail of their plan. It was relatively simple; they baited Daniels and they hooked him. They hoped they'd have him netted before he knew what was happening.

It all hinged on Wynthrope being able to play his part, and on North—and perhaps Brahm—calling in a few favors. If anyone could make it work, the three of them could.

Wynthrope might have felt sorry for leaving Devlin out of the action, but his brother didn't look all that upset. Years in the army had given him enough excitement and danger to last a lifetime. The youngest Ryland liked the quiet life he and his wife led, even though Wynthrope would rather die than live in the country all year round.

Devlin was the first to depart, anxious to get home to Blythe. North followed shortly thereafter, even though it was obvious he wanted to stay and question Wynthrope, but he had a wife waiting for him as well, and Brahm's continued presence finally forced him to go.

"What about Moira?" Brahm asked when they were alone—a state that didn't fill Wynthrope with the same animosity as it used to, although he wasn't ready to give up those old grudges just yet.

He sat down on the sofa. "What about her?"

Leaning on his cane for support, Brahm lowered himself into a chair, stretching his bad leg out before him. It must be paining him awfully. He favored it often. "It is obvious she cares for you."

A rueful smile crossed Wynthrope's lips. "You are wrong. She told me she was safer not having me in her life."

"Of course she is." He spoke as though Wynthrope was a simpleton for not seeing that himself. "There is nothing safe about love."

Wynthrope scowled at his superior tone. "What would you know of love? You have never been in love in your life."

"I was, once." Brahm massaged his thigh. All that standing must have tired his leg. "Or at least I think I was. She jilted me, remember?"

"You were a hopeless drunkard. I'm surprised you even remember her." It was harsh, but true.

Brahm smiled sadly. "I have never forgotten. You will not forget either."

No, he wouldn't. He knew that. "I do not see that there is anything I can do."

"Telling her the truth when this is all over might be a good start." Using his cane for leverage, Brahm heaved himself to his feet once more. "And you might want to try giving her back her tiara when it has served its purpose. She might appreciate the gesture. Now be a good boy and help me down the stairs before I fall down them, will you?"

Wynthrope did just that. When he returned to the dimly lit confines of his rooms, he poured himself the drink he hadn't allowed himself to have out of some foolish sense of respect for Brahm and stretched out on his sofa, glass in hand.

He felt good about confessing all to his brothers. It felt as though a huge weight had been lifted off him. He hoped their plan would work, and he could finally put his past where it belonged.

And maybe, just maybe, Moira would allow him to explain things. She might even eventually allow him to visit her again, maybe start to trust him. But if Brahm thought simply returning the tiara was going to make all of that happen, Wynthrope felt sorry for him. The poor bugger didn't know *anything* about women.

Chapter 17

Wynthrope did not return to Moira's house after the night he brought Nathaniel to her. Days had passed with no sign or word of him.

She shouldn't be surprised, nor had she call to feel any disappointment. She had told him to stay away, and he was merely adhering to her wishes. She should be pleased, and she was—to an extent. Her life was much simpler and more predictable without him in it. She had much to do with the planning for Minnie's engagement party, the last thing she needed was a man underfoot. Or rather another man underfoot. Nathaniel was still staying with her, but not for much longer it seemed. He was healing nicely, and Mr. Griggs said he should be able to go home in a day or two.

Moira would miss having him so close, but she would also appreciate having her quiet time back. Unfortunately, that time would no doubt be spent obsessing over Wynthrope

Ryland. She could only pray that these plaguing thoughts of him would go away eventually.

Or maybe the man causing them might return and confide in her the reason that he was a thief. Perhaps he would trust her with his past. Perhaps he would realize that while she had meant every word about being safer without him around, she still wanted him in her life.

Did that make her a fool? Probably, but there was a voice inside her head—or perhaps in her heart—that insisted that she had not been wrong about him in the beginning. There was no way he could have pretended all of it. They had shared wonderful moments together. They had laughed and talked and played chess. Surely it hadn't all been a lie. She couldn't have been so misguided. Some of what he revealed to her had to be real, and if that was so, then there was just as real a part of him that was the good man she had once believed him to be.

And good men did not use women and pretend to care for them. Good men did not steal—not without a reason.

So what was Wynthrope's reason?

That was something she hoped to ascertain that evening. This was not a social event he would miss. There was a dinner party at Creed House to celebrate Devlin and Blythe's impending parenthood.

Moira had been surprised to get an invitation to the party, especially since she and Blythe had known each other but a brief time. During their short acquaintance, Moira had come to like the statuesque woman very much. Apparently the feeling was mutual.

That was why she and Minnie were snuggled beneath thick fur robes, their feet resting on heated bricks as the carriage jostled along the uneven cobblestones. They were on their way to Creed House for the party. In anticipation of the event, Moira had taken extra care with her appearance—

and *not* because she wanted to look good for Wynthrope's benefit. She wanted to be in her best looks to prove to him that she had not fallen into complete disarray since learning the awful truth about him.

Her scalp hurt from the elaborate hairstyle, which felt as though it might be in danger of toppling over at any moment. Sapphires dangled from her ears and adorned her neck. Her gown was a soft, warm cream brocade that pushed her bosom up until she actually looked impressive in that area.

It wasn't on purpose that the dress accented her cleavage. It was because she had gained weight since purchasing the gown. She had bought it before meeting Wynthrope. Since then she had ceased worrying about how thin she looked and concentrated on how she felt. If she was hungry she ate. No more of this starving herself to be thin—not when she was obviously the only one who found any fault with her appearance. And even she had to admit, she liked having a more impressive bosom.

"What are you going to do if he speaks to you?" Minnie asked, her voice muffled by the fur robe tucked around her.

Moira smiled dolefully. "I do not imagine he will, but if he does, I suppose I will simply speak back."

"Are you going to speak to him then?"

She shrugged and picked a bit of loose fur from her lip. The blasted robe was shedding. "Perhaps. It would be the polite thing to do. I would hate to ruin Lord Creed's party by being cold to his brother." She didn't want to admit to Minnie that she was considering taking Nathaniel's advice and cornering Wynthrope. Not that Nathaniel had suggested she trap him, but the sentiment had been the same.

She had to know the truth. Not until then could she decide what she wanted to do. Not until then would she know if he truly had feelings for her, or if it had been nothing more than greed and a bit of lust that had driven him to her bed.

Her nerves were nowhere near as distressed as she believed they ought to be. In fact, she was strangely calm about seeing Wynthrope. It would be such a relief to get an answer from him. Either he wanted her or he didn't. Either he was willing to confide and trust in her or he wasn't. And if he didn't want her, then she was done mooning over him like a stupid girl. She would put herself to the task of recovering from her broken heart and moving forward with her life. She did not expect it to happen overnight, but it would happen. If Nathaniel could develop feelings for someone after losing the love of his life, then certainly Moira could as well.

Good Lord, she didn't actually consider Wynthrope the love of her life, did she? She had loved him, of that she was certain, but she had loved the man he pretended to be. She had to find out who he really was before she could sort out her feelings.

Who was she fooling with this sorting-out-her-feelings nonsense? She loved him. Whether it was truly him or not, she loved him. She loved him as surely as she drew breath.

Which made what she was about to do all the more frightening. Tonight she planned to ascertain whether her feelings were returned.

Creed House—or Creed Manor as some called it—was a lovely whitewashed stone manor idyllically situated in Grosvenor Square. Lamps lit the way up the drive, and more lamps illuminated the front of the house so guests could see their way up the steps in the dark. Moira and Minnie ascended the smooth stone steps to the large, carved doors. Moira rapped with the heavy brass knocker, and one of the doors opened, revealing an older man of medium height and build who was almost completely bald.

"Lady Aubourn and Miss Banning?" he inquired pleasantly.

Moira smiled. "Yes."

He stood back so they might enter. "Welcome to Creed House, ladies. May I take your cloaks?"

With their outerwear removed and entrusted to the butler, who then passed the clothing to a footman, Moira and Minnie followed the butler through the great hall, which was decorated entirely in black and white. The floor was like a huge marble chess board. Even the statues lining the perimeter of the room resembled chess pieces. No wonder Wynthrope loved the game if this was the kind of environment in which he had been raised.

A door off the hall led to a corridor. Moira's gaze drifted from left to right as she walked, glancing at the many portraits lining the walls. Ryland ancestors, no doubt, judging from the countless lopsided smiles depicted. Oddly enough, it seemed a trait predominant in the males rather than the females. Ryland women obviously were not as arrogant as their male counterparts. Either that or they were simply more adept at concealing it.

They stopped two doors from the end of the corridor. The butler announced them and held the door for them to enter. Brahm was there to greet them the minute they stepped inside.

"My dear Lady Aubourn and Miss Banning." He took both their hands and kissed them both on the cheek. Minnie blushed prettily at the attention. What woman wouldn't? Viscount Creed was an extraordinarily handsome man. While Devlin had a melancholy kind of appeal and North a rugged look, Brahm was possibly the smoothest-looking of all the brothers. He was certainly the most chiseled, and he was the most at home in elegant surroundings.

Of course, none of them could hold a candle to Wynthrope—not as far as Moira was concerned. His beauty was cynical yet vulnerable. An angel cast out of heaven. Sometimes aloof and cold, other times unrestrained and joyous.

And obviously absent, she noticed as she glanced around the room, smiling and greeting the others present. Wynthrope was nowhere to be seen, and her heart sank a little. Was he simply tardy, or had he decided to take her words to heart and avoid the gathering—and consequently her—altogether?

Well, she wasn't going to let it ruin her evening. Tonight was about celebrating Blythe and Devlin, not pining for a man who might or might not be worthy of it. At least that was her resolution of the moment. It could change at any second.

She went to Devlin and Blythe, offering both of them her sincere best wishes. She even hugged them, a task not quite so comfortable considering her cheek was flattened against Devlin's chest. One of the buttons on his coat threatened to leave a mark if he held her any tighter. Good Lord but he was a strong man. So big and dangerous. Blythe didn't seem to mind.

They were going to have giants for children. Poor Blythe. Good thing she was a strapping woman.

She wandered toward the group that contained North and Octavia, Miles and Varya, and Brahm. The topic of conversation was whether North and Octavia had any plans to start a family of their own.

"Soon," Octavia responded, flashing her husband a warm smile. "I do not wish to be one of those women who is married for years and does not have children." It was then that Octavia noticed Moira, and her face turned a mortified shade of pink.

Moira chuckled. "Oh my friend, you do not think I would take offense to that, do you?" To be sure, the remark had stung, but not because Moira was insulted, more because she had been denied a basic right of womanhood by marrying Tony—something she hadn't considered at the time.

Her friend was obviously pained. "I would hope you did not, Moira."

She waved Octavia's concern away. "I never had children because I never had children." That was an easy enough answer. One could not conceive a child without having marital relations.

Octavia patted her hand. "You might remarry yet."

Moira considered the idea. Marrying again, yes, that might be nice, having someone to spend her days and nights with. As for children, she never really gave them much thought. However, if she did wed again, she would marry for love and nothing else. Life was too short to make the same mistakes twice.

Good Lord, she didn't actually believe marrying Tony had been a mistake, did she? No, maybe she regretted some aspects of her marriage, but the fact that it got her away from her parents would always be something she was thankful for.

Her parents. Just the thought of them made her stomach cramp. They would be coming for Minnie's betrothal party. For the first time since Tony's death, Moira would have to face her mother again.

At that moment, as though reading her thoughts, North thrust a glass of champagne at her. "Here, Moira. We are going to drink to Devlin and Blythe."

Moira thanked him and took the sparkling glass. Brahm, she noticed, was drinking something other than champagne. Cider, if her nose didn't deceive her—the kind without much kick.

"You are not toasting anyone without me," came a voice from behind her—a voice that sent a tremor down her spine that was both delicious and awful.

He had arrived.

She turned, sucking in a breath at the sight of him. He looked a little tired, but other than that, he was a vision of male perfection in austere evening wear, his jaw freshly shaven, his hair neatly combed.

Grinning with genuine pleasure, he greeted Devlin and Blythe, embracing his sister-in-law and kissing her cheek. He took the glass of champagne North offered and then he turned.

And saw her. His grin, she noticed, faded a bit, but did not disappear. Either he was a good actor or he was actually somewhat pleased to see her. God knew she was somewhat pleased to see him, if the trembling in her knees was any indication. Damn his eyes, but he had a lot of nerve staring at her so boldly. Of course she was staring back.

Their eye contact was broken by the sound of Brahm's voice. He allowed Miles to make the first toast as Blythe's brother, and then Brahm toasted Devlin. North and Wynthrope followed suit, each recounting some personal story about Devlin as a child.

"To my gigantic little brother," Wynthrope finished his salute with a smile. "Someday I hope to be half the man he is."

It was a touching sentiment, until North spoke. "You already are half the man he is, in height."

Laughter filled the room, and as the guests closed in around the beaming couple of honor, Moira took the opportunity to work her way closer to Wynthrope. She had no idea what to say after telling him to go away, but she would have to think of something.

"Good evening." Not terribly original, but not awful either.

He seemed surprised by her greeting. "Yes, it is."

Lowering her head, Moira worried her lower lip with her teeth for a moment before raising her gaze to his. "I wanted to apologize for some of the things I said the last time we met."

He shook his head. "Don't. You were right when you said your life was better without me in it."

She winced as her words were tossed back at her. "I never said better."

He shrugged, and took a sip of champagne. "Safer then. You were right. You need to stay away from me for a while."

His words might have hurt more if she hadn't caught the edge in his voice. He wasn't just telling her to stay away, he was asking her to—pleading even. "Wynthrope, what are you planning?"

He didn't look at her, but gazed toward his family instead. "I cannot tell you."

Moira's chest constricted. "You still do not trust me."

Wynthrope glanced down into his champagne. "I do not."

"I see." She was cold, so very cold. Numb, actually. She couldn't feel her fingers around the stem of her glass.

"No you don't." His voice was a harsh whisper as he turned his whole body to face her. "I cannot tell because I cannot trust you not to do something foolish like try to help, or, God forbid, save me."

Save him? Dear Lord, what was he planning to do? "I would not—"

"Yes you would, because you are just that kind of woman." He downed the rest of his champagne with one swallow. "You are too good. The best thing you can do to help me right now is to stay away."

She swallowed hard. "Of course." She turned to walk away. She knew he had some frightening reason for saying these things to her, but it didn't change the fact that he still did not trust her with the truth. She didn't need it all—and she didn't need it right now. All she needed was the knowledge that he might someday confide in her; then running the risk of someone hearing this humiliating conversation would be worth it.

He stopped her by stepping in front of her, shielding both of them from potentially curious eyes. "Moira, I know I have no right to ask, but I need you to trust me. If you can do that, I promise that when this is all over I will tell you everything."

Hope bloomed in her breast. "You will?"

Wynthrope's gaze was intent, steady, and sincere. "I will."

"Fine." It was all she could do not to grin like the village idiot. Maybe he didn't trust her now, but he was going to confide in her later. Her urge to smile faded. He wasn't going to confide in her until it didn't matter anymore. That didn't quite equal trust. That would be like her telling him she had been a virgin after he discovered it for himself. What was the point?

"I will stay away and wait for you to come to me." Bitterness coated her words.

He sensed her malcontent. His eyes pleaded with her. "You will not have to wait for long."

"Mm hmm." She stepped to the side, rounding the obstacle that was him. "Do not make any more promises, Wynthrope."

He frowned. "Why not?"

She shot him a sharp glance before walking away. "I just might expect you to keep them."

What the hell was that supposed to mean?

Wynthrope watched Moira as she swished across the room, every inch a queen in a confection of cream that made her breasts look temptingly bountiful. She needn't have gone to the bother if her appearance was for his benefit—or for spite. He would find her beautiful in sackcloth and ashes.

But where did she find the nerve to tell him not to make her any more promises? He had never promised her something he couldn't, or wouldn't, deliver. She was just angry because he wouldn't tell her what he was up to. Of course he wouldn't. If he told her he was going to risk his own life to bring Daniels to justice, she would tongue-lash him within an inch of his life. She might also do something foolish to try to help him. Women did not act with reason when it came to the concerns of men. Had not Octavia confronted the very man who tried to kill North because she thought she could make a difference? Granted, Octavia had been acting out of love. Wynthrope might not be so fortunate to have Moira's love, but he knew how protective she could be of those she cared about.

She had already been sweetly foolish enough to give him the tiara. He would not have her do more, especially not at the risk of her own safety. If Daniels got ahold of her . . . Well, Daniels would end up dead, but there was no way he could guarantee Moira's protection. And he wasn't going to risk losing her, not when he had yet to win her again.

The next hour that passed was as painful as having a tooth extracted. Both Blythe and Octavia suspected he had done Moira some kind of injury, and their disapproving expressions followed him wherever he went. And then there was Moira's true champion, Minerva. If looks could kill, Wynthrope would have stuck his spoon in the wall several times over already.

It was time to leave. Moira hadn't spoken to him again, in fact she was doing a very good job of pretending he didn't exist, but that wasn't why he was leaving. He was leaving because later that evening he was going to be meeting Daniels to exchange the tiara for the information Daniels had on Wynthrope. He had to prepare. He had to make certain things were in order just in case something went wrong. He had to ensure that if he died, Moira got the chess set Brahm had given him that had been their father's. She would appreciate it, and perhaps the note he had written to go with it.

Of course there was the chance that Daniels wouldn't kill him, and then he would be able to tell her the contents of the letter in person. It was that outcome he hoped for.

He approached North as soon as he saw his brother standing alone. "I'm leaving now."

Instantly North's entire body tensed, though his expression remained the same. "Already?"

"I have a few things to take care of first."

North eyed him suspiciously. "You are not going to try to get the jump on us, are you? That would be stupid."

Chuckling, Wynthrope shook his head. "No. I will be at the house on Russell at midnight. See you then."

North grabbed his arm as he started to walk away. "Be careful."

Wynthrope smiled. "Of course. Playing the reckless hero is your style, not mine."

But as he left his brother's home, Wynthrope was aware of just how bloody reckless he was being. And all because of a woman.

The woman he'd betrayed.

The woman he didn't think he could live without.

"Do you have it?" Daniels's tone betrayed his anxiety.

It was dark inside the Russell Street address, save for a fire flickering brightly in the hearth. It did little to relieve the chill in the air, the house having been empty for some time. Would someone find the fire suspicious? Wynthrope could only hope.

It was just after midnight, and Covent Garden was a dark and dangerous place to be, even for the criminals who haunted it. For instance, if one were to barge into this place right now demanding to know what was going on, he would more than likely end up with Daniels's blade in his chest, the old man was that much on edge.

It was time to put an end to this.

Wynthrope lifted the box. "Show me the papers."

Daniels flashed a string-wrapped folder thick with pages. "Satisfied?"

Not quite, but soon. Wynthrope gestured with a nod. "Set it on the table."

"You first," The old man insisted.

Wynthrope smiled coolly. "You."

They stared at each other, and finally Wynthrope won. Daniels set the folder on the rough-hewn tabletop. Wynthrope gingerly reached out and slid it toward himself, never taking his eyes off his former mentor.

"Now you," Daniels demanded.

First Wynthrope flipped the folder open to make certain the information contained was what it should be. When he was satisfied that it was, he set the box on the table, pushing it toward Daniels.

The Irishman snatched it up, his face bright with greed and delight as he opened the lid. "Ah, boyo, ye did me proud."

Wynthrope didn't acknowledge the praise. Having earned it by losing Moira, he didn't take any pleasure in it. "You will leave England now, and never return."

The older man nodded absentmindedly. Likely he hadn't even noticed that it was an order and not a question. "Yes, yes. Whatever."

Wynthrope was just about to relax when Daniels snapped the box shut and pulled a pistol from his pocket. His heart tripped heavily against his ribs. "What now, you are going to kill me?"

Daniels made a tsking noise. "'Tis just a wee bit of insurance, lad. I just want to make certain you don't try any funny stuff as I make my escape."

"Funny stuff. Me?" The words sounded falsely innocent, even to himself. And just what the hell was "funny stuff" anyway? There was nothing amusing about this situation, although bashing Daniels's head against the table might give him a smile.

Daniels's eyes narrowed. "Aye, like tryin' to be a hero or some such nonsense. You be the type of man who would try to wrest this pretty from me to win the fair maiden's heart."

"She's not a maiden," Wynthrope replied. "And there's not enough shine in the world to win her heart." Why he was telling this bastard anything about Moira was beyond him. He knew only that the urge to defend her had outweighed any common sense that might have helped him conceal his true feelings for her.

"So she's one of those then." Daniels shot him a look of pity from behind the gun. "Too bad for you. I hope she never finds out about our transaction, boyo. She'll not forgive ye for it."

The words hit closer than Wynthrope was comfortable with. Since when was Daniels an expert on women? He had known plenty, to be sure, but he'd never had a lasting relationship that Wynthrope knew of. He knew nothing of what Moira would or would not do.

But he had struck a tender spot, that was certain.

"I would love to discuss the details of my private life with you, but you have a country to get the hell out of."

The old man smiled. "So I do. Good-bye, lad." He backed toward the door, the tiara tucked under his arm, safe in its box. At the door he reached behind his back to depress the latch, never taking his eyes off Wynthrope. Then the darkness swallowed him, the door shut, and Wynthrope was alone with the sinister shadows and crackling blaze.

He wasted no time. As soon as the door latch clicked back into place, he opened the folder and began removing the papers several at a time. He tossed them into the fire blazing in the hearth, watching with grim satisfaction as they withered and turned to ash. He was so intent on his task that he chose to ignore the commotion outside. No doubt it was better that way.

With the last of the papers gone, and the blackened remains of his past turned to ash, Wynthrope tossed the folder into the fire as well. That was it. The end.

He stirred the embers with a poker just to be certain there were no traces of evidence left before slipping on his gloves and hat. It wasn't that he was so confident that Daniels had given him the only copy of the evidence, it was simply that he did not want to be caught with those papers in his possession. Slowly he walked across the creaking floor and opened the door, stepping out into the cold, noisy night.

There were a dozen men on horseback with rifles trained on a man kneeling on the ground. Two men had just shackled his wrists and ankles and were pulling him to his feet. A third held the oaken box in his hand. Wynthrope gazed at his back as he approached, the sound of the prisoner's raving echoing in his ears.

"I had nothin' to do with it! It was all Ryland. He's the man you want. I have evidence that he's the Ghost!"

The man with the box turned as Wynthrope approached. "Is that true, Mr. Ryland?"

Daniels ceased struggling long enough to glare at him. For the second time that evening Wynthrope realized how lucky he was that looks could not kill.

Wynthrope flashed a cool smile at the chief magistrate of Bow Street. "With a brother like mine, Mr. Reed? I would never be able to conceal it."

Duncan Reed didn't look quite convinced, but Wynthrope didn't really think he cared. The Ghost was old history, and Bow Street had caught Daniels redhanded with the Viscountess Aubourn's missing tiara—reported stolen on her behalf by North Sheffield-Ryland.

"He's lying!" Daniels shouted. "I can prove he's a thief!"

Wynthrope shrugged. "I have no idea what he is talking about, but you are more than welcome to search the house as well as myself."

Reed considered that for a moment before shaking his head. "There's no need. It is obvious to me who the real villain is here. Thank you for your assistance apprehending the criminal, Mr. Ryland."

"Assistance!" Daniels fought against his restraints like a wild man as the Runners dragged him away. "You will pay for this, Ryland! I swear to God you will pay!"

His rantings were reduced to muffled, incoherent shouts as the officers loaded him into the wagon and locked the door.

With Daniels gone and the scene a tad more quiet, Reed turned to face Wynthrope. "I have a great deal of respect for your brother."

Wynthrope nodded. "I know. He respects you as well."

"I never pressed for an explanation why he left Bow Street, and I do not want one now. As far as I am concerned this investigation ends here. Am I speaking plain enough, Mr. Ryland?"

Swallowing against the dryness in his throat, Wynthrope smiled. "Perfectly." Thank God for his luck. Thank God for North and his connections. Otherwise the magistrate might be tempted to look a little deeper in Wynthrope's past.

"I would appreciate it if you could come by Bow Street in the morning. I would like to get a written statement from all involved. I am particularly interested in how Mr. Daniels thought you would steal the tiara for him."

No doubt he was. Obviously North hadn't thought to make something up, so now Wynthrope would have to. Wonderful. What the hell kind of explanation could he possibly think of?

"He knew I had been courting the viscountess and threatened to make a scandal out of our relationship if I did not help him. Of course, I went straight to my brother."

Reed nodded, his face impassive. "Of course. Good night, Mr. Ryland. I will see you in the morning."

"Good night, Mr. Reed." It wasn't until the magistrate was safely tucked away inside his own carriage and following the prison wagon down the street that Wynthrope released the breath he had been holding.

"Good job," North commented, coming up behind him. "I found a copy of the evidence in Daniels's rooms."

Wynthrope sighed as Brahm approached from the other side. "Excellent."

The sound of a thud and heavy footfalls behind them caused them all to turn. Devlin walked out of the darkness, his Baker rifle tucked under his arm.

"Where the hell were you?" Bramh demanded.

"The roof," the youngest Ryland replied. "You three didn't really think I'd stay away, did you?"

Wynthrope laughed. That whole time Devlin could have picked Daniels off like a fly and no one would have ever known what happened. Of course, his brother wouldn't kill indiscriminately. It wasn't his nature.

"Let's go," Brahm suggested, herding them all down the street to where they had left his carriage. "Morning will come quickly, and two of you have appointments with Bow Street."

"Thank you," Wynthrope said as they reached the carriage. "All of you. You have no idea how much I appreciate your help."

North clapped him on the back. "You should have come to us sooner. We could have spared you a lot of trouble." He climbed into the carriage, followed by Devlin.

Brahm stopped Wynthrope with a hand on his shoulder as he went to step into the carriage. "We could have saved you a lot of heartache if you had only trusted us."

Wynthrope managed a self-deprecating smile. "I do not trust easily."

"Well then," his brother said, elbowing him out of the way so he could enter the carriage first. "It's about time you started, don't you think?"

Wynthrope considered the suggestion as he followed him into the vehicle. Yes, it was time. Past time, in fact.

Chapter 18

⌒◯◯⌒

When the summons came early the next morning for her to come to Bow Street, Moira's heart very nearly stopped. What could Bow Street possibly want with her? Had some harm befallen Nathaniel again? Or was it Wynthrope? Had he been caught during a robbery? Had he turned himself in? Or, dear God, was he dead?

The idea of living in a world without him in it was inconceivable to her now. Even if things were never right between them, even if she never again in her life knew the sweetness of being held in his arms, she could not bear to think of him no longer existing. The pain of never seeing him again would be infinitely worse than seeing him and never being able to have him.

It was better not to think about it. It only made her chest ache and her eyes burn.

Perhaps this summons had nothing to do with him. That made more sense. Perhaps she herself had done something wrong, although she had no idea what that might have been. She dressed quickly and dashed off a note to leave on the table for Minnie, letting her know where she had gone and that she would be back as soon as possible.

Her poor coachman looked as though he was still half asleep, as he was hardly ever called for service at this time of day. Moira apologized to him for the inconvenience and bade him to make haste to number three Bow Street.

By the time she reached her destination, her feet and fingers were nearly numb from the lack of warmth in the carriage. There had been no time to send for heated bricks, and the lap robe had been cold when she draped it over her. Her nose was frozen on her face and her teeth were chattering. She should have worn thicker stockings. She should have worn a wool gown and a fur-lined cloak, but she hadn't thought of these things.

She must have looked quite a sight, judging from the reaction of the woman who met her in the open waiting area.

"You must be Lady Aubourn," she said, cupping her shoulders with warm hands. "I am Mrs. Periwinkle, Mr. Reed's new assistant. Though I'm more like a nanny than anything else." She chuckled. "Let's get you into the master's office and warm you up."

Moira couldn't have moved her jaw to argue even if she had wanted. Her limbs were stiff and uncooperative as she allowed Mrs. Periwinkle to propel her toward a closed door to the side of the room. The plump, elderly woman knocked once, not bothering to wait until she was told to enter before doing so. She practically had to shove Moira into the room.

Ah, but it was warm in here. Already, Moira could feel it seeping through her clothes. The air was rich with the smell of coffee, and beneath that, smoke and beeswax. A man sat behind the massive scarred oak desk—a shrewd man with pale, watchful eyes.

But he was not the only man in the room, Moira noticed. There were others watching her as well. Brahm Ryland, Devlin Ryland, North Ryland, Leander Tyndale—what the devil was he doing there? And Wynthrope Ryland. He didn't even offer his usual smirk.

Dear God, she had done something! Why else would they all be there? It was impossible, though. She had never broken a law in her life. Well, almost never.

A sudden, irrational thought occurred to her. Had Wynthrope accused her of some wrongdoing and convinced his brothers to stand with him against her? No. Wynthrope had done something awful to her, that was true, but he said he had his reasons and she wanted to believe that. She wanted to believe in him. More than that, a part of her *did* believe in him, and knew that he would never sink to such depths, especially not where she was concerned.

They all stood, and Mr. Reed gestured toward the one empty chair in the room. It was directly in front of his desk, with the other men flanking her on both sides. Nothing like making a lady feel as though she had no chance of escape.

"Please sit, Lady Auburn. I apologize for inconveniencing you at this early hour. Would you care for some coffee?"

Coffee would be good. And hot. "Yes. Thank you, Mr. Reed."

She moved toward the chair, careful to avoid meeting Wynthrope's gaze as she sat. "May I ask what this is all about?"

"Of course." But the magistrate waited until Mrs. Periwinkle had handed Moira her cup and left the room before saying or doing anything else.

With the door closed, sealing them inside the warmth of the office, Mr. Reed opened the top drawer of his desk, reached in, and withdrew a very familiar-looking box. Moira frowned as she sipped at her coffee, both hands wrapped around the cup for warmth. Was that what she thought it was?

"I believe this is yours, my lady."

Moira was very much aware of Duncan Reed's watchful gaze upon her. How best to act? She had not reported the tiara stolen, so it would not do to simply thank him.

She took the saucer from her lap and set it on his desk, then placed her cup on it. Trying her best to look nothing more than merely curious, she reached for the box and opened the lid.

It was the tiara, all right.

She raised her gaze to Reed's even though she wanted to turn to Wynthrope for an explanation. "Where did you get this?"

Steepling his fingers beneath his chin, the magistrate regarded her with no emotion whatsoever. "It was found in the possession of a man we apprehended last evening."

Last evening? Dear heaven, was that why Wynthrope was there as well? He had been captured? It took all her strength not to turn to him.

What did she do now? Admit to giving the tiara to Wynthrope or pretend innocence? Moira glanced at the sparkling gems and chose a less direct route. "How did you know it was mine?"

"Mr. Ryland, who aided in the apprehension, recognized it."

Moira turned to North. "Thank you." How had he managed it? Had Wynthrope tipped him off? Or had he caught his brother with it?

North smiled. "Oh, it wasn't me. It was my brother." He pointed at Wynthrope.

It was all she could do to hide her surprise. Wynthrope? Had he betrayed his partner to save himself just as he had betrayed her, or had this been his plan all along?

She cast him the briefest of glances, to look too long

would be to reveal her confusion. He simply gave her a casual tilt of his head. Instead, she turned her bewildered gaze back to Duncan Reed and waited for him to explain. She did not have to wait long.

"Apparently the thief tried to blackmail Mr. Ryland to steal your tiara or reveal your . . . *relationship* to the public. He immediately went to North here, and they concocted a plan to catch the spider in his own web."

Moira resisted the urge to let her expression say exactly what she thought of *that* explanation. They hadn't had a "relationship" until the night Wynthrope tried to rob her. He had lied to Bow Street, and now he had brought North into his little scheme as well. Was North completely innocent, or did he know about his brother's criminal past? And just what the devil were all four of the Ryland brothers doing there?

She turned to Wynthrope with a hurt expression that was more sincere than she would have liked. "You might have told me of your plans."

He shrugged. "I did not want to risk your safety, my dear."

His dear. Butter wouldn't melt in this man's mouth. Moira hated being part of this deception, but she couldn't reveal the truth, not with all these people present. She didn't want to risk saying anything that might put North in an uncomfortable situation. Octavia was her friend, and she would do anything to spare her from discomfort. Her own discomfort she could live with, at least until she could get Wynthrope alone and demand an explanation.

She didn't bother responding to Wynthrope's false endearments, but turned to Leander instead. "And why are you here, Lord Aubourn?" It felt so strange calling him by his title, but in public it was the socially expected thing.

Leander flushed to the roots of his fair hair. "For some reason, the thief claimed that I had hired him to steal the tiara."

As ludicrous as it sounded, there was something in Leander's tone that gave Moira pause. Had he been the one to hire Wynthrope and his crony? No, it couldn't be. He would never want to hurt her or Nathaniel, never. But he might not have been able to control what his hirelings did on his behalf.

Still, it didn't make sense. Why not just ask her for the tiara? He had known her for years, there would be no need for such deceit.

Moira looked at Mr. Reed. "That is simply ridiculous. The viscount is family. If he wanted the tiara, he would have asked me for it. Wouldn't you, my lord?"

Leander shifted slightly in his chair, but he met her gaze with a direct one of his own. "Why would I ask for something that means so much to you?"

Meant so much to her? It was an adornment, for heaven's sake! It wasn't as though Tony had crafted it himself. Besides, as the new viscount, didn't Leander have a right to it? It wasn't part of the jewel collection that belonged to the title, but the tiara had been in Leander and Tony's family for years. He certainly had more of a claim to it than she did. And there was something so strange in his demeanor . . .

Dear heavens, was everyone in this room something other than what he seemed?

Yes, there was something odd afoot here. Something far stranger than Wynthrope claiming to have found the tiara or suddenly being in cahoots with Bow Street. Perhaps that had been the secret he had felt he couldn't reveal to her, that he wasn't a criminal after all, but a champion of sorts.

Perhaps she was clutching at straws.

Her head was beginning to ache. "I do appreciate your recovering the tiara for me, Mr. Reed."

The magistrate held up his hands. "Do not thank me. I simply made certain my men were on hand to make the arrest. Thanks belongs to Mr. Ryland here."

Moira gazed at Wynthrope. Her expression was carefully schooled, but she knew the disappointment had not entirely vanished from her eyes. "Yes, I suppose it does."

To his credit, Wynthrope darkened at her words, as good as admitting to her that he didn't deserve the sentiment. As much as she wanted to believe he was innocent, as much as she wanted to forgive him, there was a part of her that balked at thanking him. What was she thanking him for? Trying to steal her tiara, only to return it? Or for breaking her heart and not trusting her enough to tell her why? All she had wanted was more of an explanation.

All she wanted was to know that he was sorry. He had already made some gestures that were far grander, but had yet to ask for her forgiveness. She didn't want the damn tiara. She wanted him to feel as horrible as she did, and she wanted him to promise to never hurt her like this again.

She wanted him to be the man she knew he could be, and not the one he seemed determined to continue presenting to the world. That Wynthrope wasn't a man, he was merely armor, and he certainly wasn't the man she had adored.

Her attention returned to the man behind the desk. "Is there anything else you require of me, Mr. Reed? I am afraid I have a very busy agenda this morning." That wasn't a total lie. She did have many things to do, such as shopping for Minnie's wedding and planning the betrothal party. Everything had to be perfect—not just for Minnie, but for their mother. Mama would be the first person to find fault with any of the preparations, and the last thing Moira wanted or needed right now was her mother telling her what a disappointment she was.

"No," Reed replied. "Thank you for coming in, Lady Aubourn. You as well, Lord Aubourn. Both of you are free to go."

But not the Ryland brothers. As much as Moira would

have liked to corner Wynthrope and demand an explanation, it was going to have to wait—if she ever received one at all. If he thought returning the tiara was enough to placate her, he really didn't know her at all.

"Good morning, gentlemen," she said to the brothers and the magistrate, singling out no one in particular. Let Wynthrope think she was as unmoved by the whole situation as he was. Let him think whatever he wanted. At this point she was so unsure of what to believe, it might be safer to believe in nothing.

The men all stood and wished her a good day. Wynthrope's voice was low and personal, and Moira cringed at the sound of it. He was still playing at being her lover for Reed's benefit, not for hers. She ignored him.

Outside the office, she took the arm Leander offered her and strode to the exit beside him. She waited until they were outside, the noise of the city bustling around them before speaking. They stood beside her carriage. His was parked just ahead.

"Leander, may I speak to you?"

He turned to her, his brow knitted with concern. "Of course."

How to phrase this? She had to be delicate or risk insulting him. "Tony gave me many things that I will always treasure, but this"—she held up the box—"is not one of them. I am not insinuating anything, nor do I ask you for a reply at this time, especially given the fact that we are still very much in plain sight of Mr. Reed's office, but if this tiara is something that you would like to call your own, you may call on me this evening to claim it. I ask nothing but answers in return, after which we will never speak of this again."

He stared at her, his expression a strange mixture of horror, bewilderment, and relief. It had been he, of that Moira was now certain. He was the one who hired Wynthrope—or his associate. Strangely, that made her heart sink more than the realization that Leander was inadvertently responsible for what had happened to Nathaniel.

Leander's mouth opened, but Moira cut him off before he could say anything. "Do not say anything now. If you want this box, then come to my house this evening. If not, I will put it back in my safe with the rest of my jewelry, and there it will sit until I feel like taking it out again." Which would be never. She would never wear the tiara again without thinking of Wynthrope and all the heartbreak he brought with him. She would rather not wear it than think of him every time she did.

And she would rather Leander simply take it than hire someone to try to steal it again. Even if that never happened, she would spend the rest of her life waiting for it, probably distrusting anyone who showed the least bit of interest in her.

Or anyone who warned her about a thief being on the loose. Both Leander and Wynthrope had done that.

"Now I must go. Minnie will be waiting."

"You are an extraordinary woman, Moira," Leander remarked as he handed her up into her carriage.

Moira turned to gaze out the door at him as she sat. "No more than any other, Leander. These are simply extraordinary circumstances. Good day."

With a bemused smile, he shut the carriage door and told the driver to depart. Moira waved to him as the carriage pulled away. Her gaze drifted to the window of Duncan Reed's office. A man stood behind the tiny panes of glass. It wasn't Reed. She knew who it was just as she knew that Leander would be at her house that evening.

And she didn't know which one of them had disappointed her more.

Wynthrope spent the rest of the day and the early part of the evening in his apartments, waiting for Moira to come.

It wasn't that she had sent word she would come round, or that he was even expecting her, but he had hoped that she might come by, now that she had the tiara back. Even if she did not believe all his actions had been driven by the desire to ensnare Daniels, her curiosity must be eating at her.

But she did not come. She was undoubtedly waiting for him to come to her, which meant that she was still angry with him. And still hurt. Perhaps today's scene at Bow Street had only served to turn her even more against him. Maybe now she thought him the worst kind of scoundrel. God only knew what she was thinking. She was a woman, after all, and that sex was notoriously difficult to predict.

When he was certain she was indeed not coming, he contemplated going to her, but if she was still angry, the wise idea would be to leave her alone for a bit. As much as he wanted to see her and finally confess all, he wanted her to be willing to hear it. All the truth in the world wouldn't amount to shite if she didn't want to believe it.

So he went to Brahm's instead. His oldest brother had sent a note earlier inviting him for dinner. Normally Wynthrope would decline, but Brahm mentioned that Devlin and North and their wives were going to be there as well. While he didn't want Brahm to get the wrong idea and think that they were ever going to be the best of friends, Wynthrope could not deny that he didn't want to spend the evening alone. And Brahm had done so much for him lately, he really ought to be grateful.

His brother wasn't the villain he'd always believed him to be, but he was not quite ready to name him a saint either. Probably it was petty of him, but his life had been turned upside down quite enough for this new year. He wasn't prepared to take on any more changes just yet.

The rest of the family was already present when he arrived at Creed Manor. They sat in the drawing room with a drink—except for Brahm—and waited for dinner to be announced. Everything seemed perfectly normal, but Wynthrope detected a hint of something just underneath the surface—a tension, and it was coming from North. Was his brother still angry with him on Moira's behalf? If he was, he hoped North kept it to himself tonight. He was in no mood to discuss what he had done. At the time it had seemed like the only course of action available to him. He was not going to defend himself against his own brother, especially when he was going to need all his strength to defend himself to Moira.

After dinner, Blythe and Octavia left them to coffee—rather than port—and cigars. This was definitely odd, as usually the family broke with tradition and everyone retired to the drawing room at the same time. Obviously Blythe and Octavia had things they wished to discuss—or Octavia knew that North wanted to be alone with his brothers.

Not a full minute had passed after the women left before North spoke, "Have you heard?" he demanded of the other three.

"Heard what?" Brahm asked, lifting his cup.

North leaned forward, bracing his forearms on the polished surface of the cherry tabletop. "Daniels has already been bundled off to New South Wales."

"What?" Wynthrope almost choked on his coffee. "That's impossible. Not even twenty-four hours have passed since his arrest."

North nodded, his eyes bright. "I know."

"Where did you hear this?" Devlin asked. "Your source may be wrong."

Their half brother shook his head. "I have it straight from Duncan Reed himself. He is not impressed that Bow Street has been denied the chance to question Daniels about his affiliates in London."

Thank God they didn't. Wynthrope had been very much aware from the moment he and his brothers had hatched their plan to double-cross Daniels that he was putting himself in danger. Perhaps Reed didn't believe Daniels when he first insisted he and Wynthrope were connected, or perhaps he did but could not prove it. Regardless of what the magistrate believed, it would have been only a matter of time before Daniels talked enough to raise suspicions. Reed's loyalty to North would go only so far before the lawman gave in to his morals and had them both investigated.

He and North might be masters of concealment when they wanted to be, but Duncan Reed had taught North everything he knew. There would be no hiding from him for long.

"Did Reed tell you what happened?" he asked.

North turned pale blue eyes on him. "Apparently there wasn't much to tell. No one has given Duncan any more information than they've had to."

Devlin rolled his eyes as he stirred his second cup of coffee. "Basically nothing then."

"Exactly." North's own expression was a mixture of resignation and curiosity. "Rumor has it that Pitt was involved with the decision, but that is all I have been able to find out."

Silence fell around the table as the brothers pondered the situation and drank their coffee. It was then, as the silence grew heavy, that Wynthrope realized Brahm hadn't expressed surprise at the turn of events. In fact, Brahm hadn't expressed anything at all, which was odd for his eldest brother, who generally seemed to consider himself an expert on all things.

As he stared into his cup, Wynthrope's brow knitted. Slowly he turned his head without raising it, to regard the man seated at the head of the table. Brahm appeared disinterested, cool, composed, and uncaring. Apprehension immediately bloomed in Wynthrope's chest.

When Devlin had first gotten involved with Blythe, he had knocked the senses out of the Earl of Carnover, who had been a good friend, for making improper and forceful advances on the woman who was now Mrs. Devlin Ryland. Overwhelmed by guilt, Devlin had embarked on a path of self-destruction. Everyone had gone searching for him, but it had been Brahm who had found him, feverish and chilled in a dockside tavern. It had been Brahm who, for all intents and purposes, had saved their youngest brother. He had also given Devlin the proof he needed that he had been loved by their father.

Just this past season, when North had been prepared to sacrifice his love for Octavia because of the danger associated with his profession, it had been Brahm who stepped in. And when North's nemesis, Harker, had him at gunpoint, ready to kill him, it had been Brahm who surprised everyone by slaying the villain so North didn't have to, so North's budding career in politics could continue without blemish.

Both times Brahm had surprised them all. Both times the eldest Ryland had stepped in on behalf of his brothers and changed circumstances so that each brother had been able to go on to the kind of life and love he deserved.

With Daniels gone, not only could North rest easy, but Wynthrope certainly could. There was no danger of his shameful past coming to light now. There was nothing preventing him from telling Moira everything because he no longer had to worry about her safety.

Good God.

"It was you," he whispered hoarsely.

His brothers stared at him. He could feel Devlin and North's gazes, but he kept his own focused solely on Brahm. He had thought he and North were good actors; they had nothing on their eldest brother.

Brahm's expression was perfect bewildered innocence. "I beg your pardon?"

Wynthrope wasn't affected. "You engineered Daniels's deportation. I do not know how you managed it, but it was you."

His brother appeared amused by his allegations. "I appreciate your faith in my abilities, Wyn, but how in the name of God could a pariah like me accomplish such a feat?"

"I do not know, nor do I care," Wynthrope replied. "What I want to know is why?"

Again Brahm tried to deny it, but he was stopped this time by Devlin. "He's right. It was you, wasn't it, Brahm? You are responsible for getting rid of Daniels just as you were responsible for ridding North of Harker and ridding me of the fears that kept me from Blythe."

"Christ." North's tone was thick with disbelief. "How did you manage it?"

Under the force of all three convictions, Brahm gave up all pretext. Sighing, he pushed his cup aside and slumped back in his chair.

"How is not important."

"Not important!" North stared at him, mouth gaping. "I think I would be very interested in knowing how a 'pariah' could influence some of the most powerful men in England, and you would have to in order to get Daniels on a boat so fast."

Brahm pinned him with a stare that told him there would be no further discussion. "Someone owed me a favor."

Devlin let loose a low whistle. "That must have been some favor."

Brahm smiled slightly, his lips curving up on one side in the Ryland grin. "It was."

North's eyes narrowed. "That's it? That's all you're going to tell us?"

Brahm's head nodded once. "That is already more than you need to know."

"No," Wynthrope argued. "We—I—need to know why."

Russet eyes darkened, revealing an emotion that brought an uncomfortable tightness to Wynthrope's chest. "You are my brother."

That was it? That was his explanation? "A brother who has been a complete bastard to you since we were children."

His brother shrugged his wide shoulders. "But my brother nevertheless."

"No." Wynthrope shook his head almost violently. "That is not good enough. Maybe it was good enough when you stepped in for Devlin and North because I could believe you felt so deeply for them, but not for me."

Brahm frowned. "Why not for you?"

"Because I do not believe all this brotherly love shite. You never liked me either, so why are you doing this now?"

Laughter was not what he expected in response. "We were children! I have never harbored the same resentment for you that you felt for me. And even if I did, do you honestly think I would stand by and watch your life potentially be ruined when I had it in my power to prevent it?"

Wynthrope held his gaze. "Why?"

"Why?" Devlin and North repeated in unison.

There was no escape for Brahm this time, not when faced with the three of them. "Because I owe it to you."

"Owe us?" North scowled. "What the hell does that mean?"

Shoving back his chair, Brahm seized his cane and pushed himself to his feet. For a moment Wynthrope thought he might actually leave the room. He limped over to the mantel instead and stared up at the portrait of their father that hung there.

The former Viscount Creed had been a handsome man. Brahm looked much like him, save for the brown eyes. Wynthrope had his father's eyes—North too to an extent, although much paler. Devlin and Brahm's dark eyes came from Lady Creed.

But drinking and other excesses had taken their toll on their father's looks. By the end of his life he developed a hollow look about the eyes, a puffiness to his face that all hard drinkers seemed to develop. Wynthrope could not remember ever seeing his father without a glass of brandy in his hand, or whiskey. He had preferred whiskey.

Wynthrope had tried to drink with his father one night, but the old man hadn't known when to stop, and he could drink more than the average man. Brahm was the only one who could match him. Brahm had been able to best him. At one time Wynthrope had envied his brother that ability as well, but not after seeing what it did to him. Brahm Ryland was not a man you wanted to be anywhere near when he was deep in his cups. As vicious as he could be jovial, as complacent as he could be wild, Brahm had been completely unpredictable when he drank, and totally uncontrollable.

Brahm stood beneath the portrait, staring at it for what seemed an age. His brothers exchanged questioning glances, silently trying to decide what they should do next. They were saved from having to make the decision by Brahm turning to face them.

"I owe you because I am responsible for Father's death."

His brothers gaped at him.

"That was an accident," Devlin reminded him.

"You said you didn't remember anything," Wynthrope's tone was a bit harsher than he'd intended.

Brahm nodded. "I do not—not much of it, at any rate. I do remember that we were racing Pemberton when it happened."

"When what happened?" It was North who dared ask.

Brahm turned back to the portrait, as though it helped him collect the details in his mind. "We were practically flying we were going so fast. I told Father to give me the reins. I didn't think he was in any condition to control the horses."

"And you were?" Wynthrope scoffed, earning himself a dark glance from North. Chastised, he fell silent.

Brahm shot him a rueful smile. "Perhaps not, but I believed I was. I had not imbibed as much as Father had that night."

"What happened next?" North prodded.

Leaning on his cane, Brahm turned his attention back to the painting. "I remember him laughing at me, telling me to go to hell, of course he could control his own cattle." His tone was a mixture of amusement and sorrow. "The horses were running wild. I tried to take the reins from him. We fought. Neither of us was paying attention to the road. I managed to get the reins from him at last. We swerved. I remember being tossed through the air as the vehicle tipped. Then there was nothing."

"You do not remember dragging yourself down the road for help?" North inquired incredulously.

Brahm shook his head, his back still to them. "No, although my hands were bandaged because of the cuts from the rocks. I do not remember finding anyone. I do not remember being brought back to the house. I don't even remember being told that Father was dead. All I remember is taking the reins and then waking up one morning unable to walk and being told Father was to be buried that day."

"The doctor told you to stay in bed," Devlin remarked.

Brahm glanced over his shoulder at the youngest brother. "You carried me to the chaise so I could attend the burial."

Maybe the two of them found some kind of enjoyment in reliving these memories, but Wynthrope didn't. What he remembered of that day was feeling as though his chance to ever prove himself to his father was gone. Most people probably would have felt a strange sense of loss, but all Wynthrope had felt was relief from the burden. He never admitted that to anyone, not even North. North had been the most distraught at the funeral. Of course, he had been their father's favorite, having been born to a woman the viscount actually loved as opposed to the wife he tolerated.

"What has this to do with what you have done for the three of us?" he demanded of his brother.

Brahm turned fully this time, their father hanging over him like some strange specter of the past.

"I took your father from you," Brahm explained, his voice hushed. "If I had not tried to take the reins, he might be alive today."

"Or you might both have been killed," North informed him hotly. "Good God, Brahm, you are the last person I would expect this kind of maudlin behavior from."

"Yes," Devlin agreed. "Especially after all that rot you fed me about forgiving myself."

Their oldest brother smiled sadly. "I meant it. I know I have to live with what I have done, and I think I have forgiven myself for it. But as the head of the family it is my responsibility to look after the three of you, your wives and your children. And if anyone tries to harm you, I will remove that threat."

His conviction raised Wynthrope's brows. "So you had Daniels deported out of a sense of duty?"

Brahm frowned at him. "I did what I did because you are my brother, you arse. I want you to have a good life. I want you to be happy. I do not want you to spend your days wondering if you had just done that one thing differently if you might have changed everything. I do not want you to have the regrets that I do."

"Father's death was not your fault," Devlin insisted.

"Perhaps not. It doesn't matter now. But I have done enough harm to this family over the course of my life. If I can do anything good for it . . . if I can do anything for the three of you, I will do it. Do you understand?"

Wynthrope was beginning to believe he did. This wasn't duty. This wasn't guilt. This was love. He wasn't certain he deserved it, but he appreciated it. And in his heart he swore that someday he would return the favor.

"Thank you," he said simply, meeting his brother's gaze. His brother looked surprised by the words, but Wynthrope refused to take them back. He might not always like Brahm, but he had a sneaking suspicion he was starting to love the blighter.

Chapter 19

Wynthrope allowed another two days to pass with no word from Moira before he went to see her.

It was a cool day, gray with a light drizzle thickening the air. Umbrellas were useless; the damp sunk into every pore and fiber of one's being. The rain was much like Moira herself, he thought as he sunk lower in the seat of his carriage. No matter the precautions he thought he had taken, no matter how hardened he thought he was, he had been powerless to stop her from invading every aspect of his soul.

Her house seemed too quiet and too still as he jogged up the steps and rapped the knocker against the door.

There was no Nathaniel waiting to tell him to go away as there had been before. And Chester was polite, if not his usual jovial self, as he allowed him entrance. One might think there was nothing amiss, that everything had picked up exactly where he and Moira had left it before that horrible night.

No, not horrible. Making love with Moira had been the most incredible experience of his life. It was only what happened afterward that made it so awful.

She was in her library, just where he expected her to be. Dressed in a gown of rich moss green that made her skin and eyes glow, she was the loveliest woman he had ever laid eyes on. Color bloomed high on her cheeks as she stood and watched him enter the room. She was not immune to him. That was good. Right now even her anger was preferable to nothing at all.

"Mr. Ryland," she greeted him coolly as she set her book aside and rose to her feet. "This is a surprise."

He closed the door behind him. "Is it?"

Long, elegant hands clasped in front of her. "Yes. I rather thought now that you had managed to disentangle yourself from this unpleasant situation, you would want to stay disentangled."

She didn't really believe that, did she? She had to know that he wouldn't leave things this way.

"I promised you an explanation. I have come to deliver it, if you will listen."

Her natural curiosity got the better of her, a fact that warmed Wynthrope's heart. "All right." If she had truly made up her mind against him, she would have told him to leave and take his explanation with him.

She sat down in a chair rather than the sofa she had occupied—no doubt so he could not plant himself beside her. He seated himself in a chair opposite her, the best position for looking her in the eye.

"This story goes back many years," he told her, surprised at how suddenly nervous he was. "I will try to make it as brief as possible."

"As you wish. It is your story." She said it as though she had already decided it was going to be more lies. Frustration gnawed at Wynthrope's gut. What the hell did he have to do to please this woman? He had made an awful mistake, yes, but couldn't she forgive him for it? It was as though she believed he had set out to hurt her, as though that had been his intention from the start.

He took a deep breath. "I was but a lad, just back from my Grand Tour when a man named Daniels approached me in a tavern. He asked me if I would be interested in serving my country. I should have known better than to believe him, but I was young and stupid."

He went on to tell her the whole story about how Daniels duped him, how he had trusted the old man and had been made a fool. He even told her about North's involvement and how Daniels had blackmailed him into stealing from her by threatening to reveal what he knew about North. He knew now that Moira would not repeat the information to anyone. She would not do that to Octavia. Regardless, at this moment being honest with her was more important than North or Octavia.

"So that was the reason for my behavior at Bow Street," he concluded. "I am sorry for putting you in an embarrassing situation, but I could not let Reed know the truth for North's sake."

"Of course," she replied softly, but he had no idea if she meant it or not. "Thank you for telling me. I believe I understand your motives better now. I do wish you had shared this information before, however. It would have spared a lot of pain."

Did she refer to Nathaniel or to herself? Did she blame him for her friend's injuries? She had to know he would have prevented it if he could have. He would have taken that beating himself to spare her any more pain.

"You have your tiara back; surely that must be worth something." He cringed at his own words. Christ, that was quite possibly the worst thing he could have said at this moment.

The expression on her face told him it wasn't worth much at all. "Actually, I do not. I gave it away."

"You what?" He could not have heard her properly, had he?

She made a great show of straightening her skirts, as though she couldn't bear to face his disbelief. "I gave it away."

He was practically choking on suspiciousness. After all the effort he went through to make certain she got the tiara back . . . "To whom?"

Still she did not look at him. "That is none of your concern."

"The hell it isn't!" So much for this being a dignified, calm conversation. "I risked my life to reclaim that damn thing for you."

She eyed him suspiciously. "Did you? I rather thought you reclaimed it for yourself, to save your own skin. Or perhaps you would rather I say North's skin."

"Neither." He gritted his teeth. He had bared his soul to this woman, revealed the folly of the past, and she reacted with no more emotion than if he had told her what he had for breakfast that morning. "It was for you."

Moira folded her hands in her lap like a prim and proper schoolmistress. He wanted to believe it was because they were trembling, but there was nothing at all in her looks or demeanor that would give him cause to believe that. "Well thank you, but if you had taken the time to discuss it with me, you would have found out that you needn't have bothered."

"I thought it meant something to you." Everyone thought it meant something to her. Sweet Jesus, that was one of the reasons he felt so awful taking it!

"It did." She might have smiled if she hadn't been talking

to him, he could see it in her face. "It was a lovely gift from my husband, but it was not worth the trouble and pain it brought down upon those dear to me. It was not worth Nathaniel being hurt. It now belongs to someone who cares about it a great deal more than I ever did."

Understanding washed over him, mixing with the disbelief that flooded his mind. If it were anyone else he wouldn't think it possible, but he knew better than to put anything past Moira. The tiara now belonged to the person who had wanted it so badly in the first place—badly enough to hire someone to steal it. "Aubourn. You gave it to the new viscount."

She didn't confirm his suspicion. She didn't have to. One look at her and he knew the answer.

"So Daniels was telling the truth when he named Aubourn as his benefactor." And to think he had believed it was just another of the old man's lies.

He stared her down until she blushed and nodded. "Yes."

His fist came down on the arm of the chair so hard, he felt the reverberation all the way to his shoulder. "That son of a bitch!"

"What right do you have to judge him?" Her gaze was sharp as it pinned him to the chair. "You have no right at all."

What? "So, you pity him, but not me?" He could not keep from sneering at her strange sense of loyalty. "He is responsible for this whole debacle."

Her chin came up defiantly. "Not all of it."

No, the rest of it was probably his fault, even though he had been as much a victim in some respects as she had. "So you do not blame him for the attack on Nathaniel?"

"No. He told me he had nothing to do with that and I believed him. And I told him he could have the tiara."

"Of course you did." Mocking her probably wasn't the best course of action either. "It is not as though he would lie to you."

A deep flush rose up her throat to darken her face. "Not everyone has to lie and use people to get what they want."

He ignored that barb. "He certainly wasn't honest, was he?" He wasn't about to let her act like Aubourn was some hapless pawn after all his greed had put them both through. "You said yourself, he could have simply asked you for the frigging tiara."

She flushed even darker. Whether it was due to his language or having her own words thrown back at her, he wasn't certain. She did not back down from him, however. She wouldn't be the woman he thought she was if she did.

"Leander suffered under the mistaken notion that I would never give the tiara up because Tony and I seemed to adore each other so."

"So he decided to steal it? That's sweet."

Moira's hazel eyes narrowed at his sarcasm. "He knows it was wrong. He tried to terminate his agreement with Daniels, but Daniels would not allow it. Leander never meant for anyone to be hurt, and he knew nothing of the violence against Nathaniel."

It could be true. Daniels never did like being told what to do, but it burned that she so readily believed Aubourn and not him. He hadn't even made an agreement with Daniels—not without coercion—and yet she absolved Aubourn of everything. Was she insane? The man had hired someone to steal from her. At least Wynthrope had been blackmailed into betraying her. The viscount had no such excuse.

What was it that made him so much harder to forgive than Leander Tyndale? Was it because Wynthrope had shared her bed? Or because Moira had deeper feelings for him than he dared hope?

Or maybe it was just that her pride had been bruised. She felt used and discarded, and that never sat well with a woman.

.

"You were not so understanding when you saw that I had my throat cut when I tried to refuse Daniels."

She recoiled as though he had struck her. "I gave you the tiara. Even though you lied to me and used me, I gave you what you wanted so you would not get hurt again."

"And to protect yourself, Minerva, and Nathaniel," he reminded her. Why was he being such an ass? Surely he wasn't jealous of a girl and a fop, was he?

She rose from her chair, and he did as well, uncertain of what her next move might be. She marched right up to him, sticking a trembling finger in his face. "I would have given you that godforsaken bit of shine long ago if you had only been honest with me. If you had come to me and told me about Daniels I would have given it to you without question, but you did not trust me."

Shite, were those tears in her eyes? "Of course not! We hadn't known each other that long."

"But we certainly got to know one another, didn't we?" Her voice was thick with pain. "And still you kept it from me."

Yes, he had been wrong, but why did she keep going on about it? What did she want from him? "Don't lecture me about secrets, Moira."

"Don't you dare compare, Wynthrope." There was a tremor of rage and deep emotion in her voice. "And in case you have forgotten, I did trust you with my secret. And look what it got me. Made a fool of."

He understood that feeling. Had he not confessed just as much to her minutes earlier? "Is that why you are so angry? Because you are embarrassed? That's the one thing that is different between me and your dear Leander. He didn't wound your pride. I did."

"Of course you wounded me, you cur!" The flat of her hands slammed against his chest, knocking him backward but not off balance. "You made me believe you cared about me. You made me believe I could trust you, and then you proved just how little I could trust you, and how very little you trusted me."

"I couldn't trust you not to try to help me in some way." Damn it, hadn't they been through this already?

"Of course I would have tried to help you, but not in a way that would have put you or anyone else in danger. I would have given you the tiara, and all of this might have been avoided. Nathaniel would not have been hurt. You would not have been hurt." There was such rawness in her gaze, he could scarcely stand to look at it.

"That is easy for you to say that now." As easy as it was for him to see that she was right, that he should have been honest from the beginning.

"*I* would not have been hurt." The words were practically ground out.

His throat was so tight no words could come out, even if he had known how to reply.

"It is easy for me to say those things because they are the truth. I trust the people I care about, Wynthrope." How wary and resigned she now sounded. "Even though I did not know you that well, I had already begun to care for you, and even if that was not the case, I would have helped you regardless because you are Octavia's family."

"Why?" It was nonsense to say such things. No one should be foolish enough to trust a stranger. He knew that all too well. "How could you have known you could trust me?"

"I couldn't," she admitted. "But it is a chance I would have taken. You do not understand that, do you?"

"No." What did she think he was, a total simpleton? "People can get hurt when I take such chances."

She actually looked sorry for him, as though he were the one with the foolish notions and not her. "No. People got hurt because you didn't take the chance. The only person who can get hurt by taking a chance is you, and I believe that is what you really fear."

He scowled. "That's a load of rot."

"It is not." She was like a dog with a bone, this one. "You are afraid to trust because you think you will be hurt, or worse yet that you might hurt someone else. Well, I am sorry to enlighten you, Wynthrope, but you do more danger to yourself and others when you do not trust at all."

"You do not understand." And she probably never would. The idea made him both angry and sad. How could they ever possibly have a future when neither could make sense of what the other was saying?

"I understand that you did something foolish when you were very young. Do you think you are the only person to ever make that mistake? I married a man who could never love me just to get away from my parents. How foolish was that?"

"Fine." His jaw was tight. "You want to know the real reason I didn't tell you about my past?"

"I would love to." Had she always been this caustic, or had she picked it up from him?

"You are right. I was afraid. I was afraid of what would happen when you found out. I was afraid you would not understand. I was afraid of losing you."

Her eyes were filled with sadness as she gazed at him. "I would have tried, if only you had given me the chance. And what did lying accomplish? It still ended badly, did it not?"

Ended. Wynthrope's heart faltered. Was that it? Was it really over? He had just admitted to her that he had been terrified of losing her, even so early in their relationship, and she didn't even acknowledge what a revelation it was. He had never told anyone he was afraid of losing her. It was the next thing to admitting he loved her, a notion he wasn't about to entertain. But it hurt like hell to think he might never hold her again.

Well, what had he expected? That she'd welcome him back with open arms?

"What do you want from me, Moira?" He was pathetic and whiny and he didn't care. He would do whatever she asked, whatever she demanded. He would do it if it meant she would just take him back.

Her face was stark white now, all the flush long having faded away to a wan resignation that clawed at his soul. "Nothing I have to ask for . . . No, wait."

His heart tripped again.

"I have a question I would like answered. Honestly."

"All right." Answering one question couldn't possibly make this conversation any more agonizing.

But he was about to find out that it could.

"What if I had not woken up that night?" Her gaze was clear, her chin trembling ever so slightly as she faced him down. "Was your plan to steal the tiara and continue our relationship for as long as it suited until you would not have been a suspect when I noticed the tiara gone?"

Christ, it sounded so cold when she said it. When he remembered that was exactly what he had planned, it made his flesh crawl. He wouldn't have done it to hurt her, only to protect everyone involved.

To protect himself.

But he had changed his mind. He had decided not to steal it, and that was when she woke up. Still, that didn't change his original intent—a plan he had concocted before going to her house that night.

"Your silence is answer enough." Disgust—no, *disillusionment*—colored her tone.

"Moira, you do not understand." He grabbed her arm as

she turned to walk away. He had to explain. He had to make her understand that regardless of his actions, he had never wanted to hurt her.

"No." She shook her head, casting a betrayed glance in his direction. "I do not believe I can. I want to, but I cannot."

"Tell me what to do to make this up to you and I will do it." There was that pathetic edge again.

"It does not work that way, Wynthrope," she informed him as she pulled her arm free of his grip. He let her go, even though he could have forced her to stay. "You have to want to make it up to me, and you have to do it on your own. If I tell you, I will always wonder if you were sincere, and you may regret my demanding such things of your pride."

"You cannot be serious!" He gaped at her in disbelief. She was going to toss away everything they'd had because he couldn't read her mind? What kind of logic was this?

"I am." She looked so terribly sad. "And now I think you had better leave."

Yes, he thought so too, because he would surely go mad if he stayed.

After Wynthrope left, Moira sat alone on the window seat in her library, her body spasming with quiet, soul-wrenching sobs that she could not control.

Had she been wrong to send him away? She had wanted so badly to stop fighting her instincts and simply wrap her arms around him and tell him it was all right, but she couldn't. It would have been a lie, and she would never truly know if he regretted his actions or not.

Oh, she knew that he regretted being caught, but she didn't know if he truly regretted how he had gone about setting up the situation. Even if he had never intended to hurt her. Even if he had planned to return the tiara all along, he had to have known that she would be hurt by his actions. He had to have known that she would suspect his interest in her was based on his interest in the tiara, that he hadn't meant anything he had said to her.

She'd believed him all those times he told her the depth of the effect she had on him. She believed when he said that he wanted her. Yes, he had injured her pride. Yes, that was a big obstacle in her forgiving him. An even bigger obstacle was that he didn't seem to realize that he had yet to ask her to forgive him.

He had asked many things—what she wanted from him, for example. But she wasn't about to make it that easy for him. He would tell her he was sorry the minute she requested it, and she would always wonder if he meant it. And she knew she had been right—one day he might very well come to resent her for demanding he swallow his pride in such a manner, and he might wonder if she truly forgave him.

And in a close, narrow part of her mind, she didn't give a damn what he wanted, or how things might appear to him. She was still hurt and angry, and if he didn't ask for her to forgive him as she needed him to, then resentment would fester within her until it threatened to destroy whatever kind of relationship they managed to build. No, he would have to apologize if he wanted her, or not have her at all.

It wasn't that she thought herself better than he, or more deserving of trust or understanding. She was just as foolish and distrustful as he was, but for different reasons. She truly believed he didn't trust people because it was safer for him that way. She had a difficult time trusting people, even though she wanted to, because she could never really bring herself to believe that they actually liked her. Wynthrope had started to change that. He had made her feel better about herself. When he was around she didn't care what other people thought of her, and not because his opinion was all that

mattered. No. He made her feel as though she was wonderful
and worthy. Her *own* opinion of herself had changed for a
brief moment, and she'd actually begun to think of herself as
someone good and strong and pretty.

And then he had taken it all away, leaving her feeling like
that same fat girl who could never do anything to please her
mother, who was always less than her perfect sisters. She
hated being reminded of those feelings, hated being that girl
again.

Maybe the things he said to her were false, but her reaction hadn't been. It would take some time, but she wanted
more than anything to regain that feeling of validation, the
comfort of being in her own skin. She would reclaim it
someday, but it was going to take a while. And it wasn't going to be because a man—or anyone else—gave her permission to feel that way. It would be because *she* gave herself
permission.

She would not emerge from this bowed, not when she had
walked into it fully aware that she was taking a risk by offering herself to Wynthrope Ryland. She just hadn't considered
that the risk might be to something far more vulnerable than
her social standing. She hadn't truly considered what might
happen if he broke her heart. Then again, she hadn't considered falling in love.

Perhaps she had simply wanted love so badly, she had
jumped at the chance to taste it, but if that were the case, she
would have taken a bite long ago. It wasn't as though she
had never known love. Her parents might not be the sort of
people a child wishes for, but she'd had grandparents and
aunts and uncles who loved her, especially her dear aunt
Emily. Tony had loved her, and his family had welcomed her
as one of their own. She knew what it was to be loved and
accepted, just not by a man. Not as a man loves a woman.

She still did not know, because Wynthrope Ryland did

not love her, at least not to her knowledge. As much as her heart longed for it, her mind insisted that it would be for the best if he didn't love her. If this was his idea of love, it did not bode well for their future. Nothing boded well for their future.

She cried out at last, wiped her eyes with her handkerchief, and blew her nose until she was too tired to blow anymore. Belatedly she realized it was his handkerchief she had used. How ironically appropriate. Her head ached and her eyes burned, and there was a hollowness in her chest that filled her with dread, because she knew now what it meant.

She was in love with Wynthrope Ryland.

It didn't matter that he had hurt her, she still loved him. In fact, she loved him even more for it in some ways. He had betrayed her to protect himself, yes, but his first conscious thought had been of his brother. How could she not love someone who would put family before himself? If she thought about it long enough she could understand his logic, she could even understand why he hadn't trusted her, but it didn't take away the pain. It didn't take away the feeling that everything she had thought existed between them had disappeared into smoke.

God, when would this stop? She was going to go mad at this rate. She would never risk falling in love again, not if this was what awaited her. To think that she had regretted not marrying for love. Now she was glad for it.

"I see I have arrived just in time."

She closed her eyes on a smile as Nathaniel entered the room. Despite the lingering remorse at seeing him move so stiffly, he was a welcome distraction, even though he would no doubt want to discuss Wynthrope. He was something she could cling to, siphon strength from until her own returned. He could help her make sense of the situation and tell her if she had been too harsh on Wynthrope, or not harsh enough.

He could provide rational thought, as she had lost all capacity to do so for herself.

And most of all, he could provide a shoulder for her to weep on, because even though her reservoir of tears had run dry for the time being, it would no doubt fill again.

"You are a most welcome diversion from this melancholy," she informed him as she sat down on the opposite side of the seat.

He leaned his back against the window frame and pulled her feet into his lap. "Good. Today is the first day in four that it has not rained. You deserve a respite."

She smiled at him, feeling some of the heaviness lift from her heart. Nathaniel always had a way of making her feel better.

And fortunately he looked better himself. His face looked its normal self again, save for a couple of small cuts that were still healing and the faint yellowing of a bruise or two. He had told people he had fallen on ice in front of Moira's door. That explained his injuries and why he stayed at her house in her care.

Another person lying to protect Wynthrope Ryland and his secrets. One might almost think his secrets were more important than anyone else's. True, Wynthrope's secrets were ones most people would fight to keep, secrets that could ruin him or send him to prison, but were they any worse than Nathaniel's? Her own secrets could have destroyed the life she knew and could have sent her back to the mother who had never been anything but hateful toward her. Were her secrets less than Wynthrope's? No, not in her own estimation, but then he might disagree since his secrets were, of course, his own.

"So why the tears, my love?" Nathaniel patted her lightly on the knee. "Did he not come again today?"

They both knew who "he" was. "Actually, he was here before you."

Her friend frowned in confusion. "Then why the tears? Did he not throw himself at your feet and beg you to take him back?"

She sniffed, her fingers pulling at her damp hanky. "He offered to do whatever I wanted."

Nathaniel's bewilderment did not fade. "And the problem with that would be . . . ?"

She stared at him. He did not think it obvious? "I should not have to tell him what to do, he should know!"

Her friend chuckled at her petulant tone, but it was not mocking or hurtful. "My dear girl, he is a *man*. You cannot expect him to know what you want. They never do."

Did her friend not realize that he was of that sex as well? "Anyone should know enough to apologize for their actions," she insisted, believing in her heart that it was true. "He has not. In fact, he acts as though I should jump at the chance to forgive him."

"Probably just wishful thinking on his behalf." Nathaniel's tone was wry. "Do you want to forgive him?"

"Yes, blast it all." She crumpled the damp handkerchief in her fist as her resolve crumpled within her. "I want to forgive the bounder, but I cannot."

Nathaniel nodded knowingly. "Pride."

"It is not just pride!" She yanked her feet from his lap and sat upright. How thoroughly sick she was of being told it was her pride that had been wounded. That her pride was what held her back. It was not true! "It is necessary. How can I know he is truly sorry if he does not tell me?"

He looked truly sorry for her, something Moira didn't appreciate at this moment. "By his actions, pet."

"His actions! How can I trust those? He acted like he adored me and then he stole from me!" God, her head was pounding now.

"*Tried* to steal from you."

"Do not argue minute details with me now, Nathaniel!" This was not the time to get picky about details. The intent was there, and he had as good as admitted that if she hadn't caught him she *never* would have known the truth. "All I want is a simple apology. I want him to tell me he is sorry. I want him to ask me to forgive him and have him promise that he will trust me in the future. Is that too much to ask?"

Her friend shook his head, all traces of amusement gone. "I do not think so."

Moira hung her head as tears threatened again. "I do not want my forgiveness to be taken for granted. I gave him my trust as well as my body and he took all I had to offer and more. I want him to offer himself to me. I want to know that I alone hold his heart, that he is at his most vulnerable when he is with me. Maybe that is asking too much, but it is what I want."

Nathaniel put his arm around her shoulders as tears trickled down her cheeks, and pulled her against his chest. She had to be an uncomfortable weight against his ribs, but he didn't seem to care. "Oh my dear girl. You are in love with the brute, aren't you?"

She nodded, the wool of his coat rough against her cheek. "I fear so."

He stroked her hair. "Have you any idea of his feelings for you?"

This time she shook her head as she wiped at her eyes with the back of her hand. "He must feel something, else he wouldn't be trying so hard to woo me, would he?" It might be nothing more than the hope of a fool that made her say such things, but in her heart, she believed.

"He would not."

"I am afraid to trust him, Nathaniel." Straightening, she met his loving gaze. "I am afraid to believe what he says, and even more afraid to listen to my heart, which tells me to forget my pride and beg him to love me in return."

"Begging for love is never a good idea," he replied, patting her shoulder. "It does not turn out well for the beggar, and puts the beggee at a most unfair advantage."

Somehow she managed a smile. "Speaking from experience?"

He laughed—harshly. "Of course!" Not about Tony, though, of that she was certain. And not about Matthew Sedgewick either. Someone from his past that Moira did not know about.

Sighing, Moira slumped against the cold glass of the window. "What do I do?"

Nathaniel shrugged. "Whatever you feel is best for you."

"Can you not tell me what that is?" She eyed him hopefully, brightened by the humor that rose within her. She was not totally beaten yet.

He chuckled and shook his head. "No. If I were to offer advice, however, I would tell you to give him a bit more time. He may be a typical man, but he is not stupid. If he deserves you at all, he will realize what he needs to do."

"And if he does not?" Lord, how lost she sounded!

Nathaniel's smile was sympathetic. "Then he does not deserve you, dearest."

She smiled too, despite herself. "I was afraid you would say that." His words, no matter how unwelcome, were true. She could not make Wynthrope be the man she wanted him to be. She could only hope that she had not been wrong about him from the beginning.

"Normally I would tell you that if you want him this badly you should go after him, but that would not be the right course in this matter. Not for you." He took her hand in his own. "Give yourself some time to get your thoughts in order. Give him some time to come to his senses."

"What do I do in the meantime?" She massaged her forehead with her fingers. "I feel as though I am going mad."

He didn't hesitate. "Plan your sister's betrothal party. Shop for wedding clothes. And lunch with me, of course. Get out of this house for a while."

She squeezed his hand. "What would I do without you?" Without his support she would have lost her way a long time ago.

"You would not be half as adrift as I would be without your friendship," he replied, kissing her on the forehead. "Now, why don't we ring for some sandwiches and tea? You need to eat."

"Eat?" She laughed. "Most of my gowns are getting too tight as it is."

"And you have never looked more beautiful." Standing, he pulled her to her feet as well. "We will have cucumber sandwiches, your favorite. And lots of little cakes."

As much as she did not feel like eating, it never occurred to Moira to argue. Nathaniel always knew what she needed better than she did. She pulled the bell and told Mrs. Wright what they wanted. Mrs. Wright returned not twenty minutes later with a small cart bearing sandwiches, cakes, tea, and all the necessary tableware to enjoy them.

As usual, her friend was exactly right. Food was just what she needed. It gave her something to fixate on, and it gave her strength. She felt better after a few sandwiches and a cup of tea.

"Enough about me and the melodrama of my life," she said, plucking another sandwich off the plate. "Tell me what you have been up to these last few days. You look good."

He actually pinkened at her praise. "Thank you. Since leaving your tender care, I have been spending an awful lot of time being doted on by one sweet Matthew."

Moira arched her brows. This was news. Good news. "Really? Has he given you any indication of his intentions?"

This time the flush that swept her friend's features was

acute. It made him look so young and innocent, and in love. "Let's just say that his interest has made itself known."

Moira was dying to press for details, but didn't want to pry. Oh, devil take it. "Tell me everything."

By the time Nathaniel was done expounding on the virtues, prowess, and all-around loveliness of his dear Matthew, Moira was not only extremely happy for her friend, but extremely envious as well. Nathaniel and Matthew didn't seem to have any problems trusting each other, or demonstrating emotion. Perhaps that was because they were both men. Perhaps the trouble with her and Wynthrope lay primarily with the difference in their genders.

Or perhaps it was because both of them spent so much time trying to protect themselves, they forgot how to let other people in.

"He did tell me that my claret waistcoat made me look like a puffed-up robin, though," Nathaniel confided.

Moira grinned. Matthew was right. "Oh, I am fairly certain you will find it in your heart to forgive him."

Nathaniel's expression was suddenly serious. "Which brings us back to you and your dilemma. I do not wish to beat a dead horse, but what about you?"

"What about me?" She had a vague idea what he was getting at, but wanted him to say it just in case she was wrong. She was not going to be the one to bring Wynthrope into the conversation again.

"If he asks you to forgive him, do you believe you will be able to find it within yourself to accept?"

There was the nameless but universally acknowledged "he" again. Moira's answer came without hesitation.

"Oh yes." That was what she wanted, after all. "But I do not believe he will ever ask."

Chapter 20

O n the day of Minnie's betrothal party, Moira hid in her room as much as possible. Once it came time to start preparing for the evening, it wasn't that difficult.

She was the first person to admit when she was being a coward, but that wasn't totally the case in this matter. She was hiding not because she was afraid to face her mother, but because she was afraid she might do the woman bodily harm.

Eloise Banning was like a tiny tyrant. She had swept in Moira's house and immediately tried to take over. Fortunately, Moira's servants knew better. A viscountess ranked much higher than a mere Mrs., even if that Mrs. was the viscountess's own mother. Every time Eloise issued a new order, the servants came to Moira, which made Moira's work take twice as long as it should have because she had to counter everything her mother wanted.

Normally Moira would have tried to please her mother. It was a habit she had spent most of her life developing, after all. But not now. Now all Moira wanted was to tell the old witch to stop interfering. She avoided her mother as much as possible to keep from saying just that.

Of course Moira's house wasn't decorated properly. Moira didn't wear the right clothes. The preparations for the party were all wrong. Eloise should have known better than to leave such important matters in Moira's hands.

"The decorations for the party were hand chosen by Minnie, Mama," Moira had informed her. "So if you would like to take umbrage with them you will need to do so with your other daughter."

Of course nothing was said to Minerva about the decorations.

"You have gained weight," her mother commented with a disdainful once-over of her person. "I do hope you will not get fat again."

That was the last straw. Hands on her hips, Moira faced her mother with a straight spine and the refusal to back down. "Why would you hope that, Mama?"

Eloise sniffed. "It would be an embarrassment to have a corpulent daughter when I myself am so thin. I would hate to have people refer to you as my 'fat' daughter."

Moira hated to be referred to as her daughter at all. "A little bit of extra weight makes a woman look younger, Mama. You might want to remember that."

Her mother glanced at her as though she wasn't quite certain if she had been insulted or not. Moira smiled sweetly.

With a scowl and a *hmm* of disapproval, her mother turned and walked away. Moira did not see her again for the rest of that day. It was sheer bliss.

To make matters worse, Moira and Minnie's other sisters descended on them as well, although they had the good sense to stay at an inn rather than at Moira's. For the most part Moira got on quite well with her sisters without their mother around. The girls were a bit too much like their mother when her influence was near. Why had she been the only one to be different? Minnie was proving to be more like Moira than the other Banning daughters, but even she became a little more snappy, a little more haughty when her mother was present. How many times had Moira already taken her aside and remarked on her behavior? Their sisters, and of course their mother, told Moira to leave Minnie alone.

Thank God they would all be gone the next day. A blessedly short visit, and then she wouldn't have to see them again until the wedding that summer.

One good thing to come out of all this, however, was that Moira had scarcely any time to think about Wynthrope. Minnie had invited him to tonight's party, but Moira would be surprised if he came. He was probably at home sulking— or at least she hoped he was. Had he figured out what it was she wanted from him? Did he know that she wanted his sincere repentance? That she wanted his heart on a silver platter?

Was he prepared to offer them to her? Or had he decided she wasn't worth the effort?

She glanced at the clock on the mantel in her room as her maid entered to start working on her hair.

In three hours the guests would begin arriving, and then she would find out if she was worth his effort or not.

"I am surprised that you decided to attend the party tonight."

Wynthrope looked up from his glass at the sound of North's voice. They were in the little parlor at North and Octavia's. North was sipping coffee while Wynthrope tossed back a glass of bourbon. He needed a little fortification for the evening ahead.

"Of course I am going. I was invited."

North raised his cup to his lips. "Do you think Moira will be pleased to see you?"

"No. But I am going anyway. I want her to know I have not given up on her. I have no intention of giving up."

That resolution had come to him on one of the many sleepless nights that had passed since he last saw her. Instead of brooding and whimpering like some lovestruck idiot, he was going to face the situation head on. He was not going to let her push him away. And if she wouldn't tell him what she wanted, he would keep trying until he either figured it out or stumbled on it by accident. He didn't care how long it took, she would be his again.

"I have never known you to be stubborn before," North commented with a slight frown. "Not since we were children."

Wynthrope smiled at him. "I have been pretending to be someone else for a good many years, brother. It is time I stopped."

"I understand." Maybe he did and maybe he didn't, but it was nice of him to say so. "But why the change of heart?"

"She told me that I was protecting myself more than others and that I ended up hurting myself in the process. If having Moira means giving up all pretenses, I am willing to do it."

North regarded him strangely. "Spoken like a man in love."

The mere sound of the word sent his heart pounding like mad. Wynthrope gazed into his almost empty glass. "Yes, I suppose I am." The admission felt as though the weight of an age had been lifted from his shoulders.

North was grinning now. God only knew what he was about to say. Thankfully Wynthrope was spared any ribbing from his brother because of Octavia's arrival. All of North's attention was immediately focused on his wife, who was lovely in a bronze-colored silk gown and glittering topaz and diamond jewelry.

Wynthrope made a point of not watching them as they exchanged a kiss and hushed words of adoration. They were
such a perfect couple, so at ease with each other, and yet
emotion seethed between them, so thick it was tangible. This
was love, he supposed. Would people think the same of him
and Moira someday?

God yes, if he had any say in it.

He finished off his drink and rose to his feet. The whispers behind him were becoming annoying.

"Shall we go?" he asked brightly, turning to face his
brother and sister-in-law.

Both North and Octavia eyed him with identical expressions. They thought this was amusing, his desire to be on
their way. Let them laugh. He honestly didn't care what they
thought, as long as they gave in to his will.

"Yes," North agreed. "We should be on our way. No doubt
you wish to get this evening over with."

His brother didn't know the half of it. Yes, he wanted this
evening over, but only because he hoped to have made some
kind of headway in wooing Moira by the end of it.

The journey to Moira's Mayfair address was a slow one
this evening. It had snowed earlier, and the streets were still
covered in some areas. Carriages moved at a more cautious
pace due to the slippery conditions. By the time they finally arrived at Moira's door, Wynthrope was grinding his
teeth and ready to take someone's head clean off his
shoulders.

To make matters worse, Moira, Minnie, and their family
were waiting to greet guests just outside the party rooms.
Moira would sense his discontent and no doubt blame it on
herself. Taking a deep breath, he exhaled slowly, willing
himself into some semblance of the Wynthrope Ryland the
ton was familiar with. Cool, collected, charming, if not

catty. He could do this. He could hang on to the charade for this evening, surely.

Somehow Octavia and North managed to get ahead of him in the receiving line and were already inside with other guests when Wynthrope reached the family.

Both Moira and Minnie looked surprised to see him, but a little happy too. At least he hoped that was happiness he saw on Moira's face. It was either that or she was about to go into hysterics.

Moira and her mother were first. Mrs. Banning stared at him as though he were on display in a butcher's window—a little interested, a little distasteful. Even if he had never heard anything about this woman from Moira, he would have disliked her immediately.

"Good evening, Lady Aubourn. You are exceedingly beautiful tonight." It was a bit beyond what was proper, only because of his choice of words, but he didn't care. He was staking a claim to this woman, and he wanted everyone to know that she was his.

Moira blushed prettily, obviously flustered by his attention. "Thank you, sir." She turned to her mother. "Mama, may I introduce Mr. Wynthrope Ryland? Mr. Ryland, my mother, Eloise Banning."

Wynthrope bowed over the tight-lipped crone's hand. "Madam."

Imperious brows lifted. "You are related to the Viscount Creed, Mr. Ryland?"

Something about the woman's tone gave him pause. "He is my brother."

"How unfortunate for you."

The old bitch. Her lip actually curled when she spoke, as though she were somehow better than Brahm. At one time Wynthrope might have agreed, but not anymore. She couldn't have asked North the same question—no doubt because she knew of North's illegitimacy and didn't want to acknowledge it. In fact, Wynthrope would be surprised if the old crone lowered herself enough to even speak to North.

"Actually I feel quite fortunate, madam. There are others with less appealing family connections than me." Ah, that felt good. This version of himself might never have actually been the true him, but the wit was.

She took his meaning clearly. The flushing of her cheeks and the narrowing of her eyes was proof of that.

Wynthrope turned to Moira, who was looking decidedly uncomfortable. "You have outdone yourself this evening, Lady Aubourn."

She stared at him as though she could not believe the exchange he'd just had with her mother. "Thank you, Mr. Ryland."

"Now if you ladies will excuse me, I believe I will offer my felicitations to the happy couple." As satisfying as it had been to cross verbal swords with her mother, he didn't want to put Moira in a situation any more uncomfortable than this already was.

He moved down the line, past Moira's father to Minerva and her fiancé. He spent a few moments with them, kissing the girl's cheek and shaking the young man's hand. They were genuinely in love, and very happy. Wynthrope envied them. They had such possibilities open to them. He hoped they would have many years together, free of such foolishness as pride and secrets.

He left them and entered the drawing room, which had been opened up into the music room to allow for dancing. There was a supper room as well, where they would all sit down sometime around midnight for a meal and then continue dancing and celebrating into the wee hours.

Would Moira dance with him? Would she celebrate with him?

He watched her for much of the evening, unable to get close enough to have a private conversation. She flitted around like a butterfly all evening. Her mother never seemed to be far behind, and he could tell from the strain starting to show on Moira's lovely face that the woman found fault with almost everything she did.

How could such a viper have produced his sweet, generous Moira? All Moira wanted was trust and love and someone to treat her as she deserved. He had offered that to her, but then foolishly yanked it away. Seeing her tonight, he began to understand her a little better. It was so much easier to see things clearly when he didn't allow his own pride or emotions to cloud the way.

He found himself drifting toward where Moira and her mother stood later in the evening, after having watched Moira take the crone's abuse long enough. It was time for supper, and it was obvious that Mrs. Banning had found something wrong with the table setting.

"I should have been here to make the arrangements," her mother was saying, loudly enough that many of the guests could hear. "I should have known better than to leave such important decisions to you. You have ruined everything."

Moira's face was pale, her cheeks stained with humiliation. Wynthrope would be embarrassed too, but not because she had done anything wrong, but because this yappy harpy was her mother.

"I believe Lady Aubourn made all the arrangements to Miss Minerva's preferences," he informed the woman, coming up behind Moira. "Is that not so, Lady Aubourn?"

Moira cast him a glance that begged him not to get involved, even as she nodded. "That is true, Mr. Ryland."

Mrs. Banning glared at him. Odd, but if she had only been a more pleasant woman Moira might have looked like her. But Moira could never look as mean and unforgiving as this woman.

"This has nothing to do with you, Mr. Ryland," Mrs. Banning informed him coldly. "Please mind your own business."

Quite a few of the guests were watching now, and Wynthrope didn't care. If this woman wanted someone to verbally duel with, she had picked the wrong person.

"Lady Aubourn is my friend," he replied. "And therefore she is my business."

He was well aware of a few choice glances exchanged between guests. They were speculating as to just how good a "friend" Moira was to him. Moira stared at him with something that might have been horror on her face.

Deep groves appeared in Mrs. Banning's brow. She obviously frowned a lot. "I am her mother, and this does not concern you."

Wynthrope allowed a mocking smile to tilt his lips. "Yes, I am well aware of what kind of mother you have been."

Moira clutched his arm, the bite of her fingers urging him to cease, but he ignored her. She might be willing to put up with this awful woman, but he was not about to stand by and allow her to be so poorly treated.

He went on, "I know that despite all your efforts Moira managed to grow into a sweet, generous person. I know that if you had your way she would have turned into a spiteful witch like yourself. And I know that if I were she I would have tossed you out on your arse over an hour ago, but she is a better person than I."

There were titters among the crowd. Moira was flushed, her mother was as well. "You insolent cur!" Mrs. Banning cried. "I might have expected such coarse talk from a Ryland!"

It was meant to be an insult, but Wynthrope merely

grinned. For so many years he had resented what Brahm had done to their family's reputation, now he found some pleasure in the notoriety. "Consider yourself lucky I stopped at just talk."

The woman gasped. Moira's fingers bit harder.

His grin faded as he stared her mother down. "After all you have done to her, you should get down on your knees and beg her forgiveness."

"Wynthrope," Moira whispered, her tone urgent. "Please."

He turned to her and saw the pleading in her eyes. He had embarrassed her by speaking so loudly and brashly to her mother, but she didn't seem angry with him at all. In fact, she looked as though she would dearly love to kiss him.

Was this what she had wanted from him? A public declaration of his regard? And then the answer came to him, as though planted in his mind by one of Moira's angels. Forgiveness. It was all about forgiveness. It was what he wanted from her, and he knew in that instant that all he had to do was ask. She wanted to forgive him. She wanted him to prove his love and give her reason to trust him again. It was so simple. All he had to do was swallow what was left of his pride.

He turned to her. "*I* should beg her forgiveness," he stated clearly, not caring that everyone could hear.

Moira's face went pale, and he knew his instincts had not let him down this time. She glanced at the crowd around them. It was increasing. "Wynthrope, no."

Apparently she had not completely lost her ability to see inside his soul, because she seemed to know what he was about to do.

He dropped to his knees before her, her mother now forgotten. The room was abuzz with eager whispers. He couldn't hear any of it, didn't care what they were saying. He kept his gaze focused solely on Moira, his hands loose at his sides. He had lowered himself so that he had to look up at her, had put himself at a vulnerable position in front of her. All that was left was to take the final step.

"Please stand up," she whispered, wringing her hands.

He met her gaze. "I want you to forgive me. I *need* you to forgive me. For everything I have done, for taking advantage of your goodness, for not trusting in your intelligence and your strength. For not having faith in you or your feelings, I ask your forgiveness. For not considering your emotions, for not daring to hope you might have developed feelings for me. For not trusting you with my secrets, for not being willing to sacrifice my pride just to hold you in my arms, I beg you to forgive me."

There were tears in her eyes. "Please, just get up."

He shook his head. "I will even apologize for insulting your mother, if you want. But I cannot stand up, not until I have your forgiveness. You are everything to me, Moira Tyndale, and I do not care who knows it. If I have to, I will beg your forgiveness every night for the rest of my life, but you could save my knees a lot of injury right here and now by telling this undeserving man that he may put the rest of his life to better use by showing you how much he adores and loves you."

Moira stared at him, tears streaming down her cheeks. Was that a sniffle he heard from the corner of the room? There was another. Obviously his speech had affected more than just the woman before him.

He had just made a proper fool of himself. Everyone would be talking about it tomorrow. He should probably care more than he did. Maybe he would tomorrow, when his pride had a chance to review the situation. He was going to be a laughingstock, that was for sure.

Then Moira did the most extraordinary thing. She could have simply told him she forgave him, or she could have turned her back and walked away. Either way he would still be the one they talked about on the morrow. But she did not do either. Instead she lowered herself to her knees so that they were face to face on the cold marble floor. He could scarcely believe his eyes.

Her slender hands cupped his face, her thumbs stroking his cheeks. "I will forgive you," she whispered, "but only if you forgive me for driving you to this."

His hands covered hers. "There is nothing to forgive. I would walk down Bond Street on my knees if it meant you would have me back."

She nodded. "I will have you back."

Wynthrope practically leaped to his feet, taking Moira with him. His heart was dancing a jig in his chest, threatening to burst with joy. Holding her by the hands, he pulled her along behind him, through the crowd of staring, chattering guests, through the parlor and out into the corridor and then to the stairs.

"Where are we going?" Moira demanded as she tripped along behind him, but she knew where he was taking her. She was too happy to be scandalized by his behavior, too touched by his display to chastise him now.

He had asked her to forgive him in a way she never imagined he would do. He was such a proud man, and to humble himself like that for her . . . He told her he adored her. Told everyone present that he loved her. Her heart clenched at the mere memory of it. He loved her. Nothing else seemed to matter now.

As soon as they were in her room, the door shut behind them, he turned to her and began removing her gown, his lips devouring hers.

Oh Lord, it felt so good to hold him, to feel his body against hers. But she had guests downstairs, guests who at this very moment were speculating as to where they had gone and what they were doing.

She shoved against his shoulders. "Wyn, we cannot do this. Everyone will know."

"I don't care." He shoved a hand down her bodice, his fingers instantly bringing her nipple to a hard, tingling peak. "Do you care?"   .

"Not a whit." Not when he touched her like that.

Within seconds he had her on the bed, her skirts pushed up around her hips. His trousers were rough against the inside of her legs, and the hard flesh beneath his trousers pressed deep into the softness between her thighs.

Liquid heat seemed to pool deep and low within her. How she wanted him. She wanted him with a ferocity that went beyond physical need. She had to have him, had to take him within herself and hold him there for as long as possible, just so she would know this wasn't a dream.

His coat flew across the room, followed by his waistcoat, shirt, and cravat. Beautifully bare-chested, he raised himself above her and gazed down at her with those remarkable blue eyes.

"I will never lie or keep secrets from you ever again," he told her, his voice husky. "I wish I could promise I will never hurt you, but I'm not certain anyone could keep such a promise. I give you my word that I will try my damnedest to never hurt you again."

Smiling, she ran her hands up the smooth flesh of his back. "I do not want to hurt you either, and there will be no more secrets between us, I promise."

Vulnerability softened his features as a lock of hair fell over his forehead. He looked so young, so sweet and unburdened. There were no secrets between them now, of that she was certain. "Do you love me?"

How hopeful he sounded! Did the dolt not know? How could he not know?

"From the moment I first saw you," she admitted. "Although I thought at the time that it was just infatuation."

Shifting his weight to one arm, he slid a hand up to cup her breast through the fabric of her gown. "I saw you in the street one day several months ago, do you remember?"

She nodded. "I do."

His gaze locked with hers even as his fingers worked her body into a delicious state of arousal. "You looked at me as though you could see into my soul. I knew at that moment that if you could do that and not turn away in disgust, you were a woman I wanted to know better."

Sliding her hands down low to caress the firm swell of his buttocks, Moira lifted her hips against his. "Nothing about you could ever disgust me. I do not care what you have done in the past. I only know that you make me feel like the most beautiful, intelligent woman on the earth."

He smiled. "You are."

Her throat tightened at his words. And then any further conversation was delayed by his lips claiming hers again. Talk could wait. They had their entire lives to talk. What did talk matter now? She already knew that they would sort things out between them. As long as they were honest with each other, there wasn't any obstacle they couldn't defeat.

She would never forget the look on her mother's face when he put her in her place. As embarrassing as it was, it had been delightful as well. He had come to her rescue. No one had ever rescued her before. He had done it at least twice—when he caught her when she fell from the ladder at Octavia's, and now.

Oh, and he had saved her from spending the rest of her life afraid of trusting anyone with her secret. He had saved her from being afraid to trust at all.

He removed her gown with determined fingers, cursing each tiny button as he worked. Finally he was able to peel the shimmering silk off her. He didn't toss it on the floor as he did his own clothes, but draped it over a chair, a consideration that she found strangely touching.

But removing the gown seemed to have taken all his patience, because he didn't bother with her chemise or stockings, or even her shoes. He nipped at her nipples through the thin lawn, dampening the material with his tongue until the pink crests stood tall and tight in the cool air. Every lick of his tongue, every insistent suckle sent a shock of pure lust straight between her legs.

Her hips writhed against his. His erection was rock solid against her hip as his fingers caressed the inside of her splayed thighs. She wanted those fingers inside her, stroking that part of her that ached for his touch and the shattering release only he could bring.

Finally he gave her what she wanted. He pulled the neck of her chemise low, baring a breast to his greedy mouth. As he tasted her naked flesh, his thumb slipped between the damp curls at the apex of her thighs, into the soaked cleft, to find that one spot that came so wonderfully alive at his touch. Moira gasped, lifting her hips as he stroked her.

As she pushed against his hand, he slid a finger inside her, bringing a moan to her lips. His tongue ruthlessly flicked her nipple as his hand lifted her to the heights of sensual pleasure.

Desperate to touch him, Moira slid her own hand down to the falls of his trousers. She fumbled for a few seconds and then succeeded in freeing the hot, silky length of him. He was thick and heavy in her hand, the round head slick to her touch. He groaned against her breast, thrusting himself into the tight vise she made with her fist. Awkwardly at first, she stroked him, until instinct took over and she found a rhythm that had him pistoning his finger in and out of her until she thought she might go mad with pleasure.

Then he was gone. For a moment Moira was confused. Where was he? A second ago his weight had been upon her, his sex hot in her hand, and now he was gone.

Something brushed the inside of her thigh, and Moira realized it was hair— Wynthrope's hair. Her mind had only a second to register what he was about to do before the wet, hard thrust of his tongue brought her hips off the bed, her back arching in a deep bow. His mouth was on her, his tongue inside her, thrusting as though they were making love. And then it slid upward, to bring a shaky moan to her lips as it stroked the center of her pleasure with determined pressure.

Her fingers caught in his hair as her hips undulated under his assault. The way he made her feel was indescribable. He did things that she never thought possible—or even remotely proper. She should be embarrassed, or conscious of how her body must look in such postures, but all she could think about was how beautiful he made her feel. She was beautiful in his eyes, no matter what position her body was in. To him, she had no flaws, only things that made him love her more. She understood that now, because that was how she thought of him.

And then she wasn't able to think at all because he brought her to the brink with his tongue, and the most incredible pleasure seized her, locking her muscles tight and enveloping her in a sparkling, unseeing climax.

He didn't wait for her to recover before thrusting himself inside her. Moira gasped at the intrusion, pulling her knees up to allow him deeper access to her body. The feel of him against her internal walls was like tiny shocks rippling throughout her body. Every time he withdrew only to plow into her again brought her that much closer to another orgasm.

And then it happened. Just as yet another tempest of pleasure claimed her, she felt Wynthrope stiffen atop her, the frantic pumping of his hips stilled. He shuddered, his back arched, head tossed back. Marveling in the tremors wracking him, knowing that she was the cause, Moira wrapped her legs tight around his hips, holding him deep within her as he came.

Sometime later, after their bodies had cooled, they lay in each other's arms on the crumpled counterpane, the same quilt draped over them that had covered them the first time they made love in her bed. Only this time he wasn't at her wall safe when she woke up.

Wynthrope toyed with a loose tendril of her hair as she snuggled against him. There would be no returning to the party, not like this. That was just as well; he wasn't about to share her with anyone, not now.

"That was a big risk you took, not allowing me to withdraw," he told her. A child might be the result of tonight. Oddly enough, the idea didn't fill him with the terror that he thought it ought.

Moira shrugged. "Such risks are worth taking." Lifting her head, she met his gaze with sleepy hazel eyes. "The risk you took this evening in dropping to your knees in front of the entire party, *that* was a big risk."

Smiling, he caressed the side of her face with his index finger. How soft she was. "Such risks are worth taking."

She grinned at that.

Catching sight of the painting on the far side of the room, Wynthrope's smile faded. Her safe was behind that painting.

"You should probably change the combination to your safe," he remarked. "If you haven't already."

She stared at him for a good long moment before kissing him soundly on the mouth. "There is no need. I trust you."

Her words struck him deep inside, even deeper than her declaration of love, because they meant so much more where the two of them were concerned.

"Even with your valuables?" He said it as a half joke, wanting to lighten the mood before he did something stupid, like weep.

She pressed her face into the crook of his shoulder. Her lips brushed against his skin. "With my heart. You alone possess it."

He hugged her as fiercely as he could, but it still wasn't anything compared to the band of pure love that encircled his chest.

"You have mine as well."

Silence fell between them, and he did not mind. He was content just to hold her, until sleep finally took hold of them both, and even then, he held her still.

Wynthrope left Moira's early in the morning, but he returned later that afternoon, finding her in the library.

He kissed her soundly, marveling at how she responded to him. Her lithe body molded itself against his as she melted against him. One kiss and he was already hard.

"Shall we play a game of chess?" he suggested, breaking their kiss.

She looked as though she wanted to throttle him. "Chess? You want to play chess?"

Clearly his wanton queen had something else on her mind. He had noticed that the house was curiously quiet. Had she sent everyone out so that they might have some privacy? "Yes, I do," he replied, fighting the urge to chuckle. "Shall we?"

Somewhat sullenly, Moira nodded.

"I will set up the board," he offered, going to the table where they used to play. "I assume you have no objections to me playing white?"

"Play whatever you like."

He grinned as he prepared the table for play. To know that she wanted him that badly, that her lust for him was as great as his for her was a heady realization.

He made one final adjustment to the pieces and then turned, holding his hand out to her. "Come play."

She did as he bid, her lower lip still pouty as she took his hand and allowed him to guide her to her chair.

She wasn't the least bit interested in the game. He could tell from her posture and the set of her expression as they took their seats. He made the first move—a simple relocation of a pawn. It wasn't his pieces that mattered.

Sighing, obviously resigned to not having her way, Moira looked down to decide her own move. And then she froze. Wynthrope watched her, his breath caught in his throat.

She picked up the black queen, lifting it to eye level. The golden ring around its neck gleamed in the sunlight. The large emerald set in the gold shimmered and twinkled.

"Marry me." His voice was a rasp in the silence.

She stared at him, her mouth agape.

He took the queen from her trembling fingers and lifted the ring from it. Then, he took Moira's left hand in his and poised the ring around the tip of her finger. "Say the word and I will be at your command forever."

Moira nodded, her eyes filling with tears. "Yes. But I do not want to command you."

The ring slid easily over her finger, coming to rest at the base with perfect snugness. He had been right about the size—perfectly right. He released her hand, even though he was reluctant to let her go. That she didn't want to command him didn't matter—he was her servant till his dying day.

She bolted out of her chair and came around the table. He barely had time to shove away from the table before she launched herself into his arms, covering his face with kisses that made him laugh with joy. She had said yes!

Her exuberance had them sliding out of the chair to the carpet, landing in a twisted heap with her skirts tangled around them. He was on top of her, feeling the sweet softness of her yield against him.

"I love you, Wynthrope Ryland," she whispered, her face aglow.

His heart caught at the words. His suspected it always would. "I love you, Moira Tyndale."

They shared a grin before their lips met. And as Wynthrope Ryland made love to his fiancée on the carpet beneath the little chess table, he realized that while there was pleasure to be had in stealing a heart, there was infinitely more joy in one that was freely given.

*Bring on the spring thaw with these
hot hot hot March romances
from Avon Books!*

Just One Touch by Debra Mullins

An Avon Romantic Treasure

Caroline could not have imagined that her betrothed husband would be so tender, so warm, so . . . sensual. Rogan was expecting a meek and timid wife, but instead he finds her vibrant, charming and . . . passionate. Will this arranged marriage turn into something they have secretly hoped it would be? Something like a love match?

Special of the Day by Elaine Fox

An Avon Contemporary Romance

After a hideous break-up, Roxanne Rayeaux pitches the world of modeling, diets and philanderers and moves to Virginia to open a nice quiet restaurant. She wants some peace and tranquility, but instead she inherits the restaurant's contentious but sexy bartender, Steve Serrano. Steve is so totally *not* her type . . . so why is he so irresistible?

Lessons in Seduction by Sara Bennett

An Avon Romance

Normally prim and reserved, Miss Vivianna Greentree is beside herself. The heartless (but heartbreakingly handsome) Sir Oliver Montegomery is threatening to tear down her home for orphaned children! Vivianna is prepared to persuade Oliver to keep the orphanage by any means necessary, even if she needs lessons from a notorious courtesan to accomplish her task . . .

A Kiss in the Dark by Kimberly Logan

An Avon Romance

Two people from vastly different backgrounds are about to find out that their lives are entwined. Frantic to find his runaway sister, Lord Tristan Knight reluctantly turns to Deirdre Wilks, the most notorious woman in London, for help in tracking her down. But as Deirdre becomes a part of Tristan's life, she fights to conceal a secret that threatens to end the passion fast growing between them . . .

REL 0205